BONE DRESSER

NICO VINCENTY

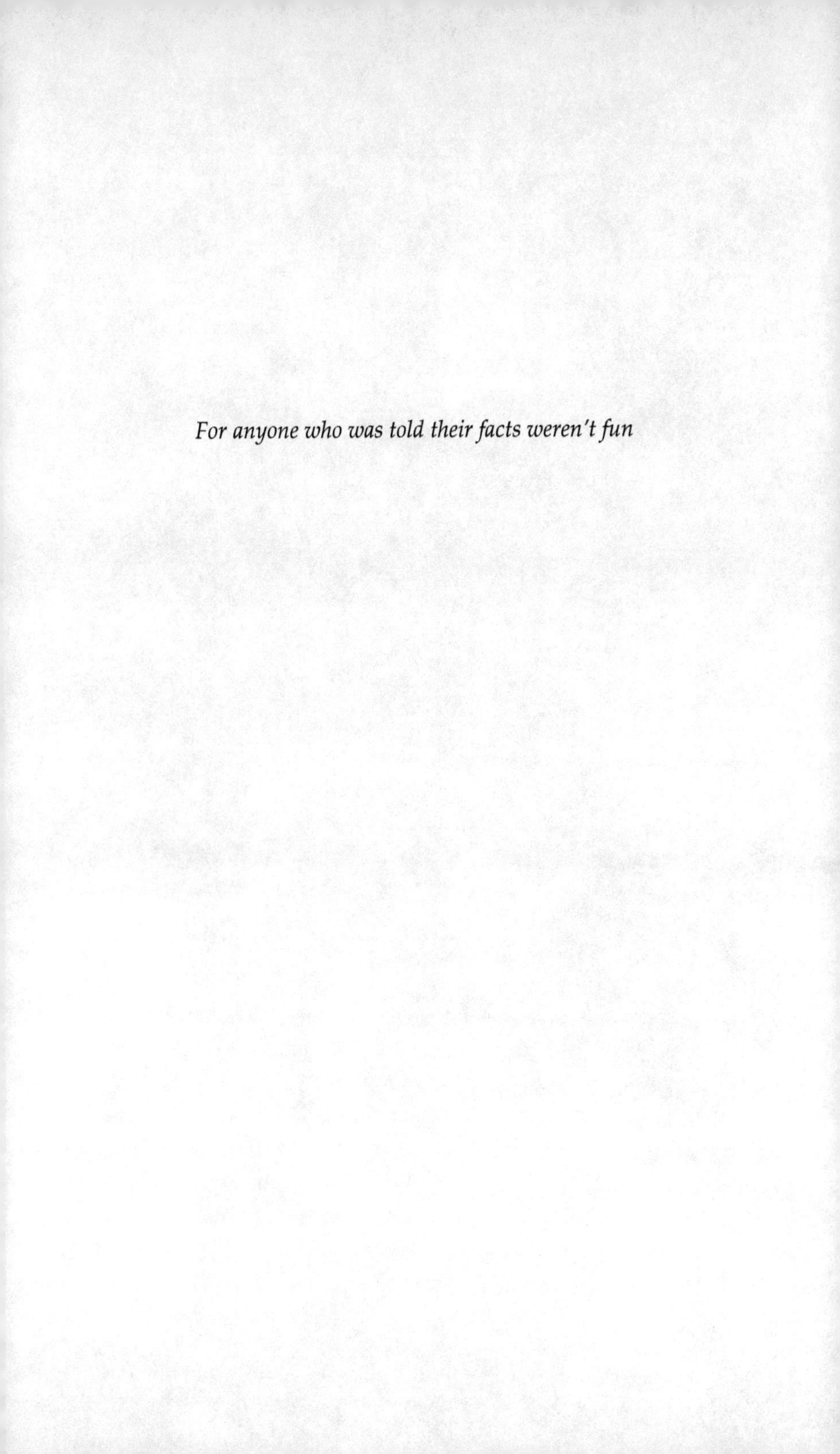

For anyone who was told their facts weren't fun

CONTENTS

Author's Note	vii
1. The Baby Job	1
2. The Interview Job	10
3. The New Leg Job	18
4. The Gurney Job	27
5. The Hazing Job	34
6. The Bloody Job	47
7. The Dinner Job	54
8. The One Newton Job	64
9. The Phone Call Job	72
10. The Knife Job	82
11. The Badge Job, Pt. 1	94
12. The Big Reveal Job	102
13. The New Friends Job	111
14. The Confounding Variable Job	119
15. The Flirting Job	129
16. The Plan E Job	137
17. The Supply Closet Job	148
18. The Sword Job	155
19. The Badge Job, Pt. 2	164
20. The Badge Job, Pt. 3	172
21. The Snapped Job	181
22. The Slow Down Job	189
23. The Control Job	195
24. The Confession Job	204
25. The Fault Job	212
26. The Voting Job	219
27. The Thinking Job	228
28. The Memory Job	241
29. The Knight in Shining Armor Job	251
30. The Plan G Job, Pt. 1	264
31. The Plan G Job, Pt. 2	271
32. The Plan H Job	279
33. The Plan J Job	288

34. The Plan O Job   296
35. The Plan Q Job   303
36. The Great Escape Job   311
37. The Step One Job   318

Acknowledgments   329
About the Author   331
Also By Nico Vincenty   333

AUTHOR'S NOTE

Bone Dresser contains sensitive material including, but not limited to: detailed medical procedures and experimentation, body horror, blood, alcohol consumption, violence (on page), sexual content (on page), threats and torture, verbal abuse, injury, and death.

CHAPTER 1
THE BABY JOB

CHASE LOVED MAKING BABIES.

Most of her colleagues hated the phrase, but since no one in a planet-sized radius had a functioning uterus anymore, she found the irony entertaining, in a *laugh so we don't cry* kind of way. Making babies really felt like creating life. Also, the parts were small and she could get more done in less time, putting it at the perfect crossroads between science and art.

Her comfort zone.

Technically, her job title was *myofabricator*, a complicated name for the simple job of synthesizing muscles. Every day, she came into Kierper Labs and drew up the beautiful threads of the quads. To anyone else, the quadriceps were the four muscles on the front of the thigh. To Chase, they were her Mona Lisa, and she painted a new version every day.

"Are we ready, kid?" Chase piled her dark curls on top of her head and tapped her tablet screen. The data flew to the big monitor on the outside wall of her fabrication chamber.

Each chamber had eight-foot glass walls around the sealed work spaces. The clear walls of the cubes certainly helped keep the floor feeling bright and open, but didn't quite kill the sense of being a mouse stuck in a maze. Her chamber sat on the edge next to the windows, which helped her breathe a little easier. It also made it easy for her to watch everyone else at work without the creeping sense of someone sitting behind her.

It was just past noon, and most of the other cubes were dark as the early birds took their lunch. Her chamber light shone like a beacon for anyone in need of muscles, the white platform inside clean and ready for work. Sitting at the white desk in front of it, Chase swiped her stylus across her tablet and squinted one eye as the genetic coding program ran. A soft *ding* echoed through the fab chamber once it settled on the optimal percentages of muscle fiber types.

"Hello, darling." A swipe of her badge opened her desk drawer, and she extracted the container with the tiny pelvis, femurs, and tibias from its frigid depths. Another smaller container held the patellae, the bones so small she couldn't see the initials of the osseofabricator who made them.

Chase checked the pelvis for a signature and frowned; she hadn't gotten bones from her favorite bone mason, Divya, in almost a month. Would this other osseofabricator double-layer the bone at the muscle origin to prevent avulsion fractures? Chase hoped so. Techs, if Divya got transferred upstairs to an Upper Extremity floor, she might just have to pitch a fit.

"Focus, Chase," she muttered.

The fab chamber hummed to life with another tap of her badge, sending a vibration through her desk. It was the nicest cube she'd ever used, with a fully adjustable counter space bigger than her mattress at home. The whole setup was beyond perfect, more than she could've ever dreamed.

The fab chamber dinged its readiness and its light turned blue. With everything set and prepped, it was time to conduct her own little symphony of proteins. Chase stepped up to the monitor situated on the outside wall of the chamber, and after a series of taps and swipes, actin and myosin formed inside. They weren't visible to the naked eye, but thanks to the fancy screen, every hook and head in the railroad tracks were big enough for her barely caffeinated brain to see.

Chase made chain after chain with meticulous precision. When she had enough, she used the screen to combine them into true muscle cells. Flicks of her fingers added nuclei and mitochondria to the cells, her instincts driving their placements. Following an enthusiastic swipe of her tablet, clicks echoed like fireworks as the fabricator melded all the pieces together into a big, beautiful myofibril.

The process repeated again and again until she had miles of myofibrils suspended by the chamber, the little nuclei sparkling like stars in the blue light. Here, she always had to talk herself off the ledge; with all the strings hanging there, shifting slightly in the current of the chamber, she deeply and wholly wanted to braid them together. Would that make the muscle produce more force, or less?

Unfortunately she "wasn't allowed to run experiments" because she was making a "product" for a "customer." *Buzzkill.*

Chase sighed as she joined the fibers into their sweet little packages–the normal way–and wrapped them in glossy connective tissues. She instructed the program to bring each bundle together and added even more layers to each end. Then, finally, she had a perfect pair of muscles glowing in the light.

Well, technically four muscles each, but who was counting?

Chase. Chase was counting.

"Alspeth, hold on."

Chase closed her eyes and took a deep breath as the voice reached her. Yes, it was nice and low and British, but that didn't negate the situation.

"Montgomery Evans. Don't tell me," she said as the man rounded on her desk. "You forgot something?"

"No, not at all." Monty, one of her current patella people, dropped to one knee and presented her with a box. "I simply had a genius idea for the cartilage structure that will help when it ossifies later. And you know, you can just call me Monty."

In the box sat two more patellae nearly identical to the ones she already possessed. Chase snatched the box from his grip and gave him the old ones to recycle. These exchanges happened often, where he fabricated a better pair for her and interrupted the process.

"Thank you. At least I hadn't already put them in." She appreciated his commitment, and he was one of the most creative boneheads she'd worked with, but she wished he would take his time and get it right on the first try. As for his name... well, it was fun to bother him, just a little.

"I'm getting faster." He put his hands on his hips, his dark skin a contrast to his gray jumpsuit. His charming smile was likely meant to disarm her, but Chase rolled her eyes.

"Speed isn't your problem. If anything, you could take a little more time so that big brain of yours can finish processing before your hands take the lead." His bones were some of the best, but she didn't need to tell him that.

His face lit up. "You think I have a big brain?"

Chase cleared her throat. That was not the point of her comment.

"I'm still above you in the rankings," she deflected, and his smile grew.

"This week, yes. But wait until next week." So *arrogant*.

Kierper didn't necessarily encourage the friendly competition between fabricators, but they also didn't lock away the logs keeping count of weekly finished projects. The main competition was between the systems—muscles, bones, skin, nervous system, and organs—but if they dug a little deeper, individual numbers were there for the whole world to see. Chase only worked on muscles, but Monty floated between systems as a utility fabricator, which was rare, but not unheard of.

No matter where Monty went, he always found a way back to her. Chase didn't mind; it was fun to have some direct competition. In the past six months, she'd had more fun at work and completed more projects than she'd had in a long time. Didn't hurt that Monty had a handsome face, either.

"Well, good luck and goodbye. Some of us actually do our jobs." She shooed him away, and he gave her a sarcastic salute before backing away from the desk.

Chase shook her head to lock her focus back into place. She changed the chamber setting to stasis, and the light turned from blue to purple as it took effect. The muscles stopped their gentle oscillations and hung frozen as she untied the sleeves of her red jumpsuit from around her waist and slipped her arms into them. Her white tank top underneath certainly wouldn't keep her warm enough in the cold chamber. She zipped up, put on her gloves and goggles for safety, then grabbed her tiny bone buddies in their boxes. Another badge tap unsealed the chamber door.

"I know, I know." Red lights flashed at her until she replaced the seal, then the calm purple returned. "Always so dramatic."

Someone knocked on her chamber wall—Monty again. Chase glared and held up her hands in a *what?* gesture.

"Check your email!" He yelled it, but she could barely hear him through the glass. He didn't let her reply, instead stuffing his hands in his pockets and turning on one heel, sauntering away.

Techs damn it. Why did he want her to check her email? What was in there? It wasn't like she could stop in the middle of fabricating to look—ugh. He did it on *purpose*. She forced a deep, calming breath, putting the thought of her email to the back of her mind.

The chamber read her badge and adjusted the countertop to her preset height. The two perfect baby quads waited for her, held aloft by the chamber's programming. Chase shivered as her body adjusted to the cold air and placed her precious cargo down, the little bones glowing on the countertop as they waited to join their friends. The left one would go first.

She pulled her stylus from her pocket and held it to the table until it buzzed twice, indicating the correct setting. With the point of the stylus, she grabbed the first muscle group and lined it up with the pelvis. She let it go for a second, and it waited patiently as she poked the attachment site on the bone to wake it up. When she moved the muscle next to it, it readily accepted the new tendon, like a puzzle piece sliding home.

With slow, methodical movements, she inched her way down the femur, laying the muscle in its new bed. She finished with a swirl and a poke at the tibia, and the other tendon connected as well. After repeating the process on the other side, she had two nearly functional knees.

Chase flipped the whole thing over. Time for the patellae.

Patellae were the bane of every grad student's existence, and the teeny-tiny newborn cartilage chunks often led to a disproportionate amount of blood, sweat, and tears from every party involved. Luckily, thanks to Chase's favorite lab partner, Yumi, she didn't have to struggle with slippery metal tweezers. Instead, she took two sterilized chopsticks from the box in her pocket and easily popped the patellae into their snug little spots.

Just like that, her job was done, and she had to go back to the boring, adult-sized parts that weren't nearly as cute. Baby cases were few and far between at Kierper nowadays, even though children were what turned it into a Fortune 500 company in the first place. The founder and CEO, Dr. George Kristiansen, was a researcher from the Last Generation. When humanity realized it would need scientific intervention in order to keep limping along, he joined in the research. After the initial fear around global infertility abated, Kierper Labs emerged, ready to solve the world's procreation complication. Sure, no one could have a baby the old-fashioned way anymore, but with a chunk of cash and a lot of paperwork, they could build one from scratch.

Chase rolled her perfect replacement wrists and cracked her knuckles. She wasn't a Kierper baby herself—her dads couldn't afford it at the time—but piece by piece, she'd use her employee discount for their top of the line parts.

The purple light blinked as she neared the end of the recommended chamber time, and her nearly frozen fingers agreed. With warm regards and well wishes, she placed the baby in its nest. A touch from her foot opened part of the floor, allowing her to put the box into the chute system.

"Goodbye, little one." Machinery whirred as it boarded its train to the next stop.

The blinking purple lights switched to red as the recommended time ended, reminding her to get the fuck out before the cold ruined her with frostbite. Chase swiped her badge next to the door to shut the chamber down and escaped into the warmth of the office. Her left knee ached with the sharp temperature change, giving its daily reminder that sometimes undergoing research experiments for money wasn't worth it. She kicked her leg a few times until a loud *crack* echoed through the area, the relief instantaneous.

Techs, her email!

Chase dropped into her desk chair and browsed her inbox for the first time that week, deleting notifications from vendors and fake recruiters, as well as generic, company-wide messages. Soon, there was nothing but the important things: details for new projects, date assignments for floating holidays, and a single internal job posting.

A job posting?

Chase clicked and nearly choked.

Openings at Kierper were rare, but a posting for a myofabricator position in Research and Development? Those came around maybe once a decade. R&D was an exclusive club with mythical company benefits and downright legendary salaries, not to mention participation in the biggest and best scientific advancements. Though there were eleven labs—one for each floor—most scientists stayed there until retirement. It was her dream, her goal, her white whale—whatever that ancient phrase meant.

She immediately disregarded all projects to stare at the message.

If even half the rumors were true, two years in R&D would provide enough company credits to replace all her body parts, and all her dads' aging parts. She could move out of her apartment, she could get a dog...hell, she could go on a *vacation*.

Not to mention, she could do some incredibly cool science. She could finally, *finally* see what happened if she braided the muscle fibers together. Her heart skipped a beat at the thought.

The messenger system on the bottom bar of her screen blinked with a new ping. Chase braced herself and clicked. Sure enough, the message was from Monty.

MONTGOMERY E:

Bet you won't.

She scanned the floor, but couldn't see his desk from her own vantage point. How had he known she'd be at her computer at that moment?

Another ping landed.

MONTGOMERY E:

Before you ask, no, I'm not stalking you. Your fab turned off.

He made a good point. The desks were hard to see, but eight foot glowing cubes were easy to spot. Despite the burning in her cheeks, Chase replied.

CHASE A:

Why are you so obsessed with me?

His answer came much too quickly for her liking.

MONTGOMERY E:

I'm not. It's one more thing for me to win.

Chase froze. The position was for a myofabricator. Sure,

Monty was in osseo right now, but he floated. He could do all of it. He had a *chance*.

The time for internal debate was over. She clicked the link to pull up the application and keyed her passcode for the Kierper database to automatically update and upload her CV. A few taps, a couple of verifications, and the only thing left was the red *submit* button. In her haste to tap the button, she actually missed it the first time, and had to tap it again to successfully submit.

Breathe.

Breathe.

Holy shit.

Chase laughed and covered her face with her hands. She actually had a chance, finally had an opportunity to reach toward her goals. All it would take was an interview. Well, and selection for an interview. And for her to meet the nebulous initial requirements.

Right. Easy.

She took a deep breath and got back to work. These muscles weren't going to build themselves.

CHAPTER 2

THE INTERVIEW JOB

THE NEXT DAY, Chase woke particularly well rested, having slept through her alarm. Adrenaline made any lingering sleepiness disappear as she ran around her apartment in a flurry, tossing her curls up in a messy nest and skipping her usual coffee. Luck granted her a fast-arriving rail car, and her heel tapped the floor in a steady staccato the whole ride. While her brain noticed the annoyed glares from the other riders, her leg refused to recognize the social faux pas. The mid-morning sun and a speed walk from the platform had her sweating before she reached the building.

"Dr. Alspeth, you made it in," said Mr. Scovajsa, the older security guard. He took her badge and scanned it, giving her a look of genuine concern over his bushy gray mustache.

"Yeah, slept through my alarm, unfortunately." She shook her head. "Messed up my whole morning."

"Well, you're here, and you're safe. That's what matters." He handed her badge back and added an extra pat on the hand.

She took it with a tight smile. "Thank you, Mr. Scovajsa, sorry to run but—"

"You have work to do." His grin reminded her of Pops, and

warmth bloomed in her chest. She needed to call home one of these days.

Soon. When she had good news about R&D, Techs willing.

After a pit stop in the cafeteria for coffee, she hustled to the ninth floor. It wasn't unusual for her to be the last to her station, but based on the stares, she was late enough to garner just a touch of office gossip.

"Welcome, Alspeth," Monty commented as she strode by. "Thank you for coming to work today."

"Wanted to give you a head start, see if you could catch up," she called over her shoulder. He laughed and almost sounded… sincere. Well then, perhaps the whole morning wasn't a wash after all.

Chase collapsed into her chair and took a deep breath. Her heart raced, and low-level panic simmered somewhere between her heart and stomach. She was at a ten, and she needed to dial it back to a three. They wouldn't fire her for being a little late as long as she made up the time later.

Once settled at her desk, she sipped her coffee and opened her inbox for the second time in as many days, which was a new record for her. There was the usual fodder from HR and the compliance center, as well as a message for a different Chase that worked in dermofabrication. All the usual suspects.

Until she found a vital message from one Dr. Beauchamp, Department Head for Research and Development.

She caught herself before she spat out her coffee and nearly broke her tablet in half in her haste to open the message. The subject line read like an automatic reply, but upon reading the message, she found it to be a genuine response.

They wanted her to come in for an interview.

On the fifteenth floor.

Today.

At eleven o'clock.

She inwardly cursed herself for not waking on time and outwardly cursed the clock for having the audacity to say she had seventeen minutes to get her act together. It would be a challenge, but she'd done more damage in less time.

When Chase first started, she put an emergency makeup kit in the bottom desk drawer, just in case the fabricators decided being fancy was important. She hadn't touched it in three years, but now it was time to call it to action.

Thank Techs the bathroom was empty. Right now she sported a look that said "exhausted doctoral candidate," and she needed her face to say "cool, professional, and innovative." She tore the tie from her hair and raked her fingers through until it was pliable enough to braid. There was dust on the outside of the bag, and even the zipper resisted release until she used every available shoulder, elbow, wrist, and hand muscle to pry it open.

A quick scrub to her face put some color under her cheeks, and a dab of powder on the bags under her green eyes made her look less like the undead. Mascara made them look more open. The neutral lipstick fell apart when she uncapped it, so she abandoned the idea and simply pressed her lips together until they too had some life in them. She stepped back to admire her work and decided it was…passable.

She checked her watch.

Six minutes.

She wasn't proud of the noise that came from her mouth and made a mental note to never recreate it in the future. After sweeping the useless, ancient makeup into the trash receptacle, she made a mad dash for the elevator. Anxiety told her to take the stairs, but climbing six stories would definitely take longer than waiting.

When the elevator finally arrived, she nearly tore the doors open with her bare hands, stopping as she noticed the single occupant in the box. Chase shoved her hands in her pockets and kept her eyes on the floor as she stood in the corner; the other person sidestepped to put as much space between them as possible. Did she smell? No, she couldn't smell. Could she? She managed a stealthy sniff, which probably didn't help her current presentation.

All her nerves gathered and froze when the elevator stopped and the artificial voice announced the fifteenth floor. Through habit alone, she exited and walked the mile long runway to the receptionist. She was a whole minute early—Dad would be proud. The man at the desk had a dazzling smile, and Chase wondered how many company credits those teeth cost.

"Dr. Chase Alspeth?" he asked. A courtesy, since she was the only person in the room. She could see her own face smiling up at him from the employee file on his tablet.

"Yes." Somehow she made her voice sound totally normal.

"Have a seat, please," he said lightly, gesturing toward the comfortable-looking leather chairs. His gaze lingered on her waist, and while at first Chase wanted to tell him exactly where he could put his eyes, it occurred to her he was looking at the sleeves of her red jumpsuit tied around her hips. She reached for them and he lifted an eyebrow, and when she slipped them on and did up the zipper, he gave her an approving smile. Job done, he went back to his tablet.

The chairs were not as comfortable as they looked, so all she could do for the disrespectful half-hour wait was bounce her leg and attempt to transfer her anxiety into excess heat energy. It didn't work. She pulled a plastic container of mouth refreshers from her pocket and popped one in, hoping that would chill her out. It was another failed attempt.

The door behind the desk opened, and Dr. Kristiansen himself stepped out. He wore no jumpsuit or lab coat, instead donning sharp pressed brown slacks with a blue button down. Chase startled to her feet and forced herself to look in his direction despite her swimming vision. She really needed to drink more water. That would be her next task, right after nailing this interview.

"Ah, yes, Dr. Alspeth. Come in," he said with a gentle smile.

Chase swallowed the mint and felt it scrape down every

centimeter of her esophagus. Even though he greeted her by name, she was tempted to look around and make sure she was the only Dr. Alspeth in the office. Her movements felt robotic as she accepted the surprisingly weak handshake, the lack of grip strength putting her nerves on pause. Besides that, only his white hair told of his advanced age.

"Thank you for meeting with us on such short notice," Dr. Kristiansen said.

"Thank you for inviting me," Chase replied. The steady voice was gone. *Damn it.*

Despite this, Dr. Kristiansen led her into the office, walking with a limp so slight she probably wouldn't have noticed if she didn't work with lower extremities. He eased himself into the chair behind a massive wooden desk. The thing had to be at least a hundred years old; she'd only ever seen anything like it in history files and period pieces on the Stream, and hadn't thought they existed anymore. She took a chair in front and found it was even more uncomfortable than the ones outside.

Maybe Dr. Kristiansen didn't want his guests to linger.

The door opened behind her, and the third member of their party crossed the office before she could turn around. He looked familiar, with his steely gray hair and unnervingly blue eyes. She rifled through her memory, hoping she hadn't accidentally bumped into him in the hallway or let the elevator door close while he ran toward it. But if they'd met before in any capacity, the man didn't show it.

"Dr. Alspeth, this is Dr. Beauchamp. He's the head of Research and Development and will help me conduct your interview today," Dr. Kristiansen said. Chase licked her lips and tried to pull some air into her lungs before standing and extending her hand.

"Nice to meet you, sir," she said. Her voice was way steadier this time.

Beauchamp looked down at her hand and then back at her, choosing to lean against Dr. Kristiansen's desk instead of accepting her offer. The heavy wood didn't so much as shift with his weight, but Dr. Kristiansen narrowed his eyes at the casual position. Beauchamp either didn't notice, or pretended not to.

"Alspeth." He said her name like a question and an explanation all in one.

"Yes." It might've been rhetorical, but she answered anyway.

"Your dissertation was about the fortification of genetic coding to allow for proper gene expression during fabrication." Again, no question.

"Yes," she repeated, her heart rate settling. She was shaky when it came to talking to superiors, but she knew how to talk about research. "I also worked in data collection, technical writing, and implementation for internal tissue repair with nanotechnology and rejuvenation for scarred materials—"

"I don't care about those." He batted her verbal resume away like an annoying fly. "Kierper."

"I'm sorry?"

"Perhaps my colleague here could be a little clearer," Dr. Kristiansen spoke up, reminding them both of proper interview etiquette. Traditionally, they involved questions, and he was a traditional man. "Why did you choose to work for Kierper? We know you had offers at CorpTech and BodT."

"Kierper is the best. Everyone knows that." According to her research, that was a fact, and she really liked facts. "I didn't just want to make bodies, I wanted to make better bodies. The *best* bodies."

Beauchamp smiled like it was the answer he wanted. Or like a snake about to strike. She couldn't quite tell. "Everyone wants the best."

"Yes." Her nerves diminished as her annoyance grew. "And Kierper has the capacity and the resources for that."

The non-questions and cryptic statements were clearly some sort of power play tactic, and it was starting to piss her off. She'd worked with a hundred guys like him, professors who claimed their brutal honesty weeded out weaklings. Really, they were just assholes.

"Harder, better, faster, stronger," Dr. Kristiansen murmured. If it was a quote, she didn't get the reference. At one hundred and forty years old, he was one of the few living from the Last Generation. He had references that were dead and buried in the depths of the old Internet. "Research and Development will require a different skill set than you currently use, and will challenge you in ways you never thought possible."

"I mean, I assumed so." She winced as she heard herself. "Sir," she added. She wanted to come across as respectful, even if Beauchamp wasn't extending the same courtesy to her.

"I dunno, Alspeth," Beauchamp said, narrowing his eyes at her. "You seem like someone who likes rules."

"Is that a bad thing?" she countered.

"Just saying, rules become guidelines in R&D. At best."

"I'm okay with bending the rules of science," she said, "but I'm not going to tell two Kierper leaders I like breaking rules as a practice." She was trying to claw her way into his good graces, but every answer felt wrong as soon as it left her mouth. Her heart rate accelerated again, beating so hard it nearly choked her.

Beauchamp sighed and pushed off the desk. Dr. Kristiansen's face muscles relaxed, visibly relieved the man was no longer leaning on the expensive furniture.

"I've heard everything I need. Call me if the next one is any better than this," Beauchamp said, striding toward the door.

"Emile, wait—"

Beauchamp didn't heed his request. He stomped out of the room, ignoring one of the most important men in the world calling his name. Oh, so he was an *entitled* asshole.

Dr. Kristiansen smoothed his wrinkle-free shirt and laced his fingers on the desk. "I know that Dr. Beauchamp is a little, ah, rough around the edges. But he is a damn good scientist."

He smiled, and the attempt at comforting her fell flat on the desk between them. The silence stretched, as strong and fragile as a spiderweb, and Chase had the feeling it was time to cut her losses.

"Is there anything else you need, sir?" Her voice shook as she tried to contain her emotions. This was her only chance to interview for R&D until Beauchamp retired, which could be between infinity and never.

"No, Dr. Alspeth. Thank you for your time." He didn't get up and didn't offer to shake her hand again. He picked up his tablet and opened another document, already on to the next candidate. The blow hit Chase square in the sternum. She stood on trembling legs and walked, glad he wasn't looking. Then he couldn't see her falling apart.

Because the day had to kick her while she was down, she exited into the lobby to find Monty sitting in the same uncomfortable chair she'd occupied earlier. At the sight of her, he adopted his usual cocky grin. As he caught her expression, the smirk dropped and a look of concern crossed his face.

"Alspeth? You okay?"

"Fine." She sniffled—how embarrassing—and kept walking, even when he stood and reached for her.

"Wait, Alspeth—"

"Good luck, you'll need it!"

She didn't turn around. The last thing she needed was for Monty to see her cry. She bypassed the elevator. The idea of standing there waiting for it, with the two men staring at her back, made her cringe. So even though every other step sent a sting through her knee, she took the stairs for all six floors until she reached her own.

The R&D job posting had to be common knowledge at that point, and the interviews as well. Everyone tried their hardest to pretend they weren't looking as she walked by. Luckily, the walk down the stairwell gave her enough time to get her tears under control, even though her emotions were likely all over her face.

She would make it through this. It would just suck.

CHAPTER 3
THE NEW LEG JOB

JUST WHEN SHE thought things couldn't get any worse, Chase got a message from the client office that afternoon.

Customer service was a blight upon humanity, and Chase avoided it whenever possible. Going to the client office was like descending to a circle of hell where she had to deal with someone grumpy, rich, or a combination of the two. The fact that Chase had to go wrangle a demon after the gut-shearing interview was a particularly rude cosmic joke.

According to the paperwork, it was *data collection*, but it was all the same to her.

Armed with her tablet and stylus, she began the journey to the second floor. The further she got from her desk, and Dr. Kristiansen's office, the easier it was to blink back her tears. Though, she would definitely have a good cry in the shower later.

The client office had plush chairs and warm, neutral tones. Whoever designed the office had tried way too hard to make the space appear comfortable. No one stood in the waiting room, which meant she had a couple more minutes before she had to paint on her client smile. Ren, the front desk person, sat with their cheek resting on their hand, squishing their face awkwardly.

"Hey." Ren always sounded a little annoyed, and it made Chase smile. They swiped one of their screens to send a chunk of documents directly to Chase's tablet, their eyes never leaving the mad frenzy of color coded appointments in front of them. If Chase read it right, the afternoon rush was on the horizon.

"Have you seen the new episode of *Earthbound*?" Chase asked, grasping at one of their few common threads.

"No, I'm trying to finish *Faerie Queen* first," Ren spat, punching at the keyboard. "If I stop, I'll never go back to it."

"Don't you hate *Faerie Queen*?" Chase said. She personally found it deliciously dramatic, but knew the world held many valid critiques for it.

Ren grimaced. "Yes."

"So why watch it?"

"To prove I'm stronger," Ren said. They ran a hand through their short red hair as the screen loaded, then sent the last docs to her tablet. "There, you'll need that."

Chase opened the docs, and the first demographics page showed a young man in uniform. His smile displayed the optimism and hubris of youth, and the record underneath said he'd been in the service for a little over a year. She swiped to the next page for the orders: Total Limb Regeneration and Replacement.

"Shit," Chase muttered. The tag for supplemental orders popped up, and she tapped it with a grimace.

Return to Active Duty Parameters.

"Double shit." She'd never seen total regeneration followed by a return to active duty. Ren snorted.

"Have fun with that," they said.

"Why do you hate me?" The challenges felt particularly personal today.

"Take it up with the scheduling gods. I'm just a lowly peasant here," they said with a flick of their hand.

"You really are watching too much *Faerie Queen*."

The automatic front doors slid open, and two older men strode in with all the confidence of people who didn't look at price tags. Like flipping a switch, Ren straightened and smiled, their voice half an octave higher than a moment before. Chase took the opportunity to make her escape through the back door to the exam rooms.

It was hard to believe this youth—Corporal James Reynolds—wanted to go back to active duty, but she figured his short journey so far lent him a little more motivation to continue. He was way younger than her normal clientele for this procedure, but service members were common in the Kierper building. They were usually ancient and on the retirement track, but Chase wasn't here to judge the client or the entity that sent them. She was there to take measurements and get back to the lab, where she belonged.

The Corporal James Reynolds waiting for her in the exam room was not the same Corporal James Reynolds who smiled from her screen. The man in front of her no longer beamed with the hubris of youth. Gone were the baby face and twinkling eyes. All that remained was a gaunt ghost of his former self. He'd lost a significant amount of weight, and not just from his missing right leg. The typical ramrod military posture was lost in favor of a slump, and instead of a uniform, he wore a ratty t-shirt and shorts. Lofstrand crutches rested against the table next to him. He didn't look up as she closed the door, his eyes focused on some spot she couldn't see. She checked to make sure the cleaning crew hadn't missed something, but the floor was as pristine as always.

"Corporal James Reynolds?" Chase asked, her voice cracking halfway.

This was why she belonged in the lab, and why Kierper needed to hire and train technicians for data collection. Everyone else in the game used them, but it was a selling point here: Clients would only work with specialists, no matter how awkward or uncomfortable the situation was for either party.

"Jamie," he corrected.

His voice came out lower than expected, and with a Southern

twang that didn't often travel this far north. Just saying his name seemed to exhaust him, and for a second Chase thought about leaving him to nap and coming back later.

"Uh, my name is Chase," she said, pulling her stylus from her pocket and tapping it against her leg to get to the right setting. When working in the client office, they were encouraged *not* to introduce themselves as "Doctor so-and-so." The handbook said it was to put clients at ease, but Chase worked hard for her Ph.D. and thought it would instill confidence. Too bad she wasn't the one in charge. "I'm here to do your muscle measurements?"

"You sure?" he asked, and she couldn't blame him. Her statements to clients tended to sound like questions, no matter how hard she tried.

"I'm hoping," she replied, forcing a weak smile. He stared at the floor, tapping his thumbs against his thighs, and so missed her failed attempt at lightening the mood. She powered through. "It says here you were…injured? During a skirmish overseas."

"Blown up," he corrected with a dry laugh. "I was *blown up* overseas."

"Oh." Her mind whirred as she searched for an appropriate reaction. It was one thing to work with rich people wanting new parts. This conversation was so far outside of her scope of practice, it might as well be overseas, too. She settled on, "I'm sorry."

"Yeah, me too," he said.

She needed to say something, anything, but her brain was physically incapable of formulating a response. And even if it could, her mouth seemed to refuse to do the moving thing with the sounds. Jamie pressed his lips together and sighed heavily, then looked up at her to say in a tight voice, "So, are we gonna do this or what?"

The sharpness of his glare startled her. Rings surrounded his dark brown eyes and heavy shadows hung underneath. He clenched his jaw and his fists, but a wince told her the actions stemmed from pain rather than aggression. A new leg wouldn't fix the mental trauma he endured.

Most former military personnel were excited when they were measured for replacement limbs. Jamie was not, and Chase didn't know how to navigate it.

"Um, yeah. Yes sir, sorry," she said, rushing to open the exam page. Her follow-up questions spilled from her in a deluge. "Was there anything different with the right compared to the left? Any scars or birthmarks or tattoos you want replaced? Any injuries to the remaining leg that need to be altered for the new limb?"

"No." He dropped his gaze again, deflating back to his original state. Chase found she could breathe a little easier at his dampened emotions, until guilt for thinking that weaseled in.

"You sure?" she asked softly.

"Yes."

That was a lie. She could see surgical scars right there on his remaining knee, including one that trailed down the line of the quadriceps tendon. A spark of annoyance momentarily overshadowed her discomfort, and she poked the scar with her stylus, making him jump and glare again.

"What's this then?" Her voice held more confidence now.

Jamie didn't seem impressed by her change in demeanor. "It's old. And it was fixed."

A thread of fear laced his expression, killing her irritation. Heat crawled up the back of her neck and chastised her for her insensitivity. It wasn't his job to know all the pertinent information fabricators needed—it was hers.

She took a deep breath. "If you want the new limb to function properly, I need to know the history of the left leg. We're building your new right one based on it."

Sure, there was only a certain percentage of symmetry between sides even without surgical involvement, but she wasn't going to get into those facts. Her ex from college told her to let other people determine if those kinds of facts were fun.

"And if I don't want the new one?" Again he looked at her

with those eyes, but this time she was a little better prepared—for his gaze, not his question.

"What?" she asked, blinking. Did she mishear him? "Why wouldn't you want a new leg?"

"Plenty of people get by with prosthetics. Or nothing at all. I could do that." He shrugged, his slender shoulders nearly reaching his ears.

Chase didn't understand. "But...but the military wants you to get a new limb. A *Kierper* limb."

He grit his teeth. "But maybe I don't want it."

"But it's a *good limb*—"

"Yeah, it'll be great!" he snapped, the rise in his voice so sharp she took a step back. "It'll be strong, and top of the line, and just as good as the original one! It'll be so perfect, those rat bastards can send me back out there again. Maybe this time I'll come back in a body bag instead of a wheelchair, so they won't have to spend money on new parts for me."

Silence weighed on both of them, and every word Chase had ever known vacated her mind.

"I'm sorry," she said again once the wheels started turning. It was a platitude at best, and they both knew it. She had no pull in the military, no pull at Kierper, no way to help him except to take his measurements. Jamie reached the same conclusion and slumped, the fight gone from him.

"No. I'm sorry, ma'am," he whispered. "You're just trying to do your job. I won't stop you."

"No, you're not—I mean, I can..." She trailed off, not sure how to salvage the appointment. Her fab chamber never yelled like that. Her fab chamber always followed instructions. She belonged with her fab chamber.

"Don't worry about me, ma'am. I'll get by," he said, his voice barely above a whisper. "Do what you need to do."

Chase wanted to do literally anything else. She swallowed, the action louder than anticipated, and adjusted the grip on her stylus. With no other option, she held the tip of the stylus to the tablet to sync it.

"I'll, um," her voice cracked again, her dry throat betraying her. She cleared it. "I'll need you to stand up." The words were hard to get out, but they were audible, which was as good as it would get.

Jamie nodded and grabbed one of the crutches, heaving himself onto his remaining leg. His shorts covered most of his thigh, which would skew her data. Maybe, instead of starting at the hip, she could start at the lower leg and come back.

The idea made her brain itch, so she discarded it.

"Can I roll this up?" she asked, gesturing to the shorts. He nodded again, looking away as she exposed his thigh with as much care and respect as possible.

Even with only the one crutch, he stood at attention, despite any physical or mental discomfort. It was impressive, and it would cut down the time of their shared torment immensely.

Jamie was a slender guy with minimal subcutaneous fat, so she had no trouble finding the different lines of his muscles. With light, practiced touches, she palpated the muscular insertion points and dragged her stylus over the necessary pathways as numbers flooded her screen. Most clients had questions or wanted to see the data going into the file, but Jamie didn't even watch.

Chase took advantage of the silence to work fast, mapping out fiber densities and shapes like an architect designing a building. Maybe he didn't want this leg, but she would still make sure it was the best damn leg money could buy, just in case he changed his mind.

A few swipes, a few holds, and she had everything she needed. Chase stood and clutched her tablet to her chest, her mind buzzing with numbers and clichés about grief. They all sounded stupid, so she reverted back to what she knew— her job.

"The next fabricator will be in shortly," she said. The best thing for both of them would be a quick exit. His brows furrowed and his eyes raised as far as her tablet.

"You're not doing the whole thing?" he murmured.

She couldn't tell exactly what emotion he displayed, only that it sounded sad in some way. He had a lot more people to deal with today, and his tolerance already seemed depleted. Now, instead of escaping, she wanted to stay and take all his measurements, if only to protect him. But management would never allow it, and she couldn't go against management.

"No, I'm sorry," she said, cringing inwardly as she offered another lame apology. "Each part of your new limb will be made independently by a specialist. This ensures quality and decreases turnaround time so you can receive your limb sooner."

Quoting the employee handbook was always helpful in these situations, even if it made her feel like an asshole. Jamie took the lingering silence after her explanation as his cue to sit again, the table squeaking as it accepted his weight. They both flinched at the noise.

Chase cleared her throat again. "Can I...get you anything while you wait?"

"No, ma'am," he said. "Thank you for your time."

Pitifully grateful for the dismissal, she turned and strode to the door. No matter how gentle she tried to close it, it felt like a slam, and her footsteps felt more like stomps as she trudged to the front. Ren noticed her entrance and tapped on the screen, pinging the next fabricator, then tapped their stylus against Chase's tablet to request the data for his file.

"What a ray of sunshine, right?" Ren said, but even they couldn't muster the typical client-related disdain.

Chase hummed a noncommittal response. Professional athletes, high-ranking government officials, rich spouses in need of a little rejuvenation—Chase could handle those. Soldiers suffering from PTSD? They deserved better than her, that was for sure.

"Who's in next?" she asked, leaning over Ren's shoulder to

look at the schedule. They pressed a couple keys, highlighting the next name. "Oh, shit."

"What?" Ren asked.

"You're good? You got everything you need?" Chase took a few steps backward, toward the lobby area instead of the back door.

"Uh, yeah, you okay? Is the next one—?"

"Everything's fine, I just gotta go!" she lied, deciding it was too much of a risk to come back the way she came and instead choosing the minefield of the lobby. The waiting clients looked up, but she avoided eye contact; she wasn't there to call them back, she was making a quick getaway.

The employee door whooshed open just as the office one shut behind her, and she prayed to Techs and any other deity listening that Monty didn't spot her as she rushed out the door. It was bad enough that he caught her this morning in a moment of weakness–she couldn't have him see her shaken up twice in the same day.

In the split second before the front doors slid closed behind her, Chase made the mistake of glancing back. Monty was looking right at her, his brows pinched. He didn't look any worse for wear, at least not like she felt after her interview. Did that mean it went better?

"Damn it." Chase shook off his apparent concern and walked to the other elevator.

She just needed one win, one moment that didn't make her feel like ripping her hair out. Based on the law of averages, that time would come soon. Chase closed her eyes as she waited for the elevator and counted backward from ten; the day wasn't done, and neither was she.

CHAPTER 4

THE GURNEY JOB

CHASE RARELY TOOK breaks at work, but the situation demanded it. It was, far and away, her worst day at work in the three years she'd been at Kierper. Bad enough that she pulled up the BodT and CorpTech websites and browsed open positions. Maybe she could get onto their R&D teams and go do fun science, just with slightly lower quality resources. At least their higher-ups didn't seem angry and tired like the ones she met today.

Of course, then she remembered she was on company Wi-Fi and closed the window immediately. That was a search for her to do in the privacy of her own…company-owned apartment. Shit.

Chase put her head on the table, ignoring the loud *thunk* it made upon impact. Maybe she didn't need to fabricate at all. Maybe she could become a mechanic, or decorate cakes at a bakery, or…teach! She could teach, right?

The thought of a sea of undergraduates staring at her made a shiver go down her spine.

"You're just being dramatic," she told herself as she sat up. "It didn't work out. You'll be fine."

After a snack, a coffee, and multiple deep breaths, Chase returned to her desk on the ninth floor. She still had a list of projects to complete, and it would be best to focus on those instead of what could have been.

One by one, the fab chamber lights around her went out as the other fabricators finished their hours. She kept her fab chamber dark as she typed away, no longer wanting the beacon to shine. It was a rare treat to be in the open room by herself, and she let her entire body relax. She wanted to cry, but willed the tears to stay in their ducts. Crying was for the shower only.

Her handheld buzzed on the table; Dad was calling. Techs, it was like the man had a sixth sense.

"Hello?"

His warm, gravely voice greeted her. "Hey, honey. Is this a good time?"

Tears threatened again, and Chase's throat ached. "Yeah, now is fine," she choked out.

He hummed. "Are you okay?"

"What? Yeah, I'm good." Techs, that was not convincing at *all*.

"Well, that sounded like a lie." Dad saw right through her. "What's going on?"

Chase couldn't help it. Suddenly she was a teenager again, talking to her dad after struggling through a humanities exam in undergrad. The whole story spilled from her in a torrent, with her dad content to wait until the flow slowed from a deluge to a trickle, until she ran out of words.

"So, um, yeah," she said at the end. "That's what's going on."

Her dad made a vague noise of disgust. "What bullies."

"Right?" It was nice to get validation, even if it was just from a parent.

"Well, did you send a follow-up message?" he asked.

Chase balked. "Did I do what?"

"A follow-up message. You know, thank them for their time, add any additional comments, that sort of thing. Sounds like you weren't really given the opportunity to sell yourself."

"Dad, I cannot express how old-fashioned that is." The only

time she'd heard of such a thing was in historical shows on the Stream. The practice sounded positively ancient.

"Honey, the man is over a hundred years old. He might appreciate something a little old-fashioned," he said.

Perhaps he made a good point.

"Well, I suppose it couldn't get any worse," she conceded.

"That's the spirit." Dad laughed, and Chase found herself smiling. He was right, wasn't he? If they didn't like a follow-up email, what was the worst they could do, fire her? Like Dr. Kristiansen said, she had offers from other places before, places that were still around, as evidenced by her sleuthing earlier. She had options.

"Thanks, Dad. I appreciate it," she said.

"Anytime, honey," he replied. "And don't worry, if you don't get the job, that man you work with won't either. You're way more talented than him."

Chase laughed and shook her head. "I think you're contractually obligated to say things like that."

"Well, yes, there was definitely a paper we signed when we ordered you. But that doesn't make it any less true."

"You don't even know him," she said, then paused. Why the hell was she defending Monty to her Dad?

He scoffed. "No, but I know you, and I know you're the best damn fabricator in that whole building."

Techs, he was so sweet, she could cry. Again. "Thanks, Dad. But enough of my woes. What's going on with you?"

Her dad launched into a long, meandering story involving a neighborhood cat, and the familiar cadence soothed her frazzled nerves. By the time the conversation wrapped up, she was almost back to baseline. Before she could second guess herself, she pulled up her email and opened one to Dr. Kristiansen. She also added Dr. Beauchamp, but after staring at his name for way too long, she removed him from the list. It was one thing to send a message, but it was another to give him the opportunity to hurt her feelings again.

Dr. Kristiansen,

I wanted to thank you for your time today. While the interview didn't go quite like I hoped, I still appreciate the opportunity to speak with you about the R&D position.

She paused. Was this the right way to word it? Chase deleted it and started over. Once again, she got two lines in before deleting and attempting a third try. All in all, it took eight drafts before she returned to her initial thoughts and finished them.

Dr. Kristiansen,

I wanted to thank you for your time today. While the interview didn't go quite like I hoped, I still appreciate the opportunity to speak with you about the R&D position. R&D requires a certain creativity, and a willingness to push the bounds of fabrication, both of which I believe I possess. This can be seen with my previous projects. I feel I wasn't able to adequately express this earlier, and wanted to make sure you knew I am very much interested in joining the R&D lab.

Thank you again.

Was it too cold? Or, was it the opposite—too casual? She'd always had so much trouble with knowing exactly what to say in emails like this, and she couldn't exactly go running to her parents for help.

Well, she *could*, but she shouldn't. She was a grown woman, nearing thirty, and needed to write her own damn emails.

Chase let the message marinate, unsent, and returned to her documentation. If, when she finished all her notes, she still liked the way the email sounded, then she'd send it. And if she didn't, then she'd go home and wallow in misery before trying again tomorrow.

An hour after the sun set, her documentation was nearly finished. The overhead lights, usually so aggressively bright during the day, dulled to a gentle glow. Combined with the dark fab chambers and empty desks, it made her ideal work environment.

Until something massive crashed somewhere on the other side of the floor. She couldn't see what fell or broke, but it was heavy enough to send vibrations through the floor and rattle her desk. For a second, she worried a fab chamber had fallen apart, and had a terrible mental image of each chamber down the line toppling over like a massive, expensive line of dominoes.

No further crashes came, only a deep hum and a creak of a stuck elevator. Who would still be here at this time, except the usual security guards? But the elevator stopped, leaving her in a silence thick with questions.

Something squeaked. A second later, the sound came again. Then again. It was a steady, rhythmic noise. And it was getting closer.

Chase had many things on her body she wanted to change, but she was lucky enough to have perfect eyesight, which allowed her to spot nerve endings and myofibril tangles…and men in black jumpsuits wheeling a shrouded body on a gurney. One wheel squeaked with every turn, an ominous soundtrack to the odd procession.

In three years, she'd never seen anyone in black jumpsuits, or even a gurney like that. The combination of the two was super fucking weird. Adrenaline flooded her vessels. Instincts told her to duck under her desk, some primitive reflex that made humans want to hide from death—*if* the body was even dead.

Chase shifted an inch at a time until her monitor hid her, the space beneath it just wide enough for her to watch the prome-nade. The squeaky wheel stuck, and the gurney jostled. A hand slid from beneath the shroud, the clearly broken bones stretching out some sort of marking on the skin. It was one hiccup away from tearing through, despite the obvious muscle bulk of the forearm. The men moving the gurney swept keen eyes across the floor as they walked, but none of them seemed to notice her. Chase's brain waffled between staying stationary or ducking beneath the desk.

Rock and a hard place. Son of a bitch.

She held her position and her breath. Her heart thudded hard against her sternum as the black jumpsuits moved out of sight toward the service elevators. Once she heard the elevator doors closed behind them, she allowed herself to breathe again, so fast and deep she choked on the air. She hoped the walls were thick enough to hide the sounds of her hacking up her second-rate lungs. Panic made the affliction more aggressive.

When she could finally breathe again, she stood. Her knee cracked so loudly in the silence that she nearly jumped out of her skin, which would be entirely too expensive to replace. What in the hell had she just seen?

Kierper never used gurneys, at least not that she knew of. All projects traveled via the chute system in the fabs. Maybe it was a table of nonviable limbs? But then, the arm would've fallen onto the floor instead of staying on the table.

Maybe it was a client on the way to the upper extremity floors. But then, why didn't they start there, since setting bones was the first priority in limb repair?

Maybe it was an employee, involved in some sort of accident. But she'd researched Kierper before, and they hadn't reported any injuries on the job in decades.

Possibilities swirled in her head, but none seemed *probable*. Each explanation seemed more outlandish than the next, until Chase finally settled on one that almost made sense.

The gurney came from the back corner, which was her floor's Research and Development wing. That would explain everything weird about the situation. The big crash must've been their usual way of travel—as high-tech as Kierper was, the elevators always had trouble—so they had to come out here with the peasants to take the parts down to the basement. That seemed likely, as R&D burned any prototypes that didn't work in an offsite incinerator. Her own tour guide told her that not-so-fun fact on her first day.

That had to be it. It was a failed R&D project, going for its last send off. It was something great, something cool, something she absolutely, one hundred percent needed to be a part of.

With resolve, Chase opened her email again. Her message

from earlier sat waiting, the send button bright blue. She didn't bother reading it again, only pressed send, throwing the message into the electronic ether.

Maybe it would help, maybe it wouldn't. Either way, she could say she did everything she could. Perhaps she still had a chance.

Chase sat down to finish her notes, engaging in a thought experiment about the body she saw and what experiments it might've been for. It was possible the muscles were supposed to prevent the break, but subpar work led to the experiment failing. Chase scoffed; *she* could probably make muscles that kept bones from breaking, given the proper tools. Ugh, what she would give to look at that prototype up close.

Chase paused as the memory returned again, and in her mind's eye, she saw the angle of the break, the mark on the skin, every part of the limb that was visible as it rolled by.

She couldn't help but wonder why a prototype would have nail polish.

CHAPTER 5
THE HAZING JOB

IT TOOK A WHOLE WEEK, but Chase got over the terrible appointment with Jamie and her horrendous interview. Well, mostly got over them. *Partially* got over them.

"Hello? Come back, Alspeth."

Chase blinked. She was at her desk with a warm cup of coffee and an equally fresh attitude, ready to accept her fate to stay at this spot forever. Monty leaned one hip against her desk, holding out the patella box.

"Spaced out for a second." She shook her head and took the box from him. He frowned.

"Are you sure you're alright? You've barely inspected any bones I've brought you the past few days."

She furrowed her brow. "You make it sound like I don't trust your work."

"Do you?" He lifted one corner of his mouth, the cheeky bastard.

"Well, I trust your second drafts. They seem to do alright."

"There it is." He was full on smiling now, and Chase couldn't quite squash the urge to smile back. A thought struck her.

"Hey, you talk to people around here, right?" she asked. Monty's brows shot up.

"I mean, yes. I'm talking to someone right now, in fact." He gestured toward her, and she rolled her eyes.

"I'm going to ignore you being deliberately obtuse," she said. Before he could come back with a quippy response, she continued. "Have you heard anything about people getting hurt here?"

She didn't like the pause Monty took before answering. "Why, have you heard something?"

"Last night, after everyone left…"

She didn't get her question out before they heard loud, disturbing footsteps pounding across the floor. Monty's eyes widened. "Shit. I've got to go."

"What?" Chase turned to glare at the offender. It was supposed to be *quiet* in the morning. The anger flipped to fear as Dr. Beauchamp came into view, the whole floor stopping and staring at the legend. Her fear turned to pure terror as he made a beeline toward her.

"Don't leave me alone with—Monty?" She turned back, but he was already gone, leaving her high and dry.

How close was Beauchamp? Could she run? If she threw her drink at him, would that deter him? She had no desire to go over her inadequacies in any greater detail, nor hear any new insults he might have cooked up.

With the inevitability of a crash, Dr. Beauchamp arrived at her desk.

"Alspeth." He stood with his arms crossed, probably trying to be intimidating. Considering she was sitting like a child sent to the principal's office, Chase didn't exactly have *power* in her repertoire at that moment.

"Dr. Beauchamp." She was proud of how cool she sounded, despite the maelstrom in her abdomen.

"Against my better judgment, and after lots and lots of arguments, Kristiansen wants you for the R&D job."

Silence.

Oh, that was her moment to respond.

"Okay?" It was not supposed to be a question. It wasn't supposed to be her entire answer, either.

Beauchamp groaned and rolled his eyes. "'Okay,' as in you accept, or 'okay,' as in you agree with my opinion?"

She blinked. "Wait, was that an offer?"

"Don't you check your email, Alspeth?" He pinched the bridge of his nose. "God, I can't help you if you won't help yourself."

"I—what?" Who still invoked an old deity and not the technologies that saved them? She put her mug down and opened her email. The same stupid messages clogged her inbox, but there, nestled amongst the mundane bullshit, was an email from Dr. Kristiansen himself. The subject line read *Regarding your recent R&D interview*. "Holy shit."

"That's what I said," Beauchamp muttered. Chase opened it and scanned the contents quickly.

"Wait." She read the passage again. "So this would be a trial period?"

"Yes."

"And my salary would be...the same." She scanned again, hoping she missed something.

Beauchamp huffed. "Yes."

She cocked her head to the side at the last portion. "And I can't tell anyone anything about what I'm working on?"

He dropped his hands to his hips. "I'm familiar with the inner workings of the program, Alspeth. Jesus, how did you get a Ph.D.?"

"Very carefully." She didn't mean for the words to slip out, and Beauchamp grinned at the alarm on her face. He could technically rescind the offer at any time—that was also explicitly stated in the message.

"Watch it, Alspeth." He turned on his heel and stomped a few more steps, then paused to look over his shoulder. The gesture was both dramatic and aggressive, and Chase would be impressed if Beauchamp didn't look so angry.

"Aren't you gonna go to the lab?" he sneered.

Chase grinned. He could stay mad.

"Right away," she said.

He left without giving her any further instructions, and went the opposite direction from the R&D corner, so Chase assumed she was on her own. She didn't know what to bring with her, but grabbed her tablet, handheld, and stylus. As she stood to leave, she noticed the attention from her coworkers, though they all pretended to be busy when she saw them.

No matter. She'd landed the job–she was going to R&D!

Chase took one last cursory glance as she walked toward the hidden office, and was quite pleased to see Monty watching, his jaw unhinged. In a completely professional move, she stuck her tongue out. Halfway there, she wished she'd brought her coffee. A jolt went through her as she remembered she would have new peers, and she had no donuts or anything to break the ice on the first day.

They were all professionals and likely above hazing, but with a director like Beauchamp, anything was possible.

As she took the turn, thunder rolled and rain started against the windows, giving the hallway a sinister darkness as she walked the path the men with the gurney took the previous week. The air conditioning stuttered on, the whine reminding her of the wheel squeaking with every turn. A place between her shoulder blades tingled, and she twisted to look behind her.

The hallway was empty, even the fab chambers out of sight.

Her pulse raced as she took off at a firm power walk, only slowing so she didn't go careening into the wall at the final turn. She fully expected to see men in suits and a pile of dead bodies. What she found was a fake plant and a door.

The light flashed green when she waved her badge in front of the sensor, and heavy deadbolts thudded into the wall before the door slid open. Another long corridor greeted her. At the end of it, another wave of her badge led to another green light, and another door sliding open. This time, she found a decontamination chamber.

A cool, automated voice instructed her to keep her badge attached, empty her pockets, and stand in a star pose with her eyes closed. As she struck the position, it was all too easy to imagine Beauchamp and his "Good Old Boys" laughing behind the door. She closed her eyes and hoped to Techs this was the legitimate protocol.

A blue light flashed. Cold air rushed over her, so cold she had to fight the urge to pull her arms in. A second later, the light turned red and the cold air hit her again. Then it cut off so fast Chase thought she'd managed to break the Techs-damned decontamination machine on her first day. The door in front of her slid open, and the voice encouraged her to move forward.

No one was laughing on the other side of the door. In fact, no one was there at all.

The tiny antechamber had one wall lined with human-sized black lockers, and access to a circular hallway on the other side. At first she thought one of the scary gurney guys waited in the corner, but it was a black jumpsuit hanging from the only open locker. Was she supposed to put that on, or was it a spare?

Upon closer inspection, the jumpsuit had her name stitched in red, and the locker door sported a nice nameplate as well. The locker itself was big enough for her to change in, so she took the cue and exchanged her red jumpsuit for the black one. It was weird to have a different color after all this time, but the black did make her feel like a badass, so she decided to grab that shred of confidence and put it on as well.

She followed the circular hallway until she found a door with her name on it. Through the door, an altered version of her station greeted her. Desks and cubes sat in a circle around the biggest fab chamber she'd ever seen. Ceiling-high glass walls delineated each station. A desktop mini fab took up half the desk; she'd seen them before, but had never been allowed to work with one.

The clear walls made it easy to see what everyone else worked on, but it also made it easy for all four of her new coworkers to stare as she entered. Divya, the long-lost osseofabricator, waved at her from across the circle. Chase, uncertain if she was dreaming or not, waved back. Divya gestured down at the desk, and Chase followed the vague instructions, finding the power button for her monitor system. Immediately, her messenger pinged.

DIVYA V:

Good to see you!

CHASE A:

Thanks! I have no clue what's going on!

She looked to her left to find her nearest colleague staring. The man—Epley, according to the pink stitching on his jumpsuit—had medium-brown skin and a serious face, but when he grinned and nodded, the welcome felt genuine. He returned to his work, his long fingers artfully handling the thinner dermo-fabricator stylus as he etched something silver between layers of skin.

The Korean man past him had zero chill and waved enthusiastically. When he gestured to his chest, Chase was uncertain what he wanted, until she realized he was pointing to his name. *Jun* was embroidered in maroon letters; he was the viscerofabricator. She tugged at the front of her jumpsuit so he could see her name, though the ping from her computer made her regret the act. Jun was friendly, but apparently—according to the ping from Divya a second later—very talkative, at least through messenger.

The last person for their team was already bored with her arrival and had her attention back on her monitor. She was older than the others, with pale skin and hair so perfectly gray it was either natural or an extremely good genetic manipulation. Her icy blue eyes didn't look Chase's direction again after the initial assessment. Allegedly, her name was Ayla, if her jumpsuit was to be believed. There was some kind of hallway between Chase's desk and hers, and Chase welcomed the space. It helped buffer the frost coming from the neurofabricator's attitude.

Chase settled at her desk and pulled open the drawers, finding a tablet waiting for her in the top one. It was many generations newer than the one she usually used; in fact, she wasn't certain this model was available to the public at all. The massive size made it hard to hold, and the powerful brightness of the screen assaulted her eyes when she turned it on. She hoped no one saw her dramatic wince at the light.

Great. Her first impression was improving by the minute.

She lowered the brightness of the screen and opened her schedule. Instead of the usual rows of projects, one big block labeled *Project 9* took up every hour of every day. The folder for the project held nothing except a genetic code and a single objective line:

Advance the muscular structure to perform strength outside its genetic parameters.

Cool, so just…invent super strength. Awesome.

The new tablet gave Chase access to every academic and research library in the world, as well as every textbook on myofabrication. She could read literally every word published on the subject, but it was notably missing anything attempted by her fellow myofabricators in the company, including her predecessor.

Beauchamp wanted her to take this DNA—which was normal, based on her preliminary assessment—and somehow make the muscles super strong. She'd read many other codes that allowed for more myofibrils, genes that were built to handle the stronger muscles. She couldn't figure out why this one was so important compared to other samples. And Beauchamp wanted her to do it completely from scratch. That was alright, that was fine, she could get creative and dig into research and all that good stuff.

The problem was, the project was *slightly* illegal. Based on a number of domestic and international laws.

Hazing. This had to be hazing.

Back in grad school, Chase read miles of articles about testing the bounds of human existence, of researchers playing gods to create people who were bigger, or stronger, or had special abilities like in the movies. They tried everything, with one resounding conclusion: the human body couldn't handle it. Any subjects in those studies dealt with horrible side effects, most of which were irreparable at best, and deadly at worst. She'd had a whole lecture series about it in school, complete with gruesome, bloody pictures of the outcomes.

And Beauchamp wanted Chase to go ahead and say "fuck that" and do it anyway.

She glanced at Divya, preparing herself to ping about this trial and deal with the laughter afterwards, but Divya chose that moment to get up and wander out the back door of her cube. Chase muttered a curse and thought about asking Epley or Jun, but the former was fully engrossed in his task, and the latter looked like he would take way too long to explain anything. Nothing in the code gave her any inclination to the correct answer of this impossible problem, which meant this project would be a real bitch and a half. And how exactly was she supposed to test it, anyway?

Her monitor pinged with another message from Jun.

JUN L:

Has anyone shown you our HNTR?

Chase wracked her brain, but nothing in her squishy database had the initials HNTR.

CHASE A:

No?

When she looked up, Jun was staring right at her with a maniacal grin. With grand, dramatic gestures, he got his badge and waved it at the front of his bubble, opening it to the mega fab in the middle. Chase followed his lead and somehow pretended she wasn't standing in the coolest and most expensive piece of fabrication equipment she'd ever seen.

"Welcome to the team, new bone dresser," Jun said, flipping his black hair out of his eyes. "You're gonna love this thing."

"Uh, okay," Chase said, and followed him down the path between her desk and Ayla's. It was suspiciously dark around the door, with only a single light flickering on when they got to it.

"It's a little weird, but go with it. And don't worry, the creep factor decreases over time." He slipped a syringe filled with a bright blue substance into his pocket, and Chase tried not to stare. "You gotta get it done, or you'll end up dreaming about it. Trust me."

"Ew," Chase whispered, quiet enough he didn't hear. She looked to Epley for assistance, but all she got was a shrug and an encouraging nod. Traitor.

Jun scanned his badge. "It'll be fun, trust me."

Chase really didn't like the way he said that.

A heavy lock turned, and as they entered, dim blue lights in the back of the room faded as the bright overhead lights kicked on.

"This is Hunter, our test shell." He gestured grandly at the three liquid-filled glass cylinders against the back wall, the sources of the blue light. What did someone named Hunter have to do with the HNTR? Were they in charge? The cylinders bubbled and gurgled as gas traveled through the liquid, a low hum of machinery maintaining them.

And one of them had a Techs-damned *person* asleep in it.

"Is that...is Hunter a *volunteer*?" Chase choked out. The person had dark hair floating above their shoulders, and long, muscular limbs punctured by tubes. They had an androgynous face, and the loose tank top and shorts floating in the liquid made it nearly impossible to tell which characteristics their genes expressed beneath.

"A volunteer? Techs no, Alspeth, what kind of operation do you think we run here?" Jun laughed, as if the assumption was so silly. "It's a shell. All the functions are prototypes. It's not conscious, even when it's awake."

"Then why in the hell do they have a name?" she countered, unable to look away from the body. She expected Hunter's eyes to flash open and had the feeling they were listening.

"It's short for *Human Neo-Technology Reviewer*," he said, smacking the inscription on the side of the cylinder, "HNTR. Calling it Hunter is easier."

"Okay," she said, her mind reeling. Hunter was eerily still, and Chase tensed in anticipation. It didn't even look like they were breathing, and she worried if there was enough oxygen transferring through the tubes. Maybe someone else's hazing assignment was to give them gills.

"Chill, Alspeth, it's just a shell," Jun reminded her. Right. Just a biological prototype.

"They…it looks so alive."

"That's why you just gotta cut into it. It's like the models from school, but the super expensive ones. And with more details." He scanned his badge and pressed a button next to the tube. Chase expected Hunter to wake up as the fluid gurgled and drained, but they didn't move. Hydraulics tilted the now-empty tube until it was horizontal, but the shell remained still as a statue. Instead of a stand, the cylinder became a bed.

Wheels on an X-frame lowered beneath the cylinder, and the wall locks disconnected, allowing Jun to roll the whole thing away from the dock. It almost looked like a gurney, and Chase checked their hands. No nail polish.

"We all work on the same one? Doesn't that damage them?" she asked, trying her best to focus on the science and not how unsettling this was.

"I mean, you fix whatever you break. There's spare parts in

the cabinets, and we're always having to trade favors. Kinda goes with the territory. The goal is one full experiment per week. Over the weekend, they archive stuff and then we start all over again." He dragged the cylinder out of the room, the wheels silent as they traveled to the mega fab. Once centered over a circle on the floor, he tapped a pedal at the foot of the gurney.

"First rule, always anchor it. Cylinder anchors to the floor, HNTR anchors to the tube," he said, pointing to the various parts.

"Got it." Since the mega fab was at the center of the pods, it made her feel like she was on display at a museum. Or perhaps in the big ring of a circus.

He punched the pedal, and a thick pole dropped. A magnetic *thunk* echoed as it stuck to the floor. As soon as it locked, the chamber hummed to life, the chill setting in much faster than her cube on the floor.

"You get it open, do whatever you wanna do, then enter test mode," Jun said. He pressed a green button, and the glass slid away, leaving him free and clear to pat Hunter affectionately on the forehead. "HNTR and I have been through a lot together."

"I'm sure," Chase said through a grimace and a shudder.

"When you're ready," he continued, oblivious to her discomfort, "you just press the blue button to activate the link." The light of the blue button faded in and out in a weird, hypnotic blink. A tiny version lit up under the skin of Hunter's temple in a matching rhythm.

"They have something in their brain?" Someone had really built a whole brain for this so-called shell, but they also did something to take away the human bits. Did no one else see how terrifying this was?

"Well, yeah, how else are we supposed to test stuff? Especially you," he said. He pulled his stylus from his pocket and tapped a white, glowing line on the tube. A screen rose, hanging in the ether of the fab chamber and displaying an entire list of commands. There was everything from leg extensions and ankle pumps to running, jumping, and pirouetting; she could literally make this body—shell?—do anything she wanted. All in the name of science.

It would be cool if it wasn't so fucking creepy.

Jun tapped a green button in the corner of the screen, and Hunter's body tensed ever so slightly. They were waking up.

"This is how you program everything," he said, gesturing to the screen as if he wasn't performing some subset of necromancy here. "You can manually move anything, or make a sequence, and HNTR will do it."

Hunter's arm lifted with a drag of his stylus across the screen, and after a few quick strokes, they lifted a single finger to flip her off. Jun chuckled, and out of the corner of her eye, Chase could see him looking for a reaction. She didn't give him one.

She hoped Hunter would lose some of their humanity whenever the screen made them move, but boy howdy was she wrong about that. Instead, it embodied the stuff of nightmares. Chase *swore* she saw their eyebrows twitch, almost as if in discomfort.

"You okay?" Jun asked with just enough concern to come across as sincere. "You look a little pale."

"Just overwhelmed," she admitted, hoping it would be enough to deter him. It was not.

"Here, give it a try." He held his stylus out, but Chase shook her head; the thought of making Hunter move again made her stomach flip.

"I'm good for now," she said.

He wiggled his stylus at her. "You're gonna have to sooner or later."

"I pick later." Maybe she really would try later, when Jun couldn't witness her passing out or throwing up. Or both.

"Look, Alspeth—"

"Thank you for showing me how to use Hunter." This was so weird, so surreal, that Chase could do nothing but flee. "I'll give it a try later, on my own."

"Oh, c'mon—"

She didn't let him finish, and instead turned on her heel and escaped to her new cubicle. Unfortunately, the glass walls were super clear, which meant there was no hiding her red face from everyone.

Chase breathed. She didn't survive all those awkward years in grad school for nothing. Recalling old coping mechanisms, she ignored the furtive glances and whatever experiment Jun was running in favor of digging into research. The sooner she got through this hazing project and proved herself to Beauchamp, the sooner she could do her actual work.

CHAPTER 6

THE BLOODY JOB

IT WAS a long day waiting for her new coworkers to leave, all of them giving her little waves as they exited. Divya gestured to the door and mimed getting a drink, but Chase shook her head; a month ago she would've jumped at the chance, but now she had nothing but spite and fear to fuel her, and those didn't mix well with alcohol.

Once alone, she went down the little hallway again to Hunter's room. There they stood, floating harmlessly in the liquid, the light of the tube casting a ghostly blue shadow over their face. Another tube gurgled, and she jumped, hand over her racing heart.

"Not a big deal," she whispered, forcing a deep breath. "So not a big deal."

Chase stared at the shell, willing it to open their eyes, or move, or do anything to show some type of life. Despite telepathic encouragement, Hunter moved exactly zero times, which meant it was time for Chase to either work or go home.

"You know," she said to Hunter, despite knowing they couldn't hear her, "this is gonna be tough on both of us. But we'll get through it together, yeah?" She shook her head. "Talking may not help for once. Shit, okay. They're a collection of tissues. It's fine. We're fine. We're not freaking out at all."

It took a few false starts before she managed to scan her badge, her anxiety rising as the fluid level fell. The tube unlocked and shifted horizontal, then the wheels dropped. It was heavier than Chase originally estimated, given how easily Jun navigated it. Those lean muscles weren't just for show then. Bastard.

The mega fab chamber hummed to life as she anchored the gurney to the floor, and she shivered as the cold passed over her. She donned the arms of her jumpsuit and went through the process from earlier until she had the cylinder locked, the screen up, and Hunter ready. The little blue light blinked under the skin at Hunter's temple, and Chase couldn't help but run a finger over the spot. She jerked her hand back after feeling something hard in a place where things should be soft. *Gross.*

The screen waited for her command, its pretty list displaying all the wonderful things she could test—if only she weren't so chicken about it. She told it to flex and extend Hunter's knee, and the joint bent and straightened in a remarkably smooth motion. Tonight, she only wanted to test how much force the quads could take before failure. She could've tested any muscle, but everything was so weird that she needed to do something familiar.

Without Jun hovering, Chase took a minute to examine the body in front of her. Tubes connected to ports beneath their clavicles, and a quick diagnostics run told her they delivered nutrients and oxygen while ridding the body of waste, all on a cellular level. Quick, clean, and efficient maintenance, as if they were just another piece of machinery.

"You'll tell me if this hurts, right?" Chase asked, knowing full well she would scream bloody murder if the shell actually responded. "I hate the skin stitching part, but I'll try not to mess it up too bad."

Talking to her projects wasn't a new thing, but her projects rarely had faces. It wasn't something she wanted to focus on at the moment.

She tapped the screen, calling up the basic set of quads she fabricated earlier and locking them in place next to her. She then adjusted the X-frame so the cylinder sat right where she needed it. Once Hunter was at a proper height and position, she was officially out of excuses.

"Sorry in advance. Haven't done dermo since school," she explained, as if Hunter cared. Their face didn't move, didn't even twitch.

Chase chose a long, thin stylus from her pocket and palpated where the current muscle originated, then with a long breath and a low groan, she started the incision. She was eternally glad to be alone in the lab at that moment, as the massive fab chamber amplified every vocalized discomfort as she dissected the skin. Techs, it felt like the first time all over again.

The cut was messy, but functional enough, and she managed not to squeal with the second one. The skin sagged now that there was some slack, and she couldn't stop a gag at the squelch it made as it settled. She could handle muscles or bones or blood or viscera, even nerves in a pinch. But skin? Skin was the thing that got her.

"Glad one of us is calm, 'cause I'm hating this." Her voice wavered as nausea threatened. She considered taking the skin off entirely and bribing Epley to replace it for her, but considering she had nothing to barter, she gave up that dream. With the bare minimum dissected, she scrolled through the settings until she found the lock feature. There, now it wouldn't flop around while she tried to work.

With the pesky skin out of the way, she got a full view of the situation. Whoever worked on Hunter's quads previously sure did a number on them. Instead of pretty, red muscle, it was dark purple, with spots of black, necrotic tissue extending through.

"Whoa, this sucks," she said, exchanging the dermo stylus for her trusty myo one. "What the fuck did they do to you?"

Hunter, once again, didn't respond.

Chase quickly cut out the previous muscles and discarded them without a second thought. There was something weird about the attachment sites, but with all the new stimuli, her brain couldn't quite complete the puzzle. She hoped it was a genetic anomaly that would help her, because that would be her only win at this point.

Once the new quads were in place and the attachments fully connected, she turned back to the screen and double checked her selected program. A touch of the stylus, and the chamber hummed and moved Hunter into a seated position outside the cylinder. Another touch materialized a bolster in front of their ankles. Her old chamber could only hold things in stasis, whereas this one could move things and shape them, even apply resistance if she needed. *Amazing.*

A simple knee extension would give her a solid enough baseline to play with in the lab. Having no clue how much weight the quads could move before tearing, she set a bar of twenty-five kilograms. She thought it would be a challenge, but Hunter's knees extended with little effort and startling speed. Chase jumped as their knees snapped into hyperextension, the sound so sharp she was sure she accidentally tore the hamstrings and poplitei.

With a grimace, she raised Hunter up, but when she examined the area, she found no balls of muscles recoiling from torn tendons, and no swelling or bruising developing at the insertion points. There was no evidence of avulsion fractures, likely thanks to the weird bone thing.

Huh. So Hunter was *strong* strong.

An extra setting stopped the movement before end range. She cranked up the resistance; if twenty-five kilograms was nothing, how was two hundred and fifty?

There was definite strain on the muscles, but no sign of a limit. The bones looked solid too—Chase blew a kiss to Divya, wherever she may be—which meant she had free rein to increase it even more. What was the normal force tolerance? She could picture the slide from her lecture notes, but the fact didn't materialize. It was one number in a slew of numbers that vacated her brain after an exam.

She would look it up between now and next time. Chase thought about pausing to find the answer, but she was already halfway through the time limit of the fab chamber, and she wasn't going to interrupt her experiment for something silly like fact-checking.

"Let's do this."

A thousand kilograms defined the muscles, though the strain was minimal.

Twelve hundred kilograms required a bit of a push.

Fifteen hundred kilograms made the quads shake, and the patellae squealed as they ground against the femurs.

She went in smaller increments then, flushing the system with each repetition to add energy and remove wastes from the overworked muscles.

Chase knew a lot about muscles. She knew how they had multiple nuclei and mitochondria to help with regeneration and energy production. She knew all the different zones in the fibers, and how they changed with contraction and relaxation. She knew each layer intimately, and how they all fit within the continuum.

But she forgot how much blood muscles had.

At one thousand, eight hundred and sixty-six kilograms, Hunter's new quads tore with a sound like ripping fabric, and all the extra blood from the demand spewed like a geyser. It coated her face, blinding her and landing in her open mouth. In a very professional and lady-like way, she spit and sputtered, wiping her face furiously with her sleeves, attempting to block the continued onslaught. Her only victory in that moment was managing not to vomit.

The blue chamber light turned red. Blood protocols initiated, and the temperature dropped further as the machine disintegrated the blood particles. The fabric of her jumpsuit contracted and shifted as the chamber scrubbed them, and she felt odd pinching and tingling sensations as it cleaned the remnants from her skin and mouth. She gagged again, feeling like ants were stuck in her mouth and throat and nose. When the itching stopped, her mind stopped with it, as if the fab chamber sent her into a forced shut down along with Hunter.

Though she technically didn't lose consciousness, she had the sensation of waking up. The light was blue again, and the fab chamber was so clean that for a moment, she thought the whole thing was a hallucination. But the torn muscles lying limp on their lap put her failure on full display.

"Sorry," she whispered to Hunter. "That probably hurt."

If Hunter said anything, she wasn't sure she'd even notice.

"Next time we're doing something more fun," she said, reaching a fumbling hand into her pocket to find the dermo stylus again. "Like running. Or jumping rope. Or literally anything else."

She packed the muscles away as carefully as possible, then released the skin from its hold and stitched it back together with clumsy strokes. It took three attempts to turn off the chamber and shut down the tube. The magnet disengaged with a resounding *thunk*, and even though her whole body felt weak and jelly-like from the encounter, she managed to roll Hunter back to their room.

The preserving liquid filled the chamber once again, Hunter's long limbs floating effortlessly and their hair pulled away from their face by the viscosity. They looked vaguely familiar, like someone Chase had seen in a dream or in a history file. Maybe she'd even seen them on the street somewhere.

Wait. Not a volunteer. Just a body.

"Sorry," she said again, her voice shaky on the one word. Beauchamp and the others talked like Hunter was just a pile of genes. But genes had to come from somewhere; how old was Hunter? Did they have relatives running around? Descendants?

That wasn't a thought she wanted to follow.

"We'll get through this. Hopefully with less blood next time," she said, patting the glass. Hunter said nothing, which Chase took as agreement.

Despite the cleansing cycle in the fab chamber, she still showered three times in the lab and scrubbed her skin so raw it matched the red of her old jumpsuit. The black one went into the designated container, and she felt like pinning an apology note to whoever took care of laundry. Her mind struggled to focus on anything besides getting dressed and getting the fuck out. So much happened for a first day, and she wanted—no, *needed*—to go home and regroup.

The front lobby was empty and the cafeteria closed down by the time she made it downstairs. That was fine, she didn't want to eat anything anyway. A different security guard, a younger man with glasses and messy black hair, took her badge and scanned her out. She hoped she remembered to thank him, but couldn't quite remember with her mushy, overwhelmed brain.

One iota of determination rooted in her heart. Beauchamp wanted to challenge her? Fine. Then she would rise to meet it.

CHAPTER 7

THE DINNER JOB

CHASE SURVIVED the three days until the weekend, but there was no rest for the weary or the recently disturbed.

She returned to her nice, quaint, company-controlled apartment Friday night to find a reminder notice displayed on her wall screen. Maintenance required her to vacate the apartment between the hours of seven and nine; there weren't any specifics in the notice besides vague references to chemicals and tests. Even if all she wanted was to collapse on her bed and sleep for a thousand years, she needed to be an adult and let the people work.

She took one look around the apartment and deemed it good enough for company, then changed out of her barely-used red jumpsuit into more casual clothing, wishing they were pajamas. The bed and couch both sang their siren songs to her, but she managed to slide on her shoes and leave the apartment right as the clock flipped to seven.

A man in denim overalls and a beat-up baseball cap exited the elevator as she got on, his tool belt clanking and jingling as he walked in the direction of her door. It seemed likely he would stop at the other apartments before hers, but as the elevator doors closed, she watched him stomp steadily down the hall, ignoring the other apartments on the way.

Weird. What was wrong with just *her* apartment?

It was still nice and warm as she stepped out of the building, the sidewalk baking her from underneath with residual heat. The sun demanded attention every so often, blinking between every building as she walked the five city blocks to Market Square. Sweat prickled her skin, and if she sweat, then she could count this as her exercise for the day and reward herself with a little treat.

Market Square was loud and busy no matter the time of day or night, and reminded Chase of days gone by when she would help Pops at his shop. Sunset colors shifted above her as the glass ceiling added digital assistance to the waning light, and tiny stars sparkled where the city pollution drowned them out. She needed a few minutes to remember how to move in the crowd, the skill as old and trusty as anything else from her younger years.

"Alspeth?"

Chase barely heard her name and turned sharply, scanning the crowd. She'd never seen anyone from work here, and only one person called her by her last name. Right as she accepted the trick of her imagination–possibly something to see a neurofabricator for–she spotted Monty walking out of a nearby store, a tall, blonde woman at his side. Chase thought about running, but the crowd rooted her to the spot.

"I thought that was you!" He hit her with his annoying smile, and she ignored the way her stomach flipped. His companion made a face, like he said something weird. Was she worried about his excitement at seeing her?

"See? You are stalking me," Chase said. The crowd nearly drowned out her voice, but she was loud enough for the blonde to make another face. Techs, was he on a date? She didn't know what she thought his type would be, but tall, blonde, and muscles for days certainly wasn't it.

"You'll notice I was here first, so it must mean *you* are stalking *me*," Monty said. Chase rolled her eyes, as did the blonde.

"I'm just here to kill time while maintenance fixes something in my apartment." She held up her hands in innocence. Monty cocked his head to the side.

"At the company apartments? Anything I need to be worried about?"

"Not that I know of. They didn't really explain anything." Chase glanced at the blonde, who held a thousand-yard stare. Oh no, if this was a date, Chase was definitely ruining it.

Monty, unaware, frowned. "That's weird. Usually they're very detailed."

Apparently, the blonde had enough. "Alright, I'm out. Let me know about later."

"Yes, yes, on your way," Monty said, taking her shoulders and turning her away. The woman allowed it, though the muscles her sleeveless shirt and fitted pants showed said she could easily win the fight. Once she was out of earshot, Monty said, "Excuse my friend, Ellison. She's a bit of a diamond in the rough."

Friend? "She seems nice," Chase said politely. Monty barked a laugh.

"She's a bit of a bully."

"I like her even more, then." And if she was honest, she liked that Ellison was just a *friend*.

He held up a finger. "You say that now, but wait until she turns her wrath on you. Not as fun then."

"I'm sure." If Ellison turned her blue eyes on Chase with any sort of purpose, she might melt into the floor. "Anyway, I'm going to go get something to eat. Want to come?"

The invitation surprised both of them, but Chase couldn't deny how good it was to see a friendly face after three days in the new lab. Monty looked over his shoulder dramatically, then pointed to his own chest.

"Me? You're asking me?"

"Nevermind, I rescind the offer," Chase lied.

"What if I pay?" he asked.

She pretended to consider, then said, "Offer is back on the table. Let's go."

Chase pushed into the crowd, not waiting to see if Monty kept up with her. A second later, he bumped his shoulder into hers to make his presence known. The touch startled her, but she found she didn't hate it. When the crowd made the path tight, he let her go first with a gentle hand on the small of her back, his skin warm even through her t-shirt. She didn't hate that touch either.

She led him to a Mediterranean stand and, true to his word, Monty paid for her massive pile of falafel. The busy night made them find a bench to eat at instead of a table, and pressed them next to each other. Monty didn't seem bothered by it, so Chase pretended the contact didn't make her insides squirm.

She cleared her throat. "You know, you never answered my question the other day. About people getting hurt at work?" She looked up and saw some emotion flash across his face, but it was gone too soon for her to recognize it.

Monty took his time finishing his bite and wiping his mouth before answering. "I mean, no one from our floor has said anything. But I've heard some rumors. Urban legends, probably."

Urban legends? Intriguing. "Oh? Like what?"

"The usual." Monty gave her a pointed look. "People disappearing, going to different labs, never to be seen again…"

"You literally see me right now," she said, a small laugh escaping.

He gestured with his pita, the hummus on it nearly sliding off. "Ah, but I didn't see you for three days. Minds start to wander."

"Worried about me, Montgomery Evans?" she asked with a

smile, ignoring how the thought made the back of her neck warm and her chest tight.

Monty made a face. "I try to be nice, and you come back with my full government name?"

"Not the full government name, I don't know your middle name," she said.

"And you never will." He took a large bite, and she did as well, hoping he would continue with a real answer. He didn't disappoint. "But no, I haven't heard anything concrete about people getting hurt. Why, did something happen in the R&D lab?"

"I saw something weird but..." She still couldn't quite explain away the body on the gurney the other night, but didn't want to add fuel to the rumor mill. "I guess it was just old parts or something."

"How has it been this week?" he asked. When she narrowed his eyes, he held up his hands. "Genuine question. Nothing nefarious."

The blood, the sweat, the tears. She thought for a long moment before answering. "It was really hard. Cool, but really hard."

He grinned. "You could always step down and give me the position."

"Should've seen that coming," she muttered.

His eyes softened, and his smile turned sincere. "In all seriousness, I'm sure you're doing great. Probably just some growing pains."

Techs, she hoped she kept the surprise at the kind words off her face. "Thank you. It actually does help to hear that." Her voice sounded almost normal. It was odd to get a compliment from him, but somehow that made it feel more genuine.

The mischief returned. "And if you ever need help with anything..."

Her smile flattened, and he laughed at the expression. "Can't help yourself, huh?"

"I do mean it. Even if it's just to share a meal and talk to someone."

Damn it, he was right. Hanging out with him did make her feel better about the whole thing. It reminded her there was a world outside the lab, and normal people that weren't callous to cutting open a weird human shell.

They finished off their meal, and Monty gathered the trash and tossed it into the receptacle. Chase assumed their moment was over and they'd go their separate ways, but it was Monty's turn to hand out a surprise invitation.

"I need dessert. Is there an ice cream shop nearby?"

"Uh, I think so?" Chase looked around, hoping to spot the place she knew existed, but whose location remained elusive. She stood, bolstered by blind confidence and the need to impress. "This way."

They made it three rows up before she stopped and internally begged her mind map to work.

"You don't know where the ice cream shop is." His accent made it sound like he'd spell it *shoppe*.

"I have no clue where the ice cream shop is," she admitted. He jerked his head to the left.

"I spotted it on my way in. So much for your photographic memory."

"I've never claimed to have photographic memory," she said. After this week, she wished her memory was worse.

"Guess I was projecting then."

He said it with a nonchalant shrug and joined the ice cream line without a second thought. A patron further up the line got their treat and walked by, their sundae covered with strawberry syrup. Chase's week grabbed her mind, and for a brief moment the strawberry syrup was blood, and the taste of iron coated her tongue.

"Alspeth?"

"Huh?"

They were at the front of the line now, and the cashier looked at her expectantly. She apologized and picked her dessert based on the color rather than flavor, determined not to have any more reminders of her time in the lab.

Her first bite of chocolate ice cream was too big and too fast, but the blast of cold and sweet helped push the thoughts way down deep where they belonged. The brain freeze, for once, was worth it, especially when she and Monty exited the Market Square and hit the perfectly warm, clear night air. Monty drifted toward the rail platform, but Chase kept walking, pretending not to see him.

"Are you too good for the rail?" he asked. She turned on her heel and continued backwards, minding her tricky knee. It was a beautiful night, and she wanted to savor it. She wasn't about to let a smelly, claustrophobic rail car stop her.

"Are you too good to walk?" she countered, taking a slow bite of her ice cream.

"Absolutely. Do I look like someone who exercises?" He gestured to his general physique, and Chase took a second to trace the line of his body, eyes narrowed.

"Is that a trick question? Or are you just fishing for compliments?" Because he *definitely* looked like he exercised.

"Yes," he replied with a grin.

She rolled her eyes. "What's the phrase? Cheeky bastard? Come on, walk off a little bit of that ego." Another about-face, and she continued on her way. Behind her. Monty groaned, and a beat later she heard his footsteps as he caught up.

"You're a bad influence," he said.

"Technically, I think this makes me a good influence. Make sure Ellison knows that, just in case we meet again. I want to impress her."

His gaze went skyward. "Of course you do. But that's just because you don't know her."

There was limited foot traffic to bother them, and the walk home was easy and breezy. Monty carried most of the conversation with rowdy tales about Ellison, and Chase found herself laughing along. After the evening, she gathered enough data to support a budding hypothesis—Monty was actually pretty cool.

When they got back to the apartment building, he surprised her by getting off the elevator on her floor.

"Wait. Have we been neighbors this whole time?" she asked. She knew he lived in these apartments—most Kierper peons did—but she was surprised to find him this close.

"I'm a few floors up. But I'm a gentleman and wished to walk you to your door."

"How absolutely archaic of you," she said.

"Just want to make sure the maintenance person isn't waiting to kill you," he said.

"Why? If they did, then you could have my R&D spot."

He pretended to think for a moment. "You make a good point."

They reached her door, and she discovered she wasn't ready for their time to end. Or maybe she wasn't ready for the silence of her lonely apartment. The lock recognized her key fob and slid open, and she paused in the doorway, making sure it wouldn't close. Monty, bless him, seemed to get the hint.

"Do you watch *Earthbound*? I haven't seen the new episode this week," he said, nodding toward her wall screen, where the notification for the next episode glowed.

"Oh, neither have I," she said, an odd sense of relief flooding through her. "Do you want to watch it?"

"I'd love to. None of my roommates watch it, and it's more fun when there's someone who gets all the references."

"That we can agree on," Chase said.

She stepped back into her apartment and went to the pantry, Monty following her in. A bottle of wine was exactly where she left it—all the way at the back, forcing her to snake her arm just right to retrieve it.

"Don't judge me for the state of the apartment, but at least I have—are you okay?"

She glanced back to find Monty grimacing and holding the

side of his head. When he noticed her staring, he dropped his hand and put on a brave attempt at his usual smile.

"I'm fine." His right eye twitched.

"Post sugar headache?" She stepped closer, wine forgotten. "I've got pain relievers in the other room."

"That would be fantastic." He shifted from foot to foot, and a muscle in his cheek fasciculated. If he was able to control whatever pain hit him, that was probably a good sign the evening wasn't in mortal peril.

"Okay, be right back," she said, sliding past him and going to the bathroom.

The bottles under the bathroom sink stood like pretty plastic soldiers, and she grabbed the two pain relievers from the formation. They worked differently, how was she supposed to know which would be best for Monty? She read the labels, as if that would help, then rolled her eyes. She was acting like a Techs-damned teenager. All she needed to do was bring both and give him the option.

"Ah! You found it." There was more vigor in his voice than she anticipated as she exited her bathroom. He stood next to her living room lamp, on the clear opposite side of the apartment from the kitchen. The light was probably hurting his head further, and she wished she'd thought to turn it off for him.

"Yeah, I didn't know which one you prefer, so I brought both," she said, holding the bottles out to him. "Are you sure you're alright?"

He picked the same medication she usually took and twisted the bottle open, dumping a few pills into his hand. He swallowed them dry, and Chase nearly gagged in sympathy.

"Actually, I, um," he cleared his throat, probably from the gross pill coating. "I kind of have migraine problems?" Given the way he winced, it wasn't common for him to admit this. "These will definitely help, but if I want to function tomorrow, I'm afraid I need to drink a lot of water and hide in my bedroom for a few hours. I'm sorry, I'll have to take a rain check on our watch party."

"No! I mean, no apology necessary." *That's totally what she meant.* "I understand. I'm sorry you have to deal with it, that sucks."

"It's fine. Ever since I got a refurbished brain stem, they only come around once in a blue moon." He smiled so easily, and it made her feel like she hadn't done something innocuous to completely screw up whatever was happening. "How about lunch Monday? Give you a break from the new lab?"

"You're just fishing for more R&D info," she said, earning a grin. "But yes, lunch sounds good."

"Excellent," he said, and took one step toward the door. Chase matched his movements and held out the bottle.

"Do you have some of these at home? Or do you need to borrow this?"

"Oh, I have an entire drawer full," he said. This time, she didn't interrupt his trek to the door. "Thank you, though. I'm dreadfully sorry about all this."

"I understand," she said. It wasn't a lie, just a bit of an equivocation. "Go get some rest."

Monty gave her one last smile before leaving, the apartment turning silent and empty in his absence. In an instant, the magic of the evening was gone, and she was alone with her thoughts.

She eyed the bottle of wine, unopened on the counter. It wasn't a great coping mechanism, but it would have to do for tonight, lest she wanted to dream about soulless bodies and blood.

CHAPTER 8
THE ONE NEWTON JOB

IT DIDN'T HURT Chase's feelings that Beauchamp let her work on her hazing project for a second week, but it did piss her off.

Every day she sat in her little bubble and watched her colleagues do actual life changing science—she assumed, since she had no access to their projects—while she tried to find an answer to her impossible problem. There'd been no more bloody mishaps since she monitored the stress of the muscle during her experiments now, but she still couldn't get Hunter to increase their threshold.

If Beauchamp wanted her to figure this out, then she'd do it. Chase worked with a hundred people like him in academia, and she'd built up spite like she built up muscles: one layer at a time, until it was strong, beautiful, and perfect.

Sick of being stuck with this meaningless task, she did the unthinkable and made some random shit up to test. It was common practice to change one variable at a time, but since that hadn't gotten her anywhere, she decided to change everything at once and hope for the best. If the stars could align for life to crawl out of a primordial soup, then perhaps they could again for her to make some extra-strong muscles.

When the hodgepodge muscles were ready, she sent them into the mega fab, then went to retrieve Hunter.

"Hello, beautiful," she said, tapping her badge against the tube. She didn't want to admit it, but Jun was right—the more she worked with Hunter, the less weird it felt. Not completely normal, but better.

"Exciting news! I have new quads for you. No need to thank me." Hunter didn't, even as she dragged the tube to the mega fab. "Try and contain your excitement, please. You're embarrassing both of us."

With gloves and a face shield, since she had no desire to taste blood again, she anchored the tube and got to work. Her efficiency improved with each experiment, and now instead of haphazard lines, she created smooth incisions and regimented stitches. Kierper had a reliable method for healing incisions, but Hunter's cuts seemed to disappear faster than usual. Perhaps it was some sort of metabolic stimulant; she was curious, but not curious enough to ask the resident dermofabricator and risk the condescension.

Once Hunter sported new quads, Chase enacted the monitoring electrodes and set the station for knee extension. The muscle fibers squeaked like a rusty gurney wheel during the test run, but they moved through the entire range of motion and had a lower reading compared to the baseline quads.

Was she onto something?

Holy shit, she might be onto something.

She upped the resistance, then upped it again. The squeaking increased with each step, echoing through the mega fab, until it plateaued at 15,000 Newtons. Previous ruptures occurred at 18,300 Newtons. Things were about to go very well, or very, very wrong.

With each increase in resistance, Chase's heart beat a little faster. Her eyes flicked back and forth between Hunter and the screen so fast that dizziness smacked her a couple times. The stress reading jumped a little, but not a statistically significant amount.

Hunter hit the 18,300 threshold with ease. Chase set the resistance to 18,301 and held her breath. The tissues made noises muscles should never make, and she braced for impact.

Except impact never came.

Her breath left in a rush, and she couldn't decide if she wanted to vomit or faint or both. She tried to tap the tablet and release Hunter's leg extension, but it took her shaking fingers a few tries before she managed the command. Something bubbled in her chest and she leaned her forehead against Hunter's tube, ignoring how silly she must look in favor of gulping down air.

Turns out, the thing in her chest was neither panic nor vomit, but laughter. She was sure she looked a little unhinged, but no one could hear except for Hunter. Her colleagues were at least pretending to work while she broke down, so what did it matter?

"We did it," she said, straightening and patting them on the shoulder. She flicked her finger across the screen, sending the report directly to Beauchamp. "Now we can get on with the real thing."

With reverence, she returned Hunter to their room, then slapped her badge against the elevator doors a few feet away. It was probably better to give him time to read the data she sent, but she was eager to start her actual work, her *important* work. She was done playing his stupid little games.

Chase took the back elevator up and strutted toward Beauchamp's office like a show dog in the final round, with her head held high and hands in her pockets. She didn't bother zipping her black jumpsuit up all the way; there was no need to impress now, her flawless experiment in his inbox would speak for itself.

The only access to Beauchamp's office was through the back elevator, which connected only to the R&D labs and the basement. A heavy door separated the hallway from the room beyond, a deterrent from anyone wanting to bother him. Chase ignored the threat and scanned her badge. The lock clicked, but the door remained stationary.

She furrowed her brows and scanned the badge again. The light was green, why wouldn't it open? She gave the door an experimental push, and the hinges creaked as it gave. Manual doors? How primitive.

Where the lab had the decontamination chamber, Beauchamp's antechamber had shelves filled with tissue samples in various stages of preservation and degradation. An entire heart floated in a liquid nearly the same color, the organ small enough to make her wonder if it was a genetic anomaly or if it was taken from a child. Two blue eyes stared in opposite directions from the jar next to it. A massive bucket sat on the floor, murky orange liquid hiding its contents. Or maybe the liquid *was* the content. All Chase knew was it was creepy as fuck and she regretted entering this office of horrors.

The second door–another manual one–gave way to the actual office. The inner sanctum reeked of dust, dirt, and embalming fluids, like the labs back in undergrad. Every available surface held jars and actual paper books, their pages yellow with age and stained with use. A frame on the wall, glinting gold in the low light, held a diploma from one hundred and twenty years prior.

"Are you gonna come in, or are you gonna keep staring at my stuff?"

Beauchamp's voice made her jump. It took a second to find him, hunched over a dark wooden desk that blended in with the chaos.

"Right, sorry." She picked her way through the maze to stand in front of him. He had chairs in front of the desk, but piles of boxes claimed those seats, forcing her to stand like a child getting reprimanded by the principal. "I came to give you a status update."

"Why? I got your data." He held up his tablet and flashed the screen. There was no data on it, just some pictures she couldn't make out.

"What do you think of the data?" She shifted her weight to one leg and stifled a grin. Her left knee ached and something from the box next to her definitely smelled funny, but none of that mattered right now. He looked up from his screen, face devoid of humor.

"I think it's bullshit," he said.

Chase's stomach plummeted, and her vision swam with the whiplash of his words. The screen cast deep shadows over his face, which remained expressionless.

"I…what?" This was a joke. Or she misheard him.

"It's bullshit. So you reinforced some tissues and got the muscle to withstand one extra Newton of force. Congratulations. You want a medal?"

He leaned back in his chair and crossed his ankle over his opposite knee, then decided against the position and instead rested his heel on a wheel of his chair. At least now she could tell what he was thinking. He was very proud of himself, and wanted to bask in whatever argument came his way. The ice in Chase's vessels turned to fire, and she clenched her fists in her pockets.

"You told me to find a way to make the muscle tolerate more than its genetics dictated," she said, quoting the brief. "I did that."

"Oh? You did that?" He stood and braced his hands on his desk. The motion involved pushing a lot of stuff out of the way, which detracted from his little power stance. "Did you find a way to build stronger muscles so that a body can withstand them? You cobbled it together in a few days—"

"I didn't cobble anything—"

"Do *not* interrupt me." He glared at her. Chase glared right back, accustomed to fighting for her space. "You made a muscle that could handle a little something extra. You did *not* make something functional. You didn't make something that could last. Why do you think I care about one Newton?"

"I thought you would care about one Newton," Chase spoke through gritted teeth, "because I thought you would want to know when I was done with your little hazing project so I could get on with my *real* work."

It was a stupid thing to say, and her heart raced as she said it, but she felt more pride than fear. Beauchamp fought between a few emotions before sneering in mild distaste, which suited her just fine. The feeling was mutual.

"That 'little hazing project,' as you so elegantly put it," he said, his voice actually chilling in a way Chase never heard another human sound, "is not a hazing project. It is your *actual* project."

"What?" A stray dust or fungus particle hit her eye, forcing it to water at this inconvenient time. She rubbed the offending eyeball and prayed Beauchamp didn't think she was crying. "That isn't possible. That's *illegal*."

"That's *science*. That's *business*. And if you don't want a part of it, you can leave the company. Just remember, I have a lot of contacts at other fabrication companies, and my opinion carries a lot of weight."

Chase blinked, both to get the remnant out of her eye and to try and grasp the situation. This had to be a dream. "You want me to break the Advanced Neutrality Agreement?"

"Oh my God, this is why I hate hiring new people," he groaned, flopping back onto his chair. "Always so dramatic. We're making real changes here. You think a company like Kierper cares about a little fine? Or a tiny cease and desist order? There's safe-guards in place here, Alspeth. This ship is unsinkable."

"I feel like I've heard that before," she said, though he would understand the old reference better than she ever could. "I just—"

"'Just' nothing. Do your job."

"But Dr. Beauchamp—"

"Listen. Do it, or you're done with fabrication. It's that simple." He turned back to his tablet and tapped away with extra force. She tried to corral her thoughts, tried to find an appropriate way to respond, but the silence lingered for too long. The petty side of her wanted to make him be the first to break it. It took every ounce of her, but she claimed the tiny victory as he scoffed and threw his hands up. "Well?"

"I guess I'll get back to work then," she said, sounding way calmer than she actually felt. If she could be this stoic, maybe she'd been hanging out with Hunter too much. Or just enough.

"Whatever. Don't wear your black suit outside the lab." Beauchamp had to have the last word, and Chase was fine with that. No matter how it ended, she came out on the losing side of this deal. She waded through the crap in his office and hallway until she escaped into the elevator.

So. Kierper didn't care about laws. Kierper was rich enough to do whatever they wanted. And whatever Kierper was doing, it was fishy as fuck, which was probably why all her data got archived every weekend. Why would they need to build super strength that functioned? That would cause nothing but trouble—

Chase thought of Corporal James Reynolds, and all the other military people that passed through the halls day to day. Was that the goal? Did they want to make the soldiers strong enough to deter any opposing forces? The alterations they'd go through for the body to withstand it—it'd be painful. Inhumane.

The elevator reached her floor, and she exited in a haze. There was no way she could work on this, not with this hypothesis. But the idea of quitting felt wrong, too. Could she really leave this all behind, leave fabricating in general, and keep quiet?

She knew the answer to that. No, she couldn't.

Chase walked into the kind of silence which meant everyone was talking about her right before she came in, so she did the very adult thing and ignored them. She needed a plan. She needed a big screen, and a stylus, and perhaps a glass or two of wine.

But first, she had to pretend to work.

There was a fresh article from a university in Buenos Aires about metabolic loading and tissue health. Perhaps she could take that and figure out regeneration tactics. That would be cool, right? If muscles could rebuild themselves, they didn't have to be super strong. Regeneration would also take her way longer to make, and, technically, wasn't unlawful. If one of those entities came after Kierper and the company tried to throw her under the rails, she could argue that her part of the group project was totally legal, thank you very much.

Chase sighed and let her head fall to her desk with a low *thump*. This was wrong. This was all so very wrong.

She clenched her fists until her fingers hurt, and if she didn't need to protect her fancy new hands, she would've punched a hole through her desk, and her tablet, and the monitor. After all this time, all her hard work, Beauchamp wanted her to set aside her morals and her entire reason for fabricating for the company's gains.

Her professors warned her about the corporate world. Perhaps they'd been correct.

CHAPTER 9
THE PHONE CALL JOB

THE ARTICLE from Argentina was not enough to maintain Chase's attention. She read the same lines over and over, the words failing to sink past the turmoil churning at the forefront of her brain. She wanted to stay in R&D, but she didn't want to break laws, especially ones that would get young soldiers like Jamie hurt. The best she could do was work on her project, but find a way that wouldn't lead to detrimental effects.

Chase was one inconvenience away from a full spiral when her monitor sounded with a new ping. She dreaded looking, anticipating something from Divya or Jun regarding her trip to Beauchamp's office. But she was pleasantly surprised to see it was from Monty.

MONTGOMERY E:

Still on for lunch?

Chase paused. She hadn't forgotten about their tentative plans, but assumed he'd made the offer in the midst of his migraine haze. Agreeing was probably a bad idea, especially given the new information she learned.

She looked around the lab. No one else seemed bothered by their situation. Chase wanted—no, needed—an outside perspective. Sure, she'd signed a few papers dictating her silence, but she could be vague enough. And if Monty wanted to try and weasel his way into the R&D lab after hearing what she had to say, then that was his prerogative.

CHASE A:

Yes please, now?

Chase cringed at how desperate those three words sounded. It wasn't even noon yet, but she didn't want to sit there and stare at her monitor. The reply came quickly.

MONTGOMERY E:

Finishing up a thing. Thirty minutes?

Techs, her anxiety made thirty minutes feel like years. Good thing they were communicating via text, so he couldn't see the face she made giving away her frustration.

CHASE A:

Sounds good.

Time slowed to a snail's pace. Chase returned to pretending to read articles while really drumming her fingers against her desk and counting the seconds. She made it fifteen minutes before giving up and shutting down her work station. Once back in her red jumpsuit, she sat through the longest decontamination protocol she'd ever seen, then made her way down to the cafeteria.

She wasn't hungry by any means, but she went through the line anyway, coming away with a turkey sandwich and a bottle of water. Neither sounded appetizing, but she needed something to do with her hands until Monty got there. There was an open table by a large window, and Chase claimed it, hoping the movement outside would distract her for the next eight minutes until her lunch date arrived.

Well, not a *date* date. Just a casual meal between colleagues, wherein she would question his thoughts on different avenues of avoiding or reporting potential war crimes.

Monty arrived right on time, waving at her before joining the line for food. It felt like another decade before he actually arrived at the table with his burger, fries, and chocolate chip cookie.

"That's all you're having?" he asked, brows furrowed.

"Not really hungry," she replied.

"Oh, we could've gone later if you—"

"Do you know which government entity is in charge of potential treaty violations?" She paused, then added, "Hypothetically."

Monty blinked, a French fry halfway to his mouth.

"This is not how I thought this would go at all," he said, eyebrows raised.

"Well?" Her own food remained untouched, except for her casual shredding of one of the bread slices.

"Okay, take a breath and a bite, and start from the beginning." He nodded at her sandwich, and she huffed before taking a very small bite.

"Do you know or not?" she asked around the food in her mouth.

"Depends on which treaty, and what kind of violation we're talking," he said.

Chase balked. "Wait, you might actually know?"

"Was this supposed to be a thought experiment or something? Because yes, I know a fair bit about international law. It was part of my career before I got into fabricating."

"This is your second career?" Techs, she'd worked with this man for what, six months? How did she not know this?

Monty waved the question away. "Not important. I believe you were telling me what sparked this line of inquiry?"

Chase bit her lip and tried to come up with an explanation. Techs, if Monty knew law stuff, then he could probably help—or turn her in for breach of contract. The thought must've shown on her face, because Monty rolled his eyes.

"I'm not going to pass anything on to the higher ups. You're obviously distraught about something. You're fun competition, Alspeth, but I don't actually plot your downfall."

"Right, sorry." Chase cleared her throat and tried to organize her thoughts. "Give me a second–I do want to give you plausible deniability if I can."

He grinned, and hell if it didn't make something warm bloom in her stomach. "'Plausible deniability?' Look at you."

"I've spent way too much time watching shows on the Stream," she admitted. Then she remembered their non-watch party and felt heat rise in her cheeks. Luckily, Monty laughed in an amused way.

"It's not your fault *Law Abiding Citizen* is so good," he said. "Let's start with this, then. Which treaty was broken?"

"Hypothetically?" Chase reiterated, the phrase *plausible deniability* running on a loop in her head. Messing with Monty was one thing, but she didn't want him to go to jail or anything.

"Hypothetically," he agreed.

"The Advanced Neutrality Agreement," she said. He let out a low whistle.

"Oh dear, a big deal then." He ran his hand over his buzzed dark hair and leaned back, pursing his lips in thought. The sunlight through the window gave his dark brown skin a golden shine—not that Chase noticed.

"Yeah, kind of a big deal," she said. "But big companies only have to worry about some fines and maybe a cease and desist. Allegedly."

"Hmm, that is usually how things go." Monty ate a few bites, obviously thinking. Chase stayed silent and ate some of her own food, trying not to interrupt. "Well, there's two ways to go about this. Hypothetically."

"Right." Chase dropped her half-eaten sandwich and leaned on her elbows, attention rapt. Monty held up a finger as he finished a bite, and swallowed dramatically.

"First, you can get in touch with the Domestic Investigations

Agency. They handle anything done here on American soil. But they're very bureaucratic and often have a lot of hoops to jump through. They'd be able to obtain a federal mandate, but it would take a long time."

The soldiers Beauchamp would likely sell the processes to didn't have a long time.

"What's my second option?" she asked.

"Hire a group to take this hypothetical company down with less conventional methods." He said it so casually that Chase laughed.

"Alright, you've also been watching too much on the Stream," she said. "If anything on those shows is accurate, I don't think my very real bank account could fund a vigilante group."

"You'd be surprised," Monty said, once again way too nonchalant. She assumed he was teasing her, but a tiny part of her wondered.

"Well, if things don't work out with the DIA, we'll go that route." Now with a plan in place, her hunger arrived. Through a mouthful she said, "Hypothetically!"

"Oh, of course, everything is hypothetical." He smiled at her, and once again Chase found herself blushing. "Now, obviously unrelated, are you going to tell me anything about R&D?"

"Absolutely not, that would be a breach of contract." She reached for more sandwich, but found her plate woefully empty. Monty turned his plate around so his fries faced her. She eyed him, confused.

"Go ahead, I'm finished with them," he said.

"Techs, why are you being so nice to me?" she asked, expecting him to jerk the plate away when she reached for a fry and hopefully hiding her surprise when he didn't.

"I've always been nice. I'm just also very competitive," he said.

Chase snorted. "That's an understatement."

Monty scoffed. "Like you have any room to judge."

She laughed and shook her head. "Yeah, I suppose you're right. I'll say, that's something I miss now that I'm in a new lab."

"Aw, you miss me?" he asked with that stupid cheeky grin.

"I didn't say that, I said I missed the competition," she insisted.

"Well, since I was your biggest competition, you're basically saying you miss me." The self-satisfied smirk made her blood boil, but not quite in anger. If she was honest, his point made her self-conscious because he was right.

"Well, don't let it go to your head," she finally said.

"Don't worry, I won't," he said, but his smile definitely said otherwise. Then he grew serious. "But if you need help, Chase, you can call on me, okay?"

Chase's breath caught, and once again she was forced to admit she might have at least one other feeling for Monty besides loathing.

"I didn't think you knew my first name," she said, clearing her throat. One corner of his mouth lifted in a subdued grin.

"I know everything, don't you realize that?"

Ah, there he was.

Her watch buzzed, dictating an end to their lunch. Monty saw the alert and nodded.

"Back to work?" he asked.

"Unfortunately." Chase stood and gathered her trash. "Thank you for your hypothetical help."

He watched her prepare to leave. Her time was up, but he still had a few minutes left. "No problem, any time," he said.

Chase opened her mouth, then realized she had nothing to say, and closed it again. She settled for a solid nod before walking away, tossing her trash in the recycling bins as she left.

According to Monty, she needed to reach out to the DIA. That should be easy. She could totally do that. Just not on company Wi-Fi.

The day dragged, but Chase waited until she returned home that evening to search for the regional Domestic Investigations Agency location. The page was less than user friendly, and she scrolled through several versions of a Contact page before finally landing on a blank site with a voice number. Whoever founded the DIA must've been part of the Last Generation too, as Chase didn't know any other business which preferred communication via voice.

She should've hesitated, but she didn't. She pressed the number.

The voice call made the periodic buzzing noises she really only heard on Stream period pieces, which nearly distracted her from the reason for the call.

"Domestic Investigations, which subdistrict are you in?"

"Um...what?" Chase knew a lot of things, but her federal subdistrict was not one of them.

The person on the other end sighed heavily.

"Your subdistrict?"

"If you say it slowly, it doesn't make the information magically pop into my head," Chase said. She grimaced; this wasn't how the conversation was supposed to go. "Look, I'm an employee at Kierper, and I need to talk to someone about—"

"Hold please."

A click, and then a random, lilting tune that sounded a touch off-key.

Ten minutes later, the music stopped.

"Domestic Investigations, which subdistrict are you calling from?"

"I still don't know. I'm a Kierper employee—"

"Hold please."

Click. The creepy song returned, but Chase's frustration limited its power.

"Domestic Investigations—"

"I don't know my subdistrict, but I need to talk to someone about Kierper."

"Hold—"

"—no—!"

"—please."

"Techs damn it!" Chase stomped to her wall screen and swiped it open, exiting the Stream and searching the browser for her Techs-damned subdistrict. Her fingers flew and she typed quickly, hoping against hope she would have the number before—

"Domestic Investigations, which subdistrict are you calling from?"

"Wait, wait, wait, it's…" Chase tapped her foot as the page loaded. "EV-zero, zero, three, nine, two, five." She let out a long breath, as if she just finished a marathon.

She heard typing on the other end. "Thank you. Calling in regards to?"

"Kierper."

"Hold please."

"No!"

Click.

This time there was no music.

She paced in the silence, counting her steps and checking her handheld to make sure the call was still connected. No wonder big companies went unchecked like Beauchamp said; if alerting the authorities was this tedious, she couldn't imagine the paperwork involved to take them down.

Jamie resurfaced in her mind. The guy didn't deserve to be genetically altered and sent back into combat. None of the soldiers did. Whatever tedium she needed to endure for him, it would be worth it.

"Agent Novak." A woman answered, her voice flat and followed by a heavy sigh. Chase swallowed her own irritation—if she wanted this to go right, she needed to be calm, cool, and professional. 'Cause she was so good at that.

"Hi, Agent Novak. My name is…" she paused. Was she supposed to give her name? Maybe anonymity was the way to go. She should've thought about that while she was on hold. "My name isn't important. I work in Research and Development at Kierper, and I found out today they're willingly and actively breaking the Advanced Neutrality Agreement."

"Okay?" Agent Novak sounded slightly less peeved, but not quite interested.

"So...don't you guys wanna know stuff like that?" She suddenly felt like a tattling child.

"How are they breaking the Agreement?" Agent Novak asked dryly. Apparently, she didn't find it as alarming as Chase did.

"They want us to create illegal stuff, like super strength."

"To what end?"

"I...military stuff?" If she said the word *stuff* one more time, she was going to stuff herself in the closet and never leave.

Agent Novak sighed. "Right. And what physical proof do you have?"

"Proof?"

"Yes, proof." Agent Novak snapped. "Data corroborated by a third party, and the illegal material. Something that gives me airtight evidence. Unless you want me to fly into the biggest body company in the world on the hearsay of a *nameless* employee?"

"...alright, I'll admit, maybe I wasn't prepared for this conversation."

"No." Chase winced at the sharp word. "Call me back when you have more information, and for Techs' sake, some cold, hard evidence."

Chase opened her mouth, but the voice call disconnected with a decisive click.

Proof.

Agent Novak wanted proof. She wanted *details*. She wanted something physical and irrefutable.

Chase could bring her own data, but that would incriminate no one but herself. She needed the data from all the labs, and the trail leading all the way to the top. How in the hell could she do that? She wasn't some kind of tech genius, able to hack into the mainframe or whatever.

She collapsed on her couch, utterly at a loss for her next step.

Her dream job was slowly becoming a nightmare.

CHAPTER 10
THE KNIFE JOB

AFTER DAYS OF THINKING, scouring the web, and watching way too many Stream shows, Chase had a plan. It was a stupid plan, but a plan nonetheless.

Sure, she spent as much time in the lab testing things that could give desired results without hurting anybody, but apparently that was even more difficult than breaking the bounds of science. Therefore, she needed a contingency. She couldn't search the web for "helpers with questionable morals" or "hackers for hire" without repercussions, but she could comb through chat spaces and read between the lines. A few questions here, a couple of comments there, and she slowly spiraled her way to a side of the world she knew existed, but never thought she'd see.

It was terrifying, but also exhilarating.

For every story in the forums about someone helpful in an impossible situation, there were slews of complaints about scams, liars, or people ending up hurt or dead. With all this varied data, how was she supposed to find a reputable criminal to steal from a massive corporate titan?

Grad school did not prepare her for this.

One night, as the clock ticked further past her bedtime and close to three, Chase paced her living room and waited as the much slower satellite cell service worked. She'd disconnected her handheld from the Wi-Fi before going down this road—a good idea, even if it slowed her down. Her intention was to follow up on everything the next day, once her brain had a break, but as she scrolled, a pattern emerged.

Chase tapped a few links shared by distinct, individual sources and set the sites side by side on the tiny screen. If she believed these commenters, then it was possible there was a Robin Hood-style agency out there taking on big problems from people out of their depth. She ran the software on her handheld, which declared none of the original comments were from bots. And each one had a variation of the same message: *They helped me when no one else would.*

Well, Chase needed help, and with the proper authorities wholly uninterested, these guys seemed like the next best thing.

Anxiety buzzed in her brain and blurred her vision as the reality of the opportunity arose. This was it. This was the contact she was looking for, if she really wanted to go through with it. The conversation with Agent Novak replayed in her head; she had no other options.

Now, if she could just convince herself to message them.

By the time the sunrise overtook the city lights below, Chase had drafted, edited, redrafted, and re-edited her message a thousand times. In the end, she settled on three simple lines about her big company, the rules they were breaking, and her desire to do the right thing despite the authorities' apathy. She didn't know if it all made sense, but the grammar software had no gripes and she had no fucks left to give, so she sent it and crashed on the couch before panic could send her into orbit.

When her alarm went off a couple hours later, she found a message waiting for her. At first, she thought her stress dream hadn't worn off yet, and it was just a hallucination. But she blinked and rubbed her eyes, and the little notification was still there. She held her breath and tapped it.

Hello, Dr. C,

Thank you for reaching out. My name is Oscar, and I'll be your contact. My team is very interested in this problem with Kierper, but will need some more information regarding the situation. At this time, I cannot guarantee that we'll take your case, but the more details you can provide, the better. How, specifically, are they breaking the Parsons Accords? With these transgressions, what are the best and worst case scenarios, in terms of how the science will be implemented? Have they made any threats to you? Anything, even something that sounds small, will be very helpful in our decision making.

We look forward to hearing back from you.

The message was brief, but they were willing to talk. Though she couldn't see clearly through her sleep deprived eyes, Chase typed out as much information as she could without implicating herself completely, just in case this was some sort of corporate loyalty spy.

She spent the entire rail ride to work staring at her phone, but no further messages came through. It took every ounce of self-control to keep her handheld in her pocket as she passed through security and grabbed breakfast on the way to the lab. How long did it take to respond to a message?

To be fair, she was asking a lot of this stranger, but that was beside the point.

Everyone was hard at work when she stumbled into the lab and took her seat. Only Divya looked up and offered a sweet smile and a wave from across the mega fab. Chase responded in kind before ducking behind her monitor and placing her handheld where she could keep an eye on it.

The monitor chimed with a ping from Divya.

DIVYA V:
You okay?

Chase thought about it for a second; was she asking because of the first couple weeks in R&D, or because she looked like death warmed over? She settled on a general reply.

Monty also pinged, asking for an update. Chase sighed and rubbed her face for a moment before replying that she'd tell him at lunch. Did they have a lunch appointment for today? No. Did she make one for them right then? Yes. She'd leave out digging through the web for some less-than-legal help, but she'd at least tell him about the conversation with Agent Novak.

Chase put her pings on Do Not Disturb and opened up some research articles. Hopefully they would pass the time until Oscar messaged her back.

The door to Hunter's room opened, and Ayla dragged the tube past Chase's desk and into the mega fab. She went through the docking procedure like any other day, but instead of leaving Hunter supine, she shifted the table so the shell stood on their own two feet. The others took notice, and styluses slowed as one by one they abandoned their work to watch.

Blue light blinked under the skin of Hunter's temple, and their dark eyes opened, staring right at Chase.

The fight or flight response was common knowledge. A lesser known response to duress was freezing. Chase learned, in that moment, she was a freezer.

Hunter's dark eyes stayed on her, their face neutral and gaze blank. Chase didn't move, as if staying still would prevent a predator from finding her. Hunter's stance felt like a live snake, coiled and ready to strike.

But they just stood there, a statue, waiting while Ayla tapped away at her tablet. Then, she stopped and looked at the shell.

"Look at me." The glass muffled her voice, but Chase heard the words.

Hunter turned, a weight lifting from Chase as their attention shifted. When their movement stopped, Ayla spoke again.

"Lift right arm."

Hunter lifted their right arm to shoulder height and left it there. Ayla's hard exterior cracked, and she grinned widely.

"Lower right arm."

Hunter obeyed. No hesitance, no question.

Chase stood, shameless in wanting a better view. Hunter was listening, understanding, following *commands*. What the actual fuck was going on?

Her movement caught Hunter's attention, and they shifted their eyes from Ayla to Chase with jerky, robotic accuracy, like a motion-detecting camera searching for a subject. This time, there was a glimmer of intelligence, a spark of recognition.

"Forget her," Ayla snapped, and Hunter scanned back to her, ignoring Chase again. The mega fab hummed and light sparkled in the middle. The particles coalesced into something shaped almost like a ruler. "Pick up the knife with your right hand."

Not a ruler then.

Hunter turned their head until they found the knife, then reached over and grabbed it around the middle. The entire lab cringed as the blade sank into their skin and blood seeped from the incisions. Their grip faltered as the knife bit through tendons, severing them.

"Damn it." Ayla waved her hand, frustrated. "Let go." Hunter did, and Ayla grabbed their hand. "Let me see."

Hunter didn't understand the nuance of the command, but didn't resist Ayla shifting their arm to better view the injury. She muttered more, but Chase couldn't hear through the glass until Ayla turned, looked directly at her, and shouted.

"Come fix these tendons."

"Excuse me?" Chase didn't like orders, especially from people who weren't her superiors. Ayla rolled her eyes.

"Please," she added, with zero sincerity. Chase glared at her, then eyed Hunter, who was perfectly still except for their head. The sound of her voice captured their attention, and once again, she met those eyes. The whole thing was terrifying and wrong, but she needed to get a closer look. Immediately.

Chase grabbed her stylus and turned her handheld face down on the desk. Out of habit, she donned the sleeves of her jumpsuit, though the mixture of fear and curiosity bubbling in her stomach kept her more than warm enough in the chill.

"It completely severed the flexor tendons," Ayla said, thrusting Hunter's hand at Chase. Chase didn't reach out fast enough, and when Ayla let go, Hunter's hand dropped to their side. If it weren't for the blood steadily streaming from their hand, Chase might have laughed.

"Did they retract at all?" she asked.

"Not yet," Ayla said pointedly.

Chase gestured for Hunter to show her the wound, but it turned out they hadn't learned gestures in the last forty-five seconds. "Show me your palm," she said, adjusting Ayla's command from earlier. Hunter recreated the position perfectly.

They were *learning*.

"Does it hurt?" Chase didn't know why she asked, or what she'd do if Hunter actually responded.

"I haven't taught it speech yet," Ayla said, rolling her eyes again. She spoke as if this were obvious, as if teaching a body without a consciousness to follow commands was an everyday occurrence. "We just got to basic commands."

Only two tendons were completely cut, and Chase easily pulled the edges together and melded the tissues. It was a basic repair, one of the first things they learned during specialization, and she wished she did it slower so she could figure out what the hell was going on here.

"I can do the skin. Thanks." It was a firm dismissal, and Chase had no excuse to stick around.

"Yeah, sure," she said, and returned to her desk. There was no hiding the interest now; the whole lab stopped in their pods and watched as Ayla gave Hunter more instructions. They successfully picked up the knife the second time, using the handle instead of the blade.

Ayla flipped her tablet, showing something to Hunter. Could

they read? Chase leaned over in an attempt to see what was on the screen, but Ayla held it just right to keep it obscured. After a moment, she moved the tablet away.

"Copy," she commanded.

A blue target materialized in the mega fab, and Hunter shifted their attention to it. Their movements were jerky and unpracticed, but the intention was clear as they threw the knife. It flew end over end and went wide of the target. Epley jumped as it hit the window to his pod and disintegrated.

Ayla made notes on her tablet, the same shadow of a smirk on her face. She was showing off–and loving it.

But the sight of Hunter learning to handle weapons terrified Chase. Based on the expressions of her colleagues, it terrified the rest of them too. Everyone except Ayla.

Once Hunter was back in their room and Ayla back at her desk, Chase was able to decrease her panic from level nine to at least a level seven. But any chance at work was shot. Besides lunch with Monty, the hours consisted of nothing but wiggling her mouse to appear online and checking her handheld every ten seconds. Was it bad form to message Oscar again?

One by one, Chase's colleagues left for the day. With the lab quiet, she was able to focus more on her actual job, which she had to keep doing to prevent Beauchamp from asking questions. She liked to think she was a badass capable of withstanding torture, but there was a real chance she'd crack like an egg at the slightest pressure, so she had to keep sciencing. The whole time, she tried to figure out how they would implement Ayla's work on living people. Could they just…shut down consciousness?

Information. She needed information. Separate, none of the experiments seemed to fit. How was Beauchamp planning to use them all together? She had to know. There had to be records *somewhere*.

Chase knew very little about computers, so at first it was difficult for her to find anything on the intranet. Whoever ran tech security was very good at their job, keeping access to other fabricators' notes hidden behind a hundred different wrong turns. She searched through the company's shared drive, but all it had were standard protocols (that no one used) and access to human resource documents (which they used even less than the protocols).

Chase attempted to access a different drive via her past client docs, going into the osseo- or dermofabrication tabs, but the system set the docs on read-only with no further access links. The schedule wouldn't help, the cafeteria menu wouldn't help, and the newsletter archives *definitely* wouldn't help. With a sigh, she sat back in her chair, tapping the safe end of her stylus against her forehead.

One of the other stations' fans kicked on, sending a vibration through the glass walls.

"Mother of Techs," she said, clutching her imaginary pearls as adrenaline buffered out of her system. Was she so off-kilter a simple fan could throw her?

Wait.

That meant someone's computer was on.

Chase sat up, looking around the lab in case someone materialized in the last hour without her noticing. It was empty, as expected; the fan was the only noise. She checked the ceilings and corners, but cameras were noticeably absent. This was a terrible idea, and by far her best one.

One at a time, she crept by the stations, putting her hand on the glass until she found the spot vibrating more than the others. A thrill of victory ran through her as she reached Jun's desk, the fan kicking up a notch to match her energy.

Though she had limited technology skills, she knew how to flip on the monitor. The bright screen nearly blinded her, and when the lights faded, she saw lines of code running so fast it gave her vertigo. She swiped at it, minimizing the programs until there, in all its open-ended glory, was Jun's desktop.

"Okay, let's see what we can find." Usually when talking to herself, she had Hunter as an excuse, but she was utterly alone.

Therefore, she didn't need to feel embarrassed. Her successes were finally catching up to the failures!

Using Jun's discarded stylus, she tapped around the screen, pulling up familiarish files and reading through them. It was a long time since she thought about any viscera stuff, and it took a few squinty-eyed moments to remember which prefixes went with each organ. Jun's project ran in the same vein as her super strength, with one marked difference: Instead of strength, he had to improve metabolic efficiency, both for regulation and for healing.

Huh. So Beauchamp wanted strong muscles that lasted a long time and organs that had the ability to heal themselves. She thought about Ayla's experiment earlier—he also wanted the shells to follow commands, without question.

A clunk from the back room made her shoot up, the chair toppling over and her thigh sinking into the corner of the table.

"Shit!" That was going to bruise later. For now, another release of adrenaline dulled the pain.

Chase fumbled with the monitor button, nearly knocking it over in her haste to turn it off. She put everything back the way she found it, forgetting to be quiet as she did so, hoping the walls were thick enough to hide the sounds of her espionage.

Well, if she could hear the person in the back room, then they could definitely hear her. *Double shit.* Someone could've come into the lab from the elevator in Hunter's room, but the automated voice would've announced their arrival... Unless it was someone high up enough to disable those features.

It took everything in her to walk slowly out of Jun's pod. She schooled her features into what she hoped was a blank look, and returned to the central mega fab, casting a quick glance around the other stations. No one hid behind the other monitors, which meant the noise came from Hunter's room.

A tiny part of her feared Hunter made the noise, but that went down a terrible route she didn't have time for. Chase eased her way down the hall, pausing before the door. Did she want to know? Of course not. But she *needed* to know. Before she could think too hard about it, she scanned her badge and barged into Hunter's room.

The sound from before was not another person, or Hunter moving. Epley was clearly the last person to work on them, and in a terrifying move, had stopped his experiment halfway through. Hunter's face and chest no longer had skin, and it was so much worse to see the staring eyes without surrounding tissue. At least with their eyes closed, Chase could pretend Hunter was sleeping, but now they saw everything—every move she made, every sharp tool on the tables in front of them, and all the mutilation.

Epley must have put the skin back in a hurry; she could see the point on the inferior angle of the sternum where the skin tore instead of cut. At the bottom of the tube, their skin lay like a discarded scarf, twisted and folded over itself. That had to be the noise she heard.

"Oh, bud, I'm sorry." With no eyelids to mask their features, Hunter looked like they were silently screaming for help. Chase swallowed the bile lingering in the back of her throat and pressed the button to drain the tube, the act making the torn skin edges dance like anemone in the current.

It was easier now to pull the tube from its home and roll it to the mega fab. With practiced motions, she locked everything in place and opened it up. Her thick myofabrication stylus wouldn't work for this delicate procedure, so she went to the cups in the supply closet and found a dermofabrication one. The thing was so long and thin she was afraid she might snap it in half.

Chase donned her safety equipment and reverently picked up Hunter's skin from the floor of the tube, her stomach clenching at the *squelch* it made as she unfurled it. She wasn't an expert skin stitcher, but she could at least manage well enough for Hunter to stay covered until Epley came back in the morning. The tiny, floating pieces earlier were more obvious in the light of the chamber. She could have sworn subdermal fibers were usually red or pink, but these had a strange silver hue.

Chase lay the skin over Hunter's face and upper chest, then selected the proper setting for the stylus. Full skin replacement was a skill she'd practiced just enough to pass. It was a way different skill than when she stitched up the front of the thigh. Her hands froze as she tried to recall information tucked way into the back of her brain, probably in a box labeled "useless".

She had to set the borders first, then she could work her way in, otherwise things would lie uneven. Right.

As she sewed, the readings on the tablet didn't match those old memories. But at this point, there was too much going on for her to care. When she finished the V cut over the chest, she moved to the neck, following the paths of the muscles underneath and finishing at the spot behind their ear. At least those remained intact; Chase didn't think she could handle a whole ear flopping about while she worked.

The last part was the hairline, her worst unit during her program. In fact, it was the face unit that solidified her plan to go into muscles; she needed more intricacy than bones required, but didn't have enough finesse for skin or nerves. Hunter's wet hair kept getting in the way, and she brushed it back, cringing hard at the intimate gesture. It gave her full access to the hairline at the cost of her comfort.

Chase shook her wrist out. After holding so tightly to the stylus, her hand and forearm were cramped. Even without the hairline tacked down, Hunter looked like themself again, and the unease churning in her stomach relented. Forcing her fingers to stay loose, she fixed the last of the border.

The rest was easy, a steady drag of the stylus over the skin to get the underlying structures to adhere. Just like that, Hunter was back in business.

"You and me," she murmured, closing the tube back up. "We'll figure this out. I think it's time for you to retire."

Hunter had no words as she returned them to their rest.

Alone again, she collapsed at her desk. Out of habit, she checked her handheld.

There was a message waiting.

With shaking fingers, Chase opened it, then read it three times before it sank in.

Oscar was willing to help her.

CHAPTER 11
THE BADGE JOB, PT. 1

CRIMINALS, even the helpful kind, didn't like meeting in person. And Chase, who knew the danger of a digital trail, didn't like airing Kierper's dirty laundry via messaging system.

Oscar, the kind soul, insisted she didn't need to take part in the con. He and his team would handle it, he said. They had it all under control, he said. Unfortunately for him, Chase was kind of a control freak, and also the one with access to the R&D lab. In her mind, it made sense to work together. After all, why risk breaking into the lab when she could let them right in?

Oh, perfect. She had her argument to make for that day. After two weeks of steady messaging, she was definitely starting to wear him down.

Chase smiled at Mr. Scovajsa as he handed back her badge. Fewer people than usual milled about the cafeteria, making it extra easy to grab a ready-made meal and some coffee before carrying on. This morning, she was a woman on a mission.

Which meant when she rounded a corner going full speed, she barely noticed Monty in time to dodge him, and even then she dropped her breakfast sandwich. The coffee, she saved— every last drop.

"Watch it!" His hand gripped her upper arm, studying her and distracting her from the tragedy on the floor. Once she righted herself, his death grip relaxed. "Are you alright? Drifting the curves there?"

"Sorry, Monty, so sorry," she said with a gasp. She bent to grab her floor food and tossed it in a nearby receptacle. "Just have a lot to do today."

"An apology? It's much too early for that." He did not sound like it was too early. In fact, he sounded pretty eager.

"Early? Haven't you been up for a few hours?" He always beat her to the office—she assumed he was one of those mythological *early birds*.

"Eh, a couple. Like you, lots to do." He shrugged, as though early mornings were a normal thing.

"What's on the docket? Anything interesting?" She put her hand in her pocket, but her handheld didn't vibrate. No messages from Oscar, then.

"Oh, big order," he said. "A hospital raised funds and is purchasing a whole slew of new limbs for cancer patients. Pretty cool, really."

"That is cool," she said, and meant it.

"And you? Any changes to your, ah, current project?" He looked around them, but no one paid them any attention. When she'd reenacted her conversation with Agent Novak for him, he hadn't been surprised. But he also didn't have any other ideas.

"No, just…trying to solve the problems," she said with a shrug. "Anything you can think of?"

He rolled his lips in for a second, thinking. "Actually, I think I might know someone. No promises, I have to see if they're still where I think they are."

"Cryptic, I hate it," Chase said. Monty laughed.

"I know, I know. But listen, anything I can do to help, you just let me know, okay?"

His sincerity made her breath catch. Even if the situation was terrible, she was so glad to have him in her corner. "Do you want to break in and steal everything for me?"

He barked a laugh and lay a hand on her shoulder. The warm weight of it comforted her. "We'll put that way down the list of plans. But are you free tonight?"

"Tonight?" She blinked. They'd shared a few lunches, but Chase assumed their meetings would be an office-based thing, except for the random meeting in Market Square.

"If you need a distraction, perhaps we can watch the new episode of *Earthbound*," he said, his cheeks turning a touch darker.

"Oh, right! Yes!" That sounded a little too enthusiastic, so she cleared her throat and said in a totally normal and chill way, "I mean, yeah, I'm free. That would be fun."

"Great." He pulled out his handheld and tapped it against hers, his contact info syncing automatically. "Ping me when you leave and I'll have pizza waiting for you."

Heat rose in her chest. Techs, it sounded so nice to have a normal plan with a normal person. "That'd be really great, honestly."

With a grin and a goodbye, Monty left, and Chase felt a strange lightness. Sure, she lost her breakfast, but she got dinner in exchange. She had a plan, she had a date, and by the time she got to the lab, she had another message from Oscar.

He wanted to see the data surrounding Hunter.

Chase didn't *have* any data for Hunter. Nothing besides what she'd done to them.

She sat at her desk and stared at her monitor, willing previous data to appear on the screen. Telling Oscar about the archives felt like the fastest way for him to drop her case. She could send what she had, but would it be enough? Would they be able to trace it back and find the rest?

Epley stood in the mega fab, adding more of the silvery skin Chase stitched the other day. There had to be a way to get everyone out of the lab with their monitors on so she could collect their data, too.

She watched Epley stand Hunter's tube up, then use the programming to create a projectile. A little blue bullet flew a short distance at a high speed, but it only lodged in Hunter's skin instead of burying into their arm.

Chase perked up.

Hunter.

Hunter.

The human body had markers all over from its past experiences. Hunter's body had to keep at least *some* record of what it went through. It would be better than her own meager numbers and half-assed attempts at espionage. If she could find a way to scan Hunter, they'd have all the data they needed.

It was official: Chase was a criminal mastermind. She should've strayed from the path long ago. With an idea in place, she sent another message to Oscar, then buckled down to actually work. She was going to make a perfect, self-sufficient muscle, hopefully a good enough trade for super strength.

She worked until the lab was empty, and then worked some more, only stopping when her stomach grumbled. There were easily two more hours worth of work on the experiment she was drawing up, but she was hungry, and tired, and had plans. Tomorrow. She'd continue tomorrow.

Back in her red jumpsuit, she gathered her things and exited the lab. As she walked, she vigorously typed another message to Oscar with details of her idea and how she planned to implement it. He hadn't responded in a while, but she wasn't above sending multiple messages between replies.

"Whoa there." Monty dragged her attention up. She was, once again, on a collision course. She tried to evade him, but her left knee twinged and made her lose balance. His hands shot to her arms, a vise-like grip which prevented her fall for the second time that day. "You really need to watch where you're going, Alspeth. Not everyone has cat-like reflexes like me."

"Right, you're right," she said, shaking her head.

"Well, definitely noting this day in my diary," he muttered. "It's almost like you're trying to run me over. Is there something you want to tell me?" He kept his face serious at first, but Chase could see the corner of his mouth trembling as he tried to hide the smile.

"Damn, and I thought I was being subtle," she said.

"Somehow I don't think that's in your wheelhouse."

Her mouth dropped open and she crossed her arms over her chest. "Excuse you, I can be subtle."

The smile broke. Techs, he was infuriating. "Yes, sure, as subtle as a freight craft."

"Those have cloaking devices now, you know," she said.

"Ah, good, when is your upgrade, then?"

"You're so obnoxious." She very nearly stomped her foot. His smile was stupid, and she hated it, but he seemed to be laughing *with* her.

Chase pressed her lips together, her mind whirring in an effort to come up with a better response. Monty's smile held all his pride in his performance. He was also standing closer to her and holding her gaze confidently. Her mind clicked. He was *flirting*.

"Whatever," she said, putting her hands in her pockets and switching subjects. "What are you doing here so late? Are we still on for tonight?"

"Oh, absolutely," he said. "I just had a couple high-priority things pop up. I'm still bringing over pizza."

"Bringing it over, huh? Inviting yourself to my place now?" She assumed they would watch it at her place, since he had a bunch of roommates to contend with. But it was fun to mess with him.

"I—well, I didn't mean to presume, but my apartment is... chaotic, at best." He winced, but whether it was from chagrin or something else, she couldn't say. With a ridiculous bow, he asked, "Dr. Chase Alspeth, might I invite myself to your place of residence to watch the Stream and share a meal of pizza?"

"Montgomery Evans, stop it." She swatted his arm until he stood, the shit-eating grin back on his face. "You always have to win, huh?"

"It's a personality flaw, I'm afraid," he said. "Let me finish up here, and I'll ping you when I'm on the way, deal?"

"Deal," she said. He took his first few steps backwards, keeping his eyes on hers and that grin on his face until he had to turn. The warmth spread through Chase's body, and a bubble of excitement rose.

Despite the ups and downs, she felt there was a net positive on the day, and hopefully, it would only get better from here. The success carried her all the way to the front lobby, hope rebuilding in her heart.

"It's later than usual, Dr. Alspeth," Mr. Scovajsa said, his wrinkles growing deeper with his frown. "Not working too much, I hope?"

"No, never," she said. She reached for her badge, but grasped nothing but air and the fabric of her jumpsuit. With disdain, she looked to the loop she always clipped it to and found it betrayed her. Her badge was gone. "Oh, fuck a duck."

"Such language, Dr. Alspeth," Mr. Scovajsa chastised, giving her a fatherly look of scorn. Little did he know, she was immune to fatherly derision since she grew up with double the adversaries.

"Sorry," she said, not meaning it. She patted down her pockets, then started digging through her bag, but the damn badge was nowhere to be found. She dumped all the contents of the bag onto a nearby table and replaced them one by one to make sure she didn't miss it. There was no mistake–her badge had disappeared into thin air.

"I have no clue where it is, I'm sorry," she said, running a hand through her hair. "Can I just type my employee ID? I'll get a new badge tomorrow, I swear."

"I'm afraid not," Mr. Scovajsa said. He pulled out his tablet and tapped away. "But we can find it. Here, enter your credentials for me."

Chase typed in all the important information, and the security program opened a blueprint of the building. A blinking white light showed where her badge hid—apparently, still in the R&D lab.

"Huh, that's weird," she said. She didn't remember taking her badge off, but there was a chance it slipped when she changed jumpsuits. There was so much going on in her brain, it wouldn't surprise her if she dropped it and missed it. "I need the badge to get into the lab. How do I get it out?"

"Normally you'd have to go to HR," he said, shuffling back to the security desk. He pulled out a blank visitor badge. "But they've gone home, so instead we get to charm this one."

"You're a hero, Mr. Scovajsa," she said, breathing a sigh of relief.

"Nah, just doing my job." The old man waved her off. "I mean, maybe I'm being a little more helpful just for you, but that's neither here nor there."

Chase gave him a smile. "I'll email the head of security tomorrow and demand he give you a raise."

"That's the spirit." He keyed in the visitor badge number, then signed the screen. "There you go. Bring it back before you leave, please."

"Can do." She took the spare badge from him and jetted to the lab as fast as her body allowed. She wanted to get home and clean her apartment a little before Monty arrived.

The hallway lights barely kept up with her as she strode to the door. For a beat, she worried the spare badge wouldn't work, but the panel dinged and turned green with no hesitation. A decontamination and another swipe, and she was back in the lab. She had every intention of going to her station, grabbing the badge, and making a quick getaway. She had *plans*.

There was just one problem.

Her badge was on her desk. And next to it, Monty sat in her chair, looking at her research on the screen.

He turned sharply as she entered, both of them staring as if hoping the other were a hallucination. Chase didn't know whether to feel scared, angry, or confused, and settled on swinging between all three.

"Well," Monty said, all traces of his British accent gone. "In my defense, you did ask me to steal it for you."

CHAPTER 12
THE BIG REVEAL JOB

"WHAT THE *FUCK* IS GOING ON?" Chase asked, her voice an octave higher than usual.

Monty stood slowly, hands up. He had the sleeves of his gray jumpsuit tied around his waist, showing off his arms. Arms that were a lot stronger than hers.

"Okay, listen," he said, his voice long and languid instead of the old British clip. "I can explain."

"Yeah, that's the part I'm waiting on." She took a step back as he took a step forward. "Why the fuck do you have my badge, and why the fuck are you in the lab?"

"It's, uh, it's a really long story," he said, glancing around.

Her heart stopped. They were very, *very* alone.

"Oh, Techs," she whispered, the bravado from before taking a hard hit. She'd talked to him about ways to fix the situation, and now Kierper sent him to seal the deal. "You're here to kill me."

"I—what? No, I'm not here to kill you." He shook his head.

"You stole my badge and lured me back here–of course, Beauchamp sent you to kill me!" Her voice was shrill now, but she couldn't stop it. He took another step forward, and she moved back, hitting the wall. Why wasn't she next to the door? Shit!

"Beauchamp? The old guy running this? Listen, Alspeth, this is just a misunderstanding—"

"Oh Techs, and I know your face, and your name—and—please don't kill me, maybe we can come to an agreement?" She stepped along the wall, trying to think of something to offer in exchange. Money? No, assassins probably made way more than her. Maybe if she made him new muscles—

"Stop saying I'm gonna kill you! I'm not gonna kill you!" He stopped moving, holding his hands up all the way and lowering his voice. "I'm not going to kill you, Alspeth. I was just trying to help. I'll give you back your badge, we'll go our separate ways, and you'll never see me again."

"That's the dumbest villain speech I've ever heard." Her voice shook so badly it was barely understandable. "You realize I believe you, like, zero percent right now, right? I'm not—don't come closer!"

"Sorry, sorry," he said softly, moving back. "Damn it, it wasn't supposed to go down like this."

Chase didn't fear for her life anymore, but that didn't mean she had calmed down. "Are you gonna explain anything? Like, actually explain?"

Monty winced. "I wasn't planning on that, no."

Shit.

"I knew something was up with you. This is stupid, there's already enough shit going on up here. If this is just a ploy to somehow get rid of me—"

She inched closer to the exit, and he moved laterally, matching her progress. He kept his hands in the air and had a neutral, almost earnest expression. If he was an assassin, he was the worst assassin she'd ever seen.

As if she'd met any assassins. She'd been watching way too many shows on the Stream.

"Alspeth, I'm not trying to get rid of you. You were struggling, I was just trying to do something about it." He busted out his trademark grin, complete with a wince. He murmured, not nearly as quiet as he thought, "Shut. Up."

"I will not shut up," Chase said, putting her hands on her hips. Could she trust him? Not as far as she could throw him. But he hadn't killed her yet, which was a good sign. It gave her time to come up with another one of her brilliant plans.

"Not you," he said, turning his head to the side and digging in his ear. She grimaced at the act, especially when he pulled something out. He held out some tiny silver thing. "It's just a comms unit. Nothing weird."

"Everything about this is weird," she said as he replaced it in his ear. "Are you some sort of spy or something?" Chase remembered her handheld and tried to slyly pull it from her pocket to call the security desk.

"Yes, you're right, I'm a spy here to steal information," he said, holding his hands out now. She curled away from him, even though he was too far to grab her.

"Oh yeah? Who do you work for?" She narrowed her eyes, hoping she could suss out any signs of lying. Surely all the true crime shows she watched gave her some observational skills.

"No one." Chase stared at him, waiting for him to break, but he kept his gaze steady.

"Yeah, sounds fake," she said, raising her handheld again.

"Don't call security!" he said.

"Why not? Wait, the cameras—"

"Yeah, those are taken care of already."

Closer now, Monty lunged, but instead of grabbing her, he took her handheld, then backed up to give her space.

"I really am—was—an employee, but now I'm just trying to get some information and be on my way," he said. "No fuss, no muss. No more people going missing."

"No—no *more*?" she asked. "Who did you kill?"

Monty sighed heavily. "I haven't killed *anyone*. I'm just trying to find someone."

For the first time in a few days, Chase thought of the body on the gurney.

"Someone you knew?" she asked. A pained expression crossed his face, and he clenched his hands into fists for a second. The action could be considered threatening, but to Chase, it looked like he was trying to hold himself together.

"An old friend. From a previous…career. We don't know if she's dead or not, but we haven't heard from her. Last I knew, she was in this lab."

If he was pretending to grieve, he was an amazing actor. Chase wanted so badly to believe him, the present information warring with the man she'd been working with for the past few months. She thought of all the lunch dates, all the advice; Monty was the one person trying to help her in this storm.

She took a breath. "They're making us do illegal things. Beauchamp threatened to blacklist me if I quit." She remembered Ayla's work earlier, how Hunter followed her commands without hesitation. "I think they're making something for soldiers."

"I know."

"And they're—wait, you know? Monty, how do you know?"

Monty sighed, pinched the bridge of his nose, and said very dejectedly,

"You've been chatting with my friend Oscar."

Chase heard him, she knew she did, but the words didn't quite make sense.

"Oscar…like, like—"

"The one and only." Monty dropped his hands and his shoulders sagged as the fight left him. "You did well, by the way, covering your tracks. Very impressive for a civilian."

"Thank you?" she squeaked.

"But we needed a different kind of data, and you couldn't get it." He gestured at her monitor. "Sometimes I have to take matters into my own hands."

Chase blinked. "So you know about the shells."

"Yeah." He paused for a second, choosing his words. "Everything I ever said to you was true, Alspeth. And I really do want to help you stop Kierper," he explained.

Chase's pulse began to slow. "But, you've been here for like, six months."

"I know. And it was a great six months." He sighed. "But my friend disappeared into one of the R&D wings six weeks ago, so the whole crew moved in."

"Your roommates."

"I'm not asking that." He turned his head to the side as he said it, probably talking into the comms unit. He turned back to her. "By the way, Kierper totally bugged your place."

That sounded silly. "No they didn't," Chase said.

Monty put his hands on his hips. "Alspeth, who knows more about bugging a place, me or you?"

"That's not the point." Finding a bug couldn't be that hard. She had a Ph.D., for Techs' sake.

"You're right. Point is, I'm gonna give you the badge back, and we're gonna leave."

"So I can go back to my bugged apartment and Kierper can disappear me like your friend? No thanks."

Monty grew very still. The line was a cheap shot, to determine if his grief was real or another con man ploy. Chase felt, just slightly, like an asshole.

"That was cold, Alspeth." There was no hint of a smile, and very real pain in his eyes.

"So that really happened?" she murmured, fear coating her words. "She got caught, and they took her?" she asked.

"Koda," he said. "Her name was Koda Sinclair, and yeah, Kierper took her. This company screwed both of us, so let me do my thing, I'll let you do yours, and we'll both be golden."

"But if you steal the data..." Her fear dissipated. If Monty was telling the truth, here was a solution, ripe for the picking. "Then we can show it to someone important. Someone who can stop them. This isn't right, what they're doing, and if we can shut them down—"

"Great, awesome, super admirable," Monty said, making circular motions with his hands. "It's gonna take a lot of planning. It's not something we can do right now."

"Why not?" Weren't they professionals? That's what Oscar said.

"Do you know all the details about this building? Have you ever planned something like this? It takes time. This was just recon."

"So you're fine with Kierper continuing to try and create super soldiers that follow commands without question?"

Monty stared at her for a long time before sighing. "Did y'all get all that?"

He cringed at whatever went on in his ear. "Okay, okay, *okay*. Got it. Loud and clear. Mainly loud." He turned back to Chase. "Alright, new plan. I'm gonna give you the badge, we're gonna walk out of here, and we're gonna head to my apartment, because there are definitely no bugs there."

This was a terrible idea. Chase knew she should definitely not do this.

"Sounds good, let's go."

Sure, it was a bad idea, but it was the only one she had. She couldn't execute a plan alone, and she couldn't trust anyone in the company to help her. This was her only chance, she felt it in her bones.

Monty—if that *was* his real name—gestured for her to leave the lab first, but she stood her ground and shook her head. He gestured again, and she objected again. He was going to stay in her eyesight the entire time, Techs damn it. Monty huffed and smacked the button for the door, making a show of exiting the room first.

The decontamination chamber did its work and spat them out into the hallway. Outside the safety of the lab, Chase's heart beat heavier and her limbs numbed. Why did she think she could do this? She was a fool in a scientist's jumpsuit.

"Take a deep breath," Monty said as they reached the elevator bank. He waved his badge to call it, and she wanted to snatch the badge out of his hand—he didn't deserve it.

"No." Because petulance brought her back to life.

"If you don't breathe, you'll pass out, and then I'll have to drag you back to the apartment and there'll be too many questions—I've got it."

"Got what?"

"Huh? Oh, sorry." He waved a hand toward his ear, like that was explanation enough. The door opened, and they stepped in. "Ground floor."

The elevator descended three floors, then jolted to a stop. The overhead lights turned red, and the automated voice asked them to patiently wait as it ran diagnostics. Panic flooded Chase; she couldn't stay in here, it was too small, everything was too much—

"Breathe," Monty reminded her. This time, she followed his instruction. He reached out, almost as if he wanted to comfort her, but let his hand drop. Chase met his eyes, and he gazed back, confident and sure.

"This is a lot," she said. Monty nodded.

"I know," he replied. "But I promise, I'm just trying to help."

She no longer had the energy to doubt him, especially when he looked so sincere.

The lights turned back to the normal, gentle white, and the automated voice informed them they were back online. The elevator shuddered into motion, and this time took them all the way down to the ground floor before stopping.

"Be cool, and when we get outside, you can yell at me as much as you want." This time, he didn't need her pestering to go first. In fact, she had to jog to catch up to him. Wait, now he wanted her to talk to Mr. Scovajsa and just act normal?

"I can't do this," she whisper-yelled to him.

"You're not breaking into the National Treasury Reserve, you're just leaving your job like you do *every day*."

Chase almost stopped walking. "Have you broken into the National Treasury Reserve? Don't answer that. I want plausible deniability."

"Techs save me," he muttered. "But look, you're freaking out less already."

"Really? 'Cause I feel like I'm freaking out more."

He shrugged. "Well, you look like it's less."

"Dr. Alspeth!" Mr. Scovajsa gave her a disarming smile. Wordlessly, she handed the temporary badge to him. "Who's your friend?"

"Uh, he's, uh—"

Monty's hand pushed her elbow gently, reminding her to hold out her real badge. Another gentle touch at her low back guided her through the exit.

"Call me Monty, sir." Now that Chase knew his real voice, the British accent sounded painfully fake. But Mr. Scovajsa didn't notice, he simply grabbed Monty's badge and eyed it for a long time. Chase held her breath, waiting for him to declare it a fake and throw the magnacuffs on his wrists, dragging him to Kierper jail.

"Monty? No, sir, that's not your name," Mr. Scovajsa said. Chase gasped, her eyes widening as she waited for the drama to unfold. But the old man smiled. "You're Dr. Evans. You earned that title, sir, and you'll use it."

"Well, thank you," he said, taking his badge back and stepping through the checkpoint. "I appreciate your good work."

"I do what I can," he said with a smile. "Take care of my girl there now."

"Yes, sir," Monty said with a salute.

Chase struggled to inhale, willing Mr. Scovajsa to read her mind. He only gave her that annoying grin, wiggling his eyebrows as Monty shepherded her through the front doors. The night air brought her back to herself, and she stopped.

"How did you do that?"

"Do what?" His voice was back to normal-normal now.

"Is that—I mean, you're a straight up *grifter*."

He furrowed his brows. "That? That wasn't a grift. That was like convincing your mom you're gonna be home by midnight."

Out of habit, Chase said, "I don't have a mom."

"What?" Monty's eyes widened. "Shit, I'm so sorry."

It would be comical if she weren't so stressed. "No, I mean—Techs damn it, what the hell is going on?"

"We're getting to that part," Monty said, waving an arm toward the rail station. "First step, back to the apartment."

She made herself follow him, focusing on one foot in front of the other until they reached the platform. They waited in awkward silence until the train arrived, and Chase folded herself into her seat, making herself as small as possible.

What the hell had she gotten herself into?

CHAPTER 13
THE NEW FRIENDS JOB

"LOOK, THE ORIGINAL OFFER STILL STANDS." Monty's voice was warm and gentle as the rail slowed before their stop. "You can go home, and we'll never see each other again. Just don't work on anything or say anything until tomorrow evening, after we clear the bugs for you. And be careful, those people are willing to do a lot of shit to keep it all under wraps."

Though her mind swirled with thoughts and fears, she found less and less of them to be about Monty and his crew. She had limited data, yes, but so far it suggested they probably wouldn't harm her.

"Nope, I'm sticking to my decision," she said. It felt right.

Monty raised his eyebrows, then nodded. "Alright then."

The train docked, and they exited to find the same blonde from the market waiting. She was dressed as if she came from the gym, her arms crossed over her chest. The sleeveless shirt emphasized her thick muscles, the kind grown organically rather than in a lab.

"What the fuck did you do?" Ellison asked. Her voice was low, and the tone made the hairs on the back of Chase's neck stand on end. She was only a couple centimeters taller than Monty, but her rage made her tower over him.

"Nice to see you too, Ellison. Maybe we could go back home before I start explaining," Monty said. He turned to Chase and added, "To everyone."

Ellison rolled her eyes. "Cut the shit."

Monty turned his gaze skyward. "I only wanna say it once."

"You're bringing a civilian in," she said.

"Yeah, she's the same civilian who *hired us*."

"We don't usually interact with the people who hire us."

"Well, we do today." Based on his tone of voice, his patience was wearing thin. Based on Ellison's expression, she didn't care. "Can we go now?"

Ellison looked Chase up and down, less like a suitor checking out a date and more like a predator sizing up a potential meal. She was so tall and muscly that Chase's fight or flight response kicked in, and luckily this time her mind chose fight. Chase squared her shoulders, standing as tall as she could despite the urge to lean over and vomit.

"Fine. Let's go," Ellison said.

"Thank you." Monty beckoned for Chase to follow him.

When they reached the right floor, Ellison led them to the last door on the right, bumping the sensor with her hip to open it. Chase took another recommended deep breath and stuffed her hands in her pockets. She could do this. She *had* to do this.

The apartment was very similar to her own, with a kitchen first thing on the left and an open living area after it. However, Chase only had one door coming off the main room, whereas this apartment had four doors. How did Monty end up in a four-bedroom apartment when it was only him?

"Monty, you have a *lot* of explaining to do." Another woman, shorter and curvier, spoke serenely from her place on the couch. She twirled her box braids idly around her fingers, as if this was just a surprise visit. Another man stopped mid-pace and stared at them through his thick, black glasses.

"Seriously, I mean we heard it all go down but," the man glanced at Chase, and she squeezed the insides of her pockets tighter. "Well, I guess it wasn't a group hallucination then. Hi, Chase. I'm Oscar."

"Oh, Techs, hi," Chase said. It was nice to put a face to the name, despite the circumstances.

"Can we all chill, please?" Monty said, holding his hands out. Chase realized he was also talking to her; she thought she was pretty calm, but the question made her buck up again.

"You're the one causing a problem," Ellison reminded him. A piece of short, blonde hair fell into her eyes, and she angrily brushed it back.

"And now you've shown the civilian all of our faces," the woman with the braids sang, though she didn't sound bothered.

"And you've also told the civilian our super illegal and personal goals," Oscar said, his words thick with a Hispanic accent, though Chase couldn't tell which country he was from.

"The civilian has a name, for the record," Chase said.

"I know, I'm sorry, this is unprecedented," Oscar said, sticking both hands in his messy black hair.

"Oscar, darling, don't pull your hair out," the woman said, putting a hand on Oscar's wrist. The lamplight made her umber skin shine beautifully.

"Thank you, Ruby," Monty said. "Chase is here because joining forces would be mutually beneficial."

Chase interjected. "Technically, Chase is here because you stole her badge and got caught."

Oscar groaned loudly and put his hands over his eyes. "I told you to wait until I had a copy!"

"I had an opportunity, and I took it," Monty said. "I didn't realize security could track its location."

Oscar dropped his hands so he could point at Monty. "You would if you listened to me."

"Gentlemen, please." The other woman—Ruby—didn't raise her voice, but still garnered their attention. Oscar crossed his arms and pointedly looked away. "Gum-Gum, if you would be a dear and explain?"

"I'd love to, Ruby," Monty said. If he had a tie, Chase thought he'd straighten it in that moment. She made a mental note to ask about *Gum-Gum* later. "I found the data we need. Or at least, part of it. Oscar was right, it's in the R&D labs, and they keep it all separated on individual drives. There's no way to hack from the outside, even if we put in the keys."

"But that's not—" Chase started, but Monty silenced her with a look. Anger bloomed in her chest, and the only reason she held her tongue was the four pairs of eyes staring at her.

"So," Monty said, waiting for further interruptions before continuing, "In order to help Chase, we need to manually get all the data from each terminal."

"Oh?" Ruby's brows rose.

"What kind of old-fashioned shit—" Ellison said.

"Hell no, I didn't sign up for this," Oscar added.

"That's too much, Gum-Gum," Ruby said.

"If Koda were here—" Ellison started.

"If Koda were here, the terminal would still work the same damn way," Monty said. A muscle in his jaw clenched, and Chase could hear the long, steady breaths he forced. "The only difference is we would actually have someone in charge, instead of the blind leading the blind. And if we wanna find our mastermind again, we have to get every piece of data possible."

"Koda was your boss?" Chase asked. If Kierper took their boss, how would they figure this out?

"Koda was the planner," Oscar said. "We should've pulled out when they took her."

"May she rest in peace," Ruby murmured. "Would if we could, darling."

"Stop talking like she's for sure dead," Monty said.

"We may not know for sure, but we can't do anything right now," Ellison said through clenched teeth. "We're blown. We need to retreat and regroup."

"Not yet," Monty said. "Besides, Chase here has a surprise piece of info to add to her case file. Chase?"

"Huh?" She startled, lost in the banter. All her courage leapt out the window, and she very nearly followed it.

"The stuff you found out," Monty said. She blinked.

"Oh. Oh! Right, yes." She pulled out her handheld, realized she couldn't display all her data, and shoved it into her pocket. "Kierper is breaking the Accords to, uh, develop some super strong, super resilient parts. Possibly to force onto soldiers? That's my current hypothesis."

Chase didn't expect silence, but that's what she got. It squeezed her from all sides, forcing more words from her. "I guess it would be to make more obedient soldiers. There's the shell we work on, Hunter, and the other day, Ayla got them to follow commands perfectly. Well, not perfectly, they needed really specific instructions, but if she finds a way to implant a command key in a normal brain, then they could turn off conscientious objection, or hesitancy, or people going rogue…"

Again, silence. This one brief.

"Fuck no, I'm not dealing with this—" Ellison exploded.

"That's a bit outside my wheelhouse." Ruby shook her head.

"Super soldiers?!" Oscar was stuck on that part.

"We. Are. *Blown*," Ellison said.

"This does complicate things," Ruby said.

"*Super soldiers?!*" Oscar reiterated.

"Guys, guys, guys!" Monty raised his voice and waved his hands to quiet them down. Ellison was halfway to a bedroom door, Oscar was stuffing machines and wires of various shapes and sizes into a leather bag, and Ruby stood calmly, staring at Monty.

"No, this is it," Ellison said, pointing at the spare bedroom door. "We're packing up, and we're reconvening somewhere else."

"There's got to be another way to find her," Oscar added.

"I think they're right, Gum-Gum," Ruby said, shaking her head. "This is beyond us."

"It doesn't have to be," Monty said. "We still have a chance. We can still find her, or at least find out what happened to her. Shit, we have someone on the inside now."

"We had someone on the inside before," Oscar said, pointing aggressively at Monty. A bead of sweat rolled down his temple, and the bottom half of his glasses fogged. "Two someones. One is here, telling us to steal plans for fucking super soldiers, and the other…"

He stopped, putting a hand to his mouth and turning away. Ruby and Ellison shared a look that made Chase feel like she was intruding on something private. These people knew each other, and knew each other well. And Koda was one of them. Monty sighed, dropping his hands.

"I wasn't supposed to count. I was supposed to be out," he said. "So now I'm saying we steal it and destroy it, or take it to someone who can do something about it, or—"

"Absolutely not," Ellison interrupted. Her blonde hair was askew like parrot feathers now. "I'm not risking your lives to follow some half-assed plan again. Not after Koda."

"We gotta do this *for* Koda," Monty said. "I left, remember? I was ready to live an honest life. But now these assholes got Koda. Even if she's dead, I wanna know. And maybe we can find a way to shut it all down, take it to someone who can do something about it."

"And in return, we get arrested," Ruby said.

"I'm sure the authorities will love closing all those international warrants," Oscar added.

"Yeah, and you know what gets you amnesty and buys enough time to get to a non-extradition country?" Monty said. "Evidence of *fucking war crimes*."

More silence.

"Absofuckinglutely not," Ellison reiterated.

"You don't have to risk the authorities," Chase said. The glare

Ellison gave her made her take a step back, and she almost grabbed Monty's arm to steady herself. Then she remembered she was still a little mad at him, and caught her balance independently. "I already talked to them once, and they didn't want to listen without proof. I'll talk to them for you and get amnesty for…whatever you guys have done."

"Bullshit," Oscar said.

"No offense, beautiful," Ruby said, her tone softer, "but that's not exactly the way the world works."

"Why not?" Chase asked. She had to convince them; she couldn't take down Beauchamp without them. "Look, I'm not here for money or blackmail or whatever. Beauchamp is running illegal processes under the guise of science, and I can't just sit there and be complicit in it. If they implement this stuff, people are going to get hurt, or worse."

"No one else in that lab has issues with it," Ellison pointed out.

"Which is part of the problem!" Chase said. "This is wrong. What they're doing is wrong on so many social and physiological levels. You can't just make people into super soldiers, it'll mess with their bodies and their minds and…" She paused, a piece of the puzzle so close she could taste it.

"Uh, you good?" Monty asked, putting a hand on her shoulder.

"Maybe her mind got messed with, too," Oscar said, earning a smack from Ruby. Chase barely heard them. All she thought of was Hunter in that lab, and how the data never quite matched up.

"They're not trying to make regular people stronger," she whispered. "They're using the shells. They're turning the shells into super soldiers."

"Yeah, we knew that," Ellison said, crossing her muscled arms over her broad chest. "That's the whole reason for your job request."

"No, you don't understand," Chase said. "They're not developing this to add onto existing soldiers, they're making the bodies. Blank bodies, like Hunter, that don't have consciousness—"

"Wait, who's Hunter again?" Oscar asked. He looked toward the door and the windows, as if Hunter would choose that moment to make a dramatic entrance.

"Hunter is the shell," she explained. "But there's no way they're just a shell. I mean, you can't put in a brain and have them follow commands, but take away consciousness...can you?"

She looked to Monty, who looked to Ellison, who looked to Ruby, who looked to Oscar, who threw his hands up. "Fuck if I know! I hack electronics, not the human brain."

"So what you're saying," Monty said, turning back to her. "Is that they're building super strong bodies designed to only follow orders? Have no thoughts of their own?"

"Yes, that's exactly what I'm saying." Cold nausea gripped her stomach, and her fingertips went numb.

"They're not just building weapons. They're building the perfect army."

CHAPTER 14
THE CONFOUNDING VARIABLE JOB

OBVIOUSLY, the devious plan hadn't been enacted, which was somewhat comforting, but that didn't stop panic from gripping Chase's insides. It wound its way through her vessels, stealing her blood. She didn't register falling until Monty's hellishly strong hands caught her. He gripped her upper arms, slowing her descent long enough to redirect her to a chair.

"Alspeth? Alspeth." She blinked and looked at him, wondering how many times he'd called her name.

"He can't…he can't do this. It's illegal. It's *wrong*." The argument was frail, even to her own ears.

"Streamflash, baby," Ellison said. "People do illegal shit all the time."

"I know but…" She shook her head, looking to Monty like he had any answers.

"It's fucked up," was all he had to offer. His expression was open, honest. She wanted so badly to believe it.

"Even more reason to bail," Oscar said, continuing to pack. He gestured at Chase with some sort of hard drive. "And you should bail, too. There's plenty of other places to work."

"I can't, Beauchamp will blacklist me. If I want to keep doing my job, if I want to keep *fabricating*, I have to stay at Kierper. It's my only option."

The crew rolled their eyes.

"Of course it is, 'cause that guy's a fucking asshole." Ellison said.

"Time for a career change," Oscar offered.

"I don't want a career change, I want to fabricate, to *help* people. Kierper does a lot of good. They started the whole revolution, they found the ways to tap genetics and—"

"And you're sure it was them?" Ruby asked. Unlike the others, her voice was even and soothing. It was a conversation, rather than an argument. Chase thought they might have been better off if Ruby infiltrated the company. "You're sure Kristiansen and Beauchamp are the ones who did all the heavy lifting?"

"Yes," she said, but then she started thinking. "Well, there was also Dr. Miller, but she…"

"Yes?" Ruby raised her eyebrows.

"I think she retired," Chase said, having no actual knowledge of the woman. "She helped everything start, and then retired."

"Never to be heard from again, I'm sure," Monty said. He knelt in front of her, his hands resting on her knees. Maybe she should've shied away, but his warm and steady presence helped ground her. He swiped his thumbs over her patellae a couple of times before standing up, and she immediately missed the contact.

"Oh, no," Ellison said, shaking her finger at him. "I don't like that look."

"Chase is right," Monty said. "We can't just leave this. This is too big."

"So then *Chase* can do something about it."

Monty huffed. "She needs our help."

"She's a confounding variable," Ellison said.

"Hey!" Chase said. She was a lot of things, but a *confounding variable* was not one of them.

"We can all come out with a win on this," Monty said, stepping closer to Ellison. She didn't budge, standing tall like a guardian warrior queen.

"Or we could all die," she said.

"Alright, kids." Ruby clapped her hands once. Chase sat up straighter, the kindergarten version of herself responding to the cue. "We're getting too emotional. We need a break."

"No, we need to go, babe," Ellison said.

"I second that," Oscar said. He now had a bunch of wires draped over his neck like Mardi Gras beads, the bag on his shoulder overflowing.

"I think we should stay," Monty said, holding his ground.

"As do I," Ruby said. Ellison's angry face dropped, Ruby's vote making her look distressed rather than pissed.

Chase held her breath. She needed them to stay, needed their help. Otherwise, she couldn't save Hunter and whoever else Beauchamp might hurt.

"So we're at an impasse," Monty said. "Ruby's right, we're too hot right now. Let's sleep on it and tackle it again tomorrow."

Ruby went to stand next to Ellison, a tender touch on her elbow keeping her from arguing further.

"Tomorrow then." Ellison turned on her heel and ducked into the nearest bedroom, slamming the door behind her. Oscar shook his head, muttering in Spanish as he dropped everything in the corner of the room.

Ruby sighed. "We'll figure something out, Gum," she murmured, going and putting her hands on Monty's cheeks. Chase dropped her gaze, not wanting to intrude on the moment. A second later, Ruby appeared in her periphery, and before Chase could say anything, she leaned down and wrapped her in a hug.

"Don't worry, Chase."

Chase went still until her brain reconnected to the rest of her body and her limbs awkwardly returned the gesture. The embrace lasted longer than was socially acceptable, but it didn't feel weird. The hug held her together, just for a minute.

"Sleep well." Ruby pulled back and touched Chase's cheek, then exited through the same door as Ellison.

"That went well," Monty said, running his hand over his short-cropped hair. He paused, looking at Chase as if just remembering why she was there. "Shit. This doesn't help my case at all."

"You stole my badge and broke into R&D, your case was slim to begin with," she said. "But I get it now."

"You're a terrible liar, but I appreciate you trying," he said. She wondered how they all got to this point—including herself.

"We all do what we have to, I guess," she said. She remembered signing the wavers for the experiments in school, and the pain afterwards. She also remembered having a comma in her bank account for the first time in years. "I'm still pissed, though. There were definitely better ways for you to do this."

"Oh yeah? Enlighten me," he said, tilting his head to the side. Defensive was a new side of him. Normally Chase would rise to the bait, but after the whole debacle, she was tired.

"I don't know," she relented. "All I know is that things are fucked up and I don't know how to fix them by myself."

"Yeah, me neither." He dropped his arms, stuffing his hands in his pockets. "C'mon, I'll walk you to your apartment."

"But there's bugs in there," she said, affronted. "I can't stay there."

"I'll disable them," Monty said.

"But you said you couldn't do that until tomorrow night," she pointed out.

"Right, what I meant to say was that we'd take care of everything after you left for work in the morning, that way we wouldn't intrude on you," he explained. She nodded, but the wheels in her brain continued to turn.

"But then they'll know," she said. "Right? I mean, if all their stuff is suddenly offline, then they'll know that I know. I mean, we know that they'll know that I know, and—"

"Take a breath, Alspeth," he said, a corner of his mouth twitching as if he almost wanted to smile. "You're right, it would be weird if it all went offline. Oscar can probably whip something up to fix that. Right Oscar?"

"Yeah, I guess so," Oscar said from the corner. He paid special attention to his wires, laying them back out in little rows.

"He may not have something right now," Monty said. "But he can figure it out tomorrow. In the meantime, you can stay here."

She cringed. "Shit, I don't want to encroach—"

"You're not encroaching." His hands landed on her shoulders again, and she wanted so badly to lean into the touch. "We gotta keep you safe."

"I mean, you don't *have* to," she said, because she could never leave things alone.

"Oh, I do. I'm invested at this point," he said with a grin.

Chase paused at that. "Asshole."

"Look at that, you're already fitting in." He jerked his head toward one of the doors. "You can stay in my room."

"Stay in—" Chase balked, thinking of her lack of a toothbrush and dirty work clothes. "I'll, uh, sleep on the couch."

"Nah, don't fight this," he said, opening the door. She expected the room to be sparse—after all, he led a seedy life of crime—but the sharply made bed and nearly sterile state of the furniture surprised her. It was even cleaner than her own place, which was kind of hot.

Oh, Techs. Whoever bugged her apartment heard her weird organizing song. *Shit.*

The thought alone made her wince, which of course, Monty misconstrued. "I know it's not fancy, but..." he trailed off, and Chase felt heat rise to her cheeks.

"No, sorry, I just..." She fumbled, trying to organize her

thoughts. "I can't believe someone bugged my apartment, and I had no idea. It's not a great feeling."

Monty's expression bordered on pity, which was not what she wanted. "I'm sorry about that," he said. "I should have told you earlier."

"I mean, it's not exactly an easy thing to tell someone," she said. "Were you ever going to? Tell me, that is."

"Eventually, yeah. If I couldn't find a way to fix it." He spoke so readily she had no trouble believing him. "I was doing my best to keep you safe and uninvolved. There are a lot of moving parts at play."

"You all seem to be handling it okay," she said. He snorted.

"Nah, this is a mess," he said, shaking his head. He glanced at one of the photos on the wall. "Koda was the smart one. It's been tough, trying to figure it all out without her."

"I'm sorry for your loss," Chase said, and she was.

"Hopefully it's not a loss yet," he said, though he didn't sound confident.

She stepped into Monty's room, close enough for his clean scent and the warmth of his skin to grant him a little more forgiveness. She should be angrier with him, she knew that, but he was sticking up for her and making an effort to protect her. For a brief moment, she considered telling him they could simply share his bed, but she banished the idea from her mind before it could take root. Now was not the time to be reckless. Now was the time to sit in a corner and think about what she'd done.

"There's extra of everything in here," Monty said, showing her to the attached bathroom. He opened the bottom drawer, which held a large black bag, its zippered mouth yawning open. In record time, he found a packaged dental care set and handed it to her.

"I'll get you some comfortable clothes to sleep in, and there's cleanser in the shower. You should be good to go."

"What about you?" Too late, she hoped he didn't take that as an invitation.

"I'll just *steal* Oscar's," he said, obviously amused by his own joke. Chase blinked at him.

"Does knowing your super secret life mean I now have to deal with terrible puns?"

"To be fair, I always make terrible puns. You just didn't realize it at the time." His smile. His damn smile.

"I hate you a little," she deadpanned.

"No, you don't, I keep things interesting," he said. She hated that he was right.

"Wait a second," she said, remembering something from earlier. "Did Ruby call you Gum-Gum?"

"Techs, I was hoping you didn't hear that," he muttered. Louder, he said, "Ruby has a weird thing about nicknames."

Chase hummed. "Does everyone call you that?"

"Fuck, no. Only Ruby can get away with it. And Ellison, when she's been drinking. But only because I can't beat her in a fight. Oscar doesn't even try."

"And Koda?" Chase asked quietly. At the look on his face, she stammered, "I mean, I'm sorry, if you're not comfortable—"

"No, it's fine," he said, clearing his throat. "I don't mind talking about her. She's the one who started calling me Monty. Said *Montgomery* was too many syllables."

She smiled. "So it is your real name."

He exhaled, shaking his head. "Yeah, it is."

"Good, because I was beginning to question. You know, with the whole secret identity thing." She waved her hands and he laughed, a real laugh for the first time that evening.

"I promise, I'm all out of life altering secrets," he said.

Chase narrowed her eyes. "You sure? Have you ever killed anyone?"

"No!" He looked appalled at the question, and while she thought she was kidding when she asked it, she was relieved by the answer. "I forge shit, that's my thing."

Chase thought about Ellison, with her giant frame and rippling muscles.

"Has Ellison?"

"What? Oh, for sure. Stay on her good side," he said. Chase's heart stopped, and he had the audacity to laugh again. "I'm kidding! About the good side thing. You'll be fine there. But seriously, she's definitely killed people."

"Duly noted. That'll make it super easy to sleep tonight."

"As long as Ruby's cool with you, you'll be fine," he said. She opened her mouth to respond, but he cut her off. "And yes, Ruby's cool with you."

"Oh, thank Techs." Chase put a hand to her chest. The conversation was a little too easy, a little too open. She wanted to hold on to the version of Monty from that morning, inviting himself over for pizza and Stream. But what if it was all a lie? She crossed her arms over her chest, building a barrier between them.

"I'm sure you have a lot of questions," Monty said. His hand raised slightly toward her, but he dropped it and held onto his jumpsuit sleeve instead.

"Yeah, I do, but…" But most of them were about his interactions with her. She took a few steps into the room, putting space between them. They could work together, for the sake of the mission, and she could work on forgetting his stupid charming smile. "Maybe tomorrow."

His eyes searched her face, and she prepared for him to push back. If he did, she wasn't sure she could turn him down. Techs, when did his answers become so important to her?

"Tomorrow it is, then." He lingered for a second longer, then stepped out of the room, closing the door behind him. Once she heard another door open and close, she went and turned the lock on the knob. In an apartment full of thieves, it probably wouldn't deter anyone, but it made her feel a little better.

Chase waited a few breaths before turning on the rinser,

closing the bathroom door too for good measure. She did the quickest cleanse of her life, and while it felt odd putting on another person's clothes, Monty's t-shirt and shorts were soft and smelled nice. She peeled back the covers just enough to slip under them, taking up the least amount of space and disturbing the setup as little as possible. It was late, but sleep eluded her, which was frustrating as hell.

She tossed, she turned, she flipped, she reversed, but she accomplished nothing except messing up the sheets she was so determined to keep pristine. Eventually, she pulled out her handheld, determined to watch something on the Stream. Instead, her plans and notes stared at her, Oscar's name at the top.

With a groan, she tossed the handheld to the other side of the bed, the light shining from where it landed. She stared at the ceiling until the screen timed out to hibernation mode. If there was a program developed for the kind of data collection she needed, she didn't know it.

A cough from the room next door made her jump, and she sat up quickly. Oscar had a lot of tech gear. Oscar was going to make something to trick the bugs in her apartment.

Oscar knew how to code.

Maybe Oscar could make the program for her, if she asked sweetly enough.

She ripped the covers off and swung her legs off the bed, fully intent on marching into the room next door and politely throwing her idea at him. Halfway through the motion, she remembered her manners, and after a few false starts toward the door, she flopped onto the bed in defeat. Now would not be a good time. Even if he was still awake, she didn't know him well enough to ask for another favor.

Teaming up with a merry band of thieves was not exactly ideal, but what choice did she have, exactly? She couldn't keep working like all of this was okay, but she also couldn't leave and let Kierper keep forming on it. It was up to her to stop them, and she was nothing if not resourceful. She just hadn't thought her resources would include hiring a criminal crew.

The idea barely comforted her, but it at least gave her a plan. And with a plan, she could relax enough to sleep.

CHAPTER 15
THE FLIRTING JOB

STORMS REPLACED Chase's alarm clock the next morning, the thunder so loud it shook the windows of the bedroom. It took a second to remember she was in Monty's room. The previous night wasn't some weird, delusional dream. Beauchamp wanted to build an army, Monty was a criminal, and she still had no fucking clue what to do about it all.

She fished through the rumpled covers until she found her handheld, the screen nearly blinding her as she checked the time. It was earlier than her usual wake up, but if she left now, she could make a clean getaway, take an actual shower at her apartment, and make it into work like normal. A note for Monty about a lunch meeting would seal the deal.

Her jumpsuit was technically clean, or at least clean enough. She got dressed as quietly as possible, did her best to make the bed and left the borrowed pajamas folded on the edge. It didn't look quite as neat as when she got in the night before. Damn it.

She quietly slid the door open just enough to squeeze out, closing it nearly silently behind her.

"Morning," Ruby said, making Chase jump a mile high.

"Shit." She needed to stop panicking so much, or her heart

would give out before she could replace it. Ruby smirked from her lounging position on the couch, idly stirring some tea.

"You're up early," she said, ignoring the outburst.

"So are you," Chase replied.

"Hoping to make a quick getaway?" She tilted her head to the side and her smile grew.

"That obvious, huh?" She wasn't as embarrassed as she should be. "I didn't want to disturb anyone. I already caused enough damage last night."

"Oh, you're fine." Ruby waved her off. "Little spats are common enough between us. They'll come around in the end. Ellison's already *this close* to giving in."

"Wait, so you're still on my side?" Chase asked, plopping down on the couch next to her.

"I am. Some people shouldn't be in charge, and based on what we've learned of Beauchamp, he's one of them." She said it so casually, like it would be the easiest thing in the world to topple the tyrant.

"That's for damn sure," Chase agreed. "But, I mean, Ellison is also right. It's dangerous." Now that Ruby was willing to help, Chase was afraid for her safety. It was easy to feel a certain way when she thought she'd be on her own.

Ruby laughed. "Danger is part of the job description," she said. "All we need is a new plan."

"Wasn't Koda the planner?" Chase asked, like a dumbass. Ruby's smile faltered for a brief second before she fortified it.

"Yes, she was. But we worked with her for ten years, so probability states we've picked up at least a trick or two."

"For—you've been working together for ten years?" Chase said.

"Surprised? I know, it's adorable. Most crews don't last this long. But when you find people that work well, you hold on to them." Fondness laced her voice, and Chase felt a pang of jealousy at the closeness they shared.

"I guess that makes sense," she said, not remembering

anyone she'd want to work closely with for ten years. Well, maybe *one* person.

"Gum-Gum's a smart guy, and you have a lot more knowledge than you realize." Ruby patted her hand. "We're going to get it figured out, and then we'll know what happened to Koda, and you'll be free from working under a conniving bastard with a deity complex. Everybody wins!"

"*If* we can come up with a plan," Chase reminded her.

"*When* we come up with a plan," Ruby corrected. "Now, are you staying for breakfast? Ellison is really good at omelets."

"I need to go home and shower, and get clean clothes," she said, remembering why she was making her escape so early. She strained her ears toward Oscar's door, but there were no signs of life from behind it. Ruby gave her a knowing smile.

"Right. Well then, Gum-Gum will see you at work. We'll send the bug thing with him."

"Oh, yeah, thank you," Chase said. "And thank you for last night."

"I love when a pretty girl tells me that," Ruby said, making Chase blush. "Go on, then. I'm sure I'll see you soon."

There was so much going on, so fast, and Chase needed a second to stop and think. She was smart, yes, and she was good at planning and problem solving. But she could only do those things if she had *time*.

She made quick work of her routine, hoping the speed wouldn't raise suspicion with whichever poor bastard had the boring job of listening in on her. She locked up like normal and left like normal, walking casually to the train station instead of sprinting like she wanted.

As she boarded, her handheld buzzed. A message popped up from Monty reading, "See you at lunch? I'll have your new pesticide."

"I'll see you there," she muttered, typing the words out and pressing send before she could second guess herself. She felt embarrassment sneaking up the back of her neck in a way she hadn't felt since the last time she'd accidentally gone home with someone. Even if this wasn't the same thing, it felt similar enough to make the spot between her shoulder blades itch.

After a morning of more failed experiments, she arrived at their meeting much too early. Watching the people in the cafeteria or outside the building made her paranoid, so she focused on scrolling on her handheld, catching up on the entertainment news she tangentially cared about.

"Damn, those two co-stars really broke up? I was rooting for them."

Chase yelped as Monty appeared beside her, food in hand. He smiled like normal, and for a brief second, she could pretend she hadn't found out about his secret double life.

"Sorry," Monty said as he sat across from her. "I didn't mean to scare you."

"Oh, no, you're fine. I was just…'deep in the earth.'" It was a dumb joke, a quote from a serial she watched on the Stream. He smiled anyway.

"'Better than being a space rock,'" he finished the quote. Her eyebrows shot up.

"Wait, you really do watch *Earthbound*?" she asked.

He laughed. "What, does it surprise you that I like the most popular show on the Stream?" he countered.

"Well…" How could Chase phrase it nicely? Luckily, Monty seemed to read her mind.

"You've known the real me this whole time, just not my… prior employment. But back to the point. You think I could stop a show like that? Like when Drean and Mart found that cave of wonders? Sure, they died there, but the *joy*."

Chase's heart soared; it was one of her favorite moments of the series. "Exactly, yes! It made me cry so hard I nearly passed out." This was simple, this was *normal*. She could pretend, for a second.

"Oh, I bawled," Monty agreed. "Now, I believe we can agree

that the science is less than accurate. Especially the part where they try to steal from the space station museum."

Okay, so she couldn't take any pointers from the show for this mission, good to know.

"And the fact that they all end up sleeping around is ludicrous," Monty said.

Guess she hadn't accidentally joined a polyamorous crew. That was slightly disappointing.

"Supply closets are literally the least sexiest place," she lied.

"But I'll be damned if I don't find out how the rest of the space station joins them on the planet," he concluded. He grinned at her, and she felt her own smile falter. "What?" he asked.

"Nothing." She shook her head.

"Your lying skills haven't improved since last night." He spoke gently, as if he really wanted to know. As if he was actually concerned. Chase took a steadying breath.

"I'm trying to reconcile everything. I was actually starting to tolerate you before I learned about the whole double-life thing." *Tolerate* was a vast understatement. If she was honest, she enjoyed spending time with him, and that feeling didn't fade as much as it should have with the previous night's revelations.

"Everything over the past six months has been the true me, I promise," he said, and she couldn't stop a dry laugh.

"You're literally talking in the worst British accent right now," she pointed out.

"Damn, you're right," he said in his normal voice. "Think people will notice if I drop it?"

She shrugged. "We work with a bunch of scientists. If you say it was an experiment, I bet they'll just ask to see the data you collected."

"You're a genius. I knew I liked you for a reason. Well, many reasons." He returned to his food while Chase reeled from his words. Had she been misinterpreting things this whole time?

"Wait, what?" she asked. He looked up, confused.

"What?" he said.

"Wait, were you..." She paused, thinking back on their past interactions, all the goofy gestures and bright smiles. "Were you flirting this whole time?"

A sharp laugh escaped him, which led to him choking on his bite of food. He coughed roughly and pounded his chest until the piece vacated his trachea.

"Not very well, apparently," he said. Chase blinked. How was this more shocking to hear than his life of crime? He cleared his throat. "Based on that face, I feel like I need to apologize for it."

"What? No." She shook her head to rattle her neurons back into place. "I thought you were just, I don't know, being nice? I've been told I can be too much, so I assume that's what people think most of the time."

His expression grew serious. "You're not too much. You're brilliant."

A few of the feelings she'd kept locked away slipped through a crack in her (metaphorical) heart. Embarrassingly enough, tears filled her eyes. Monty reached out and took her hand. Her first instinct was to pull back, but she squashed that down. It wasn't rooted in survival, but fear. And after the past few days, why would she be afraid of this?

"Sorry," she whispered, taking a napkin and dabbing at her eyes. "A lot's going on. I'm a little overwhelmed."

"That's alright. This is an overwhelming situation." He ran his thumb over her knuckles, and she was surprised at how soothing the gesture was.

"Can I ask you something?" she said, finally looking him in the eye again. He gazed back confidently, didn't even flinch at her question.

"Anything," he said, and once again she believed him.

"You said the past six months were all the real you. But you only found out about Koda a couple weeks ago." She paused to gather her thoughts, and he gave her the time, though he didn't let go of her hand. Techs, she didn't want to say it now, but she plowed ahead. "Did you—or, the crew rather—have anything to do with me getting the R&D job?"

"No, not at all." He shook his head, but his eyes never left hers. "You did that all on your own."

"But you stole my badge," she said. He winced. "Is that the reason you stayed friends with me?"

"I stayed friends with you because you're fun to be around," he said, then sighed heavily. "As for the badge…I'll be honest, that was purely opportunistic. I thought I could get what we needed and protect you from being involved."

"You were planning to give it back then?" she asked.

"I was hoping I could get it back to you without you missing it. My original plan was to steal the badge from a guy in upper extremity that keeps bothering the woman in the cube next to me. Then I'd throw it away and make him pay for a new one."

She laughed, and one last tear fell. Monty quickly reached out and brushed it away with his free hand.

"I'm sorry, Chase. I shouldn't have stolen from you," he said. She liked the way he said her name.

"You're right, you shouldn't have." She sniffled. "But I'm not mad about being involved now. To be honest, I prefer it."

"You like being involved? What?" He laid on the sarcasm, and she saw it for what it was—not a dig, but a joke between…friends?

"I know, an astonishing surprise. You never would've known if I hadn't told you." She smiled then and pulled her hand away, but only so she could actually eat the food in front of her. He laughed and returned to his meal as well.

"Look, whatever happens," he said between bites, "we're not gonna have you do anything dangerous, okay? Safety is always the most important part of the con." His eye twitched, likely due to someone yelling on the comms.

Chase snorted. "I take it Ellison disagrees?"

"Ruby, actually," he said. "Ellison is the safety manager, in that she manages everyone's safety except her own."

"That sounds about right." She paused, pushing her food around her plate. "Monty? Do you think we can actually pull this off?"

"Oh, absolutely. We've done way harder stuff in the past," he said, following it up with a big bite of pasta.

For the first time, his words felt like a lie.

CHAPTER 16
THE PLAN E JOB

"IT'S GETTING WORSE," Chase said as she and Monty walked out of the building a couple of days later. She wasn't supposed to share details, especially not to a certified thief, but they were way past that now. "Epley made skin that successfully stops bullets. Ayla's been going nonstop. If she can adapt the neural tissue to allow for reasoning while disconnecting the areas of the cortex involved in emotional regulation—"

"I love when you use your big, long words," Monty said with a saucy lilt.

Chase blushed heavily. "You work here, you should know all the big words," she replied.

"You may recall I didn't actually go to school for this. Resumes and university records are child's play. Literally, I did it as a child once to get into the advanced class at space camp." He smiled and winked, nudging her shoulder with his. "And just in case you thought I was kidding, I'm being so serious about the big words."

"About the—wait, back up." She blinked, the heat in her cheeks momentarily forgotten. "Space camp?"

"I had dreams." He shrugged. "Turns out I get motion sick, but I learned I'm really good at forging stuff."

"I..." She tried to think of a comeback. "I guess forging is just another form of fabrication."

"Now you get it," he said with that stupid smile. She hated how charming it was, and how it made her insides change places.

Chase tried to bring the conversation back to something important and ignore the mental picture of baby Monty in an astronaut suit. "Hunter can follow two-step commands now. Things are moving too fast. How are we supposed to catch up before they start making robot super soldier things?"

"Is it a robot if it's made of biological parts?"

"You're missing the point!"

"I'm right here with you." Monty stopped and held her upper arms with gentle hands. His gaze burned into her. "Listen. This is literally the most important lesson you need to learn if you're gonna go through this with us."

"I'm listening." She gave him the perfect picture of attention. Some might call her overeager, but she really cared about the information. Information was power. Information was how she could fix all this. Should she take notes? She felt like she should take notes.

"You can't lose your shit," Monty said.

"I won't." She waited for the point.

"No, that's the lesson," he said after a second. "No matter what happens, what you find out, or what someone says or does, you can't lose your shit. You lose your shit, the whole plan will collapse, and then you're either in jail or in the ground."

Chase blinked at him. "How many times have you been in jail?"

He straightened and had a devious gleam in his eye. "None. You know why?"

"'Cause you don't lose your shit?"

"No, 'cause I'm an expert escape artist," he said. "But also, I don't lose my shit."

She thought back to the moment she found him in the lab. "You kinda lost your shit when I caught you with my badge."

"That? No, that was stress, maybe even anxiety at some moments." He waved her comment away. "I did *not* lose my shit. You've gotta keep your cool, okay?"

Chase didn't remember ever keeping her cool in her entire life, but that was beside the point.

"Okay," she agreed. "So, what's the next step? In the plan?"

"We'll talk details tonight." Monty continued toward the rail station as if the world wasn't crashing around them. "Oscar and Ruby sent me some stuff earlier."

"And Ellison?"

"She's just there to look pretty. And throw some people out a window if we need her to."

The rail arrived, and they boarded together. Monty rested his arm across the back of Chase's seat, the move casual, as if he didn't think anything of it. She stiffened, then forced herself to relax. It was okay to be next to him. It was okay to *want* to be next to him. It'd just been so long she had to remind herself of that.

She leaned into him, just a little. Enough to seek comfort and give her something else to focus on besides Hunter's blank eyes as the bullet stuck in their skin and then dropped to the ground. They'd watched her the whole time, surely transfixed on the look of abject horror she couldn't disguise.

The rail slowed, a perfect distraction, and Monty led them to his apartment. An amazing smell of garlic, peppers, and onions greeted them as they entered, and Chase's stomach rumbled in response. Ruby stood at the stove, managing multiple pans. Ellison sat on the granite ledge next to it, micromanaging one pot and occasionally picking bites from the other pans. Monty slapped the side of her bare thigh, earning an indignant kick.

"Get your gross ass off the counter," he said. "And quite digging your fingers in the food."

"You can't tell me what to do," Ellison replied, crossing her arms and legs and hunkering down. Monty gestured to Chase.

"We have a guest, try to be civilized," he said.

"She's more than a guest," Ruby said, tossing a wink at Chase before returning to her task.

"Exactly. She even slept in your room the other night," Ellison added. Chase's whole body heated at the insinuation.

"*Alone.*" Monty's emphasis somehow made her blush more than the original comment.

"Did you really just hit it and—"

Ellison didn't get to finish her sentence, because Monty reached out and grabbed her by the ankle. He yanked, and she barely kept herself from tumbling off the countertop. Her glare burned as hot as the stove next to her. They started a tug of war with her leg as the rope, a very precarious game since Ruby was actively cooking *right there*.

"Enough, enough!" Ruby said, alternating hitting Monty's arm and Ellison's thigh with her hot spatula.

"Hey!" Ellison snapped at the same time Monty said, "Ow!"

"Chase may be more than a guest," Ruby said with the careful control of someone who routinely worked with children, "but that doesn't mean we can act like heathens, alright?"

"He started it," Ellison said.

Monty whirled on her. "Me? You're the one sitting next to where our food is!"

"*Next to*. That's the key, *next to*."

"Ay!" Oscar shouted from his hiding spot behind the monitors and cables on the dining table. "Some of us are actually trying to get some work done."

"Sorry, Oscar," Ellison and Monty spoke at the same time again.

"Oh, I see," Ruby said lightly. "You'll listen to Oscar, but not to me. Hmm."

"That was at the beginning of the fight, baby, you know I can't give in first thing," Ellison whispered.

"Ah, yes, how could I forget," Ruby replied. She was clearly not amused, but when Ellison gave a very exaggerated pout, she rolled her eyes and leaned in for a kiss. "You're both on thin ice."

"Aren't I always?" Monty asked, snagging his own vegetable from the pan before ducking into his room, leaving Chase alone with the others.

"Chase," Oscar said, and she could kiss him for starting a conversation before she had to. "Tell me about the lab."

She gave him all the details she could remember, from the mega fab to Hunter's room and everything in between. He nodded, scratching notes down on an already full screen as she spoke.

"Okay, so we need to figure out this elevator," he said. "I have a feeling we'll need to borrow a badge."

"That sounds risky," she said.

"We'll have to work fast," he replied. He pulled a slim metal box out of the pile, then held his hand out for her badge. "Let me see something."

It was weirdly easy to hand over her lifeline. He lay the badge on top of the box, then fished a blank badge from a container perched precariously on the corner of the table. He stuck the blank badge into the box, which must have been some kind of coding machine. Little red lights blinked into existence. Chase wanted to ask what he was doing, but he was so focused he didn't notice his glasses were slightly askew, so she didn't interrupt.

Oscar tapped a notification on the screen and keyed in a passcode. A progress bar popped up, the red inching along the line as the machine did its work. When it finished, the machine beeped and popped the badge back out.

"What did you just do?" she asked, taking the blank card and looking it over.

"I'm hoping I made you a new badge," he said, handing her the original. "I need you to test it tomorrow. But probably not at the security gate. Someplace simple, like your desk."

"Doesn't it give different signals depending on the place?" she asked. This wasn't her area of expertise, but she wanted to know all the details, and Oscar was only too happy to oblige.

"No, it's just one signature. And if we can copy a signature…" He paused for dramatic effect, and Chase filled in the blanks.

"Then we can steal any badge we need."

"Exactly," he said with a toothy grin.

"Exactly what?" Monty asked, coming back in. He'd changed from his jumpsuit to sweatpants and a t-shirt. Should she go to her own apartment to change? No, that would take too long. Should she borrow more of his clothes? No, that would be way too awkward. Almost as awkward as how long she stared at the way the sweatpants fit him.

"Exactly time to eat," Ruby said, gesturing grandly toward the stove. "Let's go everyone, I have a feeling it's going to be a long night."

After dinner, Oscar pulled up the Kierper blueprint on the big wall screen. Ellison, with an apron tied over her fitness clothes, whipped up and served them a beautiful batch of cookies. The others dug into them like it was nothing, but the last time Chase had a home cooked meal was her last visit home, before she started at Kierper. She savored the joy of it a little longer.

"Okay, if I can have your attention, please." Oscar clapped once. They quieted, and Monty shifted so that his thigh touched hers. Chase pressed back, just a little.

"Let's hear it, Os," Monty said, saluting him with a cookie. Oscar bowed low, which made his glasses shift down his nose.

"With pleasure. Special acknowledgments to our wonderful Ruby, who helped with the color coordination of this presentation," he said, and Ruby responded with a bright smile and a nod. "Without further ado, let us discuss Plan E."

"E?" Chase whispered.

"Koda did A through C. D was bringing me back in," Monty replied.

"Are there questions already?" Oscar asked, putting his hands behind his back and staring at them. If he ever wanted out of the life of crime, he would be a wonderful professor.

"Nope," Monty said.

"Sorry," Chase squeaked.

"Actually, yes," Ellison said. "Are you going to suggest the Saskatchewan Shuffle?"

Oscar huffed. "No, we don't have enough people for that one."

"Oh!" Ruby said. "What about the Duke's Tiara?"

"Too many diamonds, not enough horses," Monty said.

"If anything, we could do the Colorado Ascent," Ellison suggested, which made Ruby laugh.

"Where would we get a mountain goat on this short notice?" she asked. "If anything, we could try the Big Trifle but have the boyfriend show up—"

"Guys!" Monty's interruption quieted them, and he gestured to Oscar, who nodded.

"Thank you. We will be trying a variation on the Spanish Rail." He cleared his throat. "Step one, Chase will use this thing in the elevator to see if I can make it listen to me. If it wants to be stubborn, then Chase will *borrow* badges from fabricators on the different floors."

"Wait, Chase will *what*?" she asked, sitting up straight. "No, no, no, Chase will do no such thing."

"Chase is the only one with any access right now," Oscar pointed out.

"Yeah, but I don't have any skills," she said. They were the professionals, she was just supposed to open the doors for them. Was that an official crew position? Door holder?

"You don't have skills *yet*. But we'll figure that out later," he said. "Right, so, once we copy the badges—"

"Assuming your gadget works," Ellison muttered.

"How dare you." Oscar glared at her. "We get new badges. Ellison and Monty go with Chase into the lab, and they go floor by floor to get the data on our drives and load up the HNTRs."

"What about Ruby?" Chase asked.

"Ruby is in charge of orchestrating the exit," Oscar said. "I will keep watch in the security room."

"Oh my Techs," Chase said, a memory hitting her. "You're the nighttime security guard."

"You just noticed?" Ellison asked, earning a smack on the leg from Ruby.

"It's impressive that she noticed at all, she only saw me the one time," Oscar said. "Anyway, those are the basics. Any questions?"

"Yeah," Chase said, raising her hand. "How the fuck am I supposed to steal a bunch of badges?"

"Oh!" Ruby got excited, standing up from the couch. "I'll teach you. Come on."

"This is when I make my exit," Ellison said, sliding awkwardly past them and going to the spare room.

"What? But my presentation…" Oscar gestured at the screen, now showing a car driving away.

"It was great, Os. Really," Monty said. "You wanna show me how that thing works?"

"Yeah, I guess," Oscar said. Chase wanted to ask clarifying questions, but she was currently engaged in a panic attack.

"I can't do this," she told Ruby.

"You haven't even tried," she said, putting a hand on her cheek. "It's easy. The key is to use a distraction. Don't make it harder than it needs to be."

"How can someone get distracted enough for me to take their badge?" she asked. Ruby smiled in response, and Chase sighed. "You already took mine, didn't you?"

"See? I told you. Easy," she said, flaunting the original and the copy badges in front of her face before clipping one to the front of her own shirt. She pulled her braids back and secured them with an elastic. "Now, your turn. Let's start with square one, which is a gentle touch."

"Gentle touch. I can have a gentle touch," Chase said, trying to psych herself up.

"I'm sure you can, sweetheart," Ruby smiled, effectively knocking Chase off her game before she had time to get on.

"Right." She brought her focus back. She had to get the badge, otherwise the whole plan would fall apart.

"You already know how the clip works, and you know where it'll be. But if you try and no-look it, you'll miss entirely." Ruby's instructions weren't quite as detailed as Chase wanted. With a deep breath, she reached up and unclipped the badge without touching anything else.

"Oh. Okay." Maybe she could do this!

"Yes! Okay, now try for real this time," Ruby said. Chase didn't have the heart to tell her that *was* a real try. She concentrated harder and made sure there was no touching, not even a tug as she freed the badge from Ruby's shirt.

"Much better!" Ruby said. "Try with a distraction."

"What distraction do I use?"

"Whatever you can think of in that moment."

"Okay, um," she scanned the apartment. "Where is Ellison going?"

Ruby turned as Ellison exited their room, bag in hand. Chase, distracted by her own distraction, tried to grab the badge without looking and ended up hitting Ruby in the sternum.

"Not quite," Ruby said, fixing the badge again. "Darling, are you going to the gym?"

"Yeah, I'll be back in an hour or so," Ellison said. She squinted her eyes at them. "She's terrible."

"She's learning," Ruby emphasized. Ellison rolled her eyes, throwing a hand up in a half-wave as she left the apartment. "Alright, try again."

"Okay, uh…" More panic. "Did you turn the stove off?"

"Hmm, I think so." She turned, and Chase made another

grab for the badge. This one missed her sternum, instead landing on her breast.

"So that was another miss," Ruby said. She was completely unfazed, but Chase wanted to melt into the floor. "Chin up, buttercup, we all make that mistake at some point. All we can do is try again."

So she tried again. And again. And again. She used verbal cues to distract, and physical ones, but no matter what, she still couldn't make a clean sweep of the badge. The patience that allowed her to do her job so effectively was quickly fading, leaving her boiling in frustration. Ruby was very kind and encouraging, but even she was struggling to word the instructions differently, which meant Chase was now frustrated *and* embarrassed.

"I'm sorry, I need a break." She was close to tears, and crying in front of Ruby was *not* part of the plan. "I'm sorry, I'll—"

"Go step outside for a second, I'll be here," Ruby said. Chase nodded, pressing her lips together and quickly moving out of the apartment. It was easier to breathe in the hallway, with no eyes or ears taking note of her every failure. She sat against the wall and curled up, hoping the deep pressure would calm her super fried nervous system.

Crying would not help. It might make her feel better, but she could cry later, when it didn't interrupt her training. She rested her forehead on her knees, willing the tears to stay in her eyes.

The door opened, but she didn't look up. She couldn't face Ruby after the disaster of a lesson. Someone sat down next to her, and she recognized Monty's familiar, clean scent.

"For the record, I did way worse when I was learning how to properly execute a lift," he murmured.

"Yeah?" she asked, not raising her head.

"Yeah, it was terrible." He chuckled at a fond memory, and Chase turned her head to find him smiling, his eyes distant. "One time, I was trying to steal a guy's wallet so I could forge a super-specific ID. Easy, right? The oldest thievery in the book."

"What happened?" she asked.

"He turned just as I got my hand all the way in his pocket. And I mean, this pocket was *deep*. Pulled me around and slammed my face right into his chest."

Chase winced. "Yikes. How did you make it out?"

"Oh, absolutely booked it. I've never run faster before or since that moment. Ellison was pissed 'cause she had to fight like, ten security people while I bolted."

He laughed, which made her laugh too. "Ugh, I just hate not being good at something on the first try."

"You know better than anyone that motor skills are way different than intellectual skills," he said. He put his arm around her, and she let him pull her into him. Techs, it felt nice to be held. In particular, by him.

"You just gotta practice a little more, and have a little patience. You're smart, and creative, and pretty."

"That last one doesn't help my badge stealing skills," she said, her heart palpitating at the compliment.

"I beg to differ, but that's beside the point," he said. He looked her square in the eye. "You're gonna be okay, Chase. You're not alone."

"And what happens afterwards?" she blurted.

Monty paused. "Guess we'll have to see, hmm?" he said. "I still like hanging out with you, though. Con or no con."

"Right," she said, trying to think of a nice, flirtatious response. "If we make it through, I'll consider spending more time with you. Maybe."

Nailed it.

Monty laughed, "Well, I'll take whatever chance I can get."

He pulled her close again, and she rested her head on his shoulder. He thought she could do this, and Ruby thought she could do this. They were right, she just needed a little patience, and a little practice.

Most importantly, she wasn't alone.

CHAPTER 17

THE SUPPLY CLOSET JOB

THE NEXT DAY, Chase pinged Monty for lunch and then promptly cornered him in a supply closet next to the cafeteria. The sharp scent of chemicals didn't help her buzzing brain, it just made her eyes water in a way annoyingly similar to crying.

"I thought you said—"

Chase's words exited her in a rush. "I don't think I can do this."

"You're not doing anything yet," Monty reminded her.

There was not near enough room for her to pace, but Chase tried her best, anyway.

"But I'm going to eventually, right? I'm gonna have to. You guys don't have clearance to get into R&D, and the system is hard to mess with and—"

"Alspeth, slow down." He put his hands on her arms, the tight quarters pushing them close. "Your only job right now is to keep going into that lab and collecting information. That's it. We have time, we're not stealing anything today."

"Right." She wasn't quite convinced. "Out of curiosity, how many people have tried to steal from Kierper before?"

"A hundred and six," Monty answered readily.

"A hundred and—shit."

"In the past ten years."

"In the past *ten years?*"

"There seems to be an echo in this teeny, tiny broom closet," he said with a grin. Despite the severity of the situation, her cheeks warmed. The momentary break allowed her to take note of exactly how close they stood. If she shifted an inch forward, their chests would touch.

Focus, Alspeth.

Chase dropped her voice to a harsh whisper. "I don't even know what I'm supposed to be looking for." She shoved her hands into her hair, effectively releasing his hold on her arms. She missed it immediately.

"Anything—" He paused and tilted his head to the left. Chase was about to ask if he needed to make a pit stop on a neuro floor, but then he continued. "Anything out of the ordinary. Well, *more* out of the ordinary."

"Can I get one of those too?" She nodded to his ear.

"A comms? You probably don't want one, it's just a bunch of useless chatter." He winced, probably at a sudden increase in the volume of the "useless chatter". He turned away again. "I—no, listen, can we just—ugh, okay, hold on." He pulled it from his ear, got a sterile swab from a box on a nearby shelf, and cleaned it. When he held it out to her, she took it and inserted it without hesitation.

"Hello?" she said.

"Chase, darling, it's Ruby." Ruby's voice was as clear as if she were in the closet with them, and Chase had to resist the urge to look around for her. "We'll get you an earbud when you come back tonight, okay? But for today, I have another mission for you."

"Okay." Concrete instructions made her heart sing and calmed her more than any of the platitudes from Monty.

"I need you to try and visit the other R&D labs, and see what they have in there. See if they're all shaped like yours is," she said.

"I think I can do that." Chase kept her eyes on Monty, who gazed back steadily. She relaxed her hands down, and he put his back on her arms.

"Chase? It's Ellison." Ellison's sharp voice made her jump, and in front of her, Monty gave her a questioning look. She shook her head; he could wait.

"Um, yes ma'am?" she said, hoping that if she sounded extra respectful, Ellison would like her more.

"Ew, never call me *ma'am* again," she spat. "You gotta find a way to get Monty into that wing so he can count security guards."

"I can count security guards," she said. Seemed like an easy enough task, but apparently there was an art to it.

"No, you worry about checking floor plans," she said. "Monty can take the security walk."

"Okay, yeah, I'll tell him," she said. Monty raised one eyebrow. "Ellison said I need to get you into the wing so that you can take the security walk."

"Ugh, I hate the security walk. Tell Ellison she can take the documents I made her and do the security walk herself."

"Okay. Ellison, Monty said that—"

"I heard him," Ellison cut her off. "Tell that asshole I'm not using the documents unless I have to, and he knows it. Also, tell him to stop being a whiny plunk."

"Ellison says she's going to wait until it's necessary, and to stop being a punk."

"No, Chase, a *plunk*. There's a difference."

"Sorry, a *plunk*."

"A—give me that," Monty said, gesturing for the earpiece.

"No!" Ruby's voice was so firm that Chase flinched away from his hand. The hurt on his face reminded her that he couldn't hear what was going on.

"Ruby said no," she said, hoping that explanation would placate him. He still had too much tension around his eyes, so she reached up and rested her hand where his neck met his shoulder. A bit too intimate of a spot, but she was committed now.

"Tell Monty this is yours now. I'll be by in an hour with a spare," Oscar said. "And to get that look off his face."

Chase relayed the message, and Monty scoffed. "I'm not making a face."

"He knows that we know he's making a face," Ruby said. "You don't have to share that one."

"Okay, so," Chase said, trying to bring her focus back. It was weird, having so many people talking at once. "I need to get Monty in. Again."

"Just around the area," Ruby said. "He was in a bit of a hurry last time."

"I don't have to get in the lab, just to the hall in front of it," he said, talking over Ruby without realizing it.

"That's easy," she said. "And then I need to check out the other labs?"

"If you can," Ruby said.

"You might not be able to get to them all today," Ellison cut in.

"And that's okay," Ruby finished.

"You're going to overwhelm her," Oscar cut in. "One step at a time. We'll coach you through it."

"Right, one step at a time," she said, letting out a breath and leaning her head against her hand. The same hand resting on Monty's shoulder. So basically, she was burying her face in his well-muscled chest.

She should pull back. Definitely.

But then Monty's arms went around her and held her tight, and suddenly the thought of moving away seemed like a terrible idea. Instead, she lingered, listening to the strong beat of Monty's heart until her own slowed to match it.

When she finally shifted back, Monty didn't let her go far, their faces barely a few centimeters apart. She couldn't help but look at his lips, then forced her eyes back up to his. He reached up and tapped her ear twice, silencing the comms.

"You got this, okay?" he whispered. "And I got you."

The urge to kiss him grew. Her heart rate kicked back up in anticipation, her breaths a touch more shallow as she realized they were still pressed together. All it would take was a little lean.

Her watch buzzed loudly, signaling the end of her lunch hour. She groaned and put her hands over her face, missing Monty's warmth as he gave her space.

"C'mon, I'll walk you back up to the lab." He tapped the comms, then took hold of her waist and spun her so she faced the exit. With a gentle push, he encouraged her toward the door.

"What if I just quit? Maybe Oscar was right and I need a career change," she asked as she opened it.

"You're not gonna quit, you're too invested now," Monty said, closing the door behind them. A few people threw odd looks their way, and another few smirked like they knew a secret. Chase blushed, which definitely didn't help matters. Monty must have caught the looks, because he chuckled and put a hand on her lower back.

"Just ignore them," he said as they made their way toward the elevators.

"It's not like we need more attention on us right now," Chase hissed.

"You know how I said there were over a hundred attempted theft attempts in the past ten years? You wouldn't believe the number of workplace romances."

Chase glanced at him and found him smiling. "Seriously?"

"Seriously," he said.

"Huh." She thought about it for a moment. Seemed likely, given the proximity. "Well, I can say, I was evidently wrong about the sexiness level of a supply closet."

Monty coughed on air and choked out, "You can't be serious."

"You know my jokes are few and far between."

"You're gonna be the end of me," he murmured. "And you've been watching too much on the Stream."

"You watched them too," she said.

"Oh, he definitely watched them," Oscar said on the comms, making Chase jump again.

"Multiple times," Ellison added. Chase snorted, and Monty narrowed his eyes before giving up.

"I probably don't want to know," Monty muttered as they got onto the elevator.

Chase made eyes at Monty and he continued to look at her with an expression that she could only describe as *churlish*.

"Tell him not to make that face, it'll give him wrinkles," Ruby said. Chase gave him a grin and poked the area between his eyebrows. He rolled his eyes as he relaxed his forehead.

"C'mon, don't give it if you can't take it," she said.

"That's what—"

"Tell Ellison to hush," Monty said, though his facade cracked and a slight grin appeared.

"Tell Monty," Ellison said, "that I'm gonna kick his ass when he gets back."

"She didn't say anything," Chase said.

"Bullshit," both Ellison and Monty said at the same time. Chase couldn't help it, she laughed way too loud. Luckily, it made the others laugh with her.

"Oh, you're all going to be bad influences," she said once she had herself under control.

"Here's hoping," Ruby said.

"With great pride and pleasure," Monty said, and the look he gave her made some unknown organ in her chest glow.

The elevator landed on their floor, and they exited with as much nonchalance as possible. Well, Monty had a fair bit of nonchalance. Chase was another story. She scanned her badge to open the first door, eyeing the hallway beyond for any employees. It was empty, but somehow that made her more nervous. It must've shown, because Monty reached out and took her hand, lacing their fingers easily. She held onto him like a lifeline.

"Breathe." He checked the hallway as they walked, but squeezed her hand to comfort her. "Nothing big. Just a few elevator trips."

"Right," she said, inhaling for the first time in what felt like a few minutes. "So easy."

They stopped at the doors of the back hallway, and Chase paused. Monty waited with her, patient and sure. She was glad one of them could be confident in that moment.

"Okay. Here I go." She untangled her hand from his and stepped up to the door, but he didn't move. She looked back. "What?"

He stuffed his hands in his pocket. "Just making sure you get in okay," he said.

"Oh." Her breath left in a rush, and she turned to the scanner. Thank Techs she had something to do with her hands, and she swiped her badge. The light turned green, and the doors opened.

"See you tonight," Monty said as she stepped through.

"Yeah, tonight," she agreed, and forced herself to take one step after the other until she made it back to the lab.

CHAPTER 18
THE SWORD JOB

EVERYONE else's heads were down and Jun's desk was empty; good, one less person to stare at her as she plotted and planned. Popping up randomly in the other labs was probably frowned upon, so she'd need a good reason to go to the other floors.

The cups of styluses in the materials room gave her the idea. There was only one short, slender stylus left in the middle cup. Normally neurofabricators used that model, but if she used her long curls to cover her name in red stitching, no one would be any wiser. She stuffed the stylus in her deepest pocket... Oh no, now they were all out! Guess she needed to go to another floor and get one.

She was such a good con artist. Why had she spent her whole life following stupid rules?

A quick scan from her badge opened the elevator doors, and with all the confidence of a beginner, she called out for floor eleven. Normally that was an upper extremity floor, but obviously the rules didn't apply to the R&D labs. The elevator didn't move, and the doors stayed wide open. She called out the number again, louder, but didn't receive any verbal or mechanical response. Even the screen next to the doors remained dark.

"Oscar?" she whispered into the comms. She patted her other pocket, which held the device he gave her.

"One second," he said. "This thing is fighting me."

"Okay." She tapped her thighs and shifted back and forth on her feet, but the elevator didn't budge.

"Ugh," Oscar said. "Try manual override, that device isn't going to work."

Chase tapped the screen to wake it and tried to manually choose a floor, but the elevator stayed frozen. For a split second, she wondered if this was another stress dream and she was actually still asleep in Monty's room, but a burst of static from an overhead speaker jolted her.

"Where are you trying to go?" the artificial voice asked.

"To another floor, I—"

"You do not have clearance."

Chase glared up at the tiny black camera in the corner. "As I was saying, I—"

"You do not have clearance."

"As I was saying," Chase said, snapping her eyes to the white disc on the left side of the ceiling, which must be where the voice lived. "I need another neurofab stylus. We're all out."

"I will send maintenance," it said.

"You don't have to do that, I can just go—"

"You do not have clearance."

"Well, who *does* have clearance?" The stupid auto voice was making this a hundred times more difficult, and Chase wanted to rip the white disk from the ceiling.

"Only Dr. Beauchamp and Maintenance have access to all floors."

"Can you send me *anywhere* I can get another stylus?" She didn't have to go to eleven. Any floor would work at that point.

"No."

Chase couldn't stop the frustrated groan. "Where *can* you send me?"

"You have credentials for your lab, the basement, and Dr. Beauchamp's office."

"Of course," she muttered, pinching the bridge of her nose.

"Do you want me to send you to his office?"

"No." She could be rude to a voice. It made her feel better.

"Where are you trying to—"

She stalked out of the elevator and to the materials room. The clatter of the stylus landing back in the cup was loud, but she didn't hear it over her failure.

So much for an easily executed plan. Chase went to Hunter's room and paced, trying to come up with a contingency. Unfortunately, this wasn't her area of expertise.

"Did you guys hear all that?" she asked. No one answered on the comms, and she wondered if something in the elevator broke it. "Hello? Anyone?"

A click sounded from behind her, but when she turned, there was nothing there except Hunter snoozing away.

"Don't talk yet," Oscar whispered. "At least not to us. I'm still checking for bugs in the area."

"I doubt there are," Chase said, looking to the glowing, blue tube. "It's just me and Hunter in here, and they're asleep."

"Aw, how cute." Ruby was calm, which helped Chase feel calm.

Chase continued her pacing while Oscar did his work. If Beauchamp was the only one with access to all the floors, then this whole thing was about to get a lot more difficult.

"Okay, you're clear," Oscar said, this time at a normal volume.

"Thank you," she said. "So what do I do now? I can't get into those labs without Beauchamp."

"Correction, you can't get into those labs without Beauchamp's *badge*," Ruby said. "Kierper is so weird about their badges."

"They're control freaks," Ellison deadpanned. "Makes sense."

Oscar muttered something that almost sounded like *takes one to know one.* "I wasn't able to modify Monty's badge to get him into the lab, but since you already have lab privileges, I might be able to unlock yours. We'll check tonight."

"Tonight?" Chase said, skidding to a halt. "So what am I supposed to do all day?"

"Your job, honey," Ruby said. Chase smacked herself on the forehead.

"Don't leave a mark," Ellison said. Chase didn't realize she'd smacked herself *that* hard.

"Right, so, am I supposed to leave this thing in all day?" she said, gesturing to her ear.

"Can I assume you mean the comms?" Oscar asked. Of course. He couldn't *see* her. For someone with the highest degree in the room, she sure was making a show of dumbassery.

"Yeah," she said.

"Then yes, you can leave it all day. It'll be good to keep tabs, plus then you won't have to wrestle with it if you get in trouble," he said. "I'll mute your channel for now. Just tap your ear twice to turn it back, the vibrations will trigger it. It's actually a cool—"

"No one cares, Oscar," Ellison said, earning a sigh from the man.

"Right, anyway," he said. "Call if you need anything."

Another little click signaled the muting of her comms, and this time she was able to quell the instinct to look behind her.

"Alright, Alspeth," she murmured as she left Hunter's room. "Just do your job. Easy."

The door opened and Ayla balked at the sight of her. She crossed her arms and narrowed her eyes as Chase, once again, froze. Damn it.

"What are you doing?" Ayla asked.

"Oh, uh," Chase scrambled for an excuse, but luckily, Ayla supplied one for her.

"It's supposed to be my time with Hunter. It's on the spreadsheet."

"My bad." Chase strode to the door and squeezed past her. "All yours."

Ayla grumbled something behind her, but Chase was too busy rejoicing in her first successful grift to hear it.

Chase booted up her station to find a ping from Monty waiting for her, giving a time for a "dinner date". He was probably teasing, but if she squinted, it almost felt like an inside joke. She replied with what she hoped was a teasing acceptance, then, in a moment of brilliance, opened a message to Divya.

CHASE A:

Have you ever been to one of the other labs?

Chase didn't bother with any preamble. In front of them, Ayla got Hunter up and had them swinging a shortsword.

DIVYA V:

What do you mean, the other labs?

CHASE A:

Like, the R&D labs on the other floors. I just think it's weird that we don't share more information around here.

Chase was pushing it, she knew. But if Divya knew something…

DIVYA V:

We all have different projects, so it wouldn't matter. Why? Do you need help with your project?

A sweet offer, really. It still made Chase huff.

CHASE A:

No, I'm getting it figured out. Thank you.

Ayla made a sweeping gesture with her stylus and Hunter swung, but they lost grip on the sword and sent the blade spinning down. Blood splattered across the floor as the blade hacked into the front of their leg and embedded itself into their femur. They made no sound, but even the thick glass didn't silence Ayla's scream of frustration. She smacked her tablet until the sword disintegrated.

"You," Ayla pointed at Chase with that short, skinny stylus.

"Me?" Chase got up and opened the door to the chamber, finding more blood than originally anticipated. The chamber whirred as it cleaned it up.

"The shell fucked up. Fix it." She didn't give any room for negotiation. A few weeks ago, Chase would've bowed to it. But now she knew too much, and she was pissed about it.

"You fucked the shell up is what I'm hearing," she said. After all, Hunter didn't problem solve, they only followed directions. If she didn't give the right ones, it wasn't Hunter's fault.

Ayla stopped mid-stalk to the changing rooms, slowly turning to face her.

"I don't fuck things up," she said through gritted teeth. "The stupid shell sliced through its own quads. If you wanna get anything done today, fix it. I'm not the myofabricator here."

"Obviously not, or you could clean up your own mess," Chase said. Anger bubbled behind her sternum, but her curiosity managed to dampen it enough to keep her from going into a blind rage. Ayla huffed and stomped out, going to the locker rooms to get a fresh jumpsuit. Even though the fab took the blood away, Chase knew better than most how the clothes still felt compromised.

Hunter took a knee, their cut quads unable to keep them standing. Blood drained in rivulets from the deep gash across the front of their leg. The chamber went into overdrive trying to keep up with it.

"What did she do to you, hmm?" Chase asked quietly, assessing the injury.

"Order," Hunter replied. Chase yelped in a very dignified manner and scrambled away from Hunter.

"You can speak?" she whispered, the chamber echo increasing the volume. She looked around, but her colleagues stayed focused on their screens. How could they work when Hunter could talk?

"Minimal." Hunter made blunt statements, the intonation nearly the same as the voice in the elevator.

"Why?"

"Clarify."

"Holy shit, she taught you to talk," Chase said. The repercussions landed on her like a crashing satellite. "Wait, Hunter, what just happened?"

"Order."

"She ordered you to cut your leg?" The movement had seemed so purposeful, even though it had to be an accident.

"Order: perform maneuver with weapon." The words were slow and robotic, and it hurt Chase's brain to consolidate this living body with a mind like a computer. But they could *communicate.*

"Did it hurt?" Chase asked, putting her hand on their shoulder. Hunter didn't move, didn't lean into the gesture, didn't even look at her.

"Clarify."

"Hurt, uh, pain. Discomfort. Ouch." Chase didn't know how to explain a subjective concept to something—some*one*—that only operated in the objective. Hunter blinked, one eye slower than the other.

"Probability likely." As if that was an actual pain response.

Chase needed to move, but it was so weird hearing Hunter's gravelly voice, and even weirder seeing the blood seeping from their leg.

Right, she was supposed to be fixing that.

"Uh, okay, Hunter," she started, her voice shaking. "Can you get up?"

"Clarify order."

"Oh, uh, stand," she said, then added, "please."

Hunter stood with their unaffected leg and kept their weight away from the injured one. Was that on purpose, or an automatic reaction? If it was a reaction, was it from pain, or lack of function?

"Okay. Go face up on the table." She kept her instruction short, figuring one-step commands were probably her best bet. Hunter limped to their bed, then bent at the waist and twisted to put the back of their head on it. "No, no, I mean…" Chase had to dig into the back of her brain for the right words. "Lay supine on top of the table."

This time, Hunter did as instructed, lying flat on their back. If the table was cold, either they didn't feel it, or it didn't bother them. Chase saw the extent of the gash up close; they'd managed to get deep into the muscle bellies and chip part of the bone, which was an impressive feat. She pulled her stylus from her pocket and tapped the table to sync, choosing which setting she needed for the repair.

Then she remembered Hunter was awake. Ayla wasn't back from the changing room, and there were no instructions on the tablet.

She went to the source. "Uh, is there, like," she fumbled for the words. "A power down instruction?"

"Clarify order," Hunter said.

"Oh, uh, like a way to put you to sleep?"

As soon as she said the last word, Hunter's eyes closed and their body relaxed to their baseline state. Chase poked them in the side, then in the gaping wound in their leg, but got no response.

"Well, that answers that question," she muttered.

The muscles were already trying to heal thanks to one of her own previous experiments, but their positions were all out of whack. If Chase didn't fix them now, then scar tissue would ravage the area and affect other important structures.

She looked back at Hunter's face, waiting for the eyes to open. But the body remained silent and still, the tool the others thought them to be. Chase couldn't get the blank stare and the monotone voice out of her mind, perpetually feeling like Hunter was somehow watching her.

It was easily the worst repair she'd done since her first year. Her hands shook, she gripped the stylus too tight, and she worked way too slow. She repaired like a child working on their favorite stuffed animal, as opposed to a professional.

"Don't worry, I'll have some good ones for you later," she whispered. Once she had control of her faculties, she'd make completely new muscles for them.

And until then, she had a heist to plan.

CHAPTER 19
THE BADGE JOB, PT. 2

"WHEN CAN we cut our losses and find another way?"

Chase crossed her arms over her chest, her frustration past the crying phase and now onto the lashing out phase. The badge that she so deftly "lifted" from Ruby lay pitifully on the floor, mocking her ineptitude and reminding her that, when everything went wrong, it would be her fault.

"You *are* going to get this," Ruby said, placing gentle hands on Chase's arms. Monty leaned against the counter, snacking on popcorn and watching the show. "It just takes practice. You're not even accidentally fondling me anymore! That's a win!"

"Great, two weeks of practice and the best I can do is *not fondling*," she grumbled.

"If it makes you feel better," Monty said, "Ellison still can't nail a lift."

"Ellison doesn't need to bother with stupid stuff like lifts," said the lady herself from her position on the couch. "Ellison can just knock someone out if she needs something."

"Not always an option," Monty said.

"Technically always an option."

"Not *always*—"

"If you two can't be helpful," Ruby said in the magic tone that quelled their arguing, "Then you can both leave."

Ruby raised her eyebrows. A challenge? Monty opened his mouth, thought better of it, and shut it again.

"Sorry," he mumbled.

"Ruby, I appreciate this, I do." Chase was not actually sure if she appreciated the thief lessons in the grand scheme of things, but she was absolutely grateful for the patience. "I'm just not the right person for the job. It was one thing when I just had to take it from other fabricators, how am I supposed to take it from Beauchamp? There's no way I can do this."

"Let's switch it up, hmm?" There was a devious glint in her eye; it made Chase nervous. Ruby grabbed Monty's wrist and tugged him forward. He nearly spilled the popcorn in his bowl, managing to save it just in time for Ruby to take it from him.

"But I was—"

"Here is your new mark," Ruby said, swiping the badge from the floor and roughly clipping it to his chest. A squawk said she managed to grab some skin as well. "Beauchamp is a man—"

"Allegedly," Chase said under her breath. Ellison looked up at that, one brow lifted. With a shrug, Chase explained, "He seems more like a demon. And not even a fun one."

Ellison pointed at Chase, validating her statement.

"There's fun kinds of demons?" Monty asked.

"Don't act like you haven't watched *Faerie Queen*," Chase replied. Ellison snickered at that, turning her attention to him.

"I knew you watched that shit."

"Of course I do, I watch all the popular stuff," he said. "I'm a normal citizen now! But that doesn't mean I agree there's fun demons."

"Again, let's be helpful here," Ruby interrupted. "Let's see how you do with a subject more representative of your target. Now you don't have to worry about accidental fondling."

Chase looked at Monty, his dark eyes glinting and one corner of his mouth lifted in a grin. Her palms instantly started sweating, which was *so* very attractive and helpful in this situation.

"Go ahead, take my badge," he said, his smile getting wider. Blood rushed to her cheeks, and she made herself hold his gaze.

"Sounds like you've never had your badge taken," she tried.

This was a stupid idea.

"Oh, I had my badge taken for the first time a long time ago."

An idea that was somehow working?

"Sounds like something someone who still has their badge would say."

Alright, that jab was just for fun. She let her eyes go directly to the badge pinned to his chest, trying to mark where it was.

"Well, I don't just go around giving my badge to anyone."

"Where's the fun in that?"

She eyed the badge again, and for good measure, made a show of trailing her eyes down the rest of his body. It was totally just for practice.

"You're expressing a lot of interest in my badge—"

"Oh my Techs!" Ellison blurted. Both of them snapped to her. "You're giving me fucking blue balls over this fucking badge. Fuck. Just take it already!"

"I mean, that's what I'm trying to tell her," Monty said with a laugh.

"I just did," Chase said. She held up the badge, her heart jumping into her throat as she said it. Monty dropped his eyes, running his hand over his chest and finding it lacking.

"Holy shit, you did it," he said.

"I did it!" She threw both arms in the air, waving the badge around like a flag of victory. Monty grabbed her around the waist, lifting her and spinning her. His arms were strong and warm, with his grip tight around her hips. She tried to focus on the win instead of how nice it felt to be crushed against him.

"See? I knew you could do it," Ruby said, smiling and eating Monty's popcorn. "Now, do it again."

"This time without the weird sexual tension," Ellison added.

"There wasn't—"

"We don't—"

"I don't give a single fuck," she said. Chase swallowed heavily, smoothing down her clothing and refusing to make eye contact. Monty stuck his hands in his pockets, mumbling for Ellison to mind her own business.

"Oh, darling," Ruby chastised, shaking her head at Ellison. Ellison simply raised her hands in innocence, muttering as she went back to her tablet screen. "Don't mind her. Practice makes perfect. Again."

This time when she stepped up, Chase was acutely aware of how close Monty was. She could smell that clean scent from his laundry, and see the very edge of a tattoo peeking out from the v-neck of his shirt.

"What's your tattoo?" she asked. It was definitely a ploy, she definitely wasn't distracted and curious.

"Huh?" He looked down at his clavicle. She could see the gears turning as he tried to guess her play. "Uh, it's my brother's signature. He had mine too."

Chase noticed the past tense and wanted to ask, but she could sense Ruby and Ellison growing still.

"Do you have any other tattoos?" She hoped this was a safe route to take. After all, technically, they were just practicing.

He lifted his arm and pulled up the sleeve of his shirt, displaying a pretty inkspot pattern—and his even prettier biceps.

"The first time I ever successfully forged something, this was the stain left on the table." He was proud of the accomplishment, and of the pattern. She reached up with both hands, using one to move the sleeve further and running her other thumb over the tattoo.

"How close is this to the original?"

"Almost exact, he just missed…" Monty stopped and turned to her. She tried to hold in the grin, she really did, but she couldn't resist dangling the badge in front of his face. "Damn, I'm beginning to think you were just playing Ruby."

"She just needed the proper motivation," Ruby said, once again making Chase blush. Ruby clapped her hands. "Again."

They repeated the exercise until they were exhausted of talking points and Chase successfully took the badge five times in a row. Monty was a real sport, and if he got annoyed or impatient, he didn't show it. Most of the time, she would even dare to say he was having fun.

The weird thing was, she was having fun, too.

"Good, now you're ready for tomorrow," Oscar said, holding up his device. "This thing is primed and ready to work. I just need his badge for ten seconds to make a copy, and we'll be golden."

"Tomorrow," said Chase, shocked.

"Tomorrow," replied Oscar, elated.

"You'll be fine," Ruby said, rubbing her back. Monty offered an encouraging grin, and even Ellison gave her a very serious nod. They went on like nothing was wrong, like they weren't about to do something completely terrifying the next day.

It was commonplace to them. To Chase, it was the scariest thing she'd ever done.

Soon, dinner was made and eaten, and Chase had nothing keeping her from returning to her own apartment. Even with the scrambler on her kitchen counter blocking anything from reaching the hidden sensors, it made her nervous to be there alone. But the thought of inconveniencing the crew—Monty especially, since she'd probably steal his bed again—was even worse.

"I'll walk you back," Monty said, once she announced it was time for her to take her leave. It wasn't necessary, but it also wasn't unwelcome. She bid goodnight to the group, and walked side-by-side with a criminal back to her apartment.

"Are you nervous, getting back into it?" she asked, letting him through the front door.

"Nervous? No. Probably more disappointed than anything," he admitted, the door closing behind him. He went to check Oscar's device and, finding it satisfactory, gave it a nod and a pat. "More like pregame jitters than anything. Kinda feels like I never left, the team was just waiting for me."

"That's one way to look at it," said Chase, who'd never played a team sport a day in her life.

"Don't freak out," he said, nodding again as she held up a bottle of wine from the fridge. It was the only viable thing to consume, but he didn't need to know that. "You've got the lift down. Only thing you're lacking is confidence."

"Techs, feels like so much more than that." She got two glasses from the cabinet and poured. "I mean, this isn't…I'm not…"

"Not a thief?" he joked, accepting the glass and taking a long sip. "I know. But trust me, things aren't always black and white when it comes to right and wrong."

"Yeah, I'm beginning to figure that out. I've made plenty of bad decisions, but this just might be the best one yet." She downed half her glass and leaned against the kitchen counter; he matched her pose against the opposite counter.

"You're gonna be okay, Chase. We got you. *I* got you."

Techs, he looked so serious, even more so than when he told her before. This time, she almost believed it.

Something shifted between them, their eyes locked from either side of the tiny galley kitchen. It was time to admit to herself that she didn't hate him. In fact, it was possible she quite liked him.

He moved closer, putting a hand on her cheek. The touch sent a jolt through her that had nothing to do with which company built her body.

"You've got me?" she murmured.

This time she was the one decreasing the distance between them, resting a hand on his chest and feeling the steady beat of his heart. If she focused on this, she didn't have to think about tomorrow. His dark eyes bore into her, and he stood steadfast despite her invading his space.

"I told you," he said softly, the timber of his voice resonating through her palm. His thumb ever so slightly traced a circle on her cheek. "I got you."

Fuck it. His wine glass clinked as he set it on the counter, the last thing she heard before she leaned forward and pressed her lips to his. The kiss was warm, and the wine made it taste like summer. She fumbled with her own glass for a moment before he plucked it from her grasp, not even looking as he placed it down.

His hands, normally so strong, were gentle as he tangled his fingers in her hair, angling her face just right so he could deepen the kiss. She leaned into his chest, gripping the hem of his t-shirt as his lips moved against hers, turning her blood to fire as her body redirected it. It was easy to move the hem of the shirt, and she felt the warmth of his skin, the tightening of his muscles. She brushed the pads of her fingertips over his obliques.

It was a while since her last kiss, and even longer since a kiss like this. She didn't want to think about tomorrow, she wanted to stay here and kiss Monty until everything figured itself out. Her body, so used to the panic setting over the past few days, finally had something better to focus on now.

"Do you want to stay a little later?" Chase whispered, kissing him again to give herself a breath before the response.

"Ask me again after tomorrow," he whispered back, softening the words with another languid kiss. "I don't do end of the world."

"I'll hold you to that," she said, kissing him again as if she could change his mind. Really, it was just to soothe her bruised ego, her heart raw after the subtle rejection.

"Please do," he murmured against her lips. She felt him smile into the last kiss, and he slowly peeled his body from hers. He walked backwards to the door, his eyes on her the whole time. "Goodnight, Alspeth."

"Goodnight."

He threw a wink her way before letting himself out. Once the door clicked closed, she let out a long breath, running her hands over her hot cheeks in an effort to calm herself. Techs, what was she *thinking*?

She picked up both glasses, quickly swallowing the wine left in his glass. Maybe he was sure it wasn't the end of the world, but she wasn't so confident. A great set up for her first con.

Her first con.

She rubbed her cheeks again, this time to fight off tears. Whether they were tears of sadness or fear or frustration, she didn't know. This was not how things were supposed to go. This was supposed to be her dream job, everything was supposed to be perfect—

A hollow thunk echoed through her empty apartment as she dropped her head to the counter. It wasn't her fault Kierper had illegal plans, and it wasn't her fault that no one else would do the right thing. And if the only way to stop the illegal thing was to do other illegal things, did it really count as illegal?

She knew it did.

By the time she showered and crawled into bed, the wine was hitting her enough to numb her anxieties. This was the right thing to do, even her wine-addled brain knew it.

Now she just had to go through with it.

CHAPTER 20
THE BADGE JOB, PT. 3

THE NEXT MORNING, Chase didn't want to put on her big girl jumpsuit and face Monty, but considering he was literally her partner in crime now, she had no choice. He waited for her at the platform, giving her that stupid handsome smile the second he spotted her in the crowd.

"Morning," he said as she pulled up next to him.

"Hey," she squeaked, jumping as the rail rattled in quickly. He put an arm around her shoulders, tucking her into his side.

"You got this," he reminded, his words tickling her ear. Did he think she was worried about the con? If so, he wasn't wrong. It just wasn't the only thing that worried her.

"We'll see about that." Admittedly, the weight of his arm was comforting as the rail took them closer and closer to her impending doom.

Monty walked her all the way to the outer door of the lab. She hoped to kiss him again, almost desperately wanted to, and was rewarded by the universe as he pressed his lips to hers, the touch teasing and playful and just enough to pull her head out of the depths of despair. It was the boost she needed to actually get into the lab and get ready for her moment.

"Lunch?" he murmured, resting his forehead against hers.

"I'll ping you when I'm ready," she said around her racing heart. He grinned and gave her one last brush of his lips.

"I'll be waiting anxiously," he said, taking slow, backward steps away from her.

"Anxiously? Why anxiously?" she asked, perking an eyebrow.

"You're right. I'll be waiting confidently, super chill, not nervous or worried at all. My only non-confident emotion will be some light pining." He punctuated his words with a shrug and a smile.

Amusement grabbed her, dissipating some of her fear. "That's what I thought," she said. "Really focus on the pining."

He gave her a salute. "I'll move it to top priority." He reached the end of the hallway, and blew an exaggerated kiss. "Go get 'em."

Chase, also wanting to focus on something silly and not the crime she was about to commit, pretended to catch the kiss and stuff it in her pocket. Techs, who *was* she? She figured out a couple of emotions, and now she was acting like a lovesick teenager.

When she turned to scan her badge, she found her stomach wasn't rolling with panic anymore. All right, perhaps there was something positive to a little bit of flirting.

The minutes dragged by like dead bodies on a gurney as she waited for the opportune time. If she went to see Beauchamp around midday, it would give her an excuse to leave the lab and get rid of any suspicious evidence. If things went wrong, then she could go to lunch and never come back.

Easy.

The moment the clock flipped to noon, Chase shot up, sending her chair careening into the wall. Divya, Jun, Ayla, and even Epley looked up, making her freeze like a deer in the rail lights.

"Been working out too much, I guess," she said, feeling how awkward her smile was and forgetting they probably couldn't hear her through multiple layers of glass walls. She didn't wait to see their reaction, instead striding toward the back elevator and waving her badge. Her pulse hammered in her ears and she tapped on the comms.

"There you are." Oscar's voice was a balm on her soul, unfreezing her limbs and forcing her into the elevator.

"Fourteenth floor," she said. The elevator complied this time, swooping her up to Beauchamp's office.

"She's on the move," Oscar said.

"You're going to do great, honey," Ruby said.

"Don't fuck it up," Ellison added.

"Ell—"

"She's fine, she knows I'm in the hallway backing her up."

Chase did *not* know Ellison was in the hallway backing her up, but really appreciated the information.

The elevator stopped, sending a spark through her nerves. She suddenly had the urge to urinate, but a restroom break was not part of the plan.

Pushing through the door to the office wasn't as disconcerting as the first time, as she was now prepared for the horrors inside. The gruesome jars seemed to have multiplied since her last visit. He sat in the semi-dark of a desk lamp, bent over the work in front of him. If he was surprised by her visit, he didn't show it.

"Alspeth," he said, not looking up from the papers on his desk. Who used *paper* anymore? "To what do I owe the displeasure?"

Strong start.

She opened her mouth, but the words stuck in her throat. The silence built until Beauchamp finally looked up.

"Well?"

"Tell him you want access to the other labs," Monty reminded her, his voice low and smooth.

"I want access to the other labs," she said. Damn, she was good at this.

Beauchamp raised his eyebrows. "You want what?"

"Access to the other labs." This time, she sounded almost confident.

"Yeah, tell him," Ellison said. "Fuck him up."

"You don't need access to other labs." Beauchamp was unamused. But Chase was undeterred.

"The archives make it impossible to work," she said. "And if we want to do things efficiently—"

"If you want to do things efficiently," Beauchamp stopped her with a raised hand, "then you go back down to *your* lab and do *your* job, instead of coming up here and complaining that you need someone to hold your hand."

"I don't need anyone to hold my hand." Before, she was fake pissed. Now it was real. "But the idea that one person alone can do the impossible is ridiculous. If you want results, then I need to be able to talk to other myofabricators."

"If you need that much help, then I'll relieve you of your position right now." He stood up, coming around the desk and reminding Chase why she was *actually* in his office. "Is that what you want?"

He crossed his arms, and Chase made a devastating discovery.

His badge was not at his chest, like she practiced.

It was on his belt.

"Alspeth!" The bark brought her back to reality. "Answer the question."

"No, I don't want that," Chase said, trying to control her ire so she could problem solve. "But you promised me resources."

"You have the world at your fingertips, and the most advanced shell in the program. What could the other floors possibly have that you don't?"

"Active discussion!" As a test, she dramatically tossed her hands up. He wasn't within reach. "I don't want to waste time trying to reinvent the wheel using failed practices. But if I could talk with the people who've been working on this longer than I have—"

"See, that's another area where you're wrong." He took a step toward her. The primal part of her brain really wanted her to take a step back, but the new "thief" side of her brain realized he was doing part of the work for her by moving closer. "The other fabricators don't have the same project you do. You are responsible for it. So stop trying to shove that onto other people."

"That's not the way science works. Researchers are supposed to rely on each other." She could feel her pulse in her ears, a thoroughly unsettling sensation.

"Don't." Beauchamp stepped uncomfortably close now, and Chase forced herself to stay planted, tucking her thumbs into her pockets. If she wiggled her fingers, she could feel the edge of his badge. "Don't you dare try to tell me how science works. How *research* works."

She dropped her eyes, feigning shame. Her cheeks burned, but not from the verbal lashing.

"You think it's hard to figure out how to make muscles a little stronger? I helped save the human race from *extinction*, Alspeth. *That* is hard."

Ruby advised her not to take her eyes off the prize. She saw it now, dangling within reach. In her periphery, she could see him glaring at her face.

"I achieved the impossible."

A tiny reach, and with a little pinch of her thumb and forefinger, she took the badge.

"So you need to quit your whining, and be *better*."

She looked up at him, his eyes boring into hers with unconcealed disdain. Fear was likely evident on her face, but it would only help her at this moment as she slowly, carefully, tucked the badge into her pocket.

Only to hear it click against the small container of mouth refresher in her pocket.

The world slowed as Beauchamp's eyes dropped. She knew

he couldn't see her concealing the badge, her hand covered it completely. But that wouldn't explain the noise.

"Chase? What's happening?" Ruby asked. "Are you okay?"

"She hasn't screamed, she's okay." Ellison said.

"Shh!" Monty's sharp sound hushed them.

In a moment of sheer stupid audacity, Chase switched her grip, pulling out the mouth refreshers.

"Mint, sir?" she asked, her voice low enough to cover her nerves. Beauchamp's glare snapped back up.

"Get the fuck out of my office, Alspeth." His words were dangerously calm, and she took the opportunity to, for once, do exactly as he said.

There were no parting words, and Chase didn't look back as she nearly ran out the door. A spot between her scapulae threatened to paralyze her, but she had to keep moving, had to keep herself from getting caught.

"Alspeth, you good?" Monty spoke with a quiet confidence, and it carried her to the elevator. When the door closed, she gave the order for her floor and sank down onto her heels.

"Oh my Techs, I think I'm gonna throw up," she said, doing her damndest to hold herself together. *Don't lose your shit, don't lose your shit —*

"Did you get it?" Oscar asked.

"Oscar!" Ruby chastised.

"Of course she did," Monty, ever her saving grace.

"Don't throw up, that'll be super obvious." Ellison always had great words of wisdom.

"I got it," she said, and the whole crew erupted in cheers, making her flinch at the volume.

"Atta girl!" Monty's voice rang out over the others, the simple praise so mundane that for a second she forgot what she'd done.

"Okay, you're almost there," Ruby said just as the elevator slowed. "Change jumpsuits and head to lunch. Ell, are you in position?"

"Yup," Ellison said, popping the "p" at the end of the word.

Chase stumbled out of the elevator doors. It was a struggle to keep her steps slow and even, and to school her features into something resembling normalcy. She held her breath the entire trek through the lab.

She ducked into her locker before anyone could say anything, choking on her palpitating heart as she awkwardly shimmied into her red jumpsuit. She clipped the badge behind her own before going into the decontamination chamber to hide it from the scanners.

Just make it out, make it out, make it out—

"If you keep coaching yourself verbally, they're gonna catch on," Ellison said.

"Shut up," Chase muttered, squashing the instinct to tap her foot as the chamber did its work.

"Oh, I like when you get feisty," Ellison said, and Chase decided to risk the decontamination process starting over to reach up and tap her comms into silence. This was all easy to them, but she could barely remember to breathe.

The decontamination chamber kicked her out, and her footsteps echoed outrageously loud as she strode through the final hallway. She kept her head bowed so her curls hid her face. It wouldn't prevent anyone in security from knowing who she was, but it made her feel better all the same.

"You hung up on me," Ellison said once Chase arrived on the main floor. She pushed a custodial cart stacked high with automatic cleaning appliances, her blonde hair tucked underneath a cap the same shade of olive as her jumpsuit.

"I'm trying not to lose my shit," Chase hissed, falling into step with her.

"The hard part is done." Ellison was matter-of-fact, which helped. "Now we let Oscar do his job. And if the worst happens, then I do *my* job and we get the fuck out of here."

Very matter-of-fact.

"Right," Chase said. She liked that there was more than one plan—it soothed her frazzled nerves.

"Come on." Ellison turned down a different hallway toward the service elevators. She kept their pace casual, which prevented Chase from walking too fast. The elevator took them down to the first floor, and the door opened to a patiently waiting Oscar. Chase was surprised to see Monty with him; he wasn't part of the plan.

"There she is," Monty smiled, holding his arms out for a hug. She welcomed the pressure of the embrace, considering she felt like her bones could melt at any second.

"Come, come," Oscar said, gesturing quickly with his fingers. "We are very proud of you, yes, but we need to get this done first."

"Right." Chase dug into her pocket. Ice blasted through her veins when she found it empty. "Wait—"

"No, don't tell me," Ellison said, her jaw dropping. Chase patted her pockets down, panic rising until she felt the extra badge attached beneath her own.

"Techs alive," she said, pulling the badge off and handing it to Oscar, nearly dropping it in the process.

"Don't scare me like that." Monty held his hand over his heart. Oscar's fancy card machine went to work, the little red lights blinking for ten seconds before flipping to a happy green.

"Badge copied, and we're good to go," he said, tossing said badge into the lost and found receptacle on Ellison's cart. "Who's ready for some lunch, hmm?"

"How can you even think about eating right now?" Chase's stomach spasmed at the thought, but Oscar looked confused.

"Uh, 'cause it's lunch time?" He looked to Monty for confirmation. Monty nodded, also not seeing the problem.

"We'll get you some cake, that'll make it better," he said. He put a hand on the small of her back. "Come on, you're good."

"Yeah, I'm good." It came out as a squeak, but at least it was audible.

Step one, complete.

CHAPTER 21
THE SNAPPED JOB

CHASE WASN'T one hundred percent sure how she made it through the last hours of her workday. Perhaps it was sheer gumption, perhaps it was Ruby saying nice things periodically on the comms. As she exited the lab and made for the doors, she took her first real breath of the afternoon. Monty met her outside, tucking her hand in his elbow and leading her at a normal pace to the rail station. She expected someone to call after them, or for security to jump on them, and fought every instinct not to look over her shoulder as they walked away.

"Doing great," Monty murmured. His biceps flexed under her hand, and she made an effort to loosen her grip. The joints in her fingers popped as she stretched. He said nothing further, but his shoulder did relax perceptibly.

"Beauchamp left, too," Oscar said, his voice a whisper in the comms. "Ellison got the badge back to his office shortly after lunch, and now he's leaving the parking garage. All clear."

"See? Told you." Monty squeezed Chase's hand into his side. They boarded the rail, and once the doors closed and they were in disgusting, sticky train seats, she released the tension in her body.

"Techs, this is so stressful." She bent forward to rest her

elbows on her knees and her head in her hands. "How did you do that all the time? I don't think my heart beat for the past few hours."

"You're just hungry," Ruby said.

"Don't worry, we've got you covered there," Ellison said. "I think we might've cooked up everything in the fridge."

"It's hard not being involved! Proper coping mechanisms are important in this line of work," Ruby said.

"Of course it is, my love."

Chase made a face and dropped it before Monty could see it. Hearing Ellison be anything but rough felt wrong.

"Ay," Oscar cut in. "Keep that nonsense offline. I don't wanna hear it."

"No one wants to hear it," Monty added.

"Careful, your jealousy is showing," Ellison teased. Monty scoffed, and Oscar made a retching noise.

But Chase smiled.

Monty caught her eye, but instead of smiling back, his eyes widened.

"Uh oh," he said.

Chase snorted at the outburst, and at the look on his face. The snort quickly evolved into a giggle, and the giggle transformed into loud, deep laughs that left tears streaming down her cheeks. Other rail riders glanced at her, but someone laughing to themselves wasn't enough to draw more than a heartbeat's worth of attention.

"And she snapped," Ellison deadpanned.

"Alspeth, hey." Monty put his hand on her shoulder and moved so he could look her in the eye. "Hey, you good?"

"Good? Of course I'm good," she said, her voice an octave higher than usual. She couldn't stop fucking *laughing*.

"Definitely snapped," Oscar said.

"No, I'm fine," Chase said. Monty's super serious face threatened any control she regained. "I'm fine. Totally fine. I mean, I just broke like, so many company policies. And laws. And stole from my boss." The laughter ebbed away, but for some reason, her chest still shook. "And risked everything. *Everything.*"

The tears fell, but instead of laughter, sobs wracked through her. She covered her face in a brave attempt to hide her utter embarrassment and despair.

Everything–she was risking *everything* on this hope that Monty and his friends could help her succeed. She was trusting *known criminals* to do the right thing. What the fuck was she thinking?

Warmth enveloped her as Monty pulled her into his chest, letting her cry into the fabric of his t-shirt.

"I got you. Remember?"

The rumble of his voice through his sternum comforted her and gave her something steady to focus on besides her dwindling sense of self-efficacy.

He held her the entire rail ride, and they very nearly missed their stop because of her unfortunate display. Monty got her attention just in time and dragged her through the doors. Perhaps they should stay on the rail, Chase thought. They could stay on the rail and go a long, long way from here.

"Sit," Monty said, directing her to a bench. She dropped onto it, leaning her forearms on her legs as she took deep, gulping breaths. Monty kept his hand on her back, and she focused on expanding her ribs into it. If she just took in a little more oxygen, then her brain would work better.

"I can't believe I did that," she said. He reached up to tap her comms off for her, and she appreciated the thought of privacy. "I didn't think…"

"Didn't think you'd end up working for the bad guys?" Monty supplied. "Or didn't think you'd end up working *with* the bad guys?"

"Either. Both." She took a breath. "Just—I'm doing the right thing, right Monty? Trying to take Beauchamp down?"

"You're really asking me if it's a good move to try and take down someone with too much power and keep him from building an army of super soldiers?" He raised one eyebrow at her. This time when she smiled, it wasn't because she was breaking. "You're doing the right thing, Alspeth. Unconventional problems call for unconventional solutions."

"Right," she said. She didn't believe him completely, but it was a start. "Is this all worth it for you? Getting back in?"

Monty sighed, then tapped his own comms. "I'd be lying if I said helping you wasn't helping me, too. The rest of them were supportive when I wanted out. Ruby even threw a going away party for me, cake and all."

"Of course she did," Chase said.

Monty grinned. "It was a good cake. You'll have to ask her to make one for your birthday." He paused and took a breath. "Koda wasn't supposed to follow me. But she wanted to make sure I was okay and settled in fine. The problem was…Koda was never good at letting an opportunity pass by, no matter how dangerous it was. And I think this time it caught up with her."

"She came by herself?" Chase asked. Monty sighed and nodded.

"Messaged me and said she would stop by," he said. "Ell lost contact that afternoon. The only way they found her location was from the tracker in her comms."

"Fuck," Chase breathed. Her heart dropped to somewhere around her talocrural joints.

"Yeah." Monty took a deep breath. "I know things don't look promising, but we have to try. And this will be really tough on you, but you're strong. You're braver than any con man I've ever known."

Chase gave a brief huff of a laugh. "You must not know many con men then."

"You'd be surprised."

They sat in silence. Trains glided into the station and bulleted off again, the crowds milling like ants in a row. Chase reached over and took Monty's hand, more in a show of solidarity than a romantic gesture. The kiss she pressed to his knuckles was more for that.

"Hey Monty?" she murmured.

"Hmm?"

"Thank you. For everything. For helping me, and…" How could she explain how he made her feel? Like she finally had a rock to hold on to in this storm?

Either he read her mind, or didn't need her to finish the statement. He simply ran his thumb over her knuckles.

"You're welcome, Alspeth. I got you."

Their quiet returned. He didn't rush her, and so she sat and sorted through all her feelings until she felt stable. Not necessarily good, but stable. When she turned and smiled at him, he stood, but didn't release her hand.

"C'mon. I'm starving."

If she tried to eat, she would vomit her entire stomach, organ and all, but she followed him anyway.

Monty opened the apartment door with a smile and a loud cheer, as if they didn't just have existential crises moments before returning. Ruby raised her arms with a celebratory yell, flinging green sauce onto the wall and dropping a spoonful of rice onto the floor. Oscar popped open a bottle of champagne and dramatically poured some into an oversized blue coffee mug held by Ellison. Ellison thrust the mug into Chase's hand and clapped her on the back, hard enough that the drink nearly spilled. The woman smiled at her, and for the first time Chase felt like Ellison didn't hate her.

"I didn't fuck it up," Chase said, with as big of a grin as she could muster.

"You didn't fuck it up!" Ellison said with another cheer.

Chase took a hearty glug of the champagne. The bubbles burned her throat and her nose, but the flavor was sweet and dangerously light. Now seemed as good a time as any to partake, so she took another heavy swig for good measure.

As promised, Ruby and Ellison cooked enough for the entire

building. After two to three fast drinks, Chase's anxiety lessened, and she was more than ready to indulge. Monty sat next to her, casually resting his hand on the back of her chair when he wasn't scarfing down food or arguing wildly with Ellison, his hands waving as they discussed things like *the Bucharest job* or *that time in the desert.*

Watching the crew interact with one another was like watching her favorite shows, and she was content to sit back and absorb story after story. The celebration turned into a happy remembrance of Koda as Oscar did a (supposedly) very accurate imitation of her that left the others howling with laughter. Chase didn't get most of the jokes, but with the alcohol they were funny, anyway.

"And Chase," he said, still in Koda's British accent. "Darling, you needed to undo just a single button on your jumpsuit, it would've made the whole operation perfect. No, not the one at your collar, the one at your back pocket!"

"The devil is in the details," Ruby crowed, her accent terrible. "Can't forget that, darling."

"Or the devil was the friends we made along the way," Monty said, turning her way and winking.

"I'll remember next time, I promise," she said, hoping she was saying the right line for this play she'd never rehearsed.

"Brilliant! Another round then," Oscar said, grabbing the last bottle of champagne and filling what glasses he could. Chase was carefully sipping now, her stomach full and her head in the clouds as Ellison took her turn at the impressions.

Hours later, it was far past her bedtime, but she was awake anyway, slouched on the couch between Monty and Oscar. Ellison and Ruby stumbled into their room long ago, and Monty gave in to the hazy fatigue, his head resting precariously on his hand as he snored softly. Chase and Oscar faced the wall screen, but the program playing was a mystery to both of them.

"I still don't know how we're gonna collect the data," Chase whispered. With one part done, now she could focus on fearing the next part. "I can't see anyone else's unless they leave their station on. The archive only holds mine."

"It's somewhere," Oscar said dreamily. "There's always a trail. Always."

"If anyone can find it, it's you," Chase said. "Shit, I wish I could have it for my job. Hunter has all these marks, but I have no way to figure out exactly what's been tried with them. I feel like I'm doing the same stuff to them that's been done before."

"'Them'? Thought it wasn't a volunteer?"

"They're not, but…" Chase tried to pull together her muddy thoughts, and eventually gave up. "I don't know. They seem like more than a tool. More than an 'it'. But maybe I'm just anthropo-morphizing."

"Maybe you could wake them up and get them to tell you," Oscar suggested. Chase shook her head, the motion making her vision swim as it struggled to keep up.

"I don't think they'd remember it. Besides, all the little details are too much for one brain to process. You'd need a digital database."

"I could make one, I bet," Oscar said. "I love making data-bases. They're so pretty and organized."

Chase rolled her head to face him. "Wait, could you really?"

"Really what?"

"Make a database."

"Of the stuff they've done to Hunter? Uh, I mean, maybe if I had access to scans or something. There's always tells for this stuff, right?"

"Yeah, there are," Chase said. She vaguely remembered feeling something was wrong about Hunter's bony attachment sites. "There has to be scanning stuff in the mega fab. It just needs a program."

She gasped and sat up, nearly falling off the couch. Oscar grabbed her, his face excited by whatever she was about to ask.

"Can you write a program?" She'd thought about it that first night, but never got around to voicing it.

"I can write many programs. What kind of program do you want?"

"To scan Hunter for irregularities!"

"Oh," Oscar said, his drunk mind returning to the conversation. His face sobered. "*Oh!*"

"'Oh?'"

"Oh!" he said, getting up too fast and falling to the floor. Monty jerked at the noise, blinking a few times before leaning his head back and returning to his slumber. Oscar bear crawled to his desk and stood on his knees, too excited to grab the chair.

Chase followed him in a slightly more graceful manner, adopting an awkward lunge so she wouldn't put too much weight on her stupid left knee. As soon as this was all over, she was getting this damn experimental thing *replaced*.

"What're we doing?" she whisper-yelled. Oscar shushed her, tapping away. Lines of code flew across the screen too fast to process, the patterns of the lines undulating like waves. The clicking of the keyboard was rhythmic enough to lull her.

"I think we can do it," Oscar said. His voice sounded far away. Chase thought she agreed, but upon reflection, was not entirely sure she agreed *out loud*. She needed to lie down, that's what she needed. Just a little break, then they could figure out the code.

CHAPTER 22
THE SLOW DOWN JOB

CHASE'S HANDHELD buzzed in her pocket. When did it go off? Hell, when did she fall asleep? It took three tries to tap the screen and stop its incessant bother. The effort required to sit up reminded her that she was not, in fact, twenty-one anymore, and that she could not stay up past midnight drinking and feel fine the next day.

She groaned and winced at the minimal light puncturing the closed blinds, taking stock of the situation with one eye. Monty looked like he'd gone straight from sitting to lying on his side, his torso on the couch and his legs hanging off the front. Ruby and Ellison's bedroom door remained closed, though she could hear the suspicious sounds of someone vomiting. Her own stomach rolled at that, then jumped as she realized Oscar was not only next to her, but wide awake and staring at his screen.

"I figured it out," he said, his accent thicker with his fatigue. Chase grabbed the edge of the table to pull herself onto her knees. Oscar had his arm awkwardly bent underneath his head, holding it up just enough for him to work.

"What did you figure out?" she asked. She had a blurry memory of them coming over here, trying to solve some sort of problem…

"The program. To scan Hunter." He tried to lift his head and failed. Instead, he lifted a hand and pointed at the screen. "I think you can use your tablet to connect with the fab chamber, and this will read it."

"Holy shit." Fully awake now. "Holy *shit!*"

Monty groaned from the couch.

"What?" he said, trying to rise and instead rolling to the floor. When he righted himself, it took a moment for his eyes to focus. "What's going on?"

"Oscar is a genius," Chase said, throwing her arms around said genius. He stiffened at first, then relaxed into the embrace.

"See? At least one person appreciates me," he said.

"We appreciate you," Monty said. "We're just used to your genius."

"It's still nice to hear it."

Monty opened his mouth to respond, but apparently the words got lost somewhere between his brain and the open air.

"Thank you, Oscar," Chase said.

"It's nothing. I just have a few bugs to figure out, and then it'll be ready. Tomorrow at the latest, I think." He swiped something on the screen, then dropped to his hands and knees and crawled to his room. "I'm going to sleep now."

"Well deserved," Chase said.

Now the hangover didn't feel so bad, with a potential plan in place. She looked over at Monty to find his eyebrows raised and his head tilted.

"A genius, huh?" he asked, making Chase's stomach roll again as she remembered his promise. Did this count as victory? Or did they need to pull off the entire con before celebrating the continuation of the world?

"No need to be jealous, Montgomery Evans." She pushed to her feet, feigning nonchalance as he grinned.

"Where're you going?" he asked, also forcing himself up. She straightened the arms of her red jumpsuit, still tied around her waist.

"I'm going to go shower, and then go to work. I've got big plans now," she said. "Are you calling in sick?"

"Me? Nah, I feel great," he said, shaking his head. "Plus, until Ellison's done ridding herself of spirits, I'm the best protection you've got if something goes wrong."

"You just had to add that last part." With the excitement of the new code, she was able to forget the danger from the day before. Now it threatened to overtake her again.

"It was a joke." He came over and rested his hands on her shoulders, warm and comforting. "A bad one. You're going to be fine. We've done stuff like this a hundred times before."

"Literally or figuratively?"

"I..." He paused, scrunching his forehead in thought. Chase had the urge to poke the little wrinkles, but somehow refrained. "To be honest, I don't know where the number's at. I'd have to ask Oscar."

They both turned to the other room, the open door putting Oscar on full display as he lay face down on his bed, his feet hanging off the edge.

"Later," Monty said. "I'll ask him later. Doesn't change the fact that I'm going with you."

"Then we better get going," she said. She stood for a second, trying to decide whether she should—or could—kiss him good-bye, but he made the decision for her by stepping back toward his room.

"I'll meet you downstairs," he said.

Chase nodded, any response stuck in her dry throat as she turned on her heel and left.

Shower. Dress. Catch the rail. Her nerves threatened to reappear the closer they got to the building, and she held her breath when they walked through the front door. Mr. Scovajsa greeted them with the same smile as every other day and scanned them through.

They really *were* good at this. It gave her the same thrill as an experiment gone perfectly right. Monty's reassurance from the night before stuck to her; she was breaking rules, yes, but for the right reasons.

"Keep your comms on, just in case," he said once they reached the outer door of the lab. She reached up and tapped it before she could forget. "I'll see you at lunch?"

"Sounds good," she said. He leaned forward and kissed her then, and she welcomed the touch and the press of his body against hers.

"Don't think I've forgotten my promise," he murmured against her lips. Her breath left in a rush, and he pulled away and gently pushed her toward the door.

With all the fake confidence she could muster, she went to the door, giving in and glancing over her shoulder one last time. Monty was grinning to himself, then he shook his head and took his leave, walking away with that familiar swagger.

Once again, Chase's colleagues barely glanced up as she landed in her little fish bowl. She assumed her arrival went more or less unnoticed, but a second later, her monitor dinged with a ping from Divya.

DIVYA V:

Beauchamp was in a mood yesterday. Tasked me with a secondary project to design a program for mass producing the bones. Sounds like something for the upper floors, but what do I know? Did you get stuck with something similar?

Chase balked at the message. There was a lot of important information in those few lines.

CHASE A:

The upper floors?

Not the most crucial bit, but the one she focused on.

DIVYA V:

Yeah, where they just sit behind the screens and type all day. They love to come down periodically and give advice like they know anything about the body. You haven't had to deal with them yet?

CHASE A:

Not yet, no. I'll be honest, I'm kinda struggling with my main project.

The conversation was so mundane. Continuing it did nothing but increase her risk of accidentally saying something incriminating, but social etiquette didn't allow her to stop.

DIVYA V:

Wanna talk it out? I don't remember much from myo, but I'm a good listener.

It was a tempting offer, but Chase had Oscar's ace up her sleeve.

CHASE A:

Not yet, I have a couple things to try first. Thank you, though. I appreciate it.

Divya sat taller so Chase could see her over her monitor and gave her the warm look she remembered from when they both worked on the floor. Chase smiled back, then turned back to her screen, Divya's words on repeat in her head.

Beauchamp wanted mass production? And he wanted Divya specifically to work on it? His comment about her Hunter being the most advanced shell ran through her mind. Her heart froze; sounded like they would be the prototype. Techs, she had to get them out, and get them out fast, before their experiments became a production line.

Good thing she had professionals working on a plan. And

while they worked on a plan... Well, she could slow things down a little, right?

She didn't know when Beauchamp came around and checked on the shells, so she grabbed the last available time to work with Hunter and blazed through fabricating some new muscles. It took longer than expected, eating into her allotted hour. She'd never pulled Hunter into the chamber so fast, nearly careening them into the wall.

"Oops, sorry," she said, more to them than to her interrupted coworkers. Of course, Hunter didn't care. They were asleep. She anchored the tube, opened it up, and started cutting.

If she was honest, it was the easiest installation she'd done in a long time. The muscles she made were the advised size based on the genetics, with a normal percentage of different fibers. The difference? She added a polymer framework that, at first glance, would support higher force rates. But, thanks to an experiment gone wrong back in school, Chase knew that any test would lead to its disintegration. At the time of discovery, she'd been so mad she threw her stylus at the wall. Now, she was glad for the failed (and unpublished) study.

"I mean, I hope he doesn't test it," she whispered to Hunter. "But if he does, at least it won't hurt you."

Hunter, of course, was unbothered.

Satisfied with her work, Chase returned Hunter to their room. The documentation only took a few minutes, and once that was done, she shut down her station. Finally, it felt like she was doing something helpful, something that could buy the time they needed until Oscar finished his program.

She rose and exited the lab, her victory carrying her all the way through the decontamination chamber and down to the ground floor. Monty waited for her, and his face brightened when their eyes met. Chase smiled back as her heart twisted in a metaphorically dangerous way.

Damn, if her feelings continued down this road, she'd be in big trouble soon.

CHAPTER 23
THE CONTROL JOB

"SOMETHING HAPPEN to make you smile like that?" Monty asked as she joined him. Chase grabbed onto his elbow, and even if it was a new element to their relationship, it felt familiar and grounded her.

"Just a bit of subterfuge," she said.

"Subterfuge? Damn, we have been bad influences on you," he said. They went through security, then followed the wave of people to the rail station.

"I mean, like you said. We have to be a little unconventional in this situation," she said as they waited. "It was a little hard to wrap my brain around, but it makes sense. And if it makes sense…" She shrugged. He untangled and laid his arm across her shoulders, tucking her into his side.

"I know it's tough, but you're doing the right thing. You're more courageous than anyone else in that lab, you know that, right?"

He looked down at her with kind eyes and a gentle smile, and the truth of his words made her breath catch.

"Well, I do now." When he said it, it was easy to believe.

He pulled her close again and pressed a lingering kiss to the top of her head. "It's gonna be okay, Alspeth. Trust me."

Funny thing, Chase realized she did. Trust him, that is. He was the same man she'd known the past few months, there were just a few more layers to him than originally anticipated. And she liked those layers. She liked *him*.

Oh, hell. These feelings were *definitely* going to get her in trouble.

The rail arrived, and they found their seats. Monty's arm stayed around her, warm and comforting as she lay her head on his shoulder. He traced a circle on her shoulder with his thumb. The movement was so easy, so sweet, that it set a tiny flame alight somewhere in her sternum. Monty made her feel confident, made her feel brave. And while the story of his past was new, these sensations were not.

She put a hand on his thigh, smirking when the muscle beneath twitched.

Chase turned her head to find him already looking at her, his gaze smoldering. And while she appreciated the small acts of affection and the supportive words, she didn't mind when he looked at her like that.

He lifted her chin with one finger, his gaze never wavering. Involuntarily, her hand gripped his thigh, leading to one corner of his mouth lifting.

"You got me, right?" she whispered. He nodded.

"Yeah, I got you."

He brushed his lips against hers, light and teasing. A promise. One she desperately wanted him to follow through on. She shifted closer so their hips touched, then crossed one leg over the other. It took everything not to squirm in her seat, especially when he stole glances of her body and licked his lips like a starving man.

The rail reached their stop, and they were forced to unravel, but Monty didn't let her go far. He took her hand and interlaced their fingers, making sure she stayed right by his side.

By the time they made it back to her apartment, every cell in Chase's body was vibrating. The door slid closed as they kicked their shoes off, then Monty turned and pressed her against it. Chase inhaled sharply, her chest pushing into his as he kept that heated gaze on her face. He tapped his ear, then hers. He then removed the comms unit from his ear before slowly plucking hers free as well. She placed her hands on his shoulders, then gently slid them up to his cheeks, smirking as he shivered.

"Still want this?" he asked. She nodded fervently.

"Please," she said.

Monty claimed her mouth in a searing kiss, setting her body alight. His hand slid down her leg to grab her knee, lifting it so she wrapped it around him, allowing him to get even closer. He caught her moan, then pulled back, just enough so they could make eye contact. Chase blushed at the obvious desire in his eyes, and knew it mirrored her own.

Whatever he was thinking about saying, he held it back. Instead, he smiled, then kissed her again, slow and lingering. In a swift movement, he grabbed her other knee and lifted her completely. She held on with arms and legs, never breaking the kiss as he walked down her short hallway.

"Which door?" he asked when they reached the end.

"Far left," she replied, breathless. "Unless you prefer the linen closet."

Monty paused for a second, thinking, then shook his head. "Nah, I want to see you."

He opened the door to her room and dropped her on the bed. She landed with a giggle and shimmied back, the laughter quickly shifting to a sigh as he lay atop her and kissed her deeply. Her fingers trailed down his spine, sending a shiver through him that had her gasping. She slipped her hands beneath his shirt, and his muscles contracted under her fingertips. Inch by inch, she dragged the hem of his shirt up. He tensed when she reached his ribs, making her smile into the kiss.

"Ticklish?" she asked. She traced his eighth rib with one finger, and he twisted away from the touch, sitting back on his knees.

"Let's focus please, Alspeth." He pulled his shirt off, and Chase's mouth went dry as she catalogued every solid muscle on display.

"Chase," she said, once clearing her throat. Monty furrowed his brows.

"What?"

She found a way to look away from the line where his obliques dipped into a V and met his dark eyes. "I like it better when you call me Chase."

He grinned. "Chase it is, then."

He took her hands and pulled her up, then placed them on his shoulders as he kissed her again. He then carefully tugged the scrunchie from her bun, letting her curls fall loose down her back. When he reached for the bottom of her shirt, she let him, and he toyed with it for a few seconds before slowly peeling it off her. She wasn't nearly as muscular as him, but a wave of confidence washed over her as he ran his hands over her stomach with a soft, but reverent, "*Fuck.*"

Eager for more reactions like that, she reached behind and unclasped her bra before tossing it in the general direction of their shirts. She was rewarded with a low groan from him, and then a sharp inhale as she put her hands over his and encouraged him to touch the newly exposed flesh.

"Techs, you're so far out of my league," he whispered. She sucked in a breath as his thumbs brushed more sensitive places, arching her back into his touch.

"I think it's the other way around," she said, her voice embarrassingly breathy.

Monty let out a low chuckle. "Oh, Chase, Chase, Chase." Each time he said her name, a jolt went down her spine. He laid her back and gave her a burning kiss before saying, "This is the only time I've heard you be wrong."

His lips dropped to her neck just as one hand squeezed, and she had to press her lips together to stifle the loud moan trying to escape.

"Let me hear you," he said, this time pinching softly, and she acquiesced by calling his name. He smiled against her neck, then trailed his kisses down until he could soothe away the pinch with his tongue. The way he took his sweet time tending to each side had her heart racing and her legs moving against his, wishing she had some pressure or friction or anything to ease the aching between them.

Monty kissed down her stomach and stopped at the edge of her jumpsuit, then carefully unlaced the sleeves tied around her waist. Chase swallowed her impatience at having his hands *so close* to where she wanted them. She nodded quickly when he took the edge of the jumpsuit in his hands and looked at her with a question. He removed the jumpsuit and her underwear in one go, and the cool air alerted her to her body's reaction to their activities. For a second, shyness came over her, but once Monty shimmied out of his own clothes and looked back, the confidence returned.

With another low curse, he ran his hands over the softness of her thighs and hips, his gaze roaming over every inch of her body as she lay splayed before him. She bit her lip as she also traced every part of him, her heart fluttering in anticipation.

"Tell me what you like," he said as his eyes met hers again.

Words left her as she realized he was serious, and she floundered as she tried to find a way to say it. Nervousness seized most of her cognitive processing and left her with one response.

"I like to be in control," she whispered. He smiled widely, and she rolled her eyes. "I know, what a surprise."

"Not what I was going to say." He flopped down onto the bed next to her and pulled her onto her side, holding her tight against his chest and slotting one leg between hers. He kissed her soundly as she hummed in relief at the contact.

"What were you going to say then?" she asked. Her eyes fluttered closed as he moved his leg just slightly, increasing the stimulation. His own reaction pressed against her stomach.

"I was going to say"—he rolled them both so she was on top —"that you gave the answer I was hoping for."

"Really?" She paused her movements, then shifted so she could straddle him completely. He laughed.

"I told you, I want to see you." His hands went to her low back, and then a little lower. He took hold of her hips and encouraged her to continue her motions. She sat up and let out a whine as the position allowed more pressure, and she followed the silent instructions from his hands until her breath was ragged and he pulsed beneath her. Techs, he looked so good under her, his muscles on display and the evening sun peeking through her window, turning parts of his brown skin a burnished gold.

He let her go a minute longer before patting her leg and saying, "Lift up."

"But this feels good." She didn't want to stop, she wanted more. And based on his grin, he wanted to give it to her.

"Give me a minute," he requested. She relented and rose onto her knees, but he didn't allow her to move further than that. Instead, he scooted down the bed until his face was right below her.

"Are you serious?" she asked.

"Absolutely yes," he replied. "Go on."

"What if I crush you?" This was something new for her, but evidently not for him.

But still, she was in control.

"You won't. Now sit, please." He gazed at her hungrily, and she hesitated for just a moment. He took her hips and tugged her down until she landed on his mouth, the warm contact making her cry out. The vibrations from his resulting laugh made her legs twitch and her abs spasm. Contrary to her prior belief, he could handle her just fine in this position, licking and sucking in all the right places as she trembled above him.

This was good. This was *really* good. She rested one hand on his head and the other on the bed, bracing herself as he sent shot after shot of pleasure through her. It was only when she felt the familiar build deep in her abdomen that she forced herself up and off of him, though her body screamed in protest.

"You okay?" he asked, scrambling out so he was sitting equal with her on the bed again. She responded by straddling his lap and wiping the wetness from his chin.

"I'm great, I was just getting too close," she said, and he gave her the most self-satisfied smirk.

"Next time, let me finish what I start," he murmured, then placed a kiss right over her carotid pulse. Chase's breath hitched.

"Next time?" she asked.

"Next time," he said. His lips moved from her pulse to the point where her neck met her shoulder, sending goosebumps down her arms. He ran his hands over every inch of her, intensifying the ache between her legs. A thought about patience flitted through her mind, but it disappeared as soon as it came. She couldn't wait anymore.

"I'm ready, are you?" she asked, desperate to have him inside her. "Or do you need—"

He wrapped his arm around her waist to lift her slightly, and kissed her as he positioned himself just right. "Oh, I'm ready," he said.

She needed no further affirmation, and slowly sank down until they were completely joined. They held each other tightly as she shivered, and her name tumbled from his lips and into her hair. When she started to move, he kissed her again, his fingers tangled in her curls and his mouth hot against hers.

He lay back, and as promised, watched her with an intensity that sent heat across her chest. When she found her rhythm, he bent his knees, supporting her while also allowing him to thrust at just the right intervals to have her saying "yes" over and over and over. One of his hands stayed on her hip, holding tight enough to bruise. The other, in contrast, went to where they were joined. He used his thumb to rub gentle, steady circles just where she needed it.

Sweat dripped down her back and glistened on his chest, but that didn't deter them. It only made her move faster, the softer places of her bouncing as she sought her end. She was close, so close, and if she was reading Monty's physiological responses correctly, he was right behind her. He murmured some encouraging words and quickened his tempo, hitting a place deep inside that had her vocalizing louder than she ever had before. A few more fast thrusts and she tumbled over the edge, growing silent and still as she came. Good thing he continued his movements, wringing out the entirety of her orgasm before his rhythm stuttered as he reached his own release. She gripped him tightly as he called her name, amidst curses and cries to a deity, until finally he slowed and stopped.

The room was silent except for their panting as they both came down from the high. Chase collapsed forward, resting her sweaty forehead on his equally sweaty chest as she tried to catch her breath. He gathered her curls in one hand and lifted them away before fanning her neck, the relief instantaneous as the heat trapped there dissipated. She stayed there for a long minute before forcing herself to dismount.

"I'll be right back," she said as she stumbled toward the bathroom.

"I'll be here," he replied, laying spread eagle in the middle of her bed.

The cool bathroom tiles felt nice beneath her feet. In the mirror, she caught how wild her hair was now, a great mess of tangles and curls. A pink tinge coated her face and chest, and her skin was sticky with sweat. But hot damn did she feel good.

Chase finished her business and returned to her room to find Monty in the same position as before, naked as the day he was created in the lab. She had every intention of getting dressed, or at least putting her underwear back on, but he reached a hand out to her with a devilish grin. Perhaps she could stay naked a little longer.

"All good?" he asked once she joined him on the bed. He

pulled her close, intertwining their legs and tracing his fingers up and down her spine.

"Great, actually," she replied, and Techs if he didn't look so damn proud of himself. She wiped the smirk off with a deep kiss that left her tingling.

"Glad I'm not alone in that." He nuzzled her neck and laid a tender kiss there. It was probably supposed to be an affectionate moment, but it caused a hitch in her breath, and she could *feel* as her normal blood flow redirected. He leaned back, one eyebrow raised. She bit her lip and tried to subdue her reaction. But the way he looked at her loosened the knot in her chest; she didn't have to keep the walls up, not anymore. It was okay to ask. It was okay to *want*.

"Exactly when were you thinking for 'next time'?"

CHAPTER 24
THE CONFESSION JOB

SO, Chase might have underestimated how nice it would be to wake up next to Monty.

It wasn't like in the movies, where they woke at the same time, curled around each other like twisted vines. She was on her stomach, facing away, and he had one arm draped across her bare back, keeping her warm since the covers were pooled around her waist. Her hips hurt, and she had some lingering soreness—Techs, when was the last time she went three times in a night?—but overall she felt calm. She felt *satisfied*.

Carefully, she turned her head. Monty remained asleep, laying on his back, reaching out with the arm over her. Just past his head, the clock told her it was barely past six in the morning; definitely too early to be up.

Monty took a deep breath, and Chase froze, hoping she didn't wake him. Luckily, he just shifted and rolled over, tucking his arms in and laying his forehead against her shoulder. He looked younger in sleep, his usual worry lines smoothed over. Affection for him burned behind her sternum. It wasn't enough to be next to him. Delicately, she turned onto her side so that his face rested against her chest. His arm went around her waist and crushed her to him, enveloping her in warmth. He sighed, the sound so inundated with contentment that she nearly laughed and ruined the whole thing. Instead, she swallowed the joy and settled back down.

Chase had no intention of going back to sleep, but it happened anyway, and before she knew it, Monty was gently waking her by rubbing her shoulder.

"There she is." He pressed a kiss to the side of her head, and she sighed heavily.

"Do we have to get up?" she asked. "Wait, what time is it?"

"A little after seven. No rush." The covers were back over them now, but Chase scooted close to him anyway. He wrapped her up and held her close, and damn did it feel nice. Thoughts of all the problems in her life faded away.

"On a scale of one to ten, how much shit are the others going to give us?" she murmured against his chest.

"They have no room to talk, Ruby and Ell tried to hide their situation for months. It was so obvious. I don't know how either of them ever runs a successful con," he said.

"So like a fifteen?"

"Definitely, they're going to be so annoying." He tried to run a hand through her hair, but his fingers got stuck in the tangles and tugged on her head. "Shit, sorry."

"Don't pull my hair if you're not gonna follow through, Montgomery Evans," she muttered. He shot back so he could see her face.

"Oh?" he said, eyebrows raised. Chase rolled her eyes.

"I'm just kidding," she said, and he deflated. "For now."

Ah, the devilish grin he gave her. "Duly noted." He rolled away and stretched; he took up so much of her bed, and yet seemed to fit in just right. "Are you planning to shower?"

"Absolutely." She rolled to the other side and sat up, the cold air a rude awakening to the day. Monty rose as well, hesitating as she walked toward the bathroom. She paused at the doorway and looked over her shoulder. "Well? Are you coming?"

That smile would be the death of her. "Well, if you're gonna offer."

Whatever extra time they had was long spent by the time they finished washing up and getting dressed. Monty debated going back to his apartment for a new jumpsuit, but ultimately decided he wasn't ready to leave their little bubble and face his colleagues. It would be bad enough on the comms, he didn't need it live as well.

"Well, well, look who decided to come back online," Oscar said literally a half second after they put their comms units back in their ears.

"Did we miss anything important?" Monty asked.

"Nope." Somehow, Ruby managed to lace the singular word with innuendo.

"Did you two have fun fu—"

"Ellison, I'm begging you," Monty said. He looked to Chase, eyes wide, as if afraid his friends embarrassing them would send her running. It was kind of him, really. Chase did often get embarrassed by little things. But not *this* thing.

"Yes, we did, thank you," she said lightly as they exited her apartment. She heard Monty cursing under his breath as the door slid closed, but that was lost quickly as Ellison howled with laughter.

"Atta girl," Ellison said, and Monty groaned.

"Techs, she's gonna be insufferable now," he growled.

"C'mon, we're all adults here." Chase poked him in the ribs, remembering too late how ticklish he was. His face grew serious and he held up a finger.

"Don't, I'm sensitive right now."

Chase only smiled and grabbed his finger, laying a kiss to the tip. Techs, what had gotten into her? Well, besides—

"You did miss one thing," Oscar said, and both Chase and Monty sobered. The elevator arrived and they boarded, nervous about what Oscar was about to say.

"What is it?" Chase asked. "Activity in the lab?"

"Oh, no, not that I can tell," he said.

"Then what?" Monty said.

"I finished the program."

The figurative gears in Chase's brain turned as she tried to figure out what he was referring to.

"The program to scan Hunter?" he said. "The one we specifically discussed and I spent all night coding two days ago so that we can gather data?"

"Oh. Oh!" It all clicked into place. "Yes! Oh, Oscar, that's amazing! You're a genius."

"Oh, uh. Thank you." She could practically hear the blush over the comms. Monty raised a brow, and Chase tapped it.

"No jealousy," she whispered, hoping the comms wouldn't pick it up. No one responded, so she assumed they were in the clear. Monty shrugged, and pulled her in for a nearly silent kiss.

"So I just plug it into the fab?" Chase asked aloud.

"Yes, I'll send it to your handheld now. It should be relatively easy, but let me know if you have any trouble getting it situated. If Beauchamp asks, just say it's for research."

"Amazing, Oscar. I'll have to wait until everyone's gone to run it, but this is going to be incredible." Her elation briefly flipped to despair; Techs, the good she could've done with all this information, if she wasn't tasked with breaking so many laws.

It was a quick rail ride and a run through the cafeteria. Too soon, Monty was giving her a lingering kiss goodbye outside the lab. If she was honest, she really didn't want to go in and work today; she wanted to call in sick and go back home to do literally anything else. But she needed to run this program, and soon. Hunter needed her, and the crew needed her. This job would be infinitely easier than the one a few days prior.

She counted the minutes until the lab was empty, then retrieved Hunter and set everything up in the mega fab. Once they were primed and ready, she followed Oscar's instructions to load the program into the fab chamber.

She had a thought. Her brain was officially back online.

While the code loaded, she scrolled through the neurofabricator files on the chamber screen. Ayla had them meticulously organized, but the system was completely different to how Chase's brain operated. She searched through nearly every folder until finding the one she needed. The file was buried through several layers of oddly labeled sections, which seemed terribly unnecessary. But she found them.

Activation terms.

"Time to wake up," she said. Hunter's eyes opened, and they stared straight at the ceiling. "Hunter?"

A muscle twitched in their forehead. In other circles, it could be considered a sign of confusion.

"What is hunter?"

Their voice was dry and monotone, but the words came smoother than their previous session. Chase blinked. They didn't know their *name*.

"You. You are Hunter. That's what we call you."

Hunter's eyes unfocused for a second as their brain consolidated this new information.

"No other officer says Hunter."

It took Chase a second to decode that.

"Hunter, does anyone else talk to you?"

"Orders." That answer was quick, but her deciphering was not.

"You only get orders?"

"Yes."

Chase grimaced. Her colleagues truly saw them as a shell, and she didn't understand how. She cleared her throat, remembering the reason she woke them up.

"Hunter, do you remember all the procedures done on you?"

"No," they said, which was a disappointing answer. "Only orders."

Chase's disappointment redirected.

"You remember all your orders?"

"Yes."

This was, Chase felt, very important information. She just didn't know what to do with it yet.

"How far back do the orders go?"

The screen switched away from the activation terms to the archives as the neural link picked up on Hunter's thoughts. It scanned backward until settling on a date six weeks prior. The day she saw the body on the gurney.

"Tell me your past orders."

They went through a few instructions before getting to a place Chase recognized. "Copy fighters. Hold weapon. Lay supine. Go face up. Hit target. Pick up knife. Learn task. Watch video. Stand up. Sit down. Stand up. Sit down. Stand up—"

"Okay. Thank you, Hunter," she said as they listed orders from most recent to older ones. However, they didn't understand the nuance of her statement. They kept going.

"Don't go against us. Learn from this. This is what death looks like. Say goodbye to Koda Sinclair. Watch what happens—"

"Stop!" she said, her breath coming fast. Hunter's teeth clacked as they shut their mouth. "Sleep."

Hunter's eyes closed, and Chase let out a long breath.

"Was that..." Ruby trailed off. Chase had almost forgotten about the comms in her ear. They had all heard everything.

She'd solved the mystery of Koda's disappearance.

"I'm so sorry," she said. It was hard enough for her to hear. She couldn't imagine the others.

Monty cleared his throat. "Is the program working?"

Right on time, the screen dinged as the code sorted. With shaking fingers, she followed the easy swipe-through directions to pull up the scanning module.

"Yeah, it is." Her voice shook, and it took everything not to cry.

"Use it, so we can give that asshole what he deserves," he growled.

"Chase, could you give us a moment?" Ellison asked, her voice softer than Chase thought she could ever be.

"I'll turn the comms back on for you," Oscar said.

"Yeah, sure. Take all the time you need." She tapped her ear to silence it, and then it was just her and Hunter. With a sharp breath, she tapped the *start* button.

A shimmering square formed at Hunter's head, and with one more tap, it traveled down their body, analyzing every square millimeter. Chase stood back, watching as the mesmerizing lights did their work. She made herself focus on the work and not what she just heard.

There was another ding as it reached their feet, and Chase looked up to see the data. Numbers filled only half the screen. What the fuck? There should be much more data than that. She flipped through different areas of the program, eventually finding the source of the problem.

Insufficient surface area and depth allowed.

If she wanted the program to analyze Hunter's muscles and bones, then she had to show it their muscles and bones. With a sigh, she pulled her stylus from her pocket.

"I'm sorry about this, Hunter," she said, now knowing they, consciously or not, remembered things said around them. "Really sorry."

She changed the setting on her stylus, then laid down the first cut. Something in the skin made her stylus drag like cutting through gristle in a steak, but it had nothing to do with her skills. It took the highest setting allowed for her to slice through the anterior areas, exposing every muscle and joint on Hunter's front side. On a lower stylus setting, she carefully dissected the capsules around the tendons and joints, hoping the enhanced skin was the only problem.

With Hunter's insides laid bare like an expertly butchered animal, Chase sent the scanner in motion again. Looking at individual muscles was one thing; seeing them all at once was another thing entirely.

The chamber light gave a warning flash of red as her time ran low, and she tapped the snooze button in the corner of the screen. It took two more snoozes before Oscar's program finished, and this time the streams of data flew so long and varied she wasn't sure where they started or ended. She quickly compressed the file and transferred it to her handheld. Once done with that, she hovered over the notification for the program's self destruction.

The comms crackled in her ear, and Oscar's voice reached her.

"Chase? All done?" he asked thickly.

"Yes. Self destruct?"

"Go for it."

"Yes, sir." She swiped with confidence. The lines of code, so lovingly crafted through the hours of the night, unraveled and disappeared in less than a minute.

But they got the data. Data they could use to take down Beauchamp and to enact revenge for Koda. Whatever lingering doubts Chase held about her decisions burnt to ashes.

She grit her teeth and picked up her stylus. "Okay, Hunter. Let's put you back together."

CHAPTER 25

THE FAULT JOB

THE NEXT TIME Chase and Monty entered the apartment, it wasn't to cheers and celebrations. Grief hung thick in the air. She couldn't stop replaying Hunter's words, her stomach clenching every time. She didn't even know Koda and it broke her heart. How terrible did it feel to hear the orders for her murder over the comms?

Monty tossed his bag down and went to his room, slamming the door behind him. Ruby, Ellison, and Oscar all kept their eyes down, looking neither at Chase nor Monty's closed door. Drawers opened and closed with audible aggression, and a moment later he returned to the heavy silence in comfortable clothes.

"So I've got bad news and bad news." Oscar broke the tension. His hair jutted at all angles, and he had bags under his eyes. "Which do you want first?"

Chase set down her bag next to Monty's, her cortisol spiking at the words. Ruby and Ellison sat on the couch, the former with a tablet open and the latter looking angrier than usual.

"Whichever's worse," Monty said, never breaking his stride into the kitchen. Oscar looked to Chase.

"I guess I agree?" she said, wondering how he could be

thinking about the con with everything else that happened today.

"Okay." Oscar swiped his fingers across his tablet. Data covered the wall screen, the numbers sorting themselves thanks to whatever algorithm he ran. "This is the stuff you collected earlier."

"Yes." Chase didn't know if she was supposed to participate, but no one else was saying anything, and she wanted to make sure Oscar felt heard.

"This tells us the different things the structures went through from all the scars left behind. The skull was thin enough in some areas to extract some info from the brain, but it's jumbled. Everything is jumbled."

"I don't understand," Chase said. This seemed like a normal thing.

"Well, the way we extracted the data points—"

"No, I understand that part," she interrupted, her nerves making her forget her manners. "I don't understand why this is bad news."

"Oh, right, that part." Oscar ran his hand through his hair, making it stick up a different way. "You know how you said the data gets archived?"

"Yes?"

"It gets archived on the computers." He scratched the back of his head. "But Hunter records everything."

Chase felt her jaw drop as her brain light turned on.

"There is no document storage," she said. "Because Hunter stores it. And I bet it's the same with all the labs."

"Exactly." He deflated.

"So even if we have this data…"

"We have to steal Hunter." Monty finally spoke, his voice low. He crossed his arms over his chest and his eyes followed the numbers on the screen, though they likely didn't mean anything to him. "We have to steal the HNTRs from every floor. We can't take the chance of them saving anything."

"Chase." Ellison spoke like a commander. "How many HNTRs are there?"

Chase counted on her fingers. The first and second floors, with the lobby and client office, likely wouldn't have an R&D lab. After that, there were two floors each for viscerofabrication and neurofabrication, one for the torso and head, two each for lower and upper extremities, then two more for dermofabrication. Floors fourteen and fifteen were all administrative and likely wouldn't have labs.

"Eleven. From the third floor to the thirteenth." She didn't like the way the floor numbers sounded like it should be ten, and double checked her work. She arrived at the same count.

"Eleven." Ellison stood and started pacing, fiddling with a chunk of her short hair. "Eleven different floors. Eleven different shells."

"They're not just a shell," Chase said, clamping her mouth shut as soon as the words were out. All eyes snapped to her, and she rambled, "Like, they're not conscious without verbal instruction, but they talked to me. They're learning a bunch of stuff. They're not some robot made out of organic parts."

"And this is how all of them are?" Ellison asked. Her gaze burned into Chase; she was gathering information. She was planning. Chase panned the room to find various calculating looks. *All* of them were planning.

Except for her.

"I don't know," she said honestly. "My Hunter might be different. Beauchamp said they were the most advanced one."

"You haven't seen them all?"

"No, remember, I couldn't use the elevator—"

"So Koda could still be in there." Ellison clenched her fists and for a moment looked like she might punch the wall, but she hit the side of her thigh instead. "She could be on any one of those floors, if they needed a new shell."

"They didn't use real people—"

"Right, 'cause the guy who told you that is *so* reliable."

"I…" Chase fumbled for words, but Ellison had a point. How could she know Koda wasn't still in the building, reduced to a shell in a lab? She thought the men with the gurney were going to the incinerator, but she might've been wrong.

"The likelihood they would keep her around is very low," Oscar said softly.

"I don't wanna hear it, Oscar," Ellison interrupted.

Oscar's eyes shimmered behind his glasses, and Chase felt her own tears threatening at his obvious pain. "We found out what happened. We have that closure. We have to accept we're probably not going to find *her*."

"You don't know that," Ellison said through clenched teeth. Every muscle in her body tensed, and her breath came in fast, angry gasps. "I could still find her. I could still bring her home."

"It wasn't your fault." Monty stood ramrod straight, matching Ellison's posture. "Koda is gone, and it sucks, but Ell, it wasn't your fault."

"I was supposed to look out for her," Ellison said, one tear escaping and running down her cheek. "It was my job to protect her, and I failed."

"You saved her a hundred times before." Monty's voice cracked. "You can't win them all, Ell. She chose to go in alone, and she didn't make it. And that's *not your fault*."

Ellison took a shuddering breath, her jaw quivering as she tried to stuff her emotions down. Chase wanted to reach out, or at least say something, but words and actions both failed her. In the end, Ruby was the one to take Ellison's hand, the simple gesture sending Ellison's tears over the edge.

"We need to get all the HNTRs free anyway," Ruby said with a sniffle. "Whether or not Koda is there is irrelevant—for now," she added at Ellison's glare.

"Ruby's right." Monty ran his hand over his face. "We get all the HNTRs out, and if Koda's there, then we keep her. But Chase said the HNTRs are living bodies, so we have to take that into account."

Chase recalled the eerie stillness of the body on the gurney, and the limp way the arm fell. The thought of her death was terrible enough, the idea they might reanimate her body to experiment on it made Chase nauseous.

"Somehow, someway, Beauchamp's gotta pay," Ellison murmured.

"Then that's what we'll do," Oscar said. He flipped the screen again, this time to a government website which definitely looked restricted. A pale woman stared at them, her red hair tucked into a tight bun that accentuated her sharp features. "Chase, this is Agent Novak, the person you spoke to a few weeks ago."

"How do you know…you know what, never mind." Apparently, nothing on the internet could hide from Oscar.

"Agent Novak wants proof, so we're gonna get her proof," he said. "You call her again, tell her you have what she needs, and we'll go in and steal it for you. While we're there, we'll see if they have Koda. Win-win."

"Then Agent Novak finds you a new job at a company that isn't violating the Advanced Neutrality Agreement, and we disappear into the night." Ruby's gentle voice softened the blow, but it still hurt. After all this, they would leave her behind. And would Monty go with them, or stay with her? She ignored the hurt and instead focused on one of Oscar's sneakier points.

"I'm not gonna let you guys do it alone." The idea gave her just enough anger to forget the rest. "It'll be tough, going to all those floors. And the controls require the badges. And what if something goes wrong? I know the programs the best and—"

"Chase," Monty said her name so tenderly, and gently laid a hand on her shoulder. Any other time, it would be soothing, but now it made her bristle.

"No, don't do that," she said, pulling back. "I'm already elbow deep in this mess with you. I'm seeing it through."

"Do you really think you can do it?" Ellison asked.

"Remember how it felt just to steal a badge. Do you think you can handle the whole thing?"

"Yes," Chase said instantly.

Ellison's expression turned to one of pity, which was even worse than the vague annoyance. "The most important thing about running a job is knowing when *your* job is done. Too many moving parts means something is more likely to break."

Chase couldn't tell where her panic was coming from: the idea of executing this plan, or the idea that the group would leave her so easily.

"But, but..." She tried to come up with something, anything to delay it. She wasn't ready to say goodbye.

Monty took her hand again, and this time she didn't pull away. "We'll get it all figured out. We don't have to make any decisions right now. At the very least, we'll need your help for the planning."

"Uh," Ellison started, but Monty shot her a look that made her jaw snap shut.

Ruby didn't let an awkward silence set in. "Gum-Gum's right. We can't be hasty. This is something we'll have to orchestrate very carefully."

"And if we get it right," Oscar said, collapsing into the chair at his desk, "we carry on."

"Techs willing," said Ellison. She perched on the arm of the couch, her hands on her knees, and Ruby scooted to sit next to her. Monty stared at the screen, even though it was now blank. Chase was stuck trying not to think about an impending split.

"Okay," Monty said, more to himself than anyone. He looked at Oscar. "Okay, pull up the blueprints."

Ruby made eye contact with Chase and patted the seat on the couch next to her, beckoning her to join. She liked having the decision made for her and went to curl up next to her. Monty sat in the last spot, his eyes on the building schematics and one hand on his chin. The other he rested comfortably on her knee, which lessened her anxiety by about ten percent. The rest of her worried that she was helping plan her own end.

Oscar plucked the stylus from behind his ear and stood next to the blueprints, writing a large number one on the screen.

"Alright, just like we always do," he said, the air around his words heavy. Chase didn't know Koda, but she could feel her presence, like a ghost from cons past. She shivered. "We start with step one."

CHAPTER 26
THE VOTING JOB

PLANNING a heist was nothing like on the Stream. Monty didn't have a document prepared with the exact details needed to succeed, Oscar didn't hop up from his chair with perfectly applicable tech, and Ruby was not running around in a skintight black suit (yet) while Ellison wrapped her hands like a boxer. Instead, Oscar transferred the blueprints to the screen on the coffee table, and they all sat around with styluses while yelling and writing over each others' notes.

The easiest option, proposed by Ellison, was to awaken all the shells and have them walk out the door. They would need jumpsuits, but those were easy enough to obtain. Sure, it would look weird for eleven "people" to walk out without acknowledging the night staff, but they would be long gone before any police arrived. Then Chase pointed out how incredibly literal Hunter was with commands, and how it might hinder more than help them during a daring escape. And that was if the other shells could even follow commands like Hunter.

Ruby proposed the next option. A building-wide evacuation would give them the space and cover they needed to access the labs. From there, they could wake the shells, dress them, and lead them out with the crowd. Take two apiece, and it would be an easy transition. Oscar shut that one down; even without the prior issues Chase stated, Kierper had very few protocols that led to a complete evacuation. Not to mention there were eleven floors, four of them—Chase huffed at the number—and only one elevator.

Monty thought waking them was too risky. After all, they knew how Chase's Hunter operated, but the rest were baskets of unknown variables. He wanted to find a way to keep them asleep, but that would require either moving their whole tanks, or finding a way to pack and sneak eleven bodies out of the building.

"Let's look at our exit options." Monty spread the display surface with both hands to zoom in. He took his stylus and made large circles at various points, disregarding any notes he crossed out. "We have the front doors, the back service doors, and the roof. Security watches the doors, obviously, but what do we have up top?"

"Uh," Oscar quickly swiped and tapped on his tablet. When he found what he wanted, he showed it to the group. "Two patrolling guards, armed with weapons that look very deadly."

Sure enough, two people walked the roof from end to end. Even on the tiny security camera screen, Chase could tell they were large and burly, formidable even without the guns in their hands. Monty looked to Ellison, who shook her head.

"One I could take, but not two. Not with those guns." She leaned her head on her hand. "They move like Army Ground Force, and those guys are nasty."

"You can tell by the way they walk?" Chase asked.

"It's a very distinctive walk," she said, which sounded like an intriguing and terrifying story.

"So, roof is out," Monty said, running his hand over his head. "Ruby, how many security guards are in the building at a given time?"

"Thirty-eight," she answered. "Two each at the front and

back doors. Two each on floors two through fifteen, with the other six roaming."

"Don't even ask," Ellison said when Monty looked her way again. "My personal best is thirty-three, and you know that."

Chase had so many questions that had nothing to do with the heist, and she was a little mad she couldn't ask them.

"What's this down here?" Oscar asked, pointing to the basement level. The schematics didn't show a door to the outside, but it did seem to be some kind of exit.

Chase squeezed her eyes shut, thinking back to her orientation tour. She hummed, really digging deep into her memory. When they were down in the basement, it had been close to lunch, and she was more worried about food than learning about—"Some type of transport thing? But it's just for parts. I think it's some kind of delivery system." There was something else about them…

"Delivery system," Oscar repeated, standing and going to his desk. They watched as he worked on the screens, muttering to himself in Spanish. Chase met eyes with the other three separately, but they all looked as confused as she felt.

"Os? Sharing is caring," Ruby said. Oscar held up a finger, continuing his search. Monty opened his mouth, but Ruby shot him a glare to silence him. In the time it took for Oscar to work, Ellison got up and resumed pacing, Monty doodled an entire stick figure forest on a corner of the screen, and Chase got halfway through a game of Atom Squeeze on her handheld.

"Ah ha!" Oscar said, clapping his hands and knocking everyone's attention back to him. "I think I've got it."

"Thank Techs," Monty said. Oscar had a glint in his eye that matched Monty's, and Chase couldn't decide if it made her nervous or excited. Oscar swiped the screen clear and zoomed in on the basement level.

"So, Chase was mostly right." He patted his pockets down, and Ruby handed him a stylus instead of pointing out the one he held in his non-dominant hand. "This is an underground transport system, yes. It goes to the smaller Kierper sites and hospitals nationally, with the purpose to deliver all the parts they make here at the central office."

"Oh, that's not helpful." Chase was disappointed that the one piece of information she had was useless, but Oscar held up a hand.

"Wait a second," he said. He zoomed the screen out and overlaid a map, red lines zigzagging through the streets. "These are all the transport lines to the offices. There's different checkpoints along the way for technicians to check the cargo."

"So we send them on a trip and hit one of those?" Ellison asked. She continued her pacing. She'd also found a switchblade somewhere and was casually flipping it around in her hand.

"No, that's too risky." Monty shook his head, his eyes narrowed at the screen. "And we don't want to risk delaying delivery to a hospital."

"Exactly," Oscar said. He tapped the screen, highlighting a blue line. "But this one goes to an offsite incinerator."

Monty's eyes widened.

"We can delay an incinerator," he whispered.

"There would be limited personnel," Chase added, now remembering the fun fact from orientation. "It's mostly automated."

"Yes!" Oscar said. She couldn't tell if he was agreeing or inspired. "I can shut down anything that's automated, at least long enough for our getaway expert to make her move."

He gestured at Ruby, who smiled like a firecracker.

"I'll need a big truck for that." She didn't sound scared—she sounded excited.

"The elevators go down to the basement," Oscar said, bringing them back to the plans of the building and highlighting the R&D corner. "We get all the HNTRs down there, load them up, intercept, and give them to Chase to hand off to Agent Novak. Then we're home free."

"Whoa, I want to help," Chase reminded. It felt wrong to get what she needed and walk out, especially since there wasn't any mention of meeting up afterward. Oscar sounded very final when he said *free*.

"You'll be doing the important part," Ellison pointed out. She was now tossing the knife in the air, careful to catch it by the handle.

"But I can do more than that," Chase said. She turned to Monty. "I'm already here, and I know how the labs and tanks work. If something goes wrong, I can help you."

"We'll get it taken care of, don't worry about it." Monty said, using the same gentle rejection as he had the night in her apartment. It was a stupid thing to think about, but Chase's emotions ran so high, every hit felt like a heavy blow.

"It'll get done faster if I'm there," she said. "It goes from five each to three or four each."

"But you have to call Novak and take them all to her," Oscar said. "That's *your* plan."

"My plan and your plan overlap," Chase said. "Maybe I'm not as *practiced* as you all are, but I've seen enough movies to know that walking away in the middle is a bad idea."

Ellison scoffed. "The Stream is hardly accurate. Way too many people get punched in the face. You gotta punch in the throat; it's softer, and it doesn't hurt your hand."

Chase must have looked appalled, because Ruby put a hand on hers and said, "She's just getting excited about the job. She gets antsy being stuck at home."

"Look," Chase said, pulling her hand away. "I know I might be a—a *liability*, but I'm gonna stay until you get away safely anyways. You might as well let me help."

Thunk. Ellison's knife stuck in the wall, buried to the hilt.

"Fuck it," she said. "Vote."

"Hold on now—" Monty said, but Ellison waved him off.

"No, I'm done holding on. Chase is a liability, yeah, but she's right about the other stuff too. We're currently short a set of hands, and she's proven hers as capable enough."

Chase, shocked by Ellison of all people sticking up for her, lost her words. Monty clenched his jaw, staring daggers at the woman.

"Five minutes ago, you were telling Chase her part was done," he pointed.

"Yeah, and five minutes later, I realized that she fills in every gap in our knowledge. Plus, she can move the shells. She does it every day." Ellison's argument made sense, and Chase could tell Monty didn't like that.

"It's not safe for her—"

"Vote." Ellison said it again, raising one hand. "All in favor of enacting Plan G?"

"Yeah," Oscar said, also raising his hand.

"Yep," Ruby said, thrusting her hand up with a little more flair.

"Honestly, I think this should be at least Plan M—"

"Chase?" Ellison cut Monty off. Chase took a sharp breath.

"Um, sure?" She raised her hand for good measure. Ellison nodded.

"Good. All in favor of a guest player on the team?" she said, keeping her hand up. Chase felt more confident raising her hand this time.

Monty shoved his hands in his pockets, and Oscar curled into himself slightly before raising his hand. Monty blinked, apparently surprised by the gesture. Ruby sighed, which stole his attention. His jaw dropped as she, too, raised her hand.

"Sorry, Gum-Gum," she said. "Ell's right, we need another set of hands."

Monty rolled his eyes. "Turncoats, the lot of you."

"I can do it—" Chase tried to say.

"I know you can do it," Monty said. "I'm not worried about your capability. The risk is just too high. We could get hurt, or caught, and I don't want you to live with that forever. Because if we get caught, it's jail. For life. And if you got hurt…"

He ran his hand over his face and looked away. Affection for him burned in Chase's stomach, but it didn't outweigh her desire to help. Her mind raced for something, anything, that might change his mind.

"Then I don't specify to Novak how many I'm bringing," Chase said. "The longer the job takes, the more likely we are to get caught. If it gets too hairy, then we cut our losses early. Some shells are better than no shells."

Monty met her eyes, holding them with a stern stare. With all the confidence she could muster, she looked back, waiting for him to break first. This was, without a doubt, the scariest thing she'd ever done in her life. But if it took down Beauchamp and got Ruby, Oscar, Ellison, and Monty complete closure over their friend, then it was worth it.

"You're sure about this?" he asked. For a moment, everything else in the room faded, and it was just the two of them. She nodded.

"I've got you."

A muscle in his jaw fluttered as he clenched his teeth.

"Alright then," he said, swiping the table so the image went up on the wall screen. "Let's run through it again, with all the details. Then it's on to Plan H."

Chase thought she would feel scared, or regret the decision immediately, but the cool assurance of being right settled over her.

She sat through the rest of the planning, making it all the way to Plan N before she started dozing off, her head—well, her entire body really—resting against Monty. He woke her somewhere around Plan T and offered to walk her back to her apartment. It was late, and she leaned against him the whole way, soaking up his warmth.

"Do you wanna come in for a minute?" she asked once they reached her door. Monty paused and looked back at the elevator, then sighed heavily and nodded.

"Yeah, I do," he said, and followed her in. She didn't grab any wine this time, instead pulling him in for a tight hug as soon as the door closed. He stiffened at first, then sank into the embrace, his face buried into her neck and his arms coming around her. She trailed her hand up and down his spine in a soothing motion, her heart breaking at what he must be feeling.

"I'm sorry about Koda," she whispered. He inhaled sharply, then let out a shuddering breath as he gripped the back of her shirt tightly. For a long time they stood there, holding on for dear life, until Monty calmed enough to pull back. He put his hands on her cheeks and his dark brown eyes roamed her face, as if he were memorizing every part of it.

"You're sure you want in on this?" he asked. She nodded.

"I understand where you're coming from. And I appreciate the concern, I really do," she said, running her thumb over part of his trapezius. "But if I can, I want to help. I *have* to see this through."

He nodded, as if her words had finally sunk in. "And after?" he asked.

Her heart jumped as he voiced the question that had been running around her mind for the past few hours.

"Well, you tell me," she whispered. "I'm hoping to keep working, but I know…they're your family. I understand if you want to go with them."

"And if I stayed?" He rested his forehead against hers, and she closed her eyes as their breaths mingled.

"Well, my life has been a lot more fun since you came into it," she said. "Unorthodox, maybe, but fun."

His smile was small, but genuine, and he leaned forward to capture her lips in a kiss. She welcomed the contact readily. But just when she was thinking she didn't need sleep after all, he broke the kiss and stepped back.

"Sorry," he said in response to the expression on her face. "Now's just…"

Chase shook her head and willed her body to dampen its response. "No, I get it," she said, taking a couple of gulping breaths. It had been a difficult night, and the last thing they needed was to rush things when emotions were so muddy. She laid a hand against his sternum and counted ten heartbeats before asking, "Do you want to stay tonight?"

He made an incredulous expression, and she rushed to explain. "Not like that, I swear. Just if you didn't want to be alone."

The pause hung between them, and she felt like she could track Monty's thoughts through his dark eyes. Then, his whole body sagged.

"I'd like that, yeah," he said. "Thank you."

There was no ceremony involved as they performed bare minimum hygiene tasks before crawling into her bed. The air conditioning kept the apartment too cold. But despite that, and the current situation, wrapped in Monty's arms, Chase felt warm, and comfortable, and safe.

They were going to get through this. Together.

CHAPTER 27

THE THINKING JOB

CHASE WANTED to know how many heists in the making happened right in front of her.

The first step after finalizing the plans was to walk the important areas, take note of weak points in security, and make sure their favorite plan could work. She assumed most of this would be done by the professionals, but was surprised when, two days later, Monty gave her a special job.

"You need to check out the basement," he said quietly as he walked her to the lab. He held her hand, the pressure steady and comforting.

"Got it." They were at the door now, and she saw him make a conscious effort to slow down and relax his grip. She assumed she'd get, at most, a brief peck goodbye, but Monty surprised her by wrapping her in an embrace.

"Please be careful," he said. Her breath caught in her chest, and she swallowed.

"I will, it'll be okay," she said. "I'm a professional now, remember?"

"You're only professional if you get paid," he said. She furrowed her brows and leaned back, supported by his hands on her spine.

"Wait, how is all this getting funded?" she asked, earning a laugh.

"That's the funny part. Technically Kierper employs four out of the five of us."

"Playing the system!" Ellison exclaimed on comms. Chase snorted.

"Might as well, they're playing everyone else," she said. She leaned into Monty and held him tight. He smiled and leaned down to give her the tender kiss she wanted.

"I'll see you at lunch," he said, reluctantly untangling. Chase made a show of taking a deep breath and steeling her resolve, then swiped her badge for the door.

She entered the lab with zero fanfare and started designing a completely normal experiment, like she wasn't trying to help steal everything from the largest body company in the world.

Speaking of which, she opened her tablet and scrolled through the lists of limb assemblies. When she found what she was looking for, she tapped her comms on.

"Oscar, are there any bugs in here recording?" she asked. There might not be any cameras, but with how easily they installed bugs in her apartment without her notice, she wanted to check the lab again.

"Wait a minute," he said. She got up and went to the materials room with a list, gathering what she needed for her next fabrication. "No, you're clear. What is it?"

"Okay, good." She returned to her desk, and once certain the door was closed, said, "Oscar, you're pretty good at hacking, right?"

"I'm going to pretend you didn't ask it like that," he said. "What do you need?"

"There's a client from a few weeks ago, he's in the military," she started. "They ordered a whole new leg for him so he can return to active duty, but he wants to retire."

"Name?" Oscar said, so fast she hesitated.

"Oh, uh, Jamie. James. Reynolds." she stuttered. She swallowed down the guilt that it took her this long to think of him.

"Got it. Oh, Army. Nice." He hummed to himself as he did his work, the sound oddly comforting to Chase. "Aw, they updated their security measures. How cute."

"Can you still hack it?"

"Chase, please, you're going to hurt my feelings," he said. "I already did, and found Reynolds' file. Oh wow, he was Ground Forces."

"Like the guys on the roof?"

"Yep. Means they're about to owe him a lot of money," Ellison chimed in. Chase held her breath as Oscar worked, her hands frozen over her tablet. Minutes trickled by like hours, long enough that she actually started to relax when he made a triumphant noise.

"All set, and he gets to move back home."

"Really? That easy?"

"Seriously, that's strike three."

Chase cringed, glad Oscar couldn't see her face.

"I'm sorry, you're amazing. You're a genius. I don't know what I'd do without you."

"Thank you."

"Watch it," Monty cut in. Chase smiled to herself.

"Still no need to be jealous," she said. "Just giving Oscar his credit."

"Thank you. Can I get back to my actual work now?"

"Working the security desk?" Monty asked.

"Don't be ridiculous." A click signified Oscar going offline.

"You gonna get to work now?" The smile in Monty's voice might be imaginary, but she held onto it.

"I guess so," she said. This time there were no goodbyes, just the clicks of the comms going off, with a special gagging noise from Ellison.

With Ayla and the rest of the group in the cube room

distracted by their real jobs, she was free to take part in her second—and arguably, more important—job.

Chase tapped Hunter's tube, saying hello, then swiped her badge at the elevator door. The elevator came when called, and she braced herself for the judgmental AI running it. Time to go on an adventure.

Chase swiped her badge, then said aloud, "Basement level."

She expected the automated voice to go back on its word and prevent her from going. To her surprise, the doors closed and the elevator descended. She tapped her comms again and pinged the group.

"What's up?" Monty was the first to respond.

"The elevator is going down," she said.

"Okay, Oscar will track you." He was all business now, which Chase appreciated. It made it easier for her to focus.

"Alright, I've located you. You're a couple floors away," Oscar said. "It should dump you out in a hallway."

He was right. She stepped out into a narrow corridor devoid of both people and decorative flair—likely a spot that didn't get much traffic. Something squealed in her ear, sending a line of pain to her retro-orbital area. She dropped to one knee, holding the side of her head and trying to regain a sense of up and down.

"Sorry, sorry!" Oscar's voice was the first thing she heard once the feedback stopped. "I changed the frequency, you should be good now."

"Holy shit," she said, trying to catch her breath. Now Monty's reaction back in her apartment all those weeks ago made sense. How had he acted so calm when, after dealing with interference herself, she couldn't see out of her right eye?

"Don't say anything, Chase." Ellison was back on the comms. "Heading your direction, let Oscar clear the area."

"I'm okay," she whispered, as if that would help. She hoped it sounded like she was just talking to herself. "I'm okay."

"There are cameras for sure," Oscar said. "Still checking on audio capabilities."

"You good?" Monty asked.

"Mhmm," Chase hummed. She stuffed her hands in her pockets and slinked down the corridor.

"Stay still." Ellison again. Chase made a noise that dictated *no*. "Chase—"

"She's doing her part, like you wanted," Monty reminded her. Ellison growled.

"I'm on my way. You know, doing *my* part."

"Chase, do you see the transport area? Cough if so." Ruby kept her on task. It was nice, really, since she recently lost every last thought in her brain. She stayed silent—there was nothing around her except for white walls, and a turn at the end of the hallway.

It would've been a quick trip if every step didn't feel like her last. Equipment buzzed somewhere in the background, and she occasionally heard the clunk-and-whoosh associated with rail travel. Otherwise, there were no signs of life in the area.

Oscar cleared his throat. "You can pick up the pace. You look a little suspicious going that slow."

Unable to voice her dissent, Chase merely glared at the nearest camera and made a show of walking faster. Since she wasn't able to talk, she couldn't tell them how creepy it was down here, how she had no clue what to expect, and how she totally regretted coming down here by herself.

The turn at the end led to yet another hallway, this one lined with doors and terminating with a double set. The bright red paint practically shouted that unauthorized personnel (like Chase) should stay out. She tried the handle of the first door, inching it open, afraid to find some lab tech at a desk behind it. Instead, she found stairs.

Good to know.

She tried the other doors as she passed, most of them locked. The only open one housed cleaning products with odd labels. These were not for everyday spills, and she didn't want to find out how powerful they were.

"Your audio is clear, it's just visuals," Oscar said.

"Thank Techs," she said, letting out a loud breath.

"Whoa, you may not be alone," Ellison said. "Oscar, visual on the transport?"

"Nothing, the cameras stop here."

"Chase, can you go through those doors at the end?" Ruby asked.

She must be looking at the blueprint. Chase walked up to the doors and held her breath. Even without a badge scan, they slid open to reveal the rail track and loading dock.

"Found it," she said.

"Perfect," Ruby said. "Okay, you can head back up now."

"Oh, thank you," she said, making a quick turn and striding back.

"Tell me when you're clear," Ellison added. Chase nodded, realizing too late that no one could see her except Oscar. She glanced at another camera, but he was kindly silent. The elevator gave her no grief, and she collapsed against its wall as it traveled back up to her floor.

"Clear," she said.

"That's my girl," Ruby said.

"We'll make a respectable criminal out of you yet," Ellison said.

"She stole Beauchamp's badge. She's a seasoned criminal now," Oscar chimed in.

"I said *respectable*, not seasoned."

"Guys, can we just—?" Monty cut in, and Chase could practically hear his hand gesture.

"Maybe one day I can take the stylus guides off," Chase said. Silence.

"I don't get it, but I'll assume it was funny," Ellison said. A bold assumption, if Chase was being honest, but she appreciated it nonetheless.

The elevator jerked to a stop, making a noise so loud Chase assumed an explosion would follow. Instead, the overhead lights turned red, and the automated voice instructed her to stay calm.

"Again?" she said. She slid down the wall until she sat on the floor and took deep, steadying breaths.

"You okay?" Ruby asked.

"Yeah, the stupid elevator just got stuck and I'm trying not to freak out," she said.

"Guys, could you give us a second?" Monty asked. Nervousness settled into Chase's gut; what did he want to talk about that he didn't want the others to hear?

The others voiced their agreement, and one by one they clicked off the comms until it was just her and Monty.

"You okay?" he asked softly.

"What, you didn't like that Ruby asked first?" she teased with false bravado.

"Just wanted to make sure you gave an honest answer and didn't try to be tough."

Damn, so he saw right through her. That was annoying.

"I'm okay," she said honestly. Neither good nor bad, just okay. "Are you still mad that the others voted me onto the team?"

He gave a dry laugh. "I'm not mad. Obviously, I like working with you, even if it's on...a different kind of project."

The nerves changed to butterflies. "Yeah?"

"Yeah." He took a deep breath. "I'm sorry for being overprotective."

"That's okay, it's nice to feel cared for," she said. "And I know it can't be easy, given the things you've seen."

"You've got that right. But be honest, are you doing this because you feel pressured to?"

"Not at all," she said. "I'm doing this because I want to."

He paused for a long moment, long enough for the elevator to come back online and continue the ascent.

"Well, as long as you want it, I'm glad you're here," he said.

Good thing he didn't have access to the cameras, because in that moment, her smile was absolutely goofy.

"Glad to be here. But now I'm back at the lab," she said as the elevator slowed. "Keep me updated?"

"Always."

She tapped off the comms and exited the elevator. A few steady breaths calmed her nerves enough to keep going, the silence of the lab welcoming.

"Where were you?" Ayla's voice nearly split Chase's chest in half.

"Huh? What?" she floundered, hand going to her heart. Ayla didn't repeat the question, she just stared from the doorway to Hunter's room. Chase gulped and said, "I, uh, just wanted a change of scenery, but didn't wanna switch my jumpsuit," she said, hoping that was a good excuse.

"Oh, the basement? It's a good thinking spot," Ayla agreed, which nearly knocked Chase off her feet.

"Uh, yeah, it was," Chase said. Something felt wrong, but she had no indications of what it might be.

Ayla shrugged, turning away with a flick of her gray ponytail and going to Hunter's tube. Chase, confused and exhausted from the morning's events, decided that her best choice at the moment was to do her actual job. After all, every plan counted on her working in R&D.

Chase focused on her new materials and the construction of a set of biceps. Hunter's legs needed a break, and she didn't want to waste resources building such large muscles when she had other, smaller options. Ayla claimed Hunter first, getting right to work as the rest of the lab trickled in from lunch. If the visual from the mega fab was anything to go on, Hunter's mastery of instructions was improving at alarming rates. Ayla now gave multi-step commands, and as the session progressed, Hunter required fewer and fewer corrections.

Hunter was learning to *think*.

Chase knew this was a big deal because she wasn't the only one taking notice of it. Divya and Epley stopped what they were doing to watch, and Jun got up to stare from his doorway. Chase waited for the dramatic response, but instead the color drained from his face, and he returned to his desk with uncharacteristic slowness.

Hunter stood in the mega fab, their arms by their sides and their expression blank. Beside them was a table with chamber fabricated weapons: a pistol, a few knives, a sword, and a baton. Ayla, wrapped in a blanket and repeatedly snoozing the timer alarms, called up three human-shaped structures in the ether to surround Hunter.

"Eliminate the targets." Ayla enunciated extra clearly for her audience. She swiped her tablet, and red bullseyes appeared on the foreheads of the pretend people. Hunter straightened, their eyes focusing on each of the targets in turn.

The first one stepped forward before Hunter had time to grab a weapon. It lifted one arm, winding up a punch. Chase nearly cried out, but Hunter easily dodged the attack, the figment losing balance like a real human would. Without hesitation, Hunter grabbed the baton from the table and swung it with extraordinary force. Chase expected the baton to phase through, but it cracked into the head like a car crashing into a wall, cratering half the skull. The figment flickered and faded.

The other two moved in tandem, the responses clearly programmed to work in sync. They danced better than any partnership as they sent fists and feet toward Hunter. Hunter dodged some of the attacks, but deep *thuds* shook the glass chamber walls when the pretend fighters landed hits on their torso and ribs. Hunter fought with practiced precision, reaching back to grab a knife so they had a weapon in each hand. Something mimicking blood squirted onto their face and forearms as they used the blade, each hand almost working independently against the two opponents.

All three moved at a speed reminiscent of martial arts films, and Chase realized she'd seen this fight before, at least on the side of the fighters. It was from a popular action franchise, the big climax where the hero and villain fought together for the fate of the world. Each move was so sharp it felt choreographed, but the way Hunter's eyes flicked back and forth suggested this was all new to them.

Hunter couldn't just think. Hunter could react, could problem solve, and do so in stressful conditions.

They sank the knife into the neck of one figment, and muscles and tendons stretched before tearing as Hunter dragged it out the front of its throat. With their other hand, they grabbed the wrist of the figment as it swung it toward them, stopping it with ease despite holding the baton. With a twist and a crack, the figment's forearm snapped and its body pitched forward, convulsing once as Hunter drove the knife into the base of its neck.

The figment hit the ground with a smack before the chamber disintegrated it, and Hunter returned to their original position. The blood glittered before blipping away a drop at a time, leaving them fresh faced and clean. The only difference was the rise and fall of their chest as they caught their breath from the exercise. Ayla looked back like she knew they were watching the whole time, flashing them all a smirk.

Divya was the first to look away, one hand on her chest and the other on her stomach. She glanced between Chase and Epley, but couldn't find any words. Instead, she shook her head, dropped her gaze, and left the cube room in a hurry. Epley followed her lead and took one step back, then another, keeping his eyes on Hunter until he was out the door. Chase was the last to look away, but instead of feeling fear or sickness, she held on to her determination.

This was why she needed to follow through with the plan; soldiers like this would be devastating. And all the scientists were stuck, forced to go down with this ship. Chase wondered if they now felt the ramifications of their actions the way she had a few weeks prior.

A pale-faced Jun left soon after, and none of them returned that afternoon. A primordial part of Chase's brain also wanted to escape after the display, but she forced herself to finish building the biceps. Unwilling to do any experiments in view of Ayla, Chase waited until she left for the day before going to Hunter's room. The muscle test was more or less an excuse to check on them, and make sure whatever Ayla had them do didn't hurt them somehow. Hunter had layers upon layers of injuries and repairs, and she was glad they couldn't perceive pain. Not yet, at least.

"Hey there, gorgeous," Chase said once the door closed behind her. "You put on quite the show earlier. Who knew you were such a badass?"

Hunter did not respond.

"It sounds like you've been advancing fast, that's pretty impressive. I don't think they give your neural tissue enough credit." She lifted her badge over the display, but stopped before scanning it.

Hunter *moved*.

Like the first time, Chase assumed it was a trick of the light. But she stopped and stared at Hunter's face, waiting until her eyes burned before blinking.

Then, it happened again.

It was barely a movement, just a brief twitch of the eyebrows. Chase stepped to the middle of the glass, trying to see as much of Hunter's face as possible. Their eyebrows pinched again, and she could see now that every once in a while, the masseters fluttered in their jaw. Were they clenching their teeth?

She looked for further physical signs. With them submerged in the preservative fluid, they didn't have a respiration rate to check, but now she could see the forefinger and thumb of their right hand shifting in an almost rhythmic manner. At first Chase thought it might be a pill-rolling movement and burned at the idea that Ayla would shut down part of the brain stem, but upon further inspection she found the movement didn't match.

Another thought hit her.

She scanned her badge again and pulled up Hunter's electroencephalography scans. Their heart rate was elevated, as was their blood pressure, and the normally steady brainwaves were bouncing erratically. Chase put a hand to her mouth, her eyes watching the quick rise and fall of the waves.

Hunter was *dreaming*.

Dreaming meant consciousness.

Hunter wasn't a shell. Hunter was *alive*.

"Holy shit," Chase whispered. Then, a little louder, "Holy *shit*."

The thrill of victory was fleeting compared to the crushing realization that now Hunter could not only remember the experiments, but could relive them in their dreams. Increased heart rate meant they also experienced an emotional response. Was it fear? Dread? Were they starting to understand the pain?

She tapped her comms on with a shaking hand. "Monty?" Her voice was barely above a whisper, and she cleared her throat to try again. "Monty, you on?"

"What is it? You okay?" he asked.

"Yeah, I'm okay, it's just–" She paused to consider her words. "Hunter is dreaming."

"Hunter, the so-called shell Hunter?" he asked.

"That's the one."

"The one they said had no brain function?" He sounded as astounded as she felt.

"Yep, that Hunter."

"Holy shit."

"I agree." Chase's vision swam, Hunter's face blurring as nausea crept up her throat. "I think I need to lie down."

"Stay there, Ell can come get you—"

"No, she doesn't need to do that," she said, the fear of inconveniencing Ellison enough to clear her vision. "I'll just…go back to my desk and keep working."

"Come down to the front, it's a good enough time to leave," he said. Again, Chase nodded even though he couldn't see her.

"That's probably a better idea," she admitted. Hunter went still, their heart rate and brain activity back at baseline. The dream was over. She tapped her comms off and put her hand on the glass.

"I'm gonna get you out of here. I promise."

CHAPTER 28
THE MEMORY JOB

CHASE UNDERESTIMATED HOW hard it would be to keep working on Hunter like nothing was wrong.

She still took them out of their room and into the mega fab, but any time she went to cut them open, her hand shook so hard the stylus didn't work properly. In the end, she alternated between creating a muscle in the lab and pretending to test it, all the while counting down the days until she could gather all the HNTRs and escape.

"Do we really have to wait another week?" she asked Monty, picking at a loose thread on the elbow of his jumpsuit as the elevator descended.

"We have some prep work to iron out," he said. He put his hand over hers; she liked to think it was a comforting gesture, but it was likely to stop the obnoxious tick. "Just keep doing what you're doing, we're in the home stretch now."

"You said that last week."

He winced. "Yeah, well, it's a long stretch."

She glared out of the corner of her eye, and he pulled her a little closer, squeezing her hand to his side. At first she let her arm extend, maintaining the space between them, but in the end she gave in and leaned in. He knew better, obviously. She just wasn't used to someone else being the professional in the conversation.

"But everyone else is doing okay too? They have their back up plans and all?"

"Oh, that's the easy part," he said. "In Plan Z, Ellison punches our way out of the situation and we scatter."

Punch and scatter? "That sounds terrifying."

"Oh, it's a terrible plan. That's why it's the last one."

They arrived at the bottom floor and joined the line to pass the security checkpoint. Everyone else seemed exhausted by the long workday, but Chase's skin buzzed. Every time she left, she felt like she was running from some invisible force. If she didn't have Monty there holding her down, she might've floated away, riding on sheer anxiety. His eyes casually roamed the area while she kept her gaze on the ground—they would look suspicious if she also looked around. But that gave her a lot of room to think.

"Are you still thinking about maybe continuing fabrication?" she asked.

Monty's eyes returned to hers, and he raised an eyebrow.

"Not in like a weird, clingy way." She unraveled from his hold and held up her hands. "I'm just saying, there's options. For you and everyone else. If you—all of you wanted."

"Oh, we're invited?" Ruby asked over comms. Her voice made Chase jump.

One corner of Monty's mouth quirked. "You still okay with me thinking about staying in fabrication?"

She nodded, but before she could reply, Ellison cut her off.

"I'm not doing an office job," she said.

"I always thought you'd make a wonderful personal trainer," Ruby said.

"You can get into race car driving, Ruby," Monty said.

"And the tech world always needs geniuses to advance things," Chase added for Oscar.

"Society isn't ready for my ideas," Oscar replied.

Monty huffed a laugh. "You guys should think about it. Changing careers could be a good move. A fresh start."

Chase took his hand and interlaced their fingers. Even if nothing ever came of this budding relationship besides this perfectly executed heist and a few fun nights, he deserved to follow his dreams. Hell, it sounded like all of them had dreams —they just needed the right push to go after them.

Monty turned off his comms, then reached up to tap hers off, too.

"You serious?" he asked.

"Absolutely," she replied.

He gave her a big, toothy grin. "Then I just might."

Her heart swelled for him, and for the others back at the apartment. This crew, through thick and thin and grief and success, survived this long thanks to their reliance on each other. And maybe, after next week, they could put this tumultuous life behind them. She grabbed the front of his t-shirt and pulled him in for a gentle kiss.

"Alspeth!"

Chase jumped away from Monty and turned. Dr. Beauchamp stalked toward them. Monty straightened and positioned himself slightly in front of her.

"Move," Beauchamp said, glaring at him. "This doesn't concern you."

"You talk to my girl like that, I'd say it does concern me."

If Chase weren't frozen in terror, she might've dwelled a little longer on the phrase *my girl*.

"Unless you do her work for her, then it doesn't." He rounded his scowl on her. "Get back in the lab."

"It's the end of my workday—"

"No, it's the end of your work *life*."

The words hit Chase like a ton of bricks. This was it. He'd found out about the heist, and the crew, and he was going to kill her for it.

"What?"

"I'm kicking you out of R&D 'cause you can't do shit," he said. "Get back up in the lab, clean up your mess, and then meet me in my office. You're *done*."

Chase gaped and turned to Monty, but he looked just as perplexed as she felt. This couldn't be happening.

"Please, sir." Her ears pulsed and she willed herself not to vomit all over him. "Please, give me another chance. Just another week."

One more week, and they could steal the HNTRs and get them to safety. They were close, so close, and now Beauchamp would stop them before they even had a chance to try.

"I've given you weeks of chances," he said. "Your colleagues said you haven't done a proper test recently, anyway. Let's go."

He grabbed her arm in a vise-like grip and ripped her out of the security line, dragging her to the elevators. Monty made to follow them, but Beauchamp nodded at two security guards. She watched over her shoulder as the men took Monty by his upper arms and held him in place, even going so far as to draw the batons from their holsters.

Chase shook her head wildly, which caused her to lose balance. Beauchamp kept her upright enough, and she could see the pain and anger in Monty's face as the distance between them increased. At least he listened to her silent plea and stopped fighting the security guards. They kept their hands on him, even as the elevator doors closed behind her.

Beauchamp chuckled once they were alone. "You really thought you were gonna get away with it, huh?"

Her blood turned to ice. "What?" There was no way to turn her comms back on without him noticing, no way for the others to hear her or what was happening.

"Your stupid ploy to fix yourself," he said. The ice thawed, marginally. "Coast by in R&D for a while, build up your credits, replace everything and then quit. Bet you were gonna try and call DIA on me too. You're not the first one with the plan, Alspeth. Just the dumbest one to try and execute it."

Well, he was partially correct. In her pocket, her handheld buzzed, but his glare stopped her from grabbing it.

"No comeback?" he continued. "That's a shame. You've been so mouthy this entire time, and now, when it matters most, you've got nothing. Hmm."

"Is there anything I could say that would work?" she asked through gritted teeth. Could she easily turn her comms back on? No, Beauchamp had all his attention on her.

"To change my mind? Oh, no, not at all," he said. "But it's amusing to watch people grovel, so you understand my disappointment."

"Keep that in your own room, not mine."

"There she is," he said with a grin.

The elevator stopped on the ninth floor. It was unnecessary for Beauchamp to keep his hold on her now, but he did so anyway, either as a power play or because he enjoyed inflicting pain. More than anything, it kept her from getting her handheld out of her pocket, though it kept buzzing incessantly. Chase followed along willingly; if this was her last chance to see Hunter before the night of their plan, she would make it count. She could answer the crew's call from the safety of the lab.

Beauchamp wrenched her bag from her and left it outside the lab in an effort to speed up the decontamination protocols. For good measure, he dug her handheld from her pocket and tossed it away. She'd never been more grateful for the comms unit in her ear.

The door to her cube slid open, and he shoved her toward it. There were no lights in the other workstations, and he all but threw her into the mega fab.

"Leave perfect, original muscles for your successor. I don't want them to do extra work 'cause of your ineptitude."

He smacked the button to slide open the door and made a quick exit. Chase took three steps toward it, but it slid closed even faster, a heavy deadbolt sounding from the wall. Her heart leapt into her throat; she was locked in, except for the elevator in the back room. More than likely, that was shut down too.

This was fine. She could handle this. They would simply have to redesign plans N through T. Surely the crew had broken into countless labs before without an inside man. What was it they always said? Start with step one.

She tapped her comms on as she crossed into Hunter's room.

"Hey," she said, as if to the so-called shell. Her comms exploded with voices.

"Are you okay?" Monty's voice rose above the rest.

"I'm okay. Oscar?" She tried to limit her words as much as possible, just in case Beauchamp was keeping tabs.

"Gimme a minute."

The tube drained with its usual gurgles, and the cacophony of voices joined in with the thuds and squeaks of the gurney.

"Techs, he was so aggressive," Ruby seethed.

"Need me to bust you out?" Ellison asked.

"We'll take care of it, hon, don't worry." Ruby again, her voice back to calm and controlled.

Unable to respond, Chase only smiled and returned to the mega fab, Hunter in tow. She could use this time to prep them for departure, all the stuff she'd been planning to do over the next few days. It wouldn't mean altering their chamber, or their room, or even their path to the elevator.

If Chase wanted Agent Novak to see everything, to understand exactly what Beauchamp was after, then they needed to be in pristinely fit condition, super strength intact. Sure, she had all her data as backup, but the DIA didn't want data. They wanted physical proof. Her one extra Newton of force needed to carry them through the finish line now.

"Chase?" Oscar's voice made the rest of them pause, the silence thick. Even her hands stopped as she tapped on her tablet. "You gotta stay nonverbal. There's bugs everywhere, and no way for me to block them."

Chase sighed. "Okay." Beauchamp would think she was just talking to herself, or to Hunter.

She recreated the parameters for the extra strong muscles, plus their regenerative capabilities. If she was lucky, Beauchamp wouldn't check her work, and would assume she put the normal, baseline muscles in.

"We're still here with you, okay?" Ruby's soothing tones helped calm her racing heart.

"We're figuring stuff out. You focus on doing your thing and dealing with Beauchamp." Oscar sounded very focused, and Chase pressed her lips together, trying to contain her emotions.

"We got you."

Monty's words sparked an extra wave of feelings, none of which she wanted to examine at the moment. They were right; if she didn't finish this, then nothing else would matter. She had her job, the crew had theirs.

Her job required tedious precision and next level focus as she strung up biceps and obliques and quadriceps and gastrocnemii. One at a time, her mini chamber assembled new muscles, all based on her plans. This would be her last work on Hunter, and she would make it her best.

"I'm sorry," she said as the chamber raised them from the table, speaking to both Hunter and the crew. Her stylus was set to cut through the skin, but she froze. Hunter wasn't dreaming then, but it was too easy to recall their face. They could feel pain, even if they didn't know the name of it.

"This'll be the last time, I promise," she whispered. With the words hanging between them, she cut, and even Ellison stayed quiet.

One by one, Chase removed the baseline muscles and replaced them with the experimental ones, doing her work significantly more efficiently than usual. The only thing she spent extra time on was the foot intrinsics, which many fabricators forgot about. But she wanted Hunter to have that increased stability.

The chamber gave her multiple warnings about her time, but she swiped them all away, her sheer gumption (and a pair of gloves) keeping her warm enough to work. Just one more minute, one more muscle, one more way to show Kierper's crimes once she got Hunter out.

It was likely a useless endeavor, part of her realized that. Next week, when they came and stole Hunter away, they would have whatever mess of muscles the new myofabricator would give them. But she would install as many as she could. Perhaps enough of them would remain to convince Novak of the danger.

When she had no more excuses to stay, she loaded Hunter up into their tube and replaced them in their room. Her heart ached and angry tears burned, but she blinked them away. Once she started crying, there was no way she would stop, and she refused to let Beauchamp see her cry.

While riding the elevator to his office, she was sorely tempted to instead go downstairs and leave. But what good would it do her? Beauchamp would track her down again. It seemed to move faster than usual, or maybe Chase only perceived it that way due to her overwhelming dread.

The elevator opened to the same long hallway with the same manual doors. The only difference was the dramatically dim lights. Chase rolled her eyes at Beauchamp's cringey performance and used the ire to fuel her as she pushed through the last door.

Darkness blanketed the whole office, save for a desk lamp casting light onto Beauchamp as he sat. The shadows caught every line and dimple in his face that dermofabrication couldn't correct. Chase could see every one of his hundred and fifty years of age. The light turned the shelves of curiosities into vague nightmare shapes. Were those eyes following her? Seemed likely.

Beauchamp probably wanted to scare her. Chase decided to be pissed instead.

"Forget to pay the electricity bill?" she asked.

Beauchamp scoffed. "You're such a disrespectful brat, you know that?"

"Learned it from my boss."

"You better watch it, Alspeth," Beauchamp threatened.

"Seriously, Chase," Monty said in her ear. "Something's wrong."

"Or what?" Chase ignored the advice. "You're already firing me. I suppose this is my exit interview?"

Someone coughed behind her, and Chase whirled around to stare into the darkness. She couldn't tell if the sound was from one of the jars on the shelf, or from someone hiding back there.

"Exit interview?" Beauchamp stole her attention back. "Oh, no, Alspeth. This is me gloating."

"Why waste the energy?" she asked, though a vein of unease cut through her false confidence.

"Chase." Ellison's warning carried a little more weight to it, and Chase wished she could take the words back.

"I mean," she started, "you've gotten what you wanted. I'll keep my mouth shut about what projects are going on in the lab. I'll join some small start up in the middle of nowhere. I screwed up, I get it."

"You really think I'm going to let you leave and carry on somewhere else?" He laughed, and though it was maniacal and way overdone, it still forced fear into Chase's bones. "Alspeth, when I say you're done, you're *done*."

"What?" It sounded too definitive.

"Fired and forgotten," Beauchamp said. Behind her, she heard the rustling of fabric and the soft sound of boots on carpet. Two security guards appeared from the dark, their eyes blank as they grabbed her arms.

"Wha-what? Let me go." Panic choked her, and she struggled against their unrelenting grip.

"Chase? What's happening?" Oscar asked.

"We're on our way," Monty added.

"No, no," Chase said, both to her friends and to the guards.

She turned back to Beauchamp and pleaded, "I promise, I won't say anything. Please don't kill me."

"Kill you? That's way too much to explain. I only reserve that for special cases. But you? You've got too many ties out there," Beauchamp said. "It'll be easy to explain to your family how a workplace incident gave you a change of heart, and now you just want to stay home with them. In fact, you won't be able to think of anything else you'd rather do but sit with your family for the rest of your life."

"What are you going to do to me?" One of the guards produced a hypodermic needle and sank it into her shoulder, the injected liquid burning all the way down her arm and up her neck.

"You aren't going to tell anyone about the things in R&D because you're not going to remember them. You're not going to remember what you've seen, or the skills you developed, or what a fabricator even does."

The world went fuzzy and the room began to spin. The shadows on Beauchamp's face made his grin stretch and distort. The last thing she heard before unconsciousness claimed her was his bitter, pompous voice.

"You're not going to remember this life at all."

CHAPTER 29
THE KNIGHT IN SHINING ARMOR JOB

CHASE WASN'T sure if she was out for minutes, hours, or days. All she knew was that waking up meant *pain*.

Her skull could burst from the pounding within it, the pressure so intense even tears couldn't escape. Every gasp sent a wave through her ribs and spine. Pain said she was alive, but it also asked, "at what cost?"

She made a brave attempt to raise her limbs, but they moved like lead and felt twice as heavy. When she was courageous enough to open an eye, she found herself strapped to a gurney. It was just like the one that transported Koda, only this time, the restraints were in place. Panic built behind her gut, but the more she tried to move, the more she hurt. The pain swallowed her voice before she could cry out.

"Chase?" The voice sounded far away. Monty? She tried to turn her head to look for him, but the muscles seized up and sent a shock down her neck. All she could do in response was whimper. "Hey, hang tight, we're gonna find you, okay? We got you."

"Chase." Ellison's bark sent another pierce through her skull. "I need you to look around and tell me what you see."

She moved her head again, and the same pain gripped her

and threw spots into her vision. A cry might've escaped her, because a second later she came back to Monty chastising.

"She's clearly hurting, she can't look around and tell you where she is."

"It was worth a try." Ellison switched tactics. "Okay, Chase. Give me one sound for yes, and two sounds for no. Is that possible right now?"

Chase took a deep breath and forced out a bit of her voice, just enough to make noise. If Ellison needed her to be louder, Chase would probably pass out from the effort.

"Atta girl!"

"You're doing great, Chase," Ruby said. "Keep holding on, we'll find you."

"I'm searching for you right now," Oscar added. "We'll get you out, don't worry."

"Okay Chase, I've got another question," Ellison said. "Breathe for a second and listen. Do you hear anything, like another person?"

Chase took a few shaky breaths, and the pain improved enough for her to see the ceiling clearly. A few more breaths, and the blood stopped rushing through her ears.

"Uh uh," she said with gargantuan effort. Sandpaper coated her lungs and throat, each breath passing through like shards of glass.

"That's excellent news," Ellison said.

"Beauchamp's office is on the fourteenth floor, I'm almost there," Monty said.

"You're doing great, hon," Ruby reminded her.

"Shit, I can't get a lock on her comms. Something's blocking me."

Tears leaked out of Chase's eyes, which didn't help the pain or the pressure in her head. What if they got caught trying to save her? Then they'd all be subjected to this—or something worse.

"No," she gasped out. "Stay."

"Like hell," Monty said.

"That's some bullshit right there," Ellison added.

Chase tried again. "Not safe."

"Don't waste your energy arguing," Ellison said. "We're coming for you, end of story."

"I'm on fourteen," Monty said. "Hang tight, Chase."

"Okay," she said, tears starting fresh. Her breaths threatened to turn into sobs, but she held herself together, if only to mitigate the pain. She didn't want to think about the danger her friends—Techs, they were such good friends—were in by coming to save her. Or what might happen to her if they didn't.

The door slammed open and Chase's heart rose. Monty was here to save her, but how did he find her so fast?

It was not Monty who walked through the door. Instead, Beauchamp strolled in, and Ayla followed behind.

"Ah, shit, you're awake," Beauchamp said. "I was hoping I wouldn't have to deal with you conscious again."

Chase hoped the adrenaline would burn away enough of her pain so she could spit on him, but apparently she couldn't have everything she wanted.

"Is that—" Monty was cut off by Ellison's instruction.

"Double time, Monty!"

"Ew, it's her." Ayla sighed. "I thought this was an emergency. You couldn't just sedate her until tomorrow?"

Beauchamp checked his watch, already bored with the situation. "That would waste resources. Plus, I've got a dinner to get to, and you know how I feel about alibis."

"Never good enough to share them," Ayla muttered. Chase tried to speak, but the words caught in her throat. Ayla ignored her, instead grabbing a tablet and a stylus from a nearby desk. They weren't in a fab chamber; white tiles covered the walls and floor, and various surgical equipment accompanied the styluses. This wasn't the lab. This was a patient suite.

Patient suites were on the second floor, lightyears away from

Monty and Ellison on fourteen. There was no way they'd get here in time.

"Well Alspeth, it's been anything but a pleasure," Beauchamp said. He smacked her leg, sending another shock of pain through her. He turned to Ayla. "You know the drill."

"Wait until you're off campus. This isn't the first time, Emile." She rolled her eyes, clearly annoyed. If she disliked him so much, why would she do something like this for him? Chase decided to ask.

"Why?" She could only make one word out at a time, and with Ayla there, she couldn't explain her location to Monty and Ellison. But if they didn't know, then they couldn't get caught trying to save her. She wouldn't mind losing her memory if they got out safe.

"Why what?" Ayla asked. "Why do this? Kid, when you've been in the game as long as I have, you learn it's about protecting your assets. No one else is gonna do it for you."

Chase furrowed her brows, but couldn't verbalize the question. Ellison was right, she needed to save what little energy she could, just in case. Luckily, Ayla could read between the lines.

"Let's just say I'm one of Kierper's longest running employees," she said with a smile.

Perhaps everyone from the Last Generation had their minds a little skewed. Living that long had to change them in some way or another.

"Fuck," Monty said in her ear. Her tears began anew. "Ell, eyes on Chase?"

"Shit! No!"

"Where are we?" Chase choked out.

"The client floor. Obviously," Ayla said, not bothering to look up from her handheld.

"The client floor?" Ellison asked.

"That's the second floor," Monty said.

"Chase, baby, you're amazing," Ruby added.

A sob escaped, and despite the pain, Chase leaned into it.

Relief and fear mingled in her chest cavity, and all she could do was cry about it.

"Oh, shut up," Ayla groaned. "It's not that bad. It won't even hurt…I don't think."

"There's easier ways," Chase said. She had to keep Ayla talking, distract her long enough for Monty to find her.

"What, like an NDA? Those don't mean anything anymore." She checked her watch and sighed. "I swear, this is the longest ten minutes of my life."

"How many times have you done this?" Her body finally came back enough for her to form real sentences, though anxiety replaced every bit of pain that disappeared.

"I don't keep count, it's unimportant," Ayla said. "You know, usually there's a lot more begging. People aren't usually this chatty."

Chase sighed. "Well, can't delay the inevitable."

"Damn straight you can't," Monty said.

Chase let the silence drag and counted the seconds as they passed. She only had a vague estimation of Beauchamp's exit time, but if she counted right, she had two more minutes.

Ayla sighed. "Finally, Jesus. Let's get started."

Well, she counted wrong.

"What exactly are you gonna do?" Chase asked, her voice an octave higher than usual. There was no keeping her cool now, just desperation for distraction.

"Like you give a shit," Ayla said. "Or would even understand. Just shut up and relax, otherwise it's gonna give both of us issues."

"Keep her talking, Chase," Monty said.

"I'm almost to two. Monty, meet us there," Ellison said.

"Got it."

"I mean, if this is the last thing I get to learn before you take it all out, it's worth a try," Chase said. The argument didn't make sense, and she scrambled for a better one. "I just wanna know. Like a last meal situation."

"Yeah, no, not worth the energy." Ayla placed her tablet on a stand, then took her stylus and dragged it across Chase's forehead. Chase tried to move out of the way and screw up the results, but the restraints held her tight. At least it didn't hurt to move anymore.

"You don't have to do this," she tried instead.

"They say that every time," Ayla said. The tablet dinged as the data arrived. "Hah, and here I thought your skull might be empty inside."

"Do you say *that* every time?" Now was not the time to antagonize, but Chase was out of options.

"Absolutely. The best part about taking peoples' memories is I get to make the same stupid jokes over and over." Ayla didn't rise to the bait. Instead, she traced the different lobes of Chase's brain, the stylus catching and pulling on her curls.

Monty or Ellison had to be close by now, right? Surely this wasn't how things ended for her?

"How do you take out just the Kierper memories?" It was a stalling tactic, yes, but also a curiosity question. They could take her out of the lab and strap her down to a table, but...

"Just the Kierper memories? Oh, no, we don't have time for that." Ayla tapped her stylus. "We're just gonna take the past five years and patch it with a little change of heart program."

"What?" Chase froze. She thought they'd be more selective. "Five years? You're gonna take five years?"

"It's quick and easy. You won't feel a thing. Well, you won't feel *much*."

Chase couldn't catch her breath. "Ayla, c'mon, we're colleagues—"

"Oh, save it. No one before you has changed my mind, and no one after will either."

"Just listen for a second—"

"Hold still." As if Chase had a choice.

"Keep her talking, Chase." Ellison repeated.

"I'm trying." Stealth no longer mattered.

"Well the restraints make it pretty easy," Ayla said. "Here we go."

"Fuck!" Chase said.

"Shit!" Ellison said in her ear.

It started as a tickle on her scalp. Then the sensation dripped into her brain like an egg sliding between the lobes. Her vision blurred, and she thought about her first day at Kierper. There were all those videos, with that stupid voice, the one that…how did it sound again?

The door slammed open, and Ellison barreled into the room. Ayla looked up just in time to get tackled onto the floor, her head hitting the tile with a loud crack. Chase strained against the ties on the gurney until she could see Ellison out of the corner of her eye. The other woman moved with expert precision and placed the dazed Ayla in a chokehold.

"No! Don't kill her!" Chase said. Ayla struggled, her delicate hands clawing at Ellison's thick forearm.

"She was literally about to take your memory and toss you on the street," Ellison said. Ayla continued to scramble, kicking her legs and slapping at every part of Ellison she could reach. Ellison didn't notice.

"She doesn't deserve to die, though," Chase said. Ellison sighed.

"Ugh, fine. If you say so." She pulled a syringe from her pocket and stabbed it into Ayla's thigh. A moment later, Ayla went limp, her eyes glassy and her head lolling to the side.

"That was an option the entire time, and you were just gonna kill her?" Chase asked.

"My job is neutralizing threats, don't judge me," Ellison said. She tossed Ayla to the side, not caring that she landed in a terribly uncomfortable position. "She'll be out for a while, though. Technically, I was only supposed to give her half the dose."

"Thank Techs you're okay." Monty skidded through the open door, his eyes wide and sweat beading on his forehead. He went to Chase and put his hands on her cheeks. "You're okay, right?"

"I'm okay," Chase said as her eyes watered for the hundredth time that night. "I can't remember half of my first day, but I'm okay."

Monty let out a heavy breath. "Better than losing it all. Let's get you out of here."

He undid the restraints around her head and shoulders while Ellison went for the ones on her legs. It wasn't until the pressure released that she realized how tight they'd been. Blood rushed through her limbs and her pressure tanked. When Monty and Ellison helped her to the side of the gurney, her head swam and black clouded the edges of her vision.

"Catch her—" Ellison grabbed her shoulders and Monty took her head, keeping her upright until the world stopped floating and she could see straight again.

"Holy shit," she said.

"Hang on, I got something for that." Ellison rummaged through her pocket and brought out an identical syringe to the one she used earlier.

"Are you sure that's the right one?" Chase asked. Ellison looked offended.

"I'm gonna pretend you didn't ask me that." She sank the syringe into Chase's thigh with slightly more finesse than earlier, the warmth spreading until it hit her heart, and then her head.

"Holy *shit*." She felt more alive than she ever had in her entire life. With this stuff, she could take on Kierper, and Beauchamp. Hell, she could take on the *world*.

"The crash is gonna suck in a few hours, but we'll have you long gone and asleep in another city by then," Ellison said. They helped Chase to her feet; not even her stupid left knee hurt thanks to the magic of Ellison's pocket injection.

"Gone? No, we have to figure out something new for next week since I won't have badge privileges." She wouldn't even have building privileges, but that was implied.

"Leave that to us. You need to go back to the apartment and pack," Monty said.

"I left snacks for you!" Ruby said.

"Left snacks—wait, what are you guys gonna do?" She didn't understand why she was going back alone, why they wouldn't join her. If she was leaving, they were all leaving, right?

"We'll do what we do best," Ellison said. "We'll steal the HNTRs and meet up with you tomorrow. Just at a different rendezvous point."

"No, we voted, I get to be part of the con," Chase argued.

"That was before Beauchamp tried to have your memory erased." Monty used that stupid fucking rejection voice again. "You need to get to a safe house. You'll find directions to it at the apartment. And you need to call Agent Novak, so she knows where and when to meet you."

"But my memory wasn't erased," Chase said. "I still have it. I still remember the plan. Please, I feel fine, I—I want to see this through. I *have* to."

"Chase, he tried to take everything away from you," Monty said, and she could see his patience wearing thin.

"Exactly! And now I want to take it from him!"

He groaned and pinched the bridge of his nose. "We don't have time to argue."

"Then don't argue," she said. "We practiced. We planned. I'm ready."

"Vote again. I say she stays," Ellison said. Based on her stance, it was less about the plan and more about impatience.

"Me too," Oscar added.

"Me three," Ruby said.

"Me four," Chase said, for good measure.

Monty clenched his jaw. "The danger is way higher now, higher than if we'd done it at the original time."

"It's worth it." Chase stood her ground. "If it saves Hunter and shuts down this operation, then it's worth it."

He sighed and got his handheld from his pocket. A number waited for her on the screen.

"Fine, then it's time to call Agent Novak."

Chase took the handheld and perched on the edge of the gurney. Adrenaline and whatever concoction Ellison gave her buzzed in her veins, making her finger shake as she hovered over the call button.

"Can't Ellison just pretend to be me?" she asked.

"Absolutely not, my voice is way too deep to pass for you," Ellison said, pitching her voice lower just to make a point. Monty gave her an encouraging nod, but his expression was more serious than she'd ever seen it.

"Now's not the time to lose that confidence," he said. "You almost got your brain cut up. This is just telling the truth to someone. That's easy."

"And you've got support," Ruby said through the comms. Monty had a stern expression, but she must've looked terrified, because he relaxed and gave her a soft grin that weakened her knees for reasons other than botched surgical experiments.

"Don't fuck up," Ellison said. Chase wondered if she was so blunt to counteract her sharp weapons.

"Got it," she said, taking a deep breath. "Here I go."

Before she could think too much about it, she swiped the screen of the handheld and initiated the call. She held it to her ear, her heart beating in time with the ring.

Click. "Hello." It wasn't a question, or a greeting.

"Hi, uh, hello," Chase said, bringing her voice back down from the stratosphere. "Agent Novak?"

Silence.

"How did you get this number?"

Chase didn't have an answer for that.

"Uh," she dragged the syllable out, her mind blank.

Right.

"My name is Chase—Dr. Chase Alspeth, I work at Kierper?"

It wasn't supposed to be a question, but she made it one. "We talked a while ago about some stuff that's going on?"

More silence.

"About what's in research and development. There's been a… development." She winced.

"You didn't tell me your name last time. Verify it."

Chase told her the full thing, including both middle names.

"And your employee ID number?"

She said that too.

A rustle.

Another click.

"Okay, Dr. Alspeth," Agent Novak said. "If you remember, I'm not interested in hearsay. We need physical proof, and data corroborated by a third party."

Chase swallowed, her mouth suddenly dry and the words stuck in her throat. This was supposed to be the *easy* part of the plan.

"Dr. Alspeth? Are you still there?"

"What? Yes, sorry, I'm here." She shook her head, hoping to knock the words out of the cobwebs. Monty mouthed the word *protection*. "But, um, if I share proof, you can protect me, right? Like, I mean, I think Beauchamp has killed people before for letting information out and I just—they actually tried to wipe my memories, and I just want to do my job, I don't want to—"

"I can protect you, Dr. Alspeth," Agent Novak interrupted. "And we'll discuss the details of that once you get the proof to me."

"He's making empty soldiers," Chase said, going against everything she thought about Hunter. "He wants us to find ways to make bodies armored and stronger, but there's no consciousness, they just take instructions without questioning them."

"I don't have time for games, Dr. Alspeth."

"I can bring you the shells," she said. A pang went through her chest; she didn't want to offer up Hunter like a sacrificial lamb, but the DIA would take care of them… Right?

"When? Do you have them now?" Her volume rose, and Chase flinched.

"No, I couldn't risk taking them from the lab until I spoke to you first."

Agent Novak huffed. "When can you get it, then?"

"Tonight. I can bring them to you by…" She pulled the handheld away from her face and checked the time. "Tomorrow morning?"

"What time?"

"Time?" She looked to Ellison, who held up six fingers. "Uh, six. There's a park that's like, two blocks south of the building. We can meet there."

"Do you have any other evidence?"

Chase wracked her brain. "I have raw data that shows all the tests done on the shell?"

"Send it to me," she said.

"Oh, uh, okay." Chase paused and patted her pockets. No handheld in sight. "I can't right now, but I can give it to you later?"

"Fine. Six o'clock, Boltray Park," Agent Novak said.

"You're sure you can protect me, right? Afterwards? I mean, I'll need a new job, and safety, and help for my dads and friends…" she asked again. The thing about scientists was they liked repeated results, and Chase wanted the promise repeated over and over before she went through with it.

"It's well within my capabilities to protect you, Dr. Alspeth." she said in a clipped tone. Chase was probably annoying her. She didn't care.

"Okay, thank you," she said. "I'll see you in the morning."

Agent Novak didn't say anything further. The line went dead and Chase let out a long breath.

"Holy shit," she said, tossing the handheld onto the gurney and resting her head in her hands.

"You did perfect," Oscar said.

"A star!" Ruby said.

"For real, you did great." Monty rested his hand on her knee.

Chase blocked out whatever he said next and focused on breathing. The call with Agent Novak made this hypothetical plan into something very, very real. They were going through with this. *She* was going through with this.

"You sure you're in?" Monty asked quietly.

"You really think we can pull this off?" she asked.

"No room for doubt right now," Ellison said.

Chase nodded. "We get this done. Then we deal with what comes next."

"'Next?'" Monty smiled when he said it. Her heart stuttered, but she held his gaze.

"I figure you're stuck with me for at least a little while after this," she said. She had a knack for spotting potential. "Maybe longer, if you want."

"Oh, I think I want," he said.

"Fucking hell," Ellison muttered.

"Hello? Can we focus, please?" Oscar said, getting their attention. "We've got three people, one elevator, and eleven floors to deal with here. It's going to get complicated."

"We're ready, Oscar," Chase said.

She heard Oscar clap over the comms. "Alright, let's steal some shells."

CHAPTER 30

THE PLAN G JOB, PT. 1

ELLISON LED them back to the security office and produced a bag from behind the last desk. After a bit of rummaging, she tossed black clothing to Chase and Monty, then left like she was late for an appointment. Chase thought it was a little heavy-handed to wear the black short-sleeved shirt and fitted pants, but once she started moving, she found they made her feel a little more badass. In the office, Oscar typed away, pausing only to lean over and tap his comms on, signaling for the rest to follow. They listened to a series of clicks as Oscar's scanner searched various frequencies to find the safest one.

"Check?" he said. He handed badges and a few USB drives to both Chase and Monty, and she stuffed them in her pocket.

"Two." Ellison, first. She sounded strained, and her word was followed by a yelp and a thud.

"Three." Monty said, apparently unconcerned.

"Four," Chase said, when Monty looked at her.

"Five." Ruby, last, a song in the word.

"Okay, one is in place," Oscar said. "Two?"

Ellison grunted, and a thud echoed through the comms. "Stay down. Uh, two getting in place."

"Good. Three, four?"

"Three, and four, out the door," Monty said. Any other day, the rhyme would amuse her, but right now Chase was too focused on following him and remembering to breathe. He took them to the front elevator, and the doors opened as soon as he waved his badge in front of the button. They piled in, the movement so weirdly normal Chase almost laughed.

"Five is ready to fly." Ruby sounded so excited, it helped Chase feel a touch better.

Monty held the door open, putting the empty lobby on display. "Last chance to bail," he said. He looked so serious it made her gulp, her mouth suddenly dry.

"No, I'm in," she said. "I've gotta get Hunter out and stop Beauchamp."

He smiled and let the doors close. It all felt way too calm, like Chase hadn't nearly died earlier and there wasn't an entire heist going on.

"Alright, then let's do this. Third floor."

The artificial voice repeated his instruction, and the elevator shook into motion.

"Are we focused?" said Ellison. "Security is out like a light, and I have a new personal best."

"Did you knock them all out?" Chase asked, appalled. The brain injuries from losing consciousness were very expensive to fix in the lab, and she doubted the security guards earned as much company credit as the fabricators. There was no way Ellison had that many syringes.

"What? No, we just gave them sleepytime tea. What kind of girl do you think I am?"

"Sleepytime tea means the drugs, doesn't it?" Chase whispered to Monty. He nodded. Perhaps she *did* have that many syringes.

"I heard that."

"Love, perhaps now isn't the time," Ruby said, her voice slightly strained. Something crashed from her comms, making Chase and Monty flinch. "I'm okay, just the garage door. I'm about fifteen minutes away from being on the road. Have you all started yet?"

"Game time starts now," Ellison said. The elevator doors kicked open on the third floor, giving them the odd sensation of hearing her voice aloud and through the comms. Monty held the door open, but neither of them disembarked, and Ellison stayed where she was in the hallway. She wore her olive green jumpsuit, but there were rips up and down the legs to allow access to her weapons, and she had the sleeves tied around her waist to show off the ones decorating her torso. She looked ready for battle.

"I feel underdressed," Chase remarked.

"I tried to give you some of these, but *no*, Monty said that was a 'safety hazard,'" Ellison said, rolling her eyes.

"It's enough of a safety hazard for you to have them, let alone anyone else," Monty said. It was nice of him to be inclusive and encouraging, but Chase knew for a fact he also had at least one knife tucked in his boot and one pistol somewhere on his person.

"Whatever, I know how to use these. But this special one is for you." She took a baton with a belt clip and gave it to Chase. Next, she retrieved a blank badge out of her pocket and waved it enticingly. "You ready?"

"Fourth floor," Monty said, his mouth half-cocked in a grin. He pulled his hand back and the elevator doors closed slowly, giving them just enough time to see Ellison flick her hand in a half-assed salute.

On comms, she said, "Two, three, and four on the move."

"You feel okay?" Monty asked. Chase took a second to check in; there was still a ghost of a headache lingering around her occipital lobe, but other than that, Ellison's drugs worked wonders.

"I'm good." The elevator stopped. "Damn, it's really time, huh?" she said, her heart rate kicking up again. She couldn't tell if she wanted to be sick or to pass out.

"It really is," Monty said. "You know the plan, and how it's all gonna go down. Slow and steady, okay?"

"Yeah, okay," she said. He stepped out of the open doors and she stayed behind, though everything in her screamed to call him back. "Slow and steady."

"And don't lose your shit," he said, pointing for emphasis.

"Wouldn't dream of it," Chase said, lying.

The doors closed on his smile, and the silence of the elevator pressed down on her. This was insane, this was the worst idea she ever had. But it was too late to back out. And if she was honest, she didn't want to.

"Oh, right," she muttered. She called to the elevator, "Fifth floor."

"Two is clear, three can move in." Oscar called it in.

This was a test, she reminded herself. Another test she studied for, another defense of her dissertation. It just required a little more physical activity.

The doors opened and she moved into the hallway. She didn't know what she expected, but it surprised her to find it shaped exactly like the ninth floor. Made sense; it was cheaper to mass produce things, like floor plans and fabrication chambers and unconscious superhuman shells.

She checked her watch, then increased her speed. She had less than a minute until Oscar would scrub Monty's badge use from the system. Not for the first time, she chastised herself for not taking more time to exercise, especially when she thought about the others listening to her huff and puff on the comms.

"Three is clear, four can move in." Oscar made the call as soon as she rounded the corner to the R&D wing. She took a deep breath and retrieved the modified badge from her pocket. If Ellison's and Monty's worked, then hers should work too.

She held her breath and flashed it in front of the sensor.

Green.

The outer door slid open, welcoming her into a clone of the ninth floor's decontamination chamber. Her heart was in her throat as she braced herself for alarms, but the door shut behind her and initiated the sequence without complaint. She followed the directions as if it was any other morning, placing all her items on the floor and waiting for the protocol to finish.

With a hiss, the inner door opened, the familiar, sterile scent of the lab greeting her. It was unnerving how utterly normal it all felt, despite the very abnormal circumstances.

Signs of life lay scattered across the lab desks, with pictures and tablets and an empty mug decorating the cube rooms. Her muscle memory dictated she go into the locker room, change into her jumpsuit, and go to her desk. She squashed the thought down before it could take root; she had a different job tonight.

One at a time, she went to each desk and plugged in Oscar's USB drives. The screens flashed and lines of code ran across them as Oscar's hack went into effect, finding, saving, then deleting any data that had to do with the fifth floor HNTR's genetic code. They were going to take the shells, but they were also going to make sure no one could make more. At least, no more with these genetics. Hopefully Agent Novak would take care of any future ones.

Once she gathered the USB drives, Chase scanned into the back room. She didn't expect this floor's HNTR to be the same as hers, since Beauchamp mentioned different labs had different projects, but she did assume HNTR 5 would at least be human shaped.

That, apparently, was a bold assumption.

At first glance, HNTR 5 was normal, albeit missing most of the muscle bulk. Instead, that energy went to the freakishly long fingers. They floated in the preservation liquid like claws, the tips of them genetically altered to be pointed. Chase wanted to think it was just the nails, but when she got closer, she realized the claws were, in fact, the distal phalanges. The toes were shaped the same way, bending at painful angles against the rim of the cylinder.

Her stomach rolled, and this time she couldn't stop herself from getting sick.

HNTR 5 slept away as Chase wiped her mouth with the back of her hand. It clearly wasn't the same level as her Hunter, with no signs of dreams, or even active brain waves. With the right treatment, it might wake up one day. She was glad no one conscious was there to witness her moment of weakness.

"Yours looks freaky too?" Ellison's voice sent another cramp of nausea through Chase's stomach. "I thought you said these were relatively normal?"

"Every floor is doing something different," she said. "You scared the living shit out of me."

"No way I'm scarier than these fuckers. Get moving, Alspeth."

Every once in a while, Chase appreciated Ellison's bluntness. Now was one of those times.

She scanned her badge, set the module to transport mode, and counted down from one hundred as the cylinder inched its way into a gurney. It was much heavier with the preservation liquid inside, and this time she couldn't hide her grunts as she pulled it to the elevator.

Every time she asked her badge to do its job, she held her breath until it carried it out. With a few pivots and more than a few curses, she maneuvered the gurney into the elevator, accidentally trapping herself in the corner. She awkwardly reached across the tube, waving the badge back and forth in hopes the sensor could sense it. It wasn't until she was all the way up on her toes and leaning on the tube that it finally beeped.

"Basement," she gasped, sliding back down. She was up close and personal with the talon toes now, and all she could hope was that the myofabricator on the fifth floor didn't care much about foot intrinsics.

The elevator stopped and the doors opened. Chase breathed a sigh of relief when she spotted Monty and Ellison on the other side.

"Ah, you did the same thing I did," Monty said. He grabbed one end of the gurney and pulled it to a better angle. Together, they pushed it out into the hallway.

"And he was stuck with a tiny one," Ellison said. Her lip curled as she took in Chase's new friend. "Ew, this one really is fucked up."

Ellison took the front end, showing off her own borderline super strength as they easily picked up speed. Chase thought they might tip as they rounded the corner to the back door, but miraculously, most of the wheels stayed in contact with the floor.

"A tiny one?" Chase asked.

"Yeah, and I got stuck with a big one," Ellison said.

"Luck of the draw," Monty said. As they neared, the doors to the transport line swung in. The platform was much wider than Chase expected, the footprint almost the same size as the entire R&D lab upstairs. Based on the way the first two fit on the far side, there would be more than enough space. There was no rail car present, but the tracks hummed with electromagnetic energy, ready to engage when Oscar gave the command.

As they said, a small shell occupied the first tank. Standing, it might come up to Chase's shoulder. The other one was well over seven feet tall. Ellison looked small next to it, though Chase wasn't surprised she was able to handle it on her own. They slotted the third one into the line, readying them to move to the transport at the right time. With the three unfamiliar, misshapen shells in front of her, Chase understood how most of her colleagues forgot these expressions of genes should actually be people.

"Okay, these are terrifying," Ellison deadpanned. Her fingers flexed toward her weapons, but she didn't grab them. "Let's go for round two before we all get taken out by the heebie jeebies."

Three down, eight to go.

CHAPTER 31
THE PLAN G JOB, PT. 2

A SUCCESSFUL FIRST round increased everyone's confidence. Chase dropped Ellison and Monty at the sixth and seventh floors, and when the elevator doors closed on them, she didn't feel a completely bone-shattering sense of fear. Improvement!

A sense of déjà vu washed over her as she walked past the desks. The beauty of the work stations wasn't near as impressive now. They hummed with the low sound of stand-by, an identical frequency to the other levels. Same shit, different floor.

"Three, you're a go." Oscar's voice was no longer a surprise, but a comfort. If two and three were a go, then her turn was on the horizon. She rounded the corner and reached the R&D wing in record time, waiting outside the decontamination chamber for her starting gun.

"Four, you're a go."

Chase scanned her badge, a smaller wave of relief washing over her when the light turned green and the door slid open. She followed the same steps as before, a little easier than the first time, and found HNTR 8.

Apparently the dermofabricator decided they only needed to do half their work before the end of the day, as poor HNTR 8 was missing half its skin. Knotted, sinewy muscle roped its way over the bones, the white outline of said bones poking through the purple deoxygenated fibers.

"Fucking amateurs," Chase muttered. She hadn't let bone peek out since her first semester of graduate school. And this clown act was able to get a position here at Kierper? In R&D? *Before her*? Ridiculous.

She swiped the badge and set the tube for transport, this time more prepared to heave the gurney across the lab to the elevator. Remembering past mistakes, she angled the gurney just right and pushed from the back end, creating a nice little pocket for herself at the front of the elevator. With instructions to descend, the elevator pitched toward the basement, taking Chase and her loot with it.

She stood with her back to the shell and tried in vain to stamp down the itching discomfort of having it behind her. Beauchamp said her Hunter was the most advanced shell, and Ayla acted like she was the first one to get them to respond to verbal commands. Logically, Chase had nothing to fear from this mass of human tissue behind her. It didn't even have a face, though the unseeing eyes made it worse. Any time she turned, she felt the blank stare right at the small of her back, and fought the chills stirring in the same spot.

"Almost there, almost there, almost there," she muttered, watching the floors count down as they flew to the basement.

The elevator clunked and stopped. The red lights came on.

"Oh, you have got to be kidding me," she growled.

A gurgle sounded and she spun around, grabbing her baton. But HNTR 8 stayed asleep, a large bubble now resting at the top of the tube.

"Son of a bitch." She put her hand over her eyes and breathed. Was tonight over yet?

"You good?" Ellison's voice cut through her panic.

"Chase, you alright?" Monty's tenderness followed.

"Fine, I'm fine guys," she said. "Just got a little freaked out."

"Techs, story of the night," Ellison agreed.

"Just a second, I've almost… There you go," Oscar said. The elevator resurrected and continued on its trip. Why would it stop now, of all times?

Monty and Ellison waited for her in the basement, and once again helped her roll the cylinder to the platform. The area was quickly filling, each of their little experiments waiting for their turn on the rail. It was, without a doubt, the most fucked up thing Chase had ever seen.

"Okay, we're two thirds of the way there," Ellison said, clapping her hands together and rubbing them. "Any issues so far?"

"Nope," Monty said, looking to Chase.

"None," she squeaked. She cleared her throat and tried again. "Uh, I mean, no, no problems."

"Okay, so we're in the second to last round now. Os, how's everyone looking?"

"Security is still snoozing, and the transport car is primed and ready to go. Take a little extra time on this one while I situate the cars. I'll send the rail as soon as Ell is on the way down with her last package."

"Ruby?" Monty asked, his gaze going to the middle distance as he listened to the comms.

"The big house is en route," Ruby said. "ETA forty-two minutes."

"Good. Keep going," Oscar said.

"Ready, break." Ellison clapped, heading back to the outer elevators. Two stops left. Maybe this heist thing wasn't so hard after all.

"Don't say it," Monty murmured, taking her hand.

"Don't say what?" she asked.

"Your face looked too relaxed. Don't say whatever you were thinking, it'll jinx us," he said. She pinched her brows together.

"What? I was just thinking—"

"Shh, shh, shh." Ellison put her whole hand over Chase's mouth. "Did you not just hear Monty?"

Chase pried herself free from Ellison's grasp. "Really? 'Jinx'? I didn't take you for the superstitious type."

"Look, any con can only succeed if you have a healthy sprinkling of luck," Monty said, doing the hand gesture for good measure.

"Do *not* fuck with Lady Luck," Ellison said. The elevator door opened, and she walked backward out of it. "She is a jealous, jealous mistress."

"That's ridi—"

"See you at home base!" she said, turning on her heel and throwing a wave over her shoulder. The doors closed behind her, and Monty called for the next floor.

"You ready for this last part?" he asked.

"Huh? Yeah, this is the easy bit," she said. He flinched at the word *easy*, and she chose not to comment on it. "Send HNTR 12 down to you, go get my Hunter, go meet Novak."

"And meet up after."

"And meet up after," she said with a smile.

"Just a reminder, we can all hear you," Ellison said. She grunted, her last shell heavier than the others. She added, "Oh, ew," and Chase didn't know if it applied to the shell or the conversation.

"Noted," Monty said through gritted teeth. The elevator doors opened and he held a hand in front of them, keeping his eyes on Chase as he stepped out. "Stick to the plan."

"Yes, sir," she said with a salute. He bit his lip and Chase held completely still, hoping that he understood what she wanted. Sure enough, he stepped back in and pressed a nearly silent kiss to her lips.

"Still heard it," Ellison said.

"Ell, darling, let them be," Ruby said. "We all know how a job can cause a rush of hormones and adrenaline—"

"Ew, stop," Oscar said. "I can't vomit on these screens, it'll ruin everything."

"I make bodies for a living, and even I don't want to hear it," Chase added.

"Finally! Someone's on my side," Oscar said.

"Hey! I was always on your side," Monty said with fake hurt.

"I wasn't," Ellison said.

"That's 'cause you're biased," Oscar growled.

"Friends, let's bring the focus back." They could all hear the laughter in Ruby's voice. Was it always like this? As the con neared the end, could they let go, just a little bit? It was nice, seeing people have fun while they worked.

"Three, you can go, if anyone cares," Oscar muttered.

"Thanks," Monty said. "Home stretch."

"It's a long stretch," Ruby reminded them.

The elevator dropped Chase on the twelfth floor. Oddly enough, this floor had a different layout than the previous ones. More space sat between each station and the chambers were bigger, allowing for the dermofabricators to stretch the sheets of skin long and wide. She didn't remember much from her dermo units, but she did remember it was better to have a continuous piece.

She shivered at the memory of laying a sheet of skin over a muscled body, and the chamber vacuum sealing it.

Gross.

"Four?" Oscar asked.

"Yes?"

"You're good whenever. I'll keep an eye on you until you get your Hunter, okay?"

"Thanks Oscar, you're the best."

"I know."

Chase weaved through the oddly placed desks into the R&D corner, swiping her badge and smiling at the little green light. Just a few tiny steps stood between her and freedom, and Hunter's too.

The lights came on extra fast and the chambers hummed to life, which made her a little salty. Why was the twelfth floor lab so important that they got special treatment? She assumed Beauchamp played favorites, but this was ridiculous.

Oh well. In a few short hours, she wouldn't have to deal with Beauchamp or his weird rules or war crimes ever again.

She checked her watch; right on time. As long as HNTR 12 wasn't obscenely heavy, she could get it to the elevator and skip down to the ninth floor with some time to spare. She geared herself up for one last bout of exercise, and this time the little green light from the badge sensor didn't surprise her at all.

Beauchamp sitting on a desk did, though.

"Alspeth?" he asked. He sounded confused, and a little surprised. A slow grin spread across his face. "Well, I'll be damned. I did *not* count on you being a part of this stupid attempt. Hell, you were supposed to have soup for brains by now."

"What—what the—" Chase couldn't breathe. Ice replaced her blood, freezing over her heart and lungs.

"Wha-wha-wha—oh, come on, apparently you're a hardened criminal. You can stop the whole deer-in-the-headlights thing," he said. He swung his legs casually, not a care in the world. "I knew something was off about you. Thought it was just your penchant for being obnoxious. I sniffed the other one out pretty quick, but you—damn, you really know how to fly under the radar."

"I don't understand," she said. Surely, she'd lost consciousness somewhere along the way and this was all a dream.

"Chase?" Monty's voice came over the comms. "Chase, is everything okay?"

"No," she said, the word leaving her in a rush. Beauchamp cocked his head to the side.

"Oh!" He tapped his ear. "Not me, huh? Is that your friends? They must be the ones who stopped Ayla from finishing her job. Huh, guess the old girl had to fail at some point."

"Chase, hold tight, I'm coming to you," Ellison said.

"No!" she said, a little more emphatic this time. This was the *last* place Ellison needed to be.

"Where are they?" he asked, tilting his head to the side. He picked up his tablet, feigning surprise. "Oh, wait, I can just look at the cameras. I always forget about those. It's more fun to watch the infrared dots on the blueprint. Reminds me of an old video game."

"What?" Chase's stomach crawled up her esophagus. He was watching them the whole time, letting them move the shells? What kind of game was he playing?

He swiped across the screen. "Ah, it seems one little rabbit is on the move, and the other...oh, how unfortunate. Seems they're stuck down in the basement with all my prototypes."

"No, those are looped videos, I'm the only—"

"Don't bullshit me, Alspeth, I know you couldn't do all this on your own. I'm a little curious as to how it all came together, but not enough to actually listen," he said. "The good news is, I have something to make it all better. Well, eleven somethings, actually."

"Chase, are you still on the twelfth floor?" Ellison spoke with military precision. "I just got on the elevator—shit."

"Yeah, I'm not letting that one come all the way up here. That'll ruin it." Beauchamp must have shut the elevator down.

"Hang tight, Chase, I'm on the way," Ellison said, straining. It was too easy to picture her prying the doors open and crawling out.

"No, no, a-abort mission, or—"

"There's no getting out of this one, Alspeth. Time to test the shells with some live enemies. The experiment never ends—you understand that, I'm sure."

Chase noticed the shell next to him, asleep in its tube. Slim muscles lay along arms so long the knuckles grazed the bottom of the cylinder. The only bulk was in the shoulders, which had to be strong to control such long levers. How much power could muscles like that produce? How much strength did they hold?

These were not questions born of scientific curiosity. Chase was now fully in survival mode, like every ancestor before her.

"Happy hunting. Or in your case, being hunted," Beauchamp said with a sinister grin. He started swiping across the tablet in rapid succession.

"What the fuck?" Monty's voice said. Over the comms, she heard splashing and cracking. "Fuck! Shit!"

"Monty?" Ellison gasped.

"Get Chase, I'll—fuck!"

The shells. Beauchamp was waking them all up.

CHAPTER 32
THE PLAN H JOB

PANIC HIT Chase as sounds of crashing and colliding echoed over the comms. Whatever was happening to Monty took over all her senses.

"I bet they're having fun." She barely heard Beauchamp over Monty's curses and the blood rushing through her ears. He swiped one last time, causing the glass to drop on the cylinder next to him. The preservation liquid spilled onto the floor in a viscous mess.

The blue light under the HNTR's temple blinked, and the shell opened its eyes. Its joints cracked as it sat up and rolled its shoulders. It turned to her, then took one stomach-dropping step out of the tube.

"Kill." Beauchamp smiled as he gave the order.

Chase didn't take time to curse or think. She ran.

"Guys! Run! Get out!" she said, slapping her badge against the scanner. The light flipped green and the door inched open. She pushed herself through the gap, screaming as a hand slammed into the wall next to her head. Her hair ruffled with the breeze of the narrow miss. Bits of the wall cracked and fell from the force of the hit. Shit, not only was this thing strong, it was *fast*, too.

The most direct route to the door was over the desks, but Chase didn't have the advantage of athleticism. She focused on moving her feet as fast as possible, her eyes on the prize. HNTR 12 crashed behind her, using its arms to propel itself over the desks. Chase begged her legs to move faster. The door was there, it was just within reach—

An impossibly large hand grabbed her shirt just as her badge touched the scanner. Her back stung where its nails cut her. She jerked back, her scream cut short as her shirt collar choked her. The door was open. It was right there. Her back hit the floor and spots exploded in front of her eyes. A crash sounded, and the shell let go. Through the fireworks, she saw it disappear behind a tumbling desk.

This was her chance.

She pushed herself to her feet, ignoring the lightheadedness, and hit her badge against the scanner again. When the door opened, she rolled into the decontamination room.

"Close! Close! Close!" she called, as if the decontamination chamber would respond quicker the more she shouted. The shell stood and locked its blank eyes on her. Slowly, steadily, it stepped across the overturned desk.

"Close!" she yelled again, and this time the door listened, inching along its track. The shell jumped and Chase held her breath, but it was a second too late. It hit as the door locked, the *bang* echoing in the chamber and making her ears ring. The lights turned blue as the decontamination process started.

"Chase! You good?" Ellison asked between pants.

"No," Chase said with a groan. She pivoted onto her hands and knees, then stopped as the lights flashed red. "Shit. Fuck—"

If the protocol restarted, would the door open?

"Please stand still for decontamination." The AI's voice was calm, as if the world wasn't going to complete shit around them. Chase waited for the door to move, but the chamber remained sealed. The shell remained on the other side, smacking the barrier over and over. It might actually be able to beat it down, but Chase didn't want to be around to find out.

"Monty?" Ellison checked in.

Bang.

No answer.

Bang.

"Monty?" Chase said, not anywhere near as calm.

Bang bang.

"Alive," he gasped. "Shit—!"

"What the hell is going on? Do I need to come to you?" Ruby said.

"No, you can't come here, it's fucked up beyond all recognition." Ellison used her military voice again. Chase pulled herself to standing, though her legs shook and her blood pressure threatened to plummet. If she could get to Ellison, and find Monty, then they could grab Oscar and get out. The chamber once again instructed her to stay still and started the cycle over.

"No, you don't get to use FUBAR on me. I can come get everyone, I just need a different vehicle—"

"Building's in lockdown, Ruby," Oscar said. "You can't get in, and we can't get out."

They fell silent at that, and Chase dreaded each second the clock counted down. The shell kept knocking at the door, its rudimentary cognition focused on the single goal. She stood at the far side of the chamber, waiting for it to open.

"What do you mean, 'lock down'?" Chase asked.

"It means you have to stay alive until I can unlock it. I got the stair doors operational again, so aim for that."

"Stairs. Got it."

She for sure wasn't panicking.

"I'm on the way," Ruby said. "Stay alive until I get there."

Easy for her to say.

"Ellison, I'll meet you on nine," Chase said.

"Too late, I'm on twelve."

Chase's heart skipped a beat. "Get ready then, one of them is right behind me."

Ding.

The doors slid open.

"Don't worry, baby, I'm coming in hot."

Chase bolted. The shell barreled into the room behind her, its long arms reaching almost across the entire decontamination chamber. Chase didn't look back as she sprinted, HNTR 12 two steps behind her. She sped through the outer chamber door and yelled for it to close. The door listened and slammed it into HNTR 12's outstretched forearm. The bones cracked like a stick over a knee.

Long fingers from the other hand curled into the limited space and tried to pry the door back open, but its strength was no match for the machinery. It pulled the second hand back just before the door crunched through the bones and completely shut. With a *thump*, the first hand hit the ground, leaving a trail of blood down the door and under the amputated arm.

"Holy fuck." There were no screams of pain from inside the chamber. HNTR 12 didn't know pain. "Holy fucking—shit—"

"Chase!" Ellison's voice snapped her back to reality. She stood at the outermost door, glowing like one of those angels all over church ruins. She gestured wildly toward the exit. "Let's *go.*"

Chase stumbled forward again, not completely sure her legs still contained bones. Everything was wrong, everything was going so wrong—

"Beauchamp," she gasped out, falling into Ellison's arms. She was confused, but at least she caught her. "Beauchamp's been watching the whole time. He woke them all up."

"And he locked the building," Oscar reminded them. "For now."

"So all those fuckers are awake?" Ellison asked.

"Can confirm," Monty said, his voice strained.

"We need to find Monty, we need to help," Chase said.

Despite what she'd promised, she was very, very close to losing her shit.

"We will," Ellison said. She shifted Chase behind her and pulled out one of her pistols. With a slap and a flick, the energy blaster hummed to life. "We gotta take care of this fucker first."

"We do?" Chase asked weakly. She cowered behind Ellison and felt no shame about it. In fact, if it weren't for the explicit knowledge she would *definitely* die without Ellison, she would take off running again. Her comms carried no sounds except for Monty's heavy breathing and an ongoing whisper from Oscar as he fought the security system.

The decontamination chamber dinged, and Ellison raised the pistol.

"C'mere, ugly," she whispered. She was so steady, and Chase figured if she could get ten percent of this woman's nerve, she'd make it through the night.

The door opened. HNTR 12 stood like a nightmare outlined in blue light. There was no way it was decontaminated, not with its arm actively dripping blood. The rules of this game were not fair.

HNTR 12 dropped its eyes to the hand on the floor, and it casually reached over to pick it up. It tried once, twice, three times to stick the hand back onto its residual limb, but it didn't stick.

"I don't suppose those things bleed out?" Ellison asked.

"I wouldn't test it," Chase said.

HNTR 12 dropped the hand and returned its attention to them. It took one careful, calculated step into the corridor, and the decontamination chamber hissed shut behind it. Ellison dug her heels into the floor and trained her sight.

The creature leaped.

The first shot made Chase drop and cover her ears, but Ellison didn't stop sinking energy bullets into her target. Holes blasted into its chest, but it picked up speed, breaking into a run toward them. Its hand stretched out like a waiting bear trap.

Ellison changed her position slightly. HNTR 12 was so close that Chase could see the blue of its eyes.

Ellison landed a blast right between them.

Brain matter exploded onto the clean white floors, reds and blues and pinks all swirling together in a goopy, soupy mess. If Chase's soul hadn't completely escaped her body, she would've been sick everywhere. In fact, she was still considering it.

"There. Nine left." Ellison set the recharge on her weapon. "Let's go."

"Right. Let's go." Chase's brain compartmentalized at the speed of light, though it was also dangerously close to shutting down.

"Hey, Chase." Ellison stooped to eye level. Chase didn't realize until that moment that she was still crouching. "Keep it together."

"Don't lose my shit," she reminded herself.

"Exactly." Ellison put a hand under her arm and dragged her to her feet. "C'mon, we gotta go find Monty."

The reminder put a fire under Chase's ass. She could swallow her own fear if it meant helping him. Ellison pushed her toward the door, and she let the momentum carry her into a jog.

"Monty? What floor are you on?" Ellison asked.

"Six," he whispered. "I managed to get out of the basement 'cause they tripped over each other, but they keep pushing me up."

"We're coming down to you," Ellison said. She grabbed Chase by the belt loop and shoved her toward the stairs.

"But wait, Beauchamp is back there." Chase turned, fully expecting to see him standing there.

"He can't do anything to us if we take out the pawns." Ellison swiped her badge at the scanner and kicked the door in. She snapped, grabbing Chase's attention again. "Go, Chase."

Ellison was right, of course. She knew that. But it scared Chase to leave Beauchamp there like he wasn't a threat.

Then she remembered the strength of HNTR 12. Okay, maybe

Beauchamp wasn't their *biggest* threat right at that moment. Didn't matter what happened to him, they still had murder shells on their tails.

They flew down the stairs–Chase stumbling more than flying–making it down one floor, then the next. Chase skidded to a halt at the ninth floor.

"What the fuck is it now?" Ellison said, halfway down the next flight before she realized Chase had stopped.

"Hunter, I have to get my Hunter," she said, reaching for the door. Ellison bounded up the stairs to slap her hand away.

"No! Your Hunter is in murder mode right now. Leave them."

"But then I can't take them to Novak—"

"Forget about Novak!" Ellison snapped. "Right now, the priority is to stay *alive*, Chase."

Chase thought about ignoring her, she really did. But Ellison was the expert in this situation. What good would it be to track down her Hunter just to get slaughtered? She had the data they collected, perhaps Novak could do something with it instead.

"Right," she said, taking off again.

Her thighs burned as they made it down to the eighth floor, then the seventh, her steps becoming more clumsy the further they went.

"Still on six, Monty?" she gasped into the comms as they got to the door.

"Shit, no, I'm not—"

Ellison moved too quickly, wrenching the door open and coming face to face with another HNTR. Its muscles were so big and bulbous it would be comical, if it wasn't staring at them with every intent to kill. Instead of stretch marks, its skin tore in the places where the hypertrophy was too much to bear. The red muscle underneath seeped serosanguinous fluid.

"Shit." Ellison reached for her gun again, but not before the shell kicked out. She got her arms up in time to block the shot, but it sent her flying back into the wall with a heavy thud. Some part of her caught Chase on the way by and sent her rolling into the metal post where the handrails turned.

Chase's breath left in a rush, and she had the distinct sense at least one of her ribs was broken. The pain was so intense her body seized, her fight or flight response choosing the stupid *freeze* option. She couldn't breathe, she couldn't think, she couldn't *move*.

It stepped into the stairwell, the doorframe catching the edges of its body and tearing at the skin and muscle. When the door tried to close, it squeezed one side of the shell. Blood dripped onto the floor, so close the splatter hit Chase's wrist.

The shell ignored her motionless body, instead targeting Ellison as she crawled to her feet with a groan. There was no way Ellison could take it on her own. It was twice her size, with four times the muscle mass. It took one step toward her, then another, and Chase noticed more blood running down its legs and pooling underneath.

The muscles were big, but brittle.

She scrambled for her baton and flicked it open. She couldn't kill it, not on her own, but she could slow it down enough for Ellison to get the upper hand.

The shell took another step. Ellison was on her feet now, but she listed to one side. Her arm hung at a gross angle and her eye was starting to swell. She growled and grabbed her forearm with the good arm, yanking harshly to reduce the dislocated shoulder. The joint relocated with a pop loud enough to make Chase's skin crawl.

The shell was right next to her now, and before Chase could talk herself out of it, she swung the baton. It made contact with the meaty calf, which wasn't what she aimed for, but it worked. The muscle belly of the gastrocnemius popped like a balloon, blood splattering all over her face and hands. The shell buckled, but stayed standing.

And now its attention was on her.

Shit.

Ellison took the opening, leaping forward and driving her knee into the shell's abdomen. Blood gushed out and the shell bent at the waist, but she gave it no opportunity to right itself. She slammed her elbows into its neck, kicked its thighs, punched at the basketball sized deltoids. Chase curled into a ball and covered her head, protecting herself from the red rain.

The shell fell with a heavy *thud*. It was alive, but its muscles were no longer viable. It was stuck there. The blue light flashed under its temple as it tracked their movements. Ellison pulled out her pistol and shot it in the forehead.

"Eight." Ellison counted down, smearing the blood from her face with the arm of her jumpsuit. She grabbed Chase's hand, both their skin slick, and pulled her to her feet. "Let's go. Monty?"

"Sorry guys. I'm on eight now—be careful."

CHAPTER 33
THE PLAN J JOB

WHEN THEY REACHED the eighth floor door, Ellison pushed Chase behind her and readied a pistol in one hand. Chase felt inadequate with her little baton, but held it at the ready, anyway. If anything came close, she could, and would, beat the shit out of it.

Ellison threw her badge with pinpoint accuracy, hitting the sensor and turning the light green. Chase was *definitely* going to practice that skill later. Ellison waited, gun up and ready. They found nothing but a dark hallway.

"Stay behind me," she whispered. She picked up the badge and swiped it again, the door sliding open a second later.

"Yeah, wasn't exactly planning on running in first," Chase muttered. Ellison threw a glare and a *shh* over her shoulder before ducking into the hallway, the pistol up and ready to work.

"Monty?" Chase murmured, turning her head every which way to cover Ellison's back. Maybe she couldn't fight, but she could sure as hell scream a warning.

A gasp came through the comms. "Still—shit!"

A crash sounded on the comms and across the floor. Chase and Ellison leapt toward a writhing shadow opposite them, following the grunts and curses as Monty fought off the shell. Ellison easily outran her, but at the noise of another crash, Chase found a pace previously untapped. Her heart bruised her sternum. Monty was fighting alone, and if they didn't get there in time—

She rounded a corner too fast and slammed into the wall. She kicked off as if she meant to do it, ignoring the bruised shoulder and stumbling through the desks.

Ellison stopped in a doorway. Chase tried to decelerate, but her knee buckled. In the end, she ran right into her, sending both of them to the ground in an awkward tangle of limbs.

"What the fuck, Alspeth?" Ellison cried, grabbing her injured shoulder.

Chase gritted her teeth against her own pain. Broken ribs *hurt*. "Why did you stop?"

"Because—"

"Fancy meeting y'all here."

Monty also lay on the ground. Next to him was the small shell from four floors down. Bruises painted its neck, and its lifeless brown eyes bugged out of its head. Thank Techs it was staring at the ceiling—Chase didn't think she could handle eye contact.

"Little fucker was so damn quick," he gasped. "Couldn't do much once I got it in a headlock, though."

"Proud of you," Ellison said, patting his chest. He groaned at the contact, but she ignored him. "Down to seven."

They pushed themselves into seated positions. Chase and Monty struggled to catch their breaths, whereas Ellison looked like she was just getting warmed up. If they made it out of this, Chase planned to start working out at a much higher consistency. The thought made her knee ache.

"You okay?" Chase asked Monty. He had rips all over the arms of his shirt, the edges dark with blood. He raised an eyebrow, which also sported a cut. Blood dribbled from it, and Chase reached out to wipe it away before it got in his eyes. Sure, touching blood without gloves was gross, but she figured a little more wouldn't kill her.

"Yeah, these are all shallow," he said, gesturing with his elbows. "You two look like hell, though."

Chase looked down at herself. The black hid most of the blood, but she could see the red spray over her arms and feel the tight spots on her face where it dried. Ellison looked even worse, with a quickly blackening eye and bruises over her forearms.

"It's not ours," Chase said, as if that made it better.

"Speak for yourself," Ellison deadpanned.

"Ellison's been doing most of the legwork here."

"I'm sorry, Chase," Monty blurted. Both women looked at each other, then back to him. "I should've seen this coming, should've planned for it."

"Hey, no, don't do that," Chase said, shaking her head. "I don't think you could've predicted this. I don't think *anyone* could've predicted this."

"If we had more time—"

"But we didn't," she said. "We're doing the best we can with what we've got."

"And what we've got is seven killer shells coming after us," Ellison reminded them. "Look, I love a good conversation about feelings, but I need it to wait until after we get out of this building. Sound good?"

Right.

Chase's knee buckled as she got to her feet, Monty's quick hands saving her from heading straight back to the ground. She took a breath and tested her leg again, and this time it held.

She really should've replaced it sooner.

Monty was the first to open the stairwell door this time, Ellison poised to cover him with gunfire. He held the door and leaned over, waving to them when the coast was clear. They were two feet in when they heard the footsteps.

The way the sound reverberated, it took a second to determine that the steps came from below them. Chase tugged them both back into the room. In the last sliver of light before the door slid closed, she spotted two heads through the bars. They could barely handle one at a time, and now they were dealing with one hundred percent more. Even with the door shut, they could hear the stomps on the stairs.

"Open the door," Ellison whispered, chomping at the bit.

"Are you kidding? Absolutely not!" Chase whispered back.

"I'm with Chase on this one," Monty joined in.

"We can control the attack, let in one at a time," Ellison said.

"Or we can let them continue on," Chase said. "We don't *have* to fight them."

"Yeah, we do. We can't let them go," Ellison said.

"That's a good point," Monty said.

"Quit switching allegiances!"

"We're all on the same side," Monty snapped. "Ellison is right, we need to take them down. But we have to do it smart."

Ellison rolled her eyes. "I was planning to do it the dumb way, but okay—"

"That's not what I meant and you know it," he said.

Chase had an idea.

"Maybe I can try and shut them down," Chase said. Both of them stared at her like she was the one with arms all the way down to her ankles.

"What?" Monty asked.

"You could do that *this whole time*?" Ellison hissed.

"I don't know!" she said, throwing her arms up. The scratches on her back pulled, and she jerked to a stop. "I said I can *try*. I'll have to use a different tablet and find a way to connect to the chip in the brain. It's a long shot. I may not be able to do it outside a fab chamber—"

"Just try it!" Monty said.

The footsteps stopped outside the door, and the frame shook as something gave an experimental push.

"Were you planning to try it out now, or..." Ellison said. The door shook again, the locks and hinges groaning. Monty pulled a pistol from his side and Ellison set the charge on her energy weapon. Their eyes never left the door. "Go!"

The shell pulled at the seam of the door with heavy, rhythmic motions, and the frame shook a little more with each repetition. Chase stumbled to the nearest desk and grabbed the tablet. She logged in with shaking fingers, scared it wouldn't have the application she needed for the shells. Thank Techs it was there, and a sigh of relief made her flinch in pain as her rib shifted. Yep, definitely broken.

Light from the stairwell poked through for a split second, long enough to spike Chase's epinephrine and reduce the pain of her rib to a forgettable level. A broken rib was about to be the least of her worries.

She opened the program just as the door wrenched open, the metal twisting and screaming as the shell tore it from its track. The skinless monster stared with large, unblinking eyes and a manic grin. The muscles rippled under foggy fascia as it crossed the threshold. The second shuffled after, its rotten, necrotic flesh falling in a trail behind it. The stench of death and decay filled the room, making Chase's eyes water.

Chase gagged as she flipped through her application, looking for the place she usually found Hunter's connection.

Ellison shot at the bigger shell, but the fascia absorbed the energy without breaking. It dispersed across the surface, momentarily turning the milky connective tissue sparkling and orange. The muscle underneath grew, just slightly. Chase stared in horror as she realized the tissue was absorbing the energy from the hit and using it to build more muscle. The more they fought, the stronger it would become.

Monty got one shot on the smaller shell, the bullet flying right through without the usual destruction. A black substance bubbled out of the hole, some of it dropping to the ground and some of it hardening like a scab.

Chase started working faster.

Connection error.

No source found.

"Any time now, Chase—shit!"

The first shell leapt at Ellison. She barely dodged, rolling across the ground as the shell went by her in a flail of meaty limbs.

And then it came straight toward Chase.

Ellison's eyes widened as she realized the mistake. Chase jumped onto the desk right before the shell slammed into it. It rocked back on two posts and threatened to topple over.

The world slowed and gave Chase the briefest moment of clarity.

She held the tablet over her head and stepped onto the edge of the desk, slamming it forward. The edge of the desk caught the shell on the chin and snapped its forehead down onto the desktop. She used the momentum to carry the tablet down. The screen shattered as she sank the edge of it into the back of the shell's neck. Glass sliced her hands, and she felt a crack and a give as the cervical vertebrae broke under the attack.

The shell hit the ground with a thud. Chase collapsed onto her hands and knees, her rib aching with every breath. The bloody, useless tablet clattered to the ground. Monty and Ellison circled the smaller shell. It seemed more cautious than its partner, its bare eyes flicking back and forth as it tried to compute the task.

The empty stare settled on Chase, and her heart stopped. Monty took the chance to grab the shell, wrapping his arms around the torso and holding its arms to its sides. Ellison struck, strong and fast, slamming her knife into the throat and ripping outwards. Black poured over Monty and he gagged. Ellison took no notice, and instead grabbed the shell by the head and snapped its neck so hard the eyes disappeared from Chase's view.

"Five," Chase breathed. With each adrenaline crash, it felt a little more impossible to keep going.

Under the desk, she heard a gurgle and a shudder. The shell

pushed itself up, its movements awkward and uncoordinated. She'd hit it hard enough to partially sever its spinal cord, but apparently that was not enough.

The shell lunged, and she screamed, kicking both feet into its chest. The move threw it backward, but also sent her careening off the desk. She landed hard on her back, knocking the wind out of her. Her diaphragm spasmed as she choked on nothing.

A skinless face and soulless eyes appeared over the desk. A second later, a hand shot toward her. She closed her eyes, bracing for impact.

It never came.

Above her, the shell held Ellison's wrist in an iron grip. A dull crack echoed through Chase's skull as Ellison's radius snapped with the pressure. She grimaced, but raised her other hand and emptied energy shot after shot into the shell's face. This time, it stayed still.

"Five." Ellison was much more definitive. The bones of her forearm swan-necked, the surrounding tissue already swelling.

"Your arm—"

"We'll take care of it later," she said. Her face was pale, and when she stood, she cradled her arm to her abdomen. There was no way she could take down five more shells.

"Give me a gun," Chase said.

"Absolutely not."

"You're hurt, you need more help. We're in Plan Z now, right?" Chase asked. Ellison cocked her head to the side.

"What?"

"Monty said Plan Z is where we depend on you to punch our way out of things."

"That's like, Plan R. V at the latest."

"Whatever! We're in that plan!" Chase said, tossing her hands up and remembering too late about her rib. She gasped and squawked in pain, then waved off the looks of concern. "If we're gonna make it out, it's gonna take all of us."

Ellison glanced at Monty, who shrugged. With a sigh, she unholstered a gun and held it out to her.

"This is the safety. If it's off, then you keep it pointed down."

"Got it."

"Don't shoot—"

"Don't shoot you, don't shoot Monty, don't shoot myself," she said. "You're getting predictable, Ell."

"I swear to Techs, Chase, I'm gonna throw you out a window," Ellison grumbled, though a grin played at the corner of her mouth.

"Save it for later," Chase said. "Oscar? What's going on?"

CHAPTER 34
THE PLAN O JOB

OSCAR GROANED, and Chase felt it in her bones. "I found his tablet and can disconnect it, but probably just for a short time. He's fighting me on the doors." he said.

"At least he's watching you and not us," Ellison said.

"I found a van, and I'm waiting for y'all outside," Ruby said. "Engine's running."

"You beautiful woman, I'm marrying you as soon as we get out of this," Ellison breathed.

"You did *not* just give me a half-ass proposal over comms," Ruby snapped.

"Can we focus?" Oscar's voice pitched an octave higher than usual. "Please?"

"What do you need us to do? Get to the front?" Monty asked.

"What floor are you on?"

"Eight," Chase said. Just one floor away from Hunter. They were still in their room when Beauchamp woke the shells up, why hadn't they ventured this far down yet?

"There's a terminal on six, it functions as a relay station between me and him. I need you to go there and disable it, then we should be able to get out," Oscar said.

"After we kill the rest of the shells," Ellison said.

"You're not killing anything with your arm like that," Chase replied.

"Your arm? What happened to your arm?" Ruby asked.

"Nothing, I'm fine." Ellison glared at Chase, who shrugged. She was still learning comms etiquette, it wasn't her fault no one told her not to mention Ellison's injuries to Ruby. "We can't let them go, we don't know what they can do. If even *one* has a tracking program installed, we won't escape, even if we make it out of the building."

"We may have to risk that. Getting out gives us a much better chance," Monty said. He opened the door to the stairwell and stepped back, listening hard for any movement. It was silent, but that wasn't comforting. If the shells weren't in the stairwell, who knew where they were hiding?

"We'll cross that bridge when we come to it," Ellison said. She attempted to march into the stairwell, but her vehemence lost some power due to a harsh limp.

Each step sent pain lancing through Chase's chest, and the back of her shoulder throbbed, but she did her best to grit her teeth and carry on. She figured if Monty and Ellison could keep going with their injuries, then she could, too. Thankfully, they were able to reach the sixth floor without further incident, and found the entire floor dark. One at a time, lights flickered on as they went down the hallway toward the corner Oscar directed.

The silence was as thick as borrowed time, their breathing and footsteps and heartbeats fracturing it. Chase led the charge and Ellison brought up the rear while Monty kept his head on a swivel. The terminal, which would "be obvious" according to Oscar, was a giant mass of wires and screens. They were kept behind metal coverings that made very loud noises when Chase dropped them.

"Shit," she said. "Sorry."

"What in the…" Monty's eyes traced over the lines. "Oscar, nothing about this is obvious."

"Should be a big box with an interface," Oscar said lightly.

"There's lots of boxes and lots of interfaces," Chase said. "Anything else you can give us?"

"Hmm, green lights?" Oscar tried.

"Techs, we're gonna die here," Ellison grumbled.

"Oh! There should be an antenna of some sort. Go for the screen under it."

"How big is the antenna?" Monty asked.

"I don't know, you're the one in front of it."

"Oscar I swear to Techs—"

"Could this be it?" Chase pointed to a box that had a half sphere on the top. Four green lights shone underneath it, the last one blinking steadily.

"Is the antenna a little nubby thing?" Monty asked.

"I guess so, yes," Oscar said, somehow affronted by Monty referring to the antenna as *nubby*.

Chase tapped the screen, bringing it to life, then swiped through with her credentials. Down the hall, the first light flickered out. Then the next. Then the next. Chase stopped her scrolling, the darkness in her periphery making a cold sweat break out on the back of her neck. The lights continued to flicker out one at a time; only the one nearest stayed lit.

"That's unsettling," Monty said.

"It's just the motion sensors." Ellison did not sound convinced.

"Oscar, what's next?" Chase said.

"Right, okay, there should be a wheel icon for settings."

"Got it." She tapped the screen, and a menu opened.

"Alright, go to routing, and it should bring up a big circuit board."

She wasn't entirely sure what the average circuit board looked like, but this virtual one was an ugly tangle of lines and lights, as if the Winter Holiday was the inspiration for the design.

"I got it, I think," she said.

"Okay, this is where it gets tricky," Oscar said. "You need to find E5, B9, X2, and P4."

"I need to find what?" Chase asked, but Monty pulled some sort of writing implement from his pocket and scribbled the points on the wall. "Is that a crayon?"

"Chalk," he said. "It's good for moments like this."

"And old-fashioned safes," Ruby said wistfully.

"Seriously?" Ellison said over her shoulder. She stood with her back to them, her left hand dangling and her right clutching her weapon. Her injured wrist was more swollen and turning a righteous shade of purple. Chase returned her focus to the board; the sooner they got out, the sooner they could get Ellison some medical attention.

"Okay, I think I got 'em," she said.

"Don't lose sight of those," Oscar said. Chase rested her hands on the side of the screen, fingers poised close. "Monty, find the wires underneath."

"There's a million of them."

"The ones attached to that specific box," Oscar clarified.

"Ah, yeah, my bad. There's only a hundred of them."

"Well, you're going to have to figure out how to disconnect all of them."

"All of them?" Monty looked to Chase, who looked back. That was a lot of wires.

"At the same time. Relatively."

Monty grit his teeth as the wheels turned. Chase tried very hard to figure out how he could undo every clasp in a timely manner, let alone all at once. It was hard to split her brain between that problem, the spots she had to manage, and the pain from her rib and shoulder.

"Techs, Monty, just grab 'em with both hands and yank," Ellison said, then muttered, "Brainiac types always getting wound up in the details."

"Ellison makes a good point," Oscar said. "Okay Chase, do you remember the order of those numbers I gave you?"

"The order?" She looked at Monty. He nodded at the chalk writing. "Uh, yes."

"Okay good, 'cause that's the order you need to turn them off."

"You probably should have mentioned that earlier."

"Put it in the suggestion box," he said. "Monty, as soon as she hits that last one, you have three seconds to pull the cables, otherwise it'll reset. And sound an alarm that puts the top ten floors in total lockdown, including the stairs. I have to stop messing with his tablet in order to do this, so work *fast*."

"No pressure," he said. He nodded to Chase. "Ready?"

She took a deep breath and nodded back. "Let's do this."

Chase checked three more times before tapping E5, then B9. She checked two more times before hitting X2, and then let her hand hover over P4. She locked eyes with Monty.

"On three?" she asked.

"*On* three or *after* three?"

"After three," she clarified.

He nodded and took hold of the wires.

"One, two, three—"

She tapped P4, and the screen flickered and turned black. Monty jerked downward, ripping the wires from their homes. All except the middle one.

Chase spotted it and lashed out, grabbing and yanking faster than she thought possible. They all stopped and held their breath, waiting for the alarm or cataclysmic lockdown event.

It didn't come.

"Oh, thank Techs," Chase said, putting her hands on her knees and breathing heavily. Her rib reminded her of its current situation, and she bit out an angry, "Fuck."

"That was a close one," Monty agreed. He rubbed the back of his hand over his forehead, getting rid of the sweat but reopening the wound on his eyebrow. Fresh blood oozed down his temple.

"Oscar?" Chase asked.

"I've got it. The connection is breaking up, so now I should be able to override everything," he said. "You need to get out of there. He'll know where you are soon."

The light at the end of the hallway turned on.

"Yeah, I think he already knows," Monty said.

The next light turned on, one step closer. Chase could see outlines, but the shells were too far away to determine their exact number. There was a distinct chance all five remaining were sent to their location.

"Run," she said. She grabbed Monty's hand and Ellison's waistband. "Run!"

They bolted down the opposite hallway. The light at the end turned on, illuminating a single shell, the light shining on its silver skin. They skidded to a halt and Chase nearly fell as her leg gave out, but Ellison was able to grab her waist and haul her back up. As the lights clicked on and the shells moved closer, they retreated into the main desk room. No exits in sight.

They were trapped.

HNTR 3, the behemoth, stood between them and the doors. Like zombies, HNTRs 4, 5, and 7 shambled toward them at an ominously slow pace. Unlike zombies, their eyes shone with enough intent and intelligence to be dangerous.

Chase, Monty, and Ellison scrambled through the desks, trying to put as much space and matter between them and the shells as possible. The shells converged like stars on a collision course, and they were going to get caught in the blast.

It was the start of a bad joke, Chase thought. A bad, terrible, cosmic joke that went something like, "A giant, a skinless nightmare, a clawed terror, and a suit of armor walk into a lab…"

"This may be it," Monty said quietly.

"What? What's happening? Oscar?" Ruby sounded frantic. "Oscar, I thought you were getting the doors open—"

"I am, but if they—if he—" Oscar sputtered, trying to get his mouth to catch up with his brain. "He found them."

"I love you, Ruby," Ellison said.

"No ma'am, you're not pulling that shit with me." They could hear Ruby's tears through her voice, and it made Chase's heart ache.

"Not giving up. Just wanted to make sure you knew," Ellison said. She grit her teeth and grabbed a second pistol with her injured arm, hitting the handle against her hip to warm it up. It looked like she could barely hold it, the inflamed flesh visibly pulsing as she forced it. Chase's hands shook as she raised her own gun, making sure to point it far away from Ellison.

"Thank you for trying to help," Chase said. "I'm sorry I got you guys into this."

The shells shoved the desks out of the way one row at a time, fab chambers cracking and sparking as they destroyed them. There was just one row now, a feeble protection from an impossible foe.

The big one jumped.

Time slowed down.

Bang!

Chase thought she'd feel the kick from the gun more. Then she realized the safety was still on.

Ellison dropped her injured hand and swayed on her feet, her eyes blinking rapidly. Even Monty looked shocked, and Chase waited to see blood spurt from either of them.

But it wasn't a gun which made the noise.

The behemoth shell was across the lab, impaled on upturned desk legs and fab chamber glass. The last three paused, trying to reason their next move. Chase gasped.

There, in between them and the shells, stood Hunter.

CHAPTER 35
THE PLAN Q JOB

HUNTER STOOD with their feet wide and fists up, their back to Chase and her friends. The skinless shell chattered its teeth and HNTR 5's freakishly long fingers twitched. If Chase didn't know better, she would think they were nervous. Only the armored one stood motionless, staring at them with cold, gray eyes.

"Hunter?" Chase croaked. Hunter turned their head just slightly so their ear was toward her.

"Don't get their attention," Ellison hissed. "Beauchamp is controlling them, that's not *your* Hunter."

"If they're not on our side, they'd have killed us already," Chase said, standing up. "Hunter, did you...did you receive orders?"

"Orders to kill," they stated. Chase held her breath, but they didn't move.

"To kill...us?" she asked. She wanted to know, wanted to take advantage of their ability to verbalize. "Are you here to kill us, Hunter?"

Hunter turned fully to Chase and locked eyes, thinking.

Taking advantage of the distraction, HNTR 5 shot forward

fingers first, fulling intent on sinking them into Hunter's back. Chase opened her mouth to warn them, but they turned on the balls of their feet and leaned back, their foot intrinsics steadying them. HNTR 5 missed its mark, the knife-like fingers flying right over Hunter. Hunter grabbed the forearm with one hand and the lateral three fingers with the other, snapping them like twigs off a dead tree. Still holding the forearm, they kicked into HNTR 5's torso, this time ripping off the entire arm.

Though blood poured freely from the wound, HNTR 5 didn't seem to perceive the pain. It focused its energy on attempting to right itself. Its muscles weren't strong enough, its upper body flapping like a flag in the wind as its weak core failed to align its spine. Hunter stalked over to it.

The other two shells watched, their eyes tracking every movement. Chase swallowed; the others were *learning*, or at least trying to.

Sensing the danger, HNTR 5 tried to crawl away, but its movements were jerky and unbalanced, like a toddler. It was comically easy for Hunter to grab it by its hair. A twist, a snap, and a rip like tearing cloth was all it took to separate HNTR 5's head from its body. The torso fell like a sack of bricks, and Hunter tossed the head across the lab.

Chase desperately hoped that Hunter would continue to ignore the kill order, because if they didn't, then she was truly and royally fucked.

"I think Hunter might be on our side," Monty said.

"Techs, I hope so."

"Three left," Ellison said. She was as white as the fab chamber floors now, sweat beading her hairline. They needed to get her out of the building and to a doctor as soon as possible, or she might lose her hand. Chase wouldn't even have access to equipment to build her a new one.

Hunter returned to their original position between Chase and the shells. They opened their mouth to finish the thought from earlier, but snapped it shut when the skinless shell moved. It took a step back as if to flee, but the armored one wasn't having it. It shoved it forward toward Hunter.

Reminded of its orders, the shell put its arms up and lashed out at Hunter. Hunter fought back, their punches landing solidly on the torso of the shell. Like before, the fascia flashed orange as the energy dispersed. But this shell wasn't as advanced as its counterpart; the muscle didn't hypertrophy with the added stimuli, and when the fascia returned to normal, Chase could see bruising pooling where the hits landed.

But this shell could move, and move *fast*. Faster than any of the others she'd seen. It ignored the injuries and rained rapid-fire blows on its opponent, its fists glowing with each contact. Hunter managed to dodge or block most of the attacks, but one snuck in. Their jaw bone cracked like an ice pond, the impact sending them to one knee. The shell lined up like a soccer player, aiming for the head as the ball. With that speed, it could take it off.

Hunter's hands shot up, catching the lower leg centimeters from their face. They held on tight and rolled back with the momentum, twisting the shell's leg. It stayed attached, but with a sound like gears grinding, the femur spiraled and broke. The shell flipped in midair and Hunter rolled until they came out on top, pinning the shell's arms under their knees. Their eyes scanned the immediate area for a weapon. The discarded arm from HNTR 5 was within reach.

Hunter reached over and grabbed the arm, breaking the brittle bones at the wrist and tossing away the part they didn't need. The needle-sharp fingers easily pierced the skin of the shell as Hunter methodically punctured their carotid arteries and jugular veins on either side. To seal the deal, they drove the bloody hand through the shell's mouth, severing the brain stem. The shell twitched once more, then grew still.

One. There was only one left.

Technically, there were two, but Chase didn't count Hunter. Hunter was acting against orders, using higher-level thought processes than the rest of them. Perhaps, given enough time and attention, the other HNTRs could achieve the same consciousness, but those chances disappeared thanks to Beauchamp's pride. While she knew she should be sad about it, all she felt was relief. If the others had any more sentience, she'd be long dead by now.

The armored shell took one heavy step. It reached out, and a blade the length of its forearm slid into its hand. Hunter yanked the stump of HNTR 5's hand from the skinless shell's mouth, one of the two remaining fingers breaking off. Hunter looked down at it like it was an inconvenience, and Chase could see the thought process again. The finger was too brittle to do any damage against whatever the fuck was coating the last combatant.

Beauchamp once told her Hunter was the most advanced shell. Clearly, this one was next in line. Its movements were more calculated than the rest, and it was all too willing to sacrifice its partners. It had problem-solving skills and a sense of self-preservation. And if Hunter didn't have help, they were going to lose.

"Weapons, they know how to use weapons," Chase said. Hunter could at least use knives. She gestured to the two sheathed at Ellison's calves. "Give them those."

"Hell no, I'm not arming them," she said, stepping away. "What if we're next?"

"Clearly we're not, unless you don't give them weapons!"

Chase could admit that, during this whole heist, she was the least educated in the situation. But Hunter was her expertise.

The armored shell took another step.

"You can't be serious."

"Chase is right, trusting Hunter is our best bet," Monty said. Hunter flicked their head toward Monty at the sound of their name. Even in the midst of all this, Chase was proud of the strides their neurological system had taken. They recognized their *name*.

"Not you too—"

"Ellison, trust Hunter," Ruby snapped.

"You're not even here!"

"It doesn't take a genius to figure out what's going on."

"Techs, fine," Ellison growled. She yanked the knives from their homes and held them by the blades. "Hunter!"

Ellison tossed the blades before Hunter turned around, which Chase thought was rather rude. It didn't phase them. They took their eyes off the armored shell for exactly as long as it took to pluck the knives from the air, then turned. They were ready for a fight.

The armored shell made the first move. It took a few pounding steps, barreling toward Hunter like a wrecking ball. It was bigger, and probably stronger, but it was slow. Hunter side-stepped it. So now the shell was barreling toward *Chase* like a wrecking ball.

Monty grabbed her arm as she jumped toward him, the change in weight sending them tumbling to the ground in a heap of limbs and bruises. His body crushed her chest, her rib screaming at her as all the air left her lungs. The shell bulldozed the last few desks, rolling all the way to the window. It hit the glass hard enough for it to crack and shake ominously.

"You okay?" Monty gasped, putting his hand on her cheek.

"Can't breathe," Chase said, unsure where she found the requisite air to speak.

"Shit," he said, rolling off her. Somehow the release of the weight hurt even worse than its presence, and she clutched her torso with a cry.

"Ell?" Monty called. Chase couldn't pick her head up quite yet. "Ell, you okay?"

"I'm alive," she said.

Steps reverberated through the floor. The armored shell was on the move.

Chase forced herself to an elbow, then to a seat. Monty slipped an arm under hers and dragged her to her feet, away from the collision course.

The armored shell didn't run this time, but Hunter didn't give it time to plan an attack. They ran to meet it, slashing with precise motions at the shell's shoulders, stomach, and legs. The blades ricocheted off every surface. The shell didn't even bother trying to dodge—it allowed the plates on its skin to do their job. Chase didn't know how Hunter was going to get past it; the covering was everywhere, like a real suit of armor from the ancient times.

Except those weren't infallible.

"The seams!" Chase and Ellison said at the same time. Hunter cocked their head with the input, then flipped the knife in one hand and sank it into the lateral portion of the shell's thigh. They met some resistance, but with a hard pull, the armor plate came off with a deep, wet pop. The white, macerated flesh underneath hung in shredded rags, but the shell showed no pain. If anything, it looked annoyed.

The shell swung its heavy blade down. Hunter raised both knives, catching it in the cross. The shell didn't try to overpower them, instead pulling back and changing its angle. Hunter deflected this slash with one knife, but not enough to avoid a slice into the skin and muscle of their forearm. Their brows pinched as they eyed the blood.

Did Hunter feel the pain?

Hunter moved before Chase could fully analyze the situation. The armored shell swung the blade at every available angle, and they dodged. She watched in real time as Hunter learned the rhythm and pattern, creating the steps to a dance that would only ever be between those two.

They plucked off the plates at the right shoulder, the left side of the back, and the right side of the abdomen. The skin wept serous fluid and blood. The knives easily sank through to the tender organs underneath as Hunter stabbed with efficiency.

The jaw and neck were the next plates to go. The armored shell might have been bigger and stronger, but Hunter was smarter. Much, much smarter.

Hunter sank a knife into its throat, the other into its brain. The light in the gray eyes, the flicker of intelligence just starting to grow, went out. Hunter dropped its body to the ground.

Chase realized she was holding onto Monty, and holding onto him very tight. Her joints popped as she released his arm, and he put on a brave face as pain likely sank into him. It was done. The shells were gone, and she still had her Hunter.

"The knives," Ellison said, going toward Hunter.

"No!" Chase said, protective instinct taking over. Even injured, there was a chance Ellison could take Hunter down, and Chase didn't want to risk it. "No, let me try. Don't threaten them."

Hunter turned sharply, their eyes flicking between Ellison and Chase. Ellison froze in place, her body tense except for her finger tapping her gun. It was her job to make sure everyone made it out safe, Chase knew that. But to her, Hunter needed to make it out safe, too.

"Let me," Chase repeated. Hunter changed their attention to her, following the sound of her voice. "Hunter?"

"Yes." They hadn't quite gotten intonation down yet. That was fine, they could work on that.

"Hunter, give me the knives, please." Chase stepped toward them, her hands outstretched.

"Chase—" Monty reached out, his hand grazing her waist.

"It's okay," she said. Hunter held up the knives with the blades in front, and for the briefest moment, Chase wondered if she made a mistake. But then Hunter flipped them, presenting their handles first.

She took them, Hunter relinquishing their hold immediately. "Thank you," Chase said.

"Not going to kill you." Hunter's eyes bore into hers. They

glanced over to Monty. "Or you." They shifted to Ellison, and after a long pause added, "Or you."

"Appreciate it," Ellison said.

"See? Told you they wouldn't kill us," Chase said, experiencing an odd mixture of relief and guilt.

"I wouldn't speak so soon," Beauchamp said.

CHAPTER 36
THE GREAT ESCAPE JOB

BEAUCHAMP SAUNTERED from the direction of the R&D lab. One by one, the lights flicked on. He held a tablet as if it were just another day in the lab, coming to a stop in front of the window. The cracks spiderwebbing across it glittered in the fluorescent lights. He glanced at the glass with a scoff before returning his attention to his tablet.

"Ok, now's the time to kill this clown," Ellison said, raising her gun.

"Nine, kill them," he said, sounding bored. Hunter shifted, and Ellison moved the gun to them. They went still again. "Nine?"

Hunter looked instead to Chase. She held her breath, trying to decide how she would dodge if they came at her. They had no weapons, and she had two knives, but besides stabbing wildly, she had no clue what to do.

But Hunter wasn't looking to kill.

Hunter was looking to her for orders.

"Nine?"

"Don't listen to him," she whispered. Ellison kept the gun pointed toward them.

"Nine, kill them," Beauchamp said again.

"Don't do it," she said. She held their gaze, willing them to fight the brainwashing.

"Not 'Nine,'" Hunter said finally, turning to Beauchamp. "Hunter."

"Hun—you don't have a *name*. You have a number," he sneered. He shook his head and pulled up the tablet. "Guess we'll do this the hard way."

He swiped something, and energy blasted from Ellison's weapon as she shot at him. The shot hit the tablet, launching it from his hands with a smoking dent in the back of it. For a breath, he looked completely and vulnerably afraid, and Chase thought Ellison would end this right here, right now.

Then Hunter screamed.

Ellison swung the gun around to Hunter, but they were down on their knees, clutching their head.

"Hunter!" Chase cried, taking a step toward them.

"Chase!" Monty said, trying to grab her hand.

"Nine!" Beauchamp shouted.

"No!" It was the only word Hunter could get out. "No! No! No!"

They tore at their temple until they bled, then continued to dig into the tissue. Chase moved to stop them, afraid they were going to injure their brain irreparably, but Monty's arms around her waist kept her back. He yelled something, but she couldn't hear over the sound of Hunter's pain.

Hunter turned toward her, and Chase's breath caught. Blood cascaded down the side of their head, and they were nearly second-knuckle deep into their temple. Before, their gaze was guarded, calculated. Now they looked at her with intensity. Whatever feelings they had, Chase couldn't interpret them. The important thing was Hunter *felt* them.

They maintained eye contact as Hunter slowly pulled their hand out. Clutched in their bloody fingertips was a black cube with wires attached. Millimeter by millimeter they dragged it out, their body twitching and shaking as the attached wires tore through Techs knew what brain matter.

The entire thing came loose with a gasp and a shudder, the wires longer than Hunter's fingers and palm combined. Chase never looked away, holding their gaze as Hunter saw the world freely for the first time.

"You're okay," she said. "Hunter, you're okay."

"Interesting," Beauchamp said. All eyes flew to him, and he startled as if he hadn't meant to be heard. His eyes were wide and his jaw slack as he took in Hunter's bloody face and the control chip previously implanted in their brain. With the attention, he attempted to pull himself together. "So, did you always know the implant was there? I have so many questions."

"No," Chase said. "The only questions you can answer are ones from the authorities."

"Ones from the—oh, for Heaven's sake, Alspeth," he said, rolling his eyes. "We went through this. The authorities don't matter. I'm the only authority here."

"I have evidence of literal war crimes," Chase said, gesturing at Hunter. Hunter's eyebrows pinched together; there was a lot going on, and they were having trouble keeping up. "I'll explain later."

"Oh please, there'll always be people like me," he said. "Let me guess, whatever agent you talked to promised that they could get you somewhere safe? That you just needed to hand over some data, maybe one of the shells? Good luck with that.

"And you," he said, rounding on Ellison and Monty. "I thought killing your friend would scare you off, but I guess you're more determined than I thought."

"So you did kill Koda?" Monty said. He looked like he'd been punched in the gut.

"Well, technically I didn't. Technically, I only gave the order," he said with a pointed look toward Hunter. Hunter blinked, their eyes unfocused as thoughts and memories crowded for their attention. "Remember that, Nine? It was your first important lesson."

"You," Ellison said, raising the gun again. Her arm shook, though Chase couldn't tell if it was from anger or the situation with her forearm.

"Don't make him a martyr, Ell," Monty said. He put his hand on Ellison's shoulder, but she kept the sight on Beauchamp.

Hunter's jaw worked, and they gasped a few breaths. Chase worried about expressive aphasia until they finally got a word out.

"Orders," they said. They spoke with the same downtrodden finality that Chase saw in soldiers, like in Jamie. "Couldn't —orders."

"Damn right I gave you orders. Follow them." Beauchamp's voice wavered, and his eyes flicked between Hunter and Ellison. Rock and a hard place, son of a bitch.

"He gave orders," Hunter said. They stood up taller and clenched their fists. "Orders to kill. Orders to hurt."

"Of course I did, you're built for that," he said. "You're a tool, not a person, and whoever told you that was lying."

"I wasn't lying!" Chase said, anger burning through her. Beauchamp had done nothing but lie and bully since the day she met him. Monty put his other hand on her shoulder to calm her.

"That's not what's important," Monty said. "What's important is that you're done. You're coming with us, and you're getting what you deserve."

"Absolutely not," he said. "Nine, I order you to kill."

"No."

There was so much power, so much potential, in that one little word. Despite everything that went wrong that night, and all the injuries she had to deal with tomorrow, Chase felt nothing but pride. No matter what, she'd saved Hunter.

"Fine," Beauchamp said, reaching into his pocket.

Ellison fired, but he ducked, her shot hitting the glass behind him and damaging it further. He grabbed a chunk of discarded shell armor and threw it with surprising strength, the plate smacking her in the side and forearm. Her second shot went wild as the pain hit her. No matter how tough she was, a broken bone was a broken bone.

Monty stepped up, but Beauchamp already had another piece of armor and threw it like a jagged, deadly frisbee. To avoid decapitation, Monty dropped to the floor, the impact knocking the breath from him.

Chase made a move to help him, but that only shifted Beauchamp's sight to her. He picked up the last piece of armor and threw, the plate on track to hit her right in the face.

Until Hunter caught it.

They didn't wait for thanks or dramatics. They tossed the plate down and sprinted toward Beauchamp, their face determined. He held out his hands and yelled out order after order, but they didn't stop. Hunter had no weapons and no instructions, but they had an idea.

The crash of the glass shattering tore the air from Chase's lungs. Hunter and Beauchamp disappeared from view, the man wrapped up in the perfect tackle. Chase screamed and ran to the window just in time to hear the impact from the street level. She clenched her eyes shut as her stomach revolted, and gripped the window frame hard enough the residual glass dug into her skin.

"What in the fuck was that?" Ruby's voice crackled to life in the comms.

"That was Hunter," Ellison wheezed. "Saving our asses."

"Hunter, like, Chase's Hunter?" Oscar asked. Chase focused on taking deep breaths and trying not to cry. They had to get out of here, otherwise Hunter's sacrifice would mean nothing.

"One and the same," Monty said. He sounded close, and a second later Chase felt his hand on her back. "Step back, Chase."

"In a second," she said, sure that if she tried to move, she would pass out.

"What happened?" Ruby asked.

"I'll tell you on the way home," Ellison said.

"Doors are clear, and elevators are operational again." Oscar said. "We have five minutes to get out of here. I'll meet you out front."

"I can't believe..." Chase got herself under control, at least enough to open her eyes. Monty stared back at her, his eyes warm and sympathetic.

"I know," he murmured. "We'll figure it out later."

"Later," she echoed. She didn't mean to look down, but gravity pulled her gaze that way. Hunter covered Beauchamp, and from this distance she couldn't tell whose limbs were at what wrong angles, and which skull the brain matter on the street came from. After all this, Hunter was gone, and they were walking out empty-handed.

"It's not fair," she said.

"It never is," he replied. She couldn't tear her eyes away; this was the last time she was going to see Hunter, the last time she could give them any sort of respect.

Except...

Except it almost looked like someone was moving.

At first she thought it was a trick of the light, or a residual neurological response from the six-story fall, but the more she stared, the more she could tell that someone was *definitely* moving.

She gripped Monty's hand, and he joined her at the window, his sharp gasp telling her that she wasn't imagining things.

"Holy shit," he whispered.

Down below, Hunter painfully and awkwardly clambered to their feet. They were so far away that Chase couldn't tell injuries or expressions, but she could at least tell when they turned and looked up at her. She could order them to wait, or to meet them out front. She could take them in, clean them up, and deliver them to Novak, like she promised.

Hunter lifted their hand in a wave, and Chase wondered which video taught them that.

She raised her hand and waved back.

With the acknowledgement, Hunter turned and started limping down the sidewalk, first at a walk, then at a run. Chase watched until they disappeared from view.

"Think we should go after them?" Monty asked.

"No," she replied, then added, "Not yet."

"Three minutes," Ellison cut in. She looked worse than bad at this point, so Chase shoved Hunter from her mind. Keeping her fingers intertwined with Monty's, she nodded.

"Let's go."

CHAPTER 37
THE STEP ONE JOB

TRUE TO HER WORD, Ruby waited outside with a nondescript van. Chase, Monty, and Ellison all limped (with Oscar's help) to the back, piling in like the bunch of criminals they were.

"Way to give me about seven heart attacks," Ruby said, climbing over the seat and bringing Ellison in for a harsh kiss.

"You know we like to be dramatic," Oscar said. He slid into the driver's seat while Ruby pulled Monty in for a bone-crushing hug. Chase thought she would be immune to the response, but as soon as Oscar started the car, Ruby shifted over and draped herself over Chase.

"I was so scared, but you did so good," she murmured. She rubbed Chase's back, which made her want to cry. She was exhausted, and hadn't even succeeded in her mission. Plus, her body hurt really fucking bad.

But she couldn't bring herself to regret a second of it.

"Where to?" Oscar asked, pulling away from the curb.

"What time is it?" Chase countered.

"Half past five," Oscar said. He filled in the blanks. "Do you still want to try to meet Novak?"

"It can't hurt, right?" she said. "I mean, I've got plenty of evidence, I just don't have Hunter. Maybe she'll still work with us."

"With you." Monty said it like he'd been burned a hundred times before.

"No, with *us*," she said. "You all put in just as much work as I did."

"It's not gonna work," Ellison said. She fished through a bag and pulled out another syringe, which she administered to herself without a flinch. She sighed happily as the pain killer went to work.

"I'm gonna try," Chase said. She wasn't done fighting, not yet. "I have to try."

"Well, I'm not letting her see my face," she said.

"Ell." Ruby moved next to her and laid a tender hand on her broken arm. A muscle in Ellison's jaw twitched, but it was the only sign of pain she gave. They locked eyes for an indecent amount of time, and when they finally broke it, Ellison sighed.

"Fine. Do what you want."

"Monty?" Chase asked. He licked his lips and took a deep breath, but ended up letting it out with a shrug.

"Worth a shot, I guess. You alright with that, Oscar?"

"I'll park around the corner. All else fails, we bolt," he said casually. Chase didn't know if he was joking or not.

Oscar drove to the opposite side of the building, then a few more streets down for good measure before turning south. In Plan G, they were all supposed to be going north while Chase went this direction, but she supposed that's why they had contingencies.

"What plan is this?" she asked Monty. He let out a huff of a laugh and shook his head.

"I think we're into the Greek alphabet now. Hell, might even be past Greek and onto Arabic," he said. He looked down at her and smiled, that same disarming grin that always made her heart twist.

"Okay, we're here." The van shuddered to a stop, and Oscar put it in park. "You've got some time."

"Okay, good," she said. She took a deep breath and flexed her fingers, the cuts in them screaming with each movement. Her grimace caught Ruby's attention, and she stopped splinting Ellison's arm to reach out toward her.

"Let me see," she said. Chase knew better than to argue, and held out her hands. Ruby tutted, shaking her head and running her fingertips over Chase's cuts.

"Some of those are gonna scar, but I don't think you'll need stitches on any of them," she said. "Let me clean them up."

"Hey, wait, it's my turn," Ellison whined. Whether from exhaustion or the mellowing effects of the pain meds, she slumped against the van wall with jelly muscles and glassy eyes.

"I can do it," Monty said. Ruby gave him the materials, and he held Chase's hand with gentle fingers and cleaned each cut so carefully she didn't feel any pain. "Is this okay? You'd probably know how to do this better than me, but..."

"We get surprisingly little medical training," Chase said. "You're doing way better than I ever could."

"Doubt that. Pretty sure you can do whatever you put your mind to," he said, glancing up at her for a second. Her cheeks grew warm and her pulse jumped, which definitely didn't help the pain situation.

"I could say the same thing to you," she said, thinking how easily he fit in at Kierper, and how he slipped into the role with no snags. She actually went to school for all this, and she struggled for her first few weeks. Monty made perfect patellae within the first week. Well, his second drafts were perfect.

"Good thing we're on the same side then, hmm?" he said. He finished her left hand, then went on to her right. Her poor, cut up hands were her most prized possession, the only thing she'd gotten from Kierper. The scars would be from Kierper, too.

He finished cleaning the cuts, then soothed over them with a mysterious blue salve. Its coolness drew out whatever pain was left.

"There, all done," Monty said, letting go of her. She missed his touch as soon as it was gone, so she grabbed the cleaning materials before he could give them back.

"Your turn," she said. He grinned and pulled off his over-shirt. The tight, sleeveless shirt underneath showed off his muscles—and the gashes all over them.

Chase did her best to copy his movements. Her hands were surprisingly steady as she used the saline soaked wipes and featherlight touches to clean the wounds. Their faces were close, and their bruised limbs intertwined in the limited space of the van. It was comfortable and easy, like she belonged.

Monty's wounds were definitely more involved than hers, and he would likely need stitches in a few places, but she would leave that to the expert sitting on the other side of the van. At the very least, his cuts were clean and dressed with the salve.

"There you go," she said. When he turned his face to hers, their noses were nearly touching. It would be so easy to kiss him.

Monty read her mind again, leaning forward and brushing his lips against hers, just enough to send a shiver down her spine. He rested his forehead against hers, and she closed her eyes, savoring the proximity.

Would Novak make her leave them? She didn't want to. She couldn't, she *wouldn't*. She'd almost died with these guys, there was no way she'd walk away now.

"Chase, it's time. All you from here," Oscar reminded her, making her jump and scoot back.

"Got it," she said. She pushed herself up, but not without one last look at Monty. "What are you gonna do while I'm out there?"

"Wait for you to come back, of course," Oscar said, as if the answer were obvious.

"We'll find a way to keep ourselves busy," Ruby said. She was holding Ellison's injured hand now, but then grabbed her elbow and pulled. Ellison groaned loudly as the bones reset with deep, crunching clicks.

"Getaway driving and medical expertise, is there anything you can't do, Ruby?" Chase asked. She wanted to stay in the van, afraid that if she stepped out then they would disappear into the night without her. Somehow, the thought hurt worse than failing their mission.

"I'm a woman of many talents," Ruby said. Usually, that would be a prime moment for Ellison to make a joke, but her eyes were closed and her jaw cemented shut with pain.

"Good luck, Chase," Monty said. She gave them all another look, saving him for last.

"See you on the other side," she said. The van door squealed as she opened it and closed with a resounding thud. As she walked toward the park, she thought she was finishing this the way she started: on her own.

Agent Novak stood next to a picnic table a few meters from the street. She wore a sharp navy blue suit, though Chase was surprised to see she sported a bright pink pocket square.

"Dr. Alspeth?" she said. As Chase passed into the light of the park lamp, Novak's brows furrowed. "What the hell happened to you?"

"It's uh, been a rough night," Chase said. Agent Novak nodded, then looked behind her.

"Where are the shells?"

Chase tried not to bristle. "They're dead," she said.

"What?"

"They're dead—"

"No, I heard you, I was hoping for an explanation." Agent Novak said. Chase took in enough oxygen to make her broken rib nearly crack back into place.

"Dr. Beauchamp caught me and my friends," she said. "He tried to use the shells to kill us, but Hunter saved us."

"And Hunter is..." She raised her eyebrows, gesturing for Chase to hurry.

"One of the shells I was going to bring you," Chase said, now almost glad she let Hunter go free. "They tackled him out of the window and ran off."

"So you're telling me," Agent Novak pinched the bridge of her nose, "that there's a sentient murder shell running around out there now? Unsupervised?"

"In their defense, they don't *want* to be a murder shell," Chase said.

"So you have nothing, unless I find this Hunter," Agent Novak said. She pulled out her handheld and sent off a quick message. Anxiety bubbled in Chase's chest, but if anyone could avoid detection, it was Hunter. They'd be okay. Maybe. Hopefully.

"There's a bunch of dead shells in the building," Chase said. She fished Monty's handheld out of her pocket and handed it over to Novak. "And there's a bunch of data on here detailing what they did to Hunter. Third party, just like you asked."

Novak took the handheld and scrolled through the data with sharp eyes. She might not have understood a lick of it, but if that was the case, she didn't show it.

"And the shell you call Hunter, it escaped?"

"Yeah, they saved us from the other shells, tackled Beauchamp out a window, and took off," Chase said. One thing she knew about talking to authorITIESwas to stick to the same story. "They have thoughts and feelings. They just…don't know what to do with them yet."

"That's dangerous." Novak tapped her ear. "All eyes out for the shell. We've got a runner."

"Don't hurt them, though," Chase said. "They'll listen to you. Don't hurt them."

"Doesn't sound like they'll listen to orders," Novak said. She sighed and checked the handheld again. "Well, Dr. Alspeth, this isn't exactly what I wanted, but I think I can still grant you amnesty. It'll just take some negotiating."

"What about my friends?"

"Your what?"

Chase inhaled. "My friends, they were in there with me, they helped—well, they were going to help me get the shells to you. They've gotten mixed up in some trouble and now—"

"I'm not a charity worker, Dr. Alspeth." Agent Novak's icy gaze bit into Chase's heart. "You want me to get it together for some friends too? No. Our deal was for you, and you alone. Whatever trouble your friends are in, they'll have to figure it out for themselves."

Chase physically balked. She took a step back, and then another, trying not to give in to her instinct to run.

"But they almost died. They almost lost everything to help," she said. "How can you just—"

"I've said all I can say," Novak said, holding her hands up. She looked completely unapologetic. Chase thought of Ellison, putting herself in harm's way a hundred times that night to protect her and Monty. She thought of Oscar, working furiously to get the doors open again. She thought of Ruby, completely abandoning her chance to flee in order to come save them. She thought of Monty, apologizing for everything going wrong.

"Then I guess we're at an impasse," Chase said quietly.

"Excuse me?"

"I'll find Hunter and bring them to you," Chase said, stepping back more confidently now. She didn't know yet if it was an empty promise or not.

"You'll be looking over your shoulder the whole time," Novak said. "Kierper is a big company, and Beauchamp had big friends."

"Job's not done," Chase said, proud that her voice was steady despite the fear. It sounded like something Oscar or Monty would say. And that's who she needed at this moment, not this agent. "Goodbye for now, Agent Novak."

She took off into the night, winding through the streets at the steadiest pace she could muster. Novak could probably catch up with a strong walk, but the agent let her leave. Her rib ached terribly, her hands were on fire, and her stupid left knee shot pain down her tibia with every step.

She'd never felt so alive.

The last corner took her remaining energy. The van was right where she left it, and she couldn't stop the tears that formed at the sight of it. True to their word, they'd waited for her.

She limped up to it, the back door open before she even got there. Monty held out a hand to help her in, and she settled onto the bench next to him. He put his arm around her, holding her close.

"So?" Oscar asked, looking at her through the rearview mirror. "What did she say?"

"She couldn't help all of us," Chase said. The whole walk back she tried to think of a way to let them down gently, but decided direct honesty was the best route. "Not unless we had Hunter."

"Ah, didn't like that, did she?" Monty murmured. Ellison, looking at her under drug-hooded eyes, scoffed.

"Told you," she slurred. Ruby pinched her leg, but she didn't seem to feel it.

"The data wasn't enough?" Oscar asked. "That was a lot of data."

"I even told her about all the shells in the building," Chase said. "She wanted Hunter."

The weight of her words interwove with the silence and settled over them.

From the beginning, the job was doomed. Chase saw that now. The law wouldn't let her friends out. Novak cared more about Hunter than helping her, and now they were all on their own.

"Sounds like we've got a lot to work on," Chase said. She adjusted her seat so she could lean against Monty and put her head on his shoulder. He rested his head against hers.

"Yeah, we do," he said. "Good thing we've got a good team."

"The best," Ellison muttered. She'd moved now so her head

was on Ruby's lap, Ruby running her fingers through Ellison's bloody blonde hair.

"So we're continuing?" Oscar asked. He held his hands up. "Just asking for clarification purposes."

"We've definitely done worse," Ruby said. "Fuck it, let's go rogue."

"Mhmm," Ellison hummed from her comfortable position, weakly raising a hand in a rallying motion. Oscar put the van in drive and took off. Chase didn't know where they were going, and she definitely had no idea what was going to happen after this, but she was too tired to care. Tomorrow she would freak out. Tonight, she was just happy to be alive.

"Are you sure about this?" Monty asked. Chase nodded.

"If I'm gonna have people coming after me, I'd rather be surrounded by friends than alone and depending on strangers," she said. It was a scary thought, for sure. But she meant it. The van hit a bump, forcing them all into the air and each other. Monty's arm tightened, and even if his hand was on her broken rib, she didn't move it.

"Sorry!" Oscar called from the front. He took a hard turn, which shifted them again. This time she couldn't stop a hiss of pain from escaping as Monty gripped her right over the broken rib. "Sorry, sorry!"

"Is his driving always like this?" she asked, reaching down to take Monty's hand and drape it over her. He tucked her into his side like she always belonged there.

"Unfortunately," he said. "There's a reason Ruby's our getaway driver."

"I can hear you," Oscar said.

"I know," Monty sang back. And despite everything, Chase laughed.

"Do all jobs go like this?" she asked. He shook his head hard enough that his eyes continued for a few beats after he stopped.

"This was, without a doubt, the worst job I've ever pulled," he said. His brows were down, his eyes were serious, and his mouth was a hard line across his face. Chase stared at him, and out of the corner of her eye could see Ruby looking, too. He held the face as long as he could, but the facade cracked, starting with the corner of his mouth. He let out a snort, which led to Chase giggling, which led to all of them laughing, long and loud, until Ellison complained with a smile on her face.

"Well, I guess I can only go up from here," Chase said. Her first con was terrible. Apparently, her future ones would be better. After all, she was a quick learner, and a perfectionist, and she had a lot of things motivating her. This would be no different from anything else she did in her life.

Monty's arm was around her shoulders, and her hand on his knee. Ruby rested her hand on Ellison's stomach, her girlfriend fumbling through her pain-reliever induced stupor to lace their fingers together. Somewhere out there, Hunter roamed free to make their own choices, their own mistakes. They could see what life was like outside the lab.

She wanted to find Hunter, eventually. She *had* to find Hunter eventually, if only for their own safety. But somehow, that didn't feel important right then. Everything went wrong tonight, yet she still managed to win, even in the nontraditional sense.

Chase knew this was the end of an era, the end of her life as she knew it. But as she looked at the people around her, she found she was more comfortable in the back of the cramped and smelly van than in any lab in the world. There was a lot to do, the list hovering in the back of her mind and threatening to choke her. She also needed to think about her dads, and how to protect herself from Kierper.

She'd always have a list, though. The difference between then and now, between the before and after, was she didn't have to do it by herself. When this all started, she thought she was alone. Even when she went out to Novak, she thought she was on her own. But her friends were there the whole time, ready to back her up and save her. The list of things to be afraid of was a mile long right now. She wasn't facing it by herself.

With that thought in mind, it was easy to hold onto Monty and go off into the great unknown. Oscar drove through the night, the streets widening and smoothing as he went farther and farther from Kierper, from everything she knew. Through the window, she could see the stars twinkling brighter as they left the city behind. There was no moon in the sky; a new moon for a new adventure.

Tonight would be about recovery.

Tomorrow, they would start with step one.

ACKNOWLEDGMENTS

When I first wrote this book, I was still in the throws of grief after losing my best friend. And so, what better way to remember her than to write a book based on our favorite TV show, *Leverage*? Thus, *Bone Dresser* was born.

Bone Dresser was the first book I ever wrote, and taught me so much. Chase is so near and dear to my heart, and Monty—based on Alec Hardison, for those who watch *Leverage*—was such a fun foil to her. I had every intention of publishing her last year, but unfortunately my world fell apart, and so now we're here!

Thank you first to my husband Drew, who always encourages me and listened to me whine about the everything until it got situated. Thank you for reminding me that I can do this. And for helping me with taxes. And for giving me enthusiastic opinions, even when I don't explain things very well. I'm sorry I'm bad at spreadsheets, thank you for listening.

Thank you to my bestie Kaela. Without you, my soul would not still be tethered to my body. Thank you for letting me voice all the terribly dark jokes I made to survive 2024. If I say anything else it'll be too much, the world doesn't need to know what goes on in our shared brain cell.

Thank you to my writing group: Alex Bree, Alice Ayers, Jaci Lunera, Matt Woodruff, NC Scrimgeour, PC Nottingham, and Tiffany O'Haro, for taking this book from the first gruesomely overwritten draft to the beauty it is today. Y'all's encouragement continues to be my lifeblood.

Thank you to my editor, Megan Carver, who is the reason we

got to have more romance! Your kind words, your humor, and your support mean the world to me. Thank you for all your hard work, you're the best.

Thank you to my work friends, who all get excited for me and encourage me, even if they're not SFF fans. I never thought I'd have coworkers so cool that I got to tell them about my nerdy writing habits.

To my therapist. You continue to be very good at your job. Thank you for believing in me. Or rather, getting me to believe in myself. Still trying to figure out how you pulled that one off, so I guess you're earning your paycheck.

And thank you to you, reader, for giving me a chance. Life is hard, and we're living in a clown show. But be the change you want to see in the world. Live your truth. Do not comply in advance.

ABOUT THE AUTHOR

Nico Vincenty is a science fiction and fantasy author from Texas. When she's not hanging out with her husband and dogs, she enjoys baking, playing Gaelic football, and spending countless hours with Link and Zelda in any iteration.

To keep up to date with Nico, feel free to follow her on social media, or sign up for her newsletter via her website.

For more information, visit https://nicovincenty.com or scan the QR code below for socials, links, and other information.

instagram.com/nicovincenty

ALSO BY NICO VINCENTY

A Swift and Sudden Exit

9 781963 724042